DREAM COUNTRY

PRAISE FOR DREAM COUNTRY

'Dream Country is a boldly ambitious new take on god systems and universal mythologies. This is a fantasy that asks questions you've never heard before.'

Jordan Ifueko, New York Times bestselling author of Raybearer

'A fantastic, engaging, mythology-rich tale about family, murder, and, above all, balance and change.'

Kirkus Reviews

'A bold and captivating tale that beautifully weaves culture, family and mythology in an incredibly intricate and lush world. I've read it countless times now, and each time I discover something new.'

Reni K Amayo, Author of 'Daughters of Nri'

'Dream Country will suck you in from the first page and spit you out feeling awestruck and lost for words.'

Fae Crate

'Complex, intriguing and layered. Dream Country combines the richness of bespoke cultures with the intimacy of dysfunctional family dynamics and wraps it all up in a breath-taking fantasy. It is a definite must-read.'

WCAN

DREAM COUNTRY

BY ASHAYE BROWN

ONWE

ONWE

First published in Great Britain in 2021 by Onwe Press Ltd

This hardback edition was first published in 2021

All rights reserved; no part of this book may be reproduced in any form or by any
electronic or mechanical means, including information storage and retrieval
systems, without written permission from the publisher, except for the use of brief
quotations in a book review.

Copyright © Ashaye Brown, 2021
Maps and graphics © Onwe Press, 2021

The rights of Ashaye Brown to be identified as the author of
this work has been asserted by her in accordance with the
Copyright, Designs and Patents Act 1988.

Printed and bounded by Clays Printers (UK) Ltd.

A CIP catalogue record for this book is available from
the British Library.

eBook ISBN 978-1-9160429-9-5
Hardback ISBN 978-1-9160429-8-8

This book is sold subject to the condition that it shall not, by way of trade or
otherwise, be lent, resold, hired out, or otherwise citculated without the publisher's
prior consent in any form of binding or cover other than in which it is published
and without a similar condition including this condition being imposed on the
subsequent purchaser.

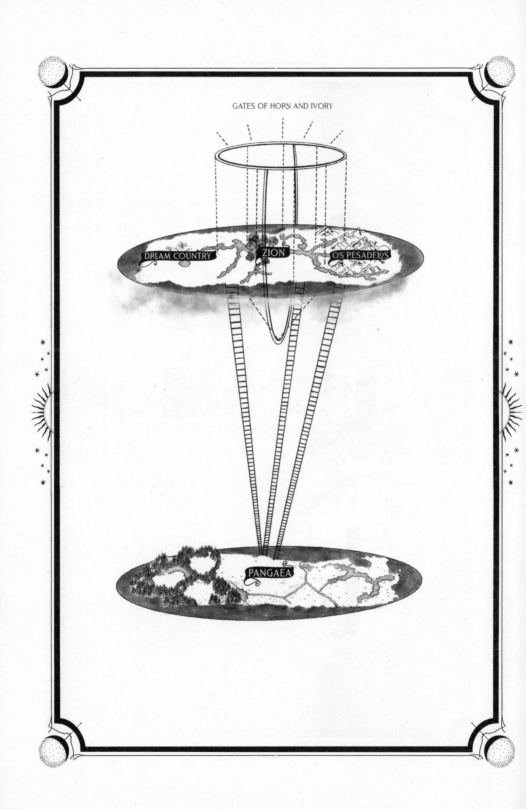

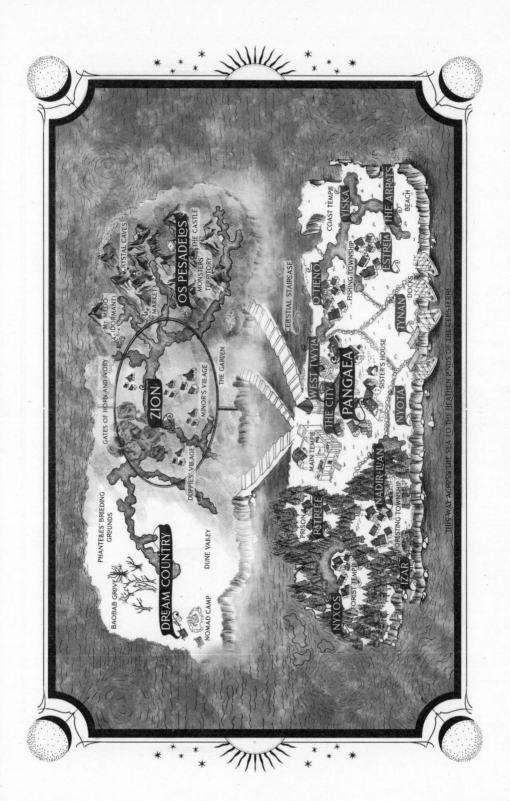

THE HOLY THEOLOGOS,
BOOK I, VERSE III.IX

On the same day that the sun rose, and rose again, another unusual thing happened. The hard ground broke open and from underneath, like plant shoots, these fences, these Gates of Horn and Ivory sprouted upwards and divided the country in three. They could not be passed through and they could not be touched. The children could only look at each other through the bars of the Gates and wonder what had happened.

There is now some country where the gods are segregated and the sun is constantly rising.

PROLOGUE

It was the island's last day to rest and the streets were, for the most part, silent. Only down one narrow avenue was there any sound at all. Bare feet slapped on the pavement as the woman looked for somewhere to hide.

Normally she would have been able to fit into the cracks in the walls. Her slim body would have slipped between the bricks and her dark skin would have blended into the shadows. They would have walked right past her. But her belly was large with pregnancy and the cracks were now too small and her skin was blanched with fear and she was now dusk instead of midnight. The woman waddled past her impossible sanctuaries and through the alley of houses. They were pressed closer together here, like broken teeth in a street thug's mouth, and the low-lying windows designed to keep out the worst of the island heat were still unlit. There was a thick, holy silence over the place: the people here kept to their beds as long as they possibly could until the day fully broke in. The woman couldn't remember the last time she'd slept, although her prayers for sleep were constant.

She also hadn't eaten in a while. Until that morning she'd been surviving off dustbin scraps and horse feed, when she'd been able to sneak into the stables. But the Magistrates had found her before she could get her next meal and she'd been forced to run, hungry. Something pounded inside her belly, but she couldn't tell if it was her stomach rumbling or the baby kicking or if her heavy heart had finally dropped too low. Whatever it was, she held a hand against the curve of her belly to calm it and to let the sensation pass without concern. She'd been having similar pains since the day before.

She left the row of houses behind and found herself on a commercial street of bakeries, carpenters, and tailors. This was civilisation, the woman knew. Where you could pay someone else to bake your bread and build your walls and mend your dresses. This was what she'd left the homeland for, spending all her life savings on a one-way boat ticket to the remote island of Pangaea, an island that the rest of the world still laughed at and called crazy. This was what the Magistrates would make her leave behind if they caught her.

She tested each door as she passed it, looking for one which was unlocked, but she was not too vigorous with her attempts, afraid to draw attention to herself with the noise. What she was really looking for, as her eyes scanned the clean cobblestone street, was a sewer. She was sure that even with her large belly she would be able to fit through the round cover grating. They would never think to look for her there; they would expect a pregnant woman to have more decency than to hide in the muck, to have self-respect like their own women had as they walked the streets with their heads held high. But the woman knew that if it gave her or her child a chance to walk like that one day, then she'd lie in as much waste as was necessary.

She had to creep down several more streets before she found what she was looking for. Often she was disoriented, confused by the labyrinthine city centre, looking up at the street signs for guidance. Although she couldn't read the Pangaean letters, she could memorise them and tell when they were different or when she'd seen them before. She was not stupid. She was a quick learner: if she got the chance she would master the language in a year.

The sewer cover was at an intersection of two roads and was square instead of round which would make it more awkward. The woman lifted the metal grating, wincing slightly as it put strain on her swollen ankles. She managed to lower herself to the ground until her legs were dangling over the edge of the opening.

The smell hit her immediately, filling her wide nostrils with the strong, almost spicy stench of the end product of a strange diet she had not yet experienced. She hesitated.

A pair of voices rose in the distance. Men's voices, and now she could hear footsteps too, reverberating under their baritone speech like a heartbeat. The woman sucked in her breath. The Magistrates had found her. Without a second thought she launched herself over the edge and down into the sewer.

The hole was not very deep and she landed safely, her fall softened by the thick stream of sewage underfoot. Stomach pain rolled around inside her again and she tensed until it passed. Standing on tiptoe, she was just tall enough to reach up and pull the cover back.

She didn't allow herself time to feel much relief at having found a hiding place. Her mind was already on the next problem and her searching hands went out, patting the moist walls, feeling for a ladder. There was nothing. She wouldn't be getting out the same way she came in. She peered off into both sides of the darkness. Shapes slowly began to form as her eyes adjusted, and she found herself staring at a wall to her left with an upright grating set into its lower bricks to let the brown stream continue to flow. There was no way through for her there. To her right the sewer floor sloped suddenly downwards, turning the stream into a river. She couldn't see how far it went but she would have to swim up to her neck in it to get anywhere.

The footsteps and voices she had heard were directly overhead now and two more voices, which sounded female, had joined them. The woman pressed herself against the wall so she wouldn't be visible if anyone looked down from above. There was no way she could risk moving away now. She'd never been the best swimmer and she would splash too much if she tried. She went very still as the footsteps stopped moving above her.

The voices were speaking more earnestly together, the Pangaean language skipping off their tongues like stones skimmed across a still lake. The woman knew she should be afraid but she found herself entranced. It was such a beautiful language. Ever since she got off the boat three days before, she'd been unable to stop herself from listening in on strangers' conversations, her mouth following theirs as she practised the new shapes and sounds. Some of them had caught her parroting them; they had frowned and turned away and said things that didn't sound so beautiful as all the rest. But there had been one handsome older man, who reminded the woman of her father, and when he overheard her he laughed and smiled and helped her correct her sounds. He'd been surprised that she already knew one word, her favourite word, and spoke it like a native.

When that kind stranger had suggested she stay with him for the night, using simple hand gestures to convey his offer, she'd gratefully accepted. She'd not minded when he'd taken her hand to guide her down the busy streets, because it reminded her once again of her father and she felt safe. But no sooner was his door closed behind her than he lifted that same hand and stroked his thumb against her full lips and cupped her breast, which was already swollen with the milk her baby would be needing in the next few days. She bit him. And then she ran.

She still remembered the sounds of the words he threw after her as she went: 'Don't worry, I'll see you again soon! And the Sisters will take that bite right out of you!' he had laughed.

Though she hadn't understood, she wondered fearfully what the words had meant and wished now that they would stop replaying in her head.

The male voices overhead said something curt, possibly a farewell as the men moved off, leaving the two women behind. The woman underground risked a glance up through the grating and her breath caught in her throat when she saw what was above her: two brown-robed Magistrates, one with her hood up so that only her angular, hard-chinned face was revealed, the other with large ringlets of blonde hair framing her face. The woman stared up at them in awe as she used one hand to rub away the ache in her stomach. She hadn't needed to stay in the city. When the boat docked in Pangaea she could have gone north, where there were fewer Magistrates around and less chance of her being spotted. But with one look at those long-sleeved brown robes she knew without a doubt that this was where she needed to be, at Pangaea's religious centre where its leaders, the Holy Magistrates, had made their home.

Even as she thought this, one of the Magistrates above her spoke in her sweet voice and said the woman's favourite word, the one she already spoke like a native:

'Majority.'

Her heart fluttered at the sound and her eyelids fell closed. Majority. The religion of the Pangaeans. And her religion too, the woman thought firmly. After all, she was here now. She'd walked away from her non-believing family, home, and country and come here where she felt the gods calling to her. Because that was the thing that made Pangaea so special and made the rest of the world hide their hatred and jealousy behind their scorn. Because here, the gods walked among the mortals.

Or so the legend went. The rest of the world laughed at what the religion called itself, laughed at the idea that one of the smallest islands in the entire world of the Celesterra would dare to consider itself the Majority of *anything*. But the woman understood that the name was not a reference to their size, but to the main gods that they worshipped, the Major gods. The gods who, every hundred or so years, on their birthday, came down to earth from the celestial realms to meet their followers in person at a festival called the Majoracle. They were the only gods in the Celesterra that did this, the only ones who didn't rely on blind faith, but instead offered concrete proof.

Of course, no non-Majority person had ever actually seen them and now the Magistrates were tracking down people like her, who might try to be the first to do so. There was a boat waiting to take them off the island.

But in fact, the woman had no ambition to see the gods. It was pure coincidence that she had arrived the same week that they were expected to appear. No, all the woman really wanted to do was build a life for herself here, to bring up her child with the same belief she had taken to her heart even before she knew that there was a name to go along with it:

Majority.

The Magistrates' conversation sounded like it was dying down. The woman looked to her right again, planning her escape route when suddenly a wave of pain rolled around from her lower back and tightened the inside of her belly. She let out an involuntary moan and quickly clasped her hands over her mouth. That pain felt a little sharper than all the rest. She glanced up again at the Magistrates. Were they finally leaving?

The hooded one half-turned as if to move away and at the exact same moment the woman felt something inside her release and a flood of water ran down the inside of her legs. She looked down at herself in confusion. And then the pain came again.

She couldn't hold it in this time, the cry escaped from her, loud and clear. Knees shaking, the woman dug her fingers into the crumbling sewer brick at her side.

Light flooded into the tunnel as the grating was lifted away and the curly-haired Magistrate bent over the hole. Her eyes widened when she saw the pregnant woman barely keeping herself up from the filth beneath her. She called something to the other Magistrate and then down to her. The woman couldn't even follow the shape of her mouth as her eyes filled with tears, blurring her vision. She'd come so close to getting away.

Another spasm rocked through her body and a string of curses left her in her native tongue. There was no point trying to abandon it anymore, now that she was going to be sent back. The curly-haired Magistrate jumped like a cat and landed next to her in the sewer. She laid a hand on the pregnant woman's shoulder and said something softly in her ear. Then she held out her hands, linked them together and mimed stepping up into it. She didn't seem to mind all the gloopy sewer water and chunks that came along with the woman's feet, she just lifted her up and the other Magistrate grabbed hold of her arms from above.

They soon got her out and laid her gently on the warm pavement. The woman screamed as another labour pain coursed through her, and as the curly-haired

Magistrate rejoined them on the ground, they looked down at her in obvious alarm. The pregnant woman wished she could help them, but this was her first child and she had no better idea what to do than they did.

The baby had gone completely still inside her and she cried out in fear. Had she killed her baby? Had all the running and the hunger and the fear killed her precious child? Should she, after all, have stayed at home and pretended that she didn't hear gods calling to her from across the sea? Gods who promised, *Rest is coming, rest is with the Majority, rest is here.*

Rest now.

She couldn't hear the gods calling to her anymore. They were as silent as her unborn child, so she screamed instead, calling up to them, and all she could hope was that they were listening.

CHAPTER ONE

Theo had been going back and forth on his decision all day. He wouldn't watch a man's legs dance from the drop of the gallows nor would he watch his head roll from the guillotine, so why would he want to watch *this*? This was *worse* than an execution, it was premeditated, public suicide. And it was all Theo's fault.

And yet here he was.

The crowd had already grown to a sickening size. Apparently no one else had suffered the doubts and hesitation that Theo had. They all *wanted* to be here. That was evident in the violin-string-taut atmosphere that hung over them all. They stood packed together in the open field as if they were the blades of grass themselves. In the distance, the rolling green hills appeared empty in comparison.

The crowd parted as they saw that it was him trying to get through. Some lifted their chins in greeting or called out a word as he passed, but there were equally as many with the same quiet sombreness showing in their eyes as Theo felt in himself. It felt wrong to see his friends and neighbours so quiet. When before had they ever gathered in such numbers without it becoming a party, a celebration? But there was no laughter and no music here today. Even the bright colours of their clothing felt wrong, as if such a rainbow should have been muted by their sorrow.

At the front of the crowd a young woman stood with brown skin as glossy as if it had been smoothed by a centuries-old current and masses of wild hair that seemed to demand not to be touched. Next to her was a man who stood out from the brown-skinned people around him, not only because of his sickly grey pallor but also because of his immense size. The pair caught Theo's eye as he approached and gestured to the space they had left between them. Theo sighed. It almost annoyed him how well his friends knew him. They knew he would come.

'He's not said a thing yet,' Iara told Theo as he reached her.

Bede, her giant companion, said, 'He won't. He was never one for words. He'd always rather get his hands around somebody's neck than have a meaningful conversation.' He shook his head in disapproval to make it clear which one of the two options he would prefer. There was a cloud of air like rotting citrus around him, the pungently sweet smell of decay. His slanted eyes sparkled above his full round cheeks. For a dead man, he always seemed so full of life.

Theo said nothing. As always, when he came to the borders of Zion, there were no words. There were just the Gates.

All along the horizon a towering fence penetrated the sky. Its bars were ornate and intricate, with an air of delicacy. Sparkling white Ivory intertwined with bone-coloured Horn, each as deadly as the other. 'The Gates of Horn and Ivory,' as the fence was commonly known, wrapped around the entire perimeter of Zion. On its other side the land was again split in two, creating three enclosed celestial realms in total. The green grass of Zion's field stopped suddenly at the border of the realm, and on one side of the fence it turned into sand while on the other it became rock. There seemed to be a shadow cast over both the other realms although the same sun touched them as shone down on Zion.

Theo shuddered and only a second later a similar quiver ran through the crowd around him as an old man stepped forward towards the Gates, supporting himself on the arm of the muscular young man next to him. As one, the crowd stood up straighter. All except Theo, who hunched his shoulders down and felt himself grow small.

He shouldn't have come.

The muscular young man stood with his back to the Gates with his head held high. He must have felt Theo's gaze because he turned and fixed him with an icy blue-eyed stare that made him shudder. Theo forced himself to maintain eye contact as he shook his head, once.

It's not too late. Don't do it.

If the other man got the message he didn't show it, but he raised his head again as if to return to his private conference with the blue sky. Iara reached for Theo's hand and squeezed it encouragingly.

'You tried,' she said softly. 'But it's better this way.'

She was right. This was his fault, but there was nothing more he could do. Theo tugged nervously at the ends of his short hair, which fell in dreadlocks to the top of his ears, and then, resigned, he met the gaze of the old man. He was fair-skinned, with two mismatched curling antlers protruding from the top of his head, one knobbly and beige like an exposed kneecap, the other smooth and pearlescent. They seemed heavy; the old man's back was bowed as if from the weight of them. His left eye was clouded over with apparent sightlessness, but he saw Theo clearly.

The Gatekeeper tapped his cane several times on the ground and the crowd fell silent.

'Gods and Goddesses of Zion. Milord Theo.' The Gatekeeper bowed so deeply in Theo's direction that his knees shook when he had to straighten again. In contrast to his fragile body, his voice was surprisingly strong, carrying all the way across the field and down to the River.

'As Gatekeeper I am honoured to guide mortals through these here Gates. Each night, as the people of our religion, the Majority, line up before me, I am the one who lets them through to either the Realm of Dreams,' he paused to let his audience's gaze wander to the sandy half of the landscape behind him, 'or the Realm of Nightmares.' Like a swinging pendulum the crowd's gaze moved again, this time accompanied by an irrepressible shudder as it settled on the stark and rocky terrain. The Gatekeeper continued. 'Or it is my honour to allow the mortals to pass a night of peace here in Zion, the Realm of Sleep. I am honoured to be able to keep Zion and its inhabitants safe, in the same way I protect the inhabitants of all three realms, by guarding these Gates. And yet today I feel no honour in the duty that brings us to these Gates.

'We are here today to bear witness to the departure of Salvador Minor who, by his actions, has forfeited his right to remain here in Zion. He has revealed himself a traitor, an attempted murderer, and a coward. And his worst crime of all, in *this* land where mortals seek their brief reprieve and the dead find their eternal rest, Salvador Minor stands accused of disturbing the peace.' An electric energy surged through the crowd as the crimes were listed before them. Jeers and taunts were thrown at the criminal from every direction. The Gatekeeper turned to the muscular young man beside him. 'Do you have anything to say for yourself, Salvador?'

Silence.

'Fine. In that case—'

'I am Salvador Minor! God of Justice! Thirteen years ago I allowed myself to be tricked. Blinded. *Put to Sleep!* I looked into the eyes of the All-Mother's murderer and I didn't see him. Justice was *not* served. I look into his eyes again today.' Salvador's blue eyes brightened and ice became fire as he locked gazes with Theo. In the depths of his rage Salvador's classical beauty was magnified, almost to the point of myth. His blonde hair shone, his muscles bulged, and Theo, who had long limbs, deep brown skin, and narrow features that made his eyes seem large and his face thin, felt small in comparison.

'Theo Major,' Salvador continued, his roar deepening to a growl, 'unnatural son, ambitious godling! To slay your own blood for her position and her power?' He looked out at the wider crowd, who cowered away. 'A few days ago, I would have torn this traitor's throat out with my bare hands, if you all hadn't stopped me. I would have woken every Sleeper and reincarnated every Duppy who prayed to him just so I could tear their throats out too! But you stopped me. Why did you stop me? Didn't you love the All-Mother, like I did? Wasn't she your world, your Goddess, and your Night?'

He held a hand up to the sky where the yellow sun burned down on all their backs. Salvador sniffed. 'I am Salvador Minor, God of Vengeance. I will avenge her.'

Suddenly Salvador's eyes filled with tears. Instead of in fear, the crowd shuffled back in embarrassment at the sight. Theo was squeezing Iara's hand much too tightly in his own, but he couldn't let go. The Gatekeeper spoke again.

'Salvador Minor, you have admitted to disturbing the peace of the Sleep realm. You have admitted to the attempted murder of the God of Sleep, Theo Major. You have also admitted that you no longer believe in Theo's innocence in the unfortunate, mysterious, and . . . *unresolved* death of his mother. Because of these three facts, you have decided that you no longer wish to be a citizen of Zion and you have decided instead to join the realm of whichever Major you now believe to be completely innocent in the All-Mother's death. You also understand that you will never be allowed back into Zion once you leave today. Is this all correct?'

Salvador nodded, not bothering to try to speak over the rising noise of the crowd.

He's really leaving, Theo thought incredulously.

'Don't go,' he blurted out, dropping Iara's hand and stepping forward. Iara and Bede quickly followed him, one on either side so they could get in the way if Salvador made any sudden moves. Theo tried to forget that they were standing there. As far as he was concerned it was just him and Salvador talking now, him and his old friend, who at one point had believed in him more strongly than anyone else. How would he be repaying him for that if he didn't try one last time to save him?

'You don't have to believe in me. Stay here and I'll give you a place in Zion where no one will disturb you. Anything you want. But please don't go over there. They'll kill you. Please.'

It wasn't right for him to beg like this, out in front of all of his people, but he didn't care. If it meant he could save the life of one Zion, he didn't mind debasing himself in front of the rest.

Salvador's lip curled into a distasteful snarl. 'I choose Dream Country.'

Theo's heart sank. The crowd broke into quick chatter and for the first time the Gatekeeper had to raise his voice to speak.

'So be it. I, Rogan Minor, God of these Gates of Horn and Ivory, open your path.'

And, just like that, part of the fence reformed behind him to become a double-doored Gate. Many in the crowd, who had never before seen the Gates opened, gasped at the sight. Rogan lay a hand on each of the newly-formed handles and Theo suppressed a shudder at the sight of contact with the poisonous materials. But these were the same materials that grew inside the Gatekeeper's own body and out of his scalp and so, unaffected, he pulled on the handles. The movement whipped up a small wind that carried the sands of the other realm onto the grass of Zion.

Salvador only stopped to spit at Theo's feet before stepping through the Gates.

Rogan reformed the Horn and Ivory behind him and the crowd immediately began to disperse. Salvador was still visible on the other side, but no one cared to see where he would go or what would happen to him next. It was none of their concern anymore, he was no longer one of them. Theo was the only one who watched him climb the ridge of a large sand dune and disappear over the other side.

CHAPTER TWO

As Theo followed Iara and Bede out of the field, they were already locked in heated conversation, which was nothing unusual for them. Even from behind, Theo could see Iara's fingers twitch with her restrained hunter's energy and it was not hard to guess who might be her prey. Bede's arms swung in wide, joyful arcs, as they always did when he knew he was getting on Iara's nerves.

'All I'm saying is that he obviously chose the better one,' Bede said as Theo finally came into earshot.

Iara frowned. 'I don't know about that.'

'Fanta at least might have some mercy. If he'd chosen Torres—'

'You don't know what you're talking about,' snapped Iara. Her anger made her brown skin take on a subtle glow, like the tinge of the coals of a dying fire.

Either Bede did not notice this, or he chose to ignore it. 'Oh, come on Iara, I was just joking. I didn't know you still—'

'Still what?' Iara glared at him, daring him to speak.

Bede only smiled, perhaps finally recognising the thin ground that he stood on. 'Theo knows what I mean, don't you, Theo?'

Theo shook his head. 'There's no good option when you're choosing how to die. I don't understand how he made the choice at all,' he said darkly. 'I should have tried harder to stop him. I should have forbidden him from leaving.'

'You shouldn't want anyone here that doesn't want to be here, Theo. You need to be able to trust everyone who lives in Zion—or else where would you feel safe?' Iara said.

'I trusted Salvador as much as I trust anyone else here.'

'And then he tried to kill you!'

Bede shook his head. 'You'd think you'd been drinking Zion water to forget that so quickly.'

Iara frowned and turned away from Theo's gaze.

But Theo hadn't forgotten. He could remember all too clearly how it had felt to have Salvador's hands around his neck, choking the life out of him, and forcing him to look into his eyes as he did it. It had taken three other Minor gods to get him to release Theo's throat. That had been only four days ago. Nothing could make him forget that, not even a long drink from the River Zion, with its properties of forgetfulness that blurred the mortals' memories of their time in the three realms. As the River Goddess, Iara knew how effective that could be.

Yet, as strong as that memory was, a more recent one was stronger—the memory of Salvador stepping through the Gate. It flooded back in and filled Theo's eyes with tears. He would have forgiven Salvador for trying to kill him, but that line, that one of Horn and Ivory, was the one that should have never been crossed.

For years Salvador had hated even to think of the other two realms. He was always preaching to Theo about war and vengeance. Theo had to constantly remind him that there was no need for that, not now, not with the Gates. With that impassable barrier between the realms, the war that had once seemed inevitable and the vengeance that had once seemed necessary were nothing more than distant memories. Ultimately that had been what divided them. Theo and Salvador's divine natures were too contrary for them to ever agree; the God of Sleep needed peace, but he would never get it with the kind of vengeance that the God of Justice wanted to impose. Salvador took Theo's pacifism as a confession of guilt and his vengeance found a new target.

The worst part was Theo could have seen it coming. He could have done something a long time ago, before Salvador's hands had found their way around his neck. He should have spoken to Salvador about the day the All-Mother died, even if he never spoke to anyone else about it. He should have answered Salvador's questions, even the ones that hurt.

What were the Major gods doing while the All-Mother was being killed?

Did you know about the weapons?

But he had chosen to keep his head down, to wait for the storm to pass. To do nothing. Because even if he chose to answer those questions, there wasn't much else he could say; the truth was that he didn't remember. He didn't remember the day his own mother died, and the guilt of his forgetfulness kept him quiet.

It could have been easy, with his power and his position as a Major, to force Salvador Minor into compliance. But Theo had never wanted to force anyone to do anything they didn't want to. After all, what if one day the Majority decided that Justice was worth more than Sleep? Or that any other of the countless powers which the Minors represented were more important than those four which their religion had celebrated above all else for centuries past: Sleep, Dream, Nightmare . . . and the Night.

Now that one of them had already fallen, it seemed to Theo that they were never more than a knife edge away from the Majority realising their mistake and directing their worship somewhere altogether more deserving.

As if she was reading his thoughts, Iara spoke again.

'Not everyone in Zion is here because they believe in you, Theo. They're just here because to them you're the lesser evil. And some of them think they could do a better job ruling Zion than you do. Do you honestly think that no one knew Salvador was coming for you that day? I've never known him to commit an act of vengeance or justice, or whatever foolishness he wants to call it, without announcing it to a room full of people first.'

Theo stiffened. 'You think there are others who want to leave?'

'No. *They* won't have to leave if they can just get rid of *you*. All I'm saying is you have to be careful, Theo. The Gates have kept out the most obvious dangers for the last thirteen years, but it doesn't mean you can let your guard down. There are still some dangerous people locked in here with you.'

'You should come to the Duppies' villages,' Bede said. 'You know you'd be safe there and we'd all protect you if any more crazy Minors came for you.'

The dead mortals like Bede—Duppies as they were called—lived on the other side of the River, their huts set up within a ring of mango trees that only partially masked their own fruity dead musk and let them believe they still had their beating hearts. Afterlife in Zion was as peaceful for them as every night's Sleep they had there when they were alive, so long as they stayed out of the gods' way. Bede was one of the only ones who could even make eye contact with Theo long enough to speak to him, which he explained was because he was more of a philosopher than a religious man when he was alive. He still regularly got into debates about the true existence of divine powers, which escalated into arguments and fistfights when the gods that sat at the table with him took offence.

Iara kissed her teeth. 'He doesn't need to *hide*, he just needs to make sure nothing like this can happen again. You should let me look into it, Theo. See if I can find out how everyone is feeling, especially right now after they all saw Salvador's display. *We* know that his speech was stupid but there might have been people in that crowd who were actually buying it. At least if I ask around a little we can be prepared.'

Theo tugged at the ends of his dreads as he nodded slowly. He didn't like the idea of spying on the other gods, but if there was anything he could do to make sure he didn't lose another friend to the other two realms, then he would do it.

Iara raised her chin in determination, empowered by the thought of her mission. As they came to the edge of the fields she immediately began to disrobe, her skin drying from too long out of her waters. The River Zion wove through its namesake realm like a central artery and its lifeblood was as blue as the grass was evergreen. The placid surface of the water shimmered and reflected the ubiquitous sun as it approached the conclusion of its second circuit.

Salvador's words came into Theo's mind: *Wasn't she your world, your Goddess, and your Night?*

There hadn't been Night in the celestial realms since Theo was six.

Out of the corner of his eye he saw Bede watching him with concern.

'Anyway . . . have you decided who you will take for a Magus yet, Theo?' Bede asked.

Theo smiled weakly at his friend, grateful for the change in conversation. 'Not yet,' he admitted.

He had let his thoughts of Salvador over the past few days distract him. He had failed in his first duty as a Major, to keep all of his Minors safe within the boundaries of his own realm, but he couldn't allow himself to fail again. Tomorrow was the start of the Majoracle, the first day of the most important week in the Majority's religious calendar. Theo was supposed to pick one mortal to spend five days with him in the celestial realms. If Theo didn't find someone by midnight, when he was expected on the mortal island of Pangaea, he would have to forfeit the entire Majoracle, not only for himself but for every Zion Minor too, meaning that none of them would get their rest. For many of the gods, the Majoracle was the only thing they had to look forward to. And the last thing he needed was another Minor mad at him.

'You only have one more day,' Bede pointed out. 'If you like, I can come with you when the Sleepers get here and help you look through them. Shouldn't they be arriving now?'

'Thanks, but I should do this on my own. I should go,' Theo said.

Bede nodded but showed no sign of surprise when Theo made no move to leave. Instead Theo sat down on the riverbank, taking off his shoes and letting his feet dangle in the cool water. He focused on the soothing feeling and tried, as best as he could, to think of nothing at all. Slowly, his eyesight began to fade and the scene around him changed.

* * *

He left his body.

The whole of Zion lay before him like a carpet at the feet of a giant. Coconut and palm trees, waterfalls and rolling hillsides spread out beneath him, the gentle wind blowing the tune of a lullaby and making the blades of grass and River water sway to its touch. Theo's eye caught every precise dancing movement. This was his paradise.

There was the River Zion with its six streams which continued on past the borders of the Gates and into the neighbouring two realms. In front of the Gates a small horned figure stood guard.

Theo found his gaze drawn to the figure of himself. There was something equally freeing and dizzying about the experience. He liked knowing that someone was watching over him from above, even if it was only himself. It reminded him of a time when there was someone up there who really did care about him, when his mother had filled the skies. But it also made him feel as if there were two versions of himself—the 'I' who was grounded, small, and disempowered by the limits of his own body, and the other, the 'I' who was limitless, powerful—a god. These two versions of himself, *I and I,* were constantly at war inside him.

From above, Theo watched the Sleepers enter the realm, popping in with bursts of displaced air. They came slowly. Once, Theo would have had the power to bring them all here, to put the world to Sleep in the blink of an eye, but nowadays, with the sun constantly shining over Zion, his power was limited. There was a natural connection between Sleep and Night, much like the connection between a mother and a son. One would be incomplete without the other.

Theo didn't let his gaze settle on anyone for too long; instead he skirted round the edges of his realm, unable even to stand the thought of another person's company. Who in Zion could understand how he was feeling right now? It wasn't just the memory of Salvador that weighed him down, it was the memory of every god he had ever given reason not to believe in him. He could have done more. But at the same time, *what more could he have done?*

If Theo could remember more clearly what had happened when Night disappeared for the final time—on the day that his mother died—he could have done more to convince Salvador and everyone else who still doubted him, of his innocence. But everything about that day was a blur. He didn't remember the first time the dawn rose twice in one day and he didn't remember the last time he saw the All-Mother paint the sky with stars. He had been six when his mother died, ancient in mortal years, but still a child for a god, perhaps too old to still curl up with his head in his mama's lap, with her fingers running through his hair as she sang to him, but that was how he spent every evening. Theo was the god of rest and peace and even now he found the easiest way for him to use his power was to conjure up that memory in his mind. As each new Sleeper entered Zion, Theo's eyes flickered behind their lids, his heartbeat slowed to the rhythm of light rain, and his body became pleasantly cool as he remembered the feeling of his mother's fingers in his hair.

Theo remained disembodied even as his physical form felt the chill of the realm's crosswinds meeting at the riverside like sharpened blades in a duel. He watched Iara swim away with the currents of her waters and he watched Bede wander off in the direction of the Duppy villages, winking up at the sky before he left, his own small farewell.

He told himself he was looking for a Magus, but he was really just looking for an escape. He liked how easy it was for him to observe the Sleepers from this distance. Usually, he felt like the one under a magnifying glass with the gazes of thousands of admiring mortals watching his every move. That was the treatment he would have to endure later in the day, when he went down in person to the mortal realm to attend the Majoracle initiation ceremony, but while they were here in his realm, he was free.

Theo's realm sight took him to a place where the grass grew wild with flowers of red hibiscuses covering the ground. A Sleeping girl of about eighteen mortal years was running her hands over the drooping petals, absently raising her fingers to her nose to inhale the lingering scent. As Theo looked closer, her head snapped up, reminding him of a startled squirrel. He pulled back in surprise until he had reminded himself that she couldn't see him. He came closer again, curious. She had a pale face with a strong jawline and grey-brown hair. Her eyes were wide and brown, with deep bags set beneath them. Theo could see the grey aura of an insomniac around her. Whenever he came across someone this tired his mind automatically reached out to soothe them, but he could see it would take more than one touch to pull this girl out of the pit of exhaustion that she was so obviously trapped in. She looked like she hadn't Slept in a year or more, which was probably why Theo was struggling to grasp her name. Usually, as soon as Theo saw a mortal's face, he would know when they had last been in his realm and what their name was. But not with her.

'Who are you?' Theo whispered and, while the question still hung on the lips of his abandoned body, the edges of the girl's soul shimmered and faded until she disappeared into wakefulness. Her slender hand was the last thing to go, still resting on the tops of the hibiscuses, and Theo was left alone to answer his own question.

My Magus, Theo thought. *She's my Magus.*

She was everything Theo had been looking for, even when he hadn't bothered to look at all. She needed him: he could make sure that she was never tired again.

I need to speak to Rogan.

In a rush, Theo's vision collided back into his body. He took a moment to readjust to the limited first-person perspective and then, once he was used to his eyes again, he got to his feet. He found the nearest crossing point on the River where several large stepping stones zigzagged over the placid surface. He covered two stones with every stride, until he came to the opposite bank where the wet ground made obnoxious sucking noises with each step.

Without thinking he went in the direction he had last seen Rogan with his realm sight hours before. When a Magus was chosen, Rogan was the one who had to be informed before anyone else, so that he knew which mortal was allowed access through the Gates when everyone else was locked out. But Theo also just wanted to talk to him because Rogan was always someone who he *could* talk to. The Gatekeeper was less deferential than a mortal, less judgemental than the other Minors, and more understanding than his friends. He had been Theo's voice of wisdom for as long as he could remember.

'Good morning, Milord,' said that voice.

Theo spun around and was shocked to find Rogan standing behind him. Rogan never left the Gates and especially not a few hours before the start of the Majoracle.

'Rogan? What are you doing here?' Theo asked in a rush.

'Looking for you. Well, actually I had already found you,' Rogan said, and his one clouded left eye seemed to wink at Theo as he spoke.

Although his eye looked blind, it actually held a second sight even stronger than Theo's, since Rogan's was not obstructed by the borders of the Gates and could see across all three celestial realms.

I guess someone still is watching over me from above.

Theo swallowed nervously and resisted the temptation to ask the Gatekeeper to look into Dream Country at that very moment. Maybe he would tell him he could see a lone figure still wandering aimlessly over the dunes. Or maybe he would tell him that the Dream Country Minors had already found him. Or—

Theo didn't ask.

'I was looking for you too,' he said instead. 'I found a Magus.'

Rogan raised an eyebrow. 'Good timing.'

That was an understatement. There were only a few hours left until midnight, when all the Sleepers would wake and not go to Sleep again for five days.

Rogan started walking and Theo fell into step with him.

'Actually, it could be terrible timing if I don't find out her name before midnight.'

'Find out her name?'

'It's the strangest thing. Her name just wouldn't come to me. Even now, I can't quite figure it out.' Theo groaned in frustration. 'I feel like I'm forgetting the name of my childhood best friend.'

'You're stressed. A lot has happened in these last few days and you know you're always the most tired right before you're due for a Majoracle. It's taking its toll on your mind—but you should try to relax. The name will come to you. Until then, focus on other things.'

Theo sighed. He could think of a million other things to focus on, none of them relaxing. At that moment, Rogan produced a wrapped package from one of his deep pockets. He bowed. 'For you, Milord.'

Theo frowned. 'It's just us here, Rogan.'

Laughter glinted in the Gatekeeper's clear eye. 'Apologies. Happy birthday, my boy.'

And there it was. The switch that could never be made in public; the closeness of their relationship that had to be kept secret. Rogan was the Gatekeeper, the only god without borders, the only one who was not supposed to show preference to one of the three realms. And yet in that one simple switch of a word, Theo stopped being 'Milord' and became 'my boy.'

But the bow remained. It was the only physical gesture ever made between them, since actual contact was impossible. Rogan's skeleton, made of the same materials as the Gates, was deadly to Theo. Horn, the material of Nightmares; Ivory, the material of Dreams. As Rogan handed over the gift, he was careful not to touch Theo; nonetheless, a nauseating tugging sensation rose up Theo's throat and crawled across his skin from the mere proximity of Rogan's hand.

Theo hurried to put five paces back between himself and Rogan before opening his gift.

Inside the package, a thin wooden box lay inside a cotton nest. Theo pulled it out, feeling the ridges of the engraved wood along a surface the size of his palm. Theo smiled down at it, remembering, and pressed the slightly rounded sides. A blade swung out smoothly, its sharp point lengthening the knife to match Theo's entire handspan.

It seemed like just yesterday that Theo watched Rogan cutting leaves and small roots with this same knife, a kettle already boiling for the tea he would make with his harvest. Theo remembered how quickly that warm cup had calmed his shaking hands as he took his first sip, how Rogan's tea and care had allowed him to forget that he was six years old and motherless. One sip from that cup and Theo had been able to leave behind everything that had happened that day and just focus on Rogan's hands and the knife that seemed to fit so perfectly well into them. He had wondered when he would be old enough, both to be allowed to hold something so sharp and to have it fit perfectly in his own hands.

'Nineteen already . . . where did the time go?' Rogan said, as if reading his mind.

Theo looked up and was surprised to see how old Rogan looked in that moment. Nineteen god years was a much longer stretch of time than nineteen mortal years, and every second of that span seemed to show on Rogan's face. In the time it had taken for Theo's hands to grow to adult size, the Gatekeeper's had become wrinkled and shaky. Suddenly Theo didn't want to accept the gift he had once pined for. He flipped the blade back down and replaced it in its box.

'Maybe you should keep it. For a few more Majoracles at least . . .'

Rogan seemed amused. 'If you're not old enough by now, you never will be. It's just an old knife. I'll make myself a new one if I need to.'

Theo admired the tool once more before slipping it into his back pocket. 'Thank you.'

'Look,' Rogan said, stopping suddenly and pointing over to some waist-high leafy bushes of peppermint. 'Why don't you go try it out?'

Theo smiled and left Rogan behind as he went over to the bushes. He bent down and flicked open his knife to cut the thin stalks. When he had a handful of peppermint he straightened up from the bush and looked around for anything else he could cut nearby. It was only then that he realised where he was: in the centre of the biggest Minor village. He was surrounded by huts with thatched roofs and branch-lined walls, and on the opposite side of the village were a few scattered plots of farmland. The only sound came from the laundry, recently washed in the River Zion and hung out of windows to dry, which flapped gently in the breeze. Theo looked around in confusion. No wonder he hadn't noticed where he was. There was no one else here. Where was the huddle of old Minors playing dominoes around the bark of a bent palm tree? Where were the young gods and goddesses kicking up dust with their shuffling feet as they danced to the sound of the steel-pan drums?

'Hello?' he called out.

Not even an echo answered him. Theo's heart began to stutter nervously, his mind going straight to Salvador.

They've left too, he panicked, but immediately chided himself for the thought. What was the chance that every single one of the hundreds of Minors had decided to follow Salvador's example and leave Zion and Theo behind? There must be a better explanation for where they all were.

Theo spun around and rushed back to the place where he had left Rogan.

'Rogan, where is every—'

But Rogan was gone.

Check your realm sight, a voice of reason, that sounded surprisingly like Rogan, said in his head.

Just as Theo took a deep breath and prepared to let his eyesight fade, every hut's door and shuttered window crashed open around him and the Minor gods and goddesses of Zion yelled together:

'Surprise!'

CHAPTER THREE

The twelve mountains of *Os Pesadelos* huddled together for warmth. Their peaks were snow-capped, jagged, and treacherous, regularly sending avalanches of ice and rock to the bottom. The people had learned to live with this risk. If an avalanche took out their favelas, there was rarely anyone left behind to complain about it. Besides, a bit of snow was nowhere near the most dangerous thing in the Nightmare realm.

Only the third mountain held no favelas. Everything about *Os Pesadelos* that made mortals shiver, and made the weak and superstitious too scared to pronounce its name, was thick around this mountain. It wasn't the largest of the range, but the climb was the most treacherous with plenty of smooth edges and steep inclines to discourage anyone from making the trip. Two branches of the River Zion wrapped around its base like the body of a slingshot framing a pebble. The air was crisp and white as folded paper.

At the mountain's peak was a small castle. The walls were carved directly out of the living rock, the first two storeys stocky and square, the last storey rising into a single turret with a conical roof. Three large arched windows looked directly out onto a sheer cliff drop.

Behind the first-floor window was the castle dining room. A long table held enough seats for twenty people, but their backs were dusty from so long without ever having been pulled out. A candle chandelier hung above the table, unlit. The walls were lined with tapestries, all turned around so that their beige backs faced outwards.

Presently, Torres Major was sitting on the floor of the dining room, barely feeling the cold from the exposed rock floor under him. Rows of drinking glasses were lined up on the floor against the opposite wall. At random points, gaps appeared in the lines, and piles of shattered glass filled the spaces, like disgraced soldiers fallen from position. Torres picked another pebble from the pile at his side and aimed it up against his eye.

Clash! He hit the stem of a glass in the third row which toppled backwards and shattered the one behind it as well.

'Killing two birds with one stone,' he muttered to himself.

'I'm not sure I appreciate the metaphor, *Senhor*,' Abilo said from his perch on the back of one of the chairs.

Torres raised a mildly amused eyebrow at the crow and then immediately forgot that he was there as he picked up another pebble.

Idle ruin had always been a favourite way to dull his mind when there were too many thoughts jostling for room inside his head. At what point, Torres wondered, was a glass not considered a glass anymore?

How many shattered pieces of itself would need to be put back together for it to be considered whole again?

It was that, that transition point between meaning and mess, definition and destruction, that fascinated him. Unthreading clothing worked just as well for a distraction as shattering glass, as could be seen by the loose and mangled ends of his long sleeves. Even melting ice could help when his mind was too crowded. And if there was nothing else around then, well, there was always himself.

When Torres was whole he was the God of Nightmares, but cut down to his parts, skin, blood, bone . . . what did he become then?

Torres sighed and shifted his weight, the first significant movement he'd made all day. He was in need of prolonged distraction today, because every elbowing, attention-seeking thought started the same way.

Majoracle . . . Majoracle . . . Majoracle . . .

At first glance it would seem like any other day in his realm. There was no celebration for him in *Os Pesadelos*, and by his own orders there hadn't been one for his past four birthdays. His candles were the smashing glasses and only Abilo was there to watch him make a wish. When he got to nineteen, he started counting all over again. And again. And. Again.

'Perhaps you would like to go out today, *Senhor*? We can visit some of the other mountains. *Senhora* Barrera just came by to see you this morning and I'm sure some of the other Minors would love to see you around again. *CAAW!*' There was a hint of self-consciousness in the bird's otherwise mellifluous voice. The occasional croaking syllable and the unintentional crowing made him clear his throat and dip his head, embarrassed, as if no one would have noticed he was a bird if not for these small defects.

Torres didn't answer for a while, until eventually, he said quite simply, 'I hate them.'

'But, *Senhor*, surely you don't mean that. Your Minors are your most devout followers and kindest friends. Remember, it was they who came to your defence when others wished to place the blame of your mother's death on you. It was they who helped to purge this realm of all trace of what it once was when still a part of Zion, and to form it into what it is now.'

'I hate this realm, too. I mean it, Abilo. I don't belong here.'

There was a realm that was perfect for him. A place where he could finally be himself, if he could just get through. There had been some mistake when the realms were divided—no, the mistake was made further back than that, when his mother named him and gave him this power. This wasn't him. He wasn't supposed to be here. If he could just leave *Os Pesadelos* behind and get through to that realm that was truly his, then, then he could be happy.

'You just need to get out of the castle for a while. You've been cooped up in here for far too long.' Abilo cleared his throat. 'Will you be attending the island ceremony tonight?'

Torres looked at him curiously out of the corner of his eye as he tested the throwing weight of another pebble against his palm. He could tell Abilo was only trying to distract him from his unending game, as he had been trying all day. Perhaps the other crows had informed him that the kitchen was running out of glasses. But why would he choose *that*, of all things, as a topic of distraction?

'I can arrange for transport down the mountain now if you'll be needing it,' Abilo said, as if he hadn't noticed he'd said anything strange. His beady black eyes met Torres's gaze steadily.

'To the ceremony? So I can sit there and watch Theo and Fanta take their Magi while every *fulano* pretends I don't exist?'

'It's been a while, *Senhor*. Maybe if you asked again—'

'No. I won't humiliate myself again. They have both made it very clear that I will never be given a Magus. There will be nothing for me at the Majoracle carnival.'

He had been forced to come to terms with that a long time ago. For the first few years of his life Torres hadn't even heard the term *Nightmare Magus*. If he thought about it at all, he would have thought it was a phrase that couldn't exist, like *Dead All-Mother*, or *double sunrise*. Long after two impossibilities came true, he began considering a third. He thought that if he could have a Magus, if he could show them that a mortal *could* survive, even enjoy a week with him in his realm, then they would stop treating him like his very existence was a crime.

Only one thing, one person, ever stood in his way.

'Do you still think I should go, Abilo?' Torres asked curiously.

'I think it would be good for the Majority to see you again, *Senhor*.'

'Of course. Because how can they fear what they can't put a face to, right?'

Abilo shook his head. 'You can't expect them to worship a god they never see, *Senhor* 'Mare.'

Torres knew Abilo only used the nickname to soften the suggestion. The regular inhabitants of *Os Pesadelos* had stopped referring to him as a Nightmare

God ever since Night stopped coming in the realms. Now he was just *Senhor* 'Mare.

He shrugged. 'I never asked for their worship.' He threw another pebble and missed.

Should he have had to? What other god had to *ask* their followers to respect them? To remember them? Torres couldn't remember the last time he'd received a genuine prayer. Not one of those mandatory ones, where his name came nestled in between the other two like an item on a checklist. No, a genuine, spur of the moment, *oh Torres please*, or *dear Torres thank you*. There were caves at the edge of *Os Pesadelos* where natural formations of crystal sprouted from the rock. They could be as tall as a man and as clear as air. In one particular cave, if Torres entered and closed his eyes, letting his mind go in the same way he did when he engaged his realm sight, he could hear every prayer that was directed to him. They resonated off the crystals like music. He hadn't been down to the caves in a while, because even though the silence that he imposed within these four walls was as heavy as the mountain itself, he knew it was easier to bear than the silence that would be waiting for him down there.

Torres froze suddenly in his thoughts and body as he felt a familiar feeling take over him.

It rose up inside him like an overfilled dam about to burst. He stiffened and the noises in the room became muffled and distant. When the feeling passed and he opened his eyes, Abilo cocked his head quickly to both sides. Torres knew the bird's movements well enough to know when a question was coming. And, knowing Abilo, it would be a question that he already knew the answer to.

'Are they getting worse, *Senhor*?'

Torres smiled weakly. 'Not too bad for me to handle.'

Abilo opened his beak as if to say something else but changed his mind and snapped it shut instead. Torres knew what he wanted to say. Another question. Why was he doing this to himself? It didn't make sense for him to suppress them. A Nightmare God was supposed to let the Nightmares out.

There were images in Torres's mind that he would never be able to unsee. They were the result of the deepest fears of everyone around him mixed with somebody's sick imagination—*his* imagination, he realised but hated to admit. But ever since he stopped letting them out, at least he was the only one that had to see them. He was starting to build up a new power in himself, to counteract the other one that came so naturally to him. Day by day, fewer and fewer Nightmares were getting out into *Os Pesadelos*. He intended to use the upcoming Majoracle days while the mortals were gone to practice his containment capacity further. What a surprise it would be for the mortals to come back and find there were hardly enough Nightmares to go around anymore! Wouldn't they call his name then? Wouldn't they praise his strength and his love? *Thank you, Torres, for taking our Nightmares away! We never should have doubted you!*

He'd spoken honestly to Abilo when he said he didn't want their worship. But he didn't want their fear either.

He bet they were not afraid of Dreams.

Torres got to his feet and stretched out his back. With the lingering images of Nightmares in his mind, he no longer felt like throwing pebbles.

'I need some air,' he said, moving quickly towards the door in a way that told Abilo clearly enough that he wanted to be alone.

The castle corridor ended at a large spiralling staircase, leading up to the library floor and then up again to the turret, turned into an aviary, where Abilo and the other crows had made their home. The smell of dead meat sometimes drifted down from the turret after the crows had a big meal. There were no bedrooms in the castle. They were not needed—Sleep was not Torres's domain. On the ground floor there were three doors, one from the dining room, another for the kitchen. Torres headed for the third door that led outside.

The chilly air hit him like a slap in the face and he shivered within his thin jumper. He hadn't realised how cold it was today. The castle was always warm inside without the need for fires. Torres sometimes imagined that it was really a dormant volcano, biding its time. From this high up, he could see right to the borders of his realm, and even a little past the Gates that surrounded it and to the other side. As always, his eyes were drawn to one realm in particular. It looked so beautiful over there, almost unreal. What would it be like to walk on that ground? To feel that air against his skin? Of course, he had walked there before, but that was a long time ago, when things were different. He knew that if he ever got a chance to go back, it would be like coming home.

To the right of the castle's entrance the precipice sloped downwards, only just wide enough for a person to stand on. To the left it disappeared suddenly into a sheer drop. Torres looked over the edge and caught sight of some crows returning with a bundle gripped in between their beaks.

More glasses? Torres wondered in amusement. At least his servants were prepared for his lasting moods.

Torres stuck his hands in his front trouser pockets to warm them up. A small goat-pen lay against the side of the castle. In theory the goats were there for transport, in case Torres ever felt like going further than his front doorstep. But right now they were only used for their milk, and Torres went towards the pen already thinking of the fresh glass that would warm his stomach. His teeth were chattering so loudly that he almost didn't hear the grotesque munching sound coming from behind the pen's fence. Torres frowned and approached the noise.

'Hey!' he cried out.

Inside the pen, a goat lay on its side in a pool of its own blood. Its flesh had been ripped open, revealing a mush of blood and bone. Its organs spilled out over its two forelegs, into the hands of the thing crouching over it.

The thing turned its head at Torres's shout and the black slits of its enormous fiery red eyes expanded in shock as it met Torres's gaze. It was a young one, the horns on its head hadn't even broken through the skin yet. The creature's serpentine body was swollen and purple around the midsection like an infected wound, the scales of its skin rippling slightly as it let out an acidic belch with the stench of digestive juices.

'*Senhor* 'Mare!' the creature said, wiping the blood from its mouth. It looked at the savaged goat in front of it and then innocently over at the other two who stood shaking and bleating pathetically in the far corner. 'Are these . . . *your* goats?'

Torres folded his arms. 'You know very well that they are.'

The creature grinned awkwardly, trying to avoid tearing its upper lip with the protruding sharpness of its lower teeth. It rose up onto the two hind pairs of its eight limbs and clasped the front pair together in supplication. 'I didn't know. I didn't know. *Me perdoe*,' it begged.

The creature switched between the two native languages of *Os Pesadelos*, as if this would make it sound more sincere. But Torres wasn't believing the act for one second. 'This mountain has had a *boitatá* ban for years. And now, you owe me for that goat.' Torres's eyes scanned over the *boitatá*'s revolting body.

There wasn't much he could take from it, even if he really wanted anything, but he also couldn't let it get away with eating one of the goats without penalty. If he did that today, then tomorrow there would be three *boitatás* up here, all expecting no more than a gentle reprimand for their raw and bloody poaching.

Around one of the *boitatá*'s scrawny left ankles, two Horn bracelets knocked against each other with every hopping movement that the creature made. Torres himself didn't follow the *Os Pesadelos* fashion of wearing Horn for decoration. In fact, he avoided the material almost as if it was the poisonous Ivory. Having it near reminded him too much of who he was.

'I didn't know,' the creature repeated.

Torres frowned. 'There's no reason for you to come up here, you get enough food below.'

The monsters of *Os Pesadelos* had made their home at the mountain bases so that when the Minors who lived above missed their step, they came tumbling straight into their eager open mouths. It seemed to Torres a horrible way to go but he could not ban the practice. All of his subjects had a right to eat.

The *boitatá* hopped on springy back legs to get closer to Torres, staying crouched the whole time so that when it spoke it was addressing its navel.

'There's food but no *taste*. There's no point eating from the other mountains when it's like this,' it hissed. '*Estou com fome.*'

'I've told you before. This is the way things are now.'

'But it's not right! It was better before. When you just let the Nightmares happen . . .' The *boitatá* stuck out a slug-like tongue to wet its lips. 'Things have not been so bad for us here since the time of the . . .'—the creature gulped—'. . . the *morte-de-ouro!*'

The *morte-de-ouro* was the *boitatá*'s natural predator, a monster that killed with flames and without mercy. They had become extinct long ago.

Torres shook his head. There had been some unintended side effects to holding back the Nightmares. Nothing harmful to the people of *Os Pesadelos*, but, well, nothing they were too happy about either.

'You'll get used to it.'

The *boitatá* gurgled in protest then tried to grab onto Torres's ankle as he pushed it aside.

'You can't do this to us, *Senhor* 'Mare! ¡*Por favor, tenha piedade!* We'll starve! We'll die!'

Carefully avoiding the puddle of drying blood, Torres lay a calming hand on one of the remaining goats' backs and pulled up his milking stool.

'No,' he said quietly, as if speaking to the goat, 'we'll survive.'

CHAPTER FOUR

It was a saying as old as the Night that when music played in Zion, all of the Celesterra danced. Steel-pan drums and the rasping baritone voices of their players sent the thrumming vibrations of the birthday song through the bones of anyone that heard it. Everyone danced in pairs, standing so close to their partners that even their sweat was shared. And as constant as the music was the laughter, the playful shouts from one side of the village to the other, and the occasional anger of rapid voices raised in argument that soon settled once again into a lazy kind of peace.

Theo walked through it all, feeling at once a part of it and completely separate. Several hours into the party, he felt he had finally recovered from his initial shock. He had never had a surprise party before because nothing could be organised without him seeing it through his realm sight. He still had no idea how they had managed to pull it off, although he knew Rogan must have been behind the plan by the way he had so subtly led him into the ambush. Rogan himself hadn't stayed for long, never liking to be far from the Gates before the start of a Majoracle.

Theo was just glad that the other Minors hadn't asked him to make a speech. It was a lot easier for him to stand in front of a group of Minors than it was to face a similar number of mortals, but his palms still got sweaty when he found himself in a crowd.

'Mister Theo!' a teasing voice called over the noise. 'Come now, man, play a couple hands with us.'

It was Tarone, the Minor God of Travellers, rocking back in his chair as he held a hand of dominoes close to his chest. A scent of earthy smoke clung all around him. Around the makeshift playing table with Tarone were Fiorel, the Minor Goddess of Healing, and Raeni, the Minor Goddess of Wealth. They too beckoned him over.

'Soon come,' Theo said, speaking casually to appease them, even as he walked away. The Wealth Goddess was a cheat at dominoes and he had no desire to be swindled by her today.

Instead he made his way to the five round buffet tables that lined the edge of the village, all laid so heavily with food that the legs bowed under the weight. Eating was a well-appreciated activity in Zion, where it was well known that a full stomach always led to a deep slumber. All around the tables, hens and rabbits wandered freely around their feet, pecking at the dropped crumbs. These animals felt safe, knowing that they were more likely to be guests than dishes at this banquet. Most Zions followed an Ital diet, eating only that which comes from the ground around them. Steaming bowls of sweet potato curry, golden-yellow ackee, and heaping piles of rice and peas were just a few of the dishes that caught Theo's eye, but it was on the cubes of freshly cut mango that his gaze came to rest. Just as he reached out to grab one, a large grey hand came from nowhere and slapped away his wrist.

'Thirst before hunger, Theo! Toast before the meal!'

Theo spun around. Bede clapped Theo on the back and laughed at Theo's jumpiness. It was an old Zion superstition to never let a Duppy walk up on you from behind, lest they steal life back from the gods. While the older gods took it more seriously and hated having Duppies around for this very reason, Theo and Bede had made it into a game, to see how many times the dead man would have already stolen Theo's life by catching him unaware. Bede was winning.

Bede waved a cup of red Zionese brew under Theo's nose. The floral scent alone made Theo a little light-headed and judging by the stench that came from Bede's breath as he spoke, he had passed the light-headed stage a long time earlier. The water that formed the base of the Zionese brew was taken straight from the crystalline River itself, and the natural properties of oblivion found in the water, plus the relaxing qualities of whatever herbs were chosen to be added to it, delivered a sucker punch both to the taste buds and to the mind. For a mortal, as Bede once was, one sip too many of this drink of the gods was enough to make him forget the world.

Theo took the cup. 'What shall we toast to?'

'To you, my friend, on your birthday! Another year older, another year wiser, and you know what they say: the older the moon, the brighter it shines!' He raised his own cup to his lips and took a large gulp, but before Theo could follow suit Bede stopped his hand again. 'Seriously, Theo, how do you do it? You're as old as the Celesterra itself, yet you don't look a second older than the day I met you.'

The dead man muttered a bitter curse as he ran a palm over the rough edge of his jaw. He had died on a morning before he got a chance to shave and now he always looked slightly unkempt. But he had not looked this way the day that he and Theo first met. Theo remembered it clearly, how Bede, then only twenty-five years old, had been dragged into the temple on the first day of the sixteenth Majoracle with a parent on either side of him. How they had fallen to their knees and pulled him down with them and begged Theo to cure their son of his—what did he call it?—*atheism*.

Theo took Bede for his Magus, but he never did cure him, and Bede took his scepticism to his grave with him when he returned to Zion. It wasn't that Bede denied the existence of the gods—no right-minded person in the Celesterra could do that—but, he asked, what made them gods in the first place? Yes, they created things like Sleep and Dreams and Nightmares, but mortals created things every day. Did that make them worth praying to?

It hadn't taken long for Theo to realise that he didn't *want* to do what Bede's parents had asked him to. He liked the kind of questions that Bede asked; he liked that for the first time he could hear them somewhere outside of his own head.

What makes me a god? What makes me worth praying to?

Bede cleared his throat, coming out of his nostalgic reverie and finally raising his cup into the air for the toast. 'Happy birthday, Theo! And many more!'

Theo smiled and brought his own cup to his lips—

And was left drinking only the air as the cup was smacked out of his hand. The blood-red contents soaked slowly into the ground at his feet.

'Are you mad, *Duppy*?' In her anger, Iara made the word an insult as she turned on Bede. 'What do you think you're doing giving him a drink without testing it first? You know there are people at this party who want him dead.'

'We don't know that for sure,' Theo said, but he was ignored.

'I've spent this entire time going around listening to what people were saying and making sure no one suspicious got too close to Theo. If you're not going to help me, at least don't help the assassins.'

'You know,' Bede said, slurring his words, 'for gods who are supposed to be *immortal*, you do spend a lot of time worrying about death.'

'Save your philosophy, atheist. You know as well as anyone that gods are only immune to natural sickness and old age. We can still die of murder. And, if anything, it's worse for us than for mortals. At least you know what happens afterwards.'

Dead gods didn't come to Zion. Instead their power was reincarnated into the next god to be born in the realms. Only one deity had ever died without ever being replaced, and the evidence of that anomaly was written above all their heads in the depths of the blue sky.

'That's ridiculous!' Bede shouted suddenly, making Iara and Theo flinch. 'How can it be worse for you just because you don't know what happens?

The unknown is always better than the known, because it can never affect you. If a tree falls in a forest with no one around to hear it, does it make a sound?'

Theo shared a glance with Iara and shrugged. Bede was always saying things like that and Theo rarely knew what they meant.

'So we're just choosing to believe that someone is definitely trying to kill me now?' Theo said, managing to make himself heard at last and immediately regretting it. Iara turned on him.

'You should know better, Theo. I don't know why you would want to drink Brew anyway. Your memory is precious, you shouldn't let anything take it away from you unless it has to. From now on, if anyone hands you a drink, you spill it. Understand?'

Theo rolled his eyes. Spilling was an old custom, in which whenever someone else prepared a god a drink, they were supposed to spill some and see what it did to the ground. If there was poison in the cup, it would burn the ground in the same way it would have done to the drinker's stomach. The practice went back to a time when gods were dropping like flies and a poisoned cup was considered the civilised way to solve a problem. A time before the Gates.

'Go easy on him, Iara. Between Salvador trying to throttle him and Fanta waiting to pounce as soon as he gets down to the island, the last thing he needs is you convincing him his birthday party is a death trap.'

Theo's whole body went tense. Iara glared at Bede and the realisation of what he had just said succeeded in penetrating the haze of his drunkenness.

'Okay, bad joke,' he said, shamefaced.

Iara kissed her teeth in annoyance. 'Ignore him, Theo. You know Fanta wouldn't try anything in front of the Majority. That's not her style. As long as she can keep them convinced she's their perfect, innocent goddess, she'll have them wrapped around her little finger. I've always said, if there's anyone you need to be worried about at these ceremonies it's . . . but he hasn't shown up for the last four Majoracles, so I doubt he'll show his face now.'

Theo noticed how Iara skipped over saying Torres's name, but he knew better than to comment on it. He needed no reminder that sometimes the past was best left firmly in the past.

Bede reached over a plate of fried plantains and lifted a heavy ceramic jug of Brew with one hand.

'Don't worry,' he said to Iara, 'we'll spill it this time.'

Just as he said this, he stumbled on his feet and the jug flew out of his hand and crashed to the floor. Theo reached out to catch him as Iara laughed.

'All-Mother, how much Brew have you ha—'

A loud groan filled the air, like a giant door creaking on its hinges. Theo barely had time to look up before the ground began to shake. A terrible tremor tore through the village, knocking Theo off his feet, and Iara and Bede fell right after him.

Theo pulled Iara, who was closest, under the table with him to shield them from the avalanche of falling plates and cups. Even though her mouth was right by his ear, Iara's voice was almost drowned out by the clamour of the earthquake.

'What's happening!' she yelled.

But Theo couldn't answer her. The sound of his heartbeat drumming in his ears drowned out the cacophony of destruction. All the while only one thought was clear in his own mind: it was finally happening. Zion was under attack. Which realm was behind it? Which of the Major had finally made the first move? *How did they get past the Gates?*

Theo opened his second sight. The scene in the Minor village was duplicated across the entire Sleep realm. The earth spasmed and tore like a spider's web against a breath of air. Narrow fissures were opening up between the villages and the River. Throughout the realm, Zions were huddling together or running about in useless panic. Many of them were calling for help, for answers, or just calling Theo's name.

He sent his gaze to the borders: the Gates were as resolute as ever against the destruction surrounding them. Theo allowed relief to flood his senses only for a second before he pulled his realm sight away, all too aware that the earthquake was continuing, despite the Gates. But before he could move, the slightest of movements caught his eye. Uncertainly, he narrowed in on the Gates once more.

And he saw the Horn and Ivory shake.

Theo snapped his sight back into his body. He was no longer under the table. The weak legs had collapsed into a timber pile and Bede's arms were around him, having just dragged him out. A young goddess screamed as a hut came tumbling down in the distance. Iara ran to help.

Theo didn't register any of it. He pulled himself from Bede's grasp and wiped the thin sheen of sweat from his brow. All he could think of was what he had just seen at the Gates.

I have to get to Rogan.

The Gatekeeper would know what was happening and which of Zion's neighbours were behind this attack. And more importantly, if Theo hadn't imagined it, if he really had seen the Gates shake, Rogan would know how to stop it.

'Theo!' Bede said, shaking his shoulder. His voice was hoarse with a desperation that showed he had obviously been calling to him for a while. 'Can't you hear that?' he asked.

Theo stared at his friend in bewilderment. What sound was he referring to? The tearing of Theo's earth? The screams of his people? He could hear all of that.

But then he did hear it, a noise draped over the commotion, like a thin quilt over a bed. The sound of a baby crying. Now that he could hear it, it was *all* that he could hear. He turned north, where the cries seemed loudest. Then without a second thought, he ran towards it.

The Sleep God ran—and destruction chased him across his realm. Sometimes the violent ground shook him as if to delay him from his course or whatever doom lay at the end of it. The clouds opened up suddenly, flooding his path with rain. But his feet were steadied by his determination and under his long stride he soon covered the breadth of land that led him to the evergreen forest.

Theo pushed through the trees, stumbling over the uprooted saplings which had been too young and too small to withstand the earthquake. All the while as he ran, the baby's cries tugged at him like a leash. At last he came to a clearing in the forest. And there, lying out in the open, young and small, the baby cried.

A Sleeper!

The baby lay on his back, naked and angry, kicking out at the world he was destroying, crying so harshly that Theo felt sick. He got closer to the child. He was tiny, his skin like spilled ink. Theo reached out to him, but the closer his hand came to the baby the harder it was to move, as if the very air itself was obstructing him. But still he stretched out his arm until just one fingertip brushed against the child's cheek and he felt the skin, smooth and waxy under his touch.

With his realm breaking apart around him, Theo put everything he had into his touch on that newborn cheek and into his voice as he commanded:

'Wake up.'

THE HOLY THEOLOGOS, BOOK ONE, VERSE II.II

During the All-Mother's pregnancy She commanded Her servants to bring Her one of everything that existed and then She proceeded to eat it all. She did not eat hurriedly, out of craving or compulsion, but She did not tell anyone why She ate either. It was only as She came to the last month of Her pregnancy that She called her servants to Her and confided in them thus:

'You may have noticed my seemingly endless appetite over the past few months. The reason that I have been eating so expansively is so that I may expose my unborn children to everything that exists so that they may know it, and once they know it, it may not harm them. There are only two things that exist that I have not yet consumed. Find these things and bring them to me before I give birth.'

And so her servants searched but they could not find what they were looking for. The last week of the All-Mother's pregnancy arrived and She despaired. But then one of her servants brought to her a strange beast, which went about on four legs and had two long antlers protruding from its skull.

'The bones of this beast contain the elements you are missing, All-Mother.'

The All-Mother rejoiced. However, before she allowed herself to eat of the beast She asked its permission, as She had of every sentient creature thus far. But this animal refused Her. The All-Mother eclipsed Herself with Her fury, but before She could release Her anger, this animal said:

'I will give you what you ask for, All-Mother, if only you would do something for me in return. Make me, and all of your servants who have worked so hard for you during your pregnancy, into Minor gods.'

The All-Mother agreed to this and She gave the beast a human shape, before she made him a god. She then snapped his antlers and began to eat of them, Horn from one and Ivory from the other. But before She was done, her waters broke, flooding the island of Pangaea below. And because She did not finish the Ivory, only one of Her three children gained immunity from it, and because She did not finish the Horn, only one of Her three children gained immunity from it.

The last child was immune to neither.

CHAPTER FIVE

Silence descended with the rain, spattering the mossy carpet of the forest. It fell in droplets on the suddenly still ground, on Theo's hands and the back of his neck as he knelt on all fours, unable to raise his head. It fell and formed puddles on the ground in front of him, in the indented shape of a baby's back, where no baby lay any longer. Theo had cut the palms of his hands when he fell, and now without thinking he released a wave of Sleep energy in himself to knit up his wounds, as well as making his hair and nails grow slightly, as his mind clouded with drowsiness. His thoughts felt slow and heavy and the child's cries still resonated in his ears, but he knew it was just an echo, a memory, a shadow. The boy's absence was clear, a great relief to him, like a weight lifted from Zion's shoulders. Yet Theo still could not raise his head.

It was only when a hand landed on his shoulder that he was able to look up. His heart sank a little to see Bede standing next to him. He had hoped for Rogan. He needed him. But Theo shook off the feeling and replaced it with the appropriate relief at seeing his friend unharmed.

'Is everyone okay?' Theo asked. His voice came out as barely a whisper.

'Iara is checking on them,' Bede said solemnly. He helped him to his feet. 'What was that, Theo?'

Theo shook his head. He couldn't think. Bede must have seen the distress in his face because he didn't let go of his arm as he led him back to the village.

Minors were gathered around the remnants of someone's hut. Most stood talking anxiously between themselves, while others lay on the ground tending small injuries or simply in shock, as Theo was. No one seemed seriously hurt. Iara had climbed onto the pile of timber that had once been someone's walls, trying to get everyone's attention.

'There he is!' she announced with relief when she saw Theo approaching.

Bede led him up to join her on the make-shift stage. A hundred voices rose at once towards them.

'What *was* that?'

'—an earthquake?'

'Did you know that was going to happen?'

'Just look at my hut!'

Iara stuck two fingers in her mouth and whistled loudly. 'Everyone shut up!' She looked angrily down at her neighbours. Only Theo could tell that the anger was a mask for her own fear. 'You're all overreacting. Now, I'm sure—'

'Is it happening, Theo? Is it war?'

Theo looked out at the crowd. The old god who had spoken, his voice ringing out like a bell, stared anxiously up at him.

The word he had plucked from everyone's mind left them all speechless. War. Once, when there was nothing to separate hate from hate, it had seemed inevitable, but now . . .

Could it be? Had Zion come under attack?

Theo thought back to the clearing in the forest. Was that his enemies' weapon of choice? An infant, a newborn *mortal* child? If it was, then Theo was insulted.

And he was terrified.

'Now, hold on. No one said anything about war,' Iara said. 'We're at peace—'

'There was never any peace, there was just the Gates!' someone else said.

'Which are right there!' Iara pointed to the horizon.

Theo's head snapped up. She was right, the Gates were still there. He'd seen them shake, but they were still standing. He almost collapsed with relief. But the crowd was not so easily subdued.

'Where's the Gatekeeper then?'

'We all knew it was coming.'

'Fanta and Torres—'

'There was a boy,' Theo said suddenly. He didn't speak loudly but everyone heard. 'A child. I woke him up.'

'A Sleeper?' Bede frowned.

Theo nodded.

'And you think this came from him?' Iara asked.

Theo shook his head. 'I don't know. But it all stopped when I woke him up.'

It seemed incredible. Theo looked out at the villages and hardly recognised them. There was destruction in every direction; the usually clean Zionese air was dusty and thick. The rain hadn't stopped.

'So,' Iara looked quickly around, then lowered her voice so that only the three of them could hear, 'what happens when he falls asleep again?'

Theo sucked in a breath. The slow fog that had descended over his brain in the forest blew away and he was able to think once more. The boy would fall asleep again. And then . . .

'I have to get down to the island.' He jumped down from the debris and began pushing his way through the crowd. Bede followed without hesitation, but Iara called him back.

'Theo, wait!' He heard her speak sternly to the other Minors. 'Theo says to start clearing everything up, rebuild, and tend to the injured. We're going to investigate this further.'

A wall of answering murmurs rose up at Theo's back. By the time he and Bede were out of the crowd, Iara had caught up to them.

'What are you going to do?' she asked, as they walked briskly through the village.

'I have to find the boy. Make sure he doesn't fall asleep again.'

And find out what he is. Theo had to know, had to be able to put a name to what he had laid his hand on in the forest.

'How are you going to do that?'

'The Magistrates will help,' Bede said.

They moved past further Minor villages. There was destruction in all of them, but less serious than around Theo's party. It seemed the damage had been worse closer to the child. The outskirts of Zion should have been completely unaffected.

Then why did the Gates shake?

Theo shook his head. He could only handle one mystery at a time.

They quickened their pace to avoid the other Minors who tried to stop them. Sometimes Iara called to them, issuing the same instructions she had already invented in Theo's name. Theo was glad to have her there. She made it seem like he had everything under control.

They were going towards the edge of the realm, to a place called the Garden— the only cultivated land in Zion. The grass was kept uniformly trimmed here and the flowerbeds had been planted by colour. Unlike the hardy brush that grew everywhere else, the plants that grew in the Garden were delicate, protected from the double sun exposure by the wooden canopies that had been erected to give them shade for half the day. A stone pathway meandered through the Garden like a dry replica of the River Zion, which didn't come this far inland. And, at the end of this path, golden railings had been erected around an area of ground that fell away into nothingness. Here was the staircase that linked the celestial realms to the world of the mortals.

Theo, Bede, and Iara approached the chasm as the staircase glowed softly from its depths. The first five steps were clearly visible, but the rest disappeared into darkness.

Theo paused at the top and looked down. Today was the day he would usually go down to Pangaea to claim his Magus so the Majoracle could officially start.

He would be excited: rest lay at the bottom of that staircase, if nothing else. But now he was standing here several hours earlier than usual. And he wasn't sure what was waiting for him down there.

'If I don't come back in time . . . I mean, if the child falls asleep again before I find him . . . Iara, will you—'

'I'll take care of everything,' she said, without looking away from the staircase. She too seemed entranced by its depths; unlike Theo, she had never been down. The staircase was just for Major gods.

'And find Rogan. He'll help. If this was planned by the other two realms, we'll need him.'

Iara frowned. 'Are you sure we can trust him? He's not one of us, Theo. And if this really was an attack by one of the other two, the only way they could have got past the Gates is if he—'

'Don't,' Theo said, cutting her off. Iara was always suspicious, but he wouldn't have her turning her suspicions on Rogan. He knew that Rogan wouldn't let anyone hurt him or Zion—and if he couldn't trust Rogan, he couldn't trust anyone.

Iara seemed to read this all on his face and the recent events must have shaken her up more than Theo suspected as, surprisingly, she relented. 'Okay then. Good luck.'

'Be careful,' Bede said.

Theo nodded. He took a deep breath. He stepped onto the first stair. Five steps later, darkness surrounded him.

* * *

On the mortal island of Pangaea, the Majority had constructed a temple tall enough for them to reach their gods. In theory. The longest spire on the domed roofs fell just short of the sky, but still they called it the Staircase Spire. No one had ever seen the real celestial staircase and it was the best substitute they had.

The real celestial staircase actually emerged in the temple's basement closet. As always, Theo hit his head on the exposed roof beams as he fumbled in the dark for the door. Outside of the closet, the basement was cavernous and musty, nothing better than an old disused storage room. There were boxes stacked in corners with the frayed edges of brown robes peeking out from where they had been folded away before either being sent for repair or deemed beyond use. Three-legged chairs were covered with grey moth-eaten sheets and both of the doors in the basement, the one that hid the staircase in the closet and the one leading up to the temple's main floor, were made of thick old wood. Theo remembered an old woman who had been First Magistrate long ago, the Majority's religious leader. She'd wanted to convert the basement into something more grandiose, with plush red carpets and incense candles burning along the stone walls. Theo had asked her not to do it. The whole purpose of the basement entrance was to be inconspicuous and it did that well as it was.

Sandalled footsteps flapped on the floorboards overhead as Magistrates hurried about with last-minute Majoracle preparations. Theo wasn't sure exactly what time it had been when he left Zion, but he guessed he was around three hours early. No one knew that he was there and he soon realised that there was no way for him to inform the appropriate people. The basement stairs led up to the hallway where he could hear all those people passing. He couldn't risk emerging from this unmarked door and revealing to a bunch of lesser Magistrates the location of the gods' entrance.

Theo tugged at his dreads in frustration. Normally the First and Second Magistrate would be waiting there to take him up when the hallways were already cleared, and the Magistrates and congregation were gathered in the main prayer room. From there they could believe that he manifested from any spore of dust or climbed down any god-reaching spire that pleased them. Theo groaned softly and sank into one of the covered chairs by the door, exhausted by his own comparisons between normality and today. It was obviously not a normal day.

So did he have time to worry about revealing the entrance? The boy could already be falling asleep again while he was down here juggling his indecision. Theo shuddered at that, the scariest thought so far. Would he be able to feel it if Zion were being destroyed again? If that unnatural boy, who could shake both Zion and the Gates around it, was already back in his realm, would Theo know?

Theo looked back at the closed closet door.

There was a tiny thud from behind it, then a voice hissed a curse and the handle began to turn. Theo froze. Had Iara followed him down? Was he too late already?

But before he could acknowledge another thought the closet door swung open and Torres Major, God of Nightmares, stepped into the room.

Torres froze at the same time that Theo sprang to his feet.

Torres raised an eyebrow. 'Jumpy,' he observed. 'And I didn't even have to say *boo!*'

Theo flinched which made Torres smile. There was a glint in the Nightmare God's eye as he spoke, a glint that Theo remembered, one that showed how Torres found the whole world funny, even if he was the only one laughing. The glint was like the oil in his tightly coiled hair and neatly trimmed goatee. There even seemed to be a mocking shine glowing through his skin, a golden brown compared to Theo's deeper umber hue. Torres's chiselled jaw quivered with the joke that only he could hear.

Had he been laughing like that, by himself, since four Majoracles ago?

Theo gulped and tried to recover some sense of calm. He wanted to sound completely in control when he spoke, as if unaffected by the presence of someone he hadn't seen since his fifteenth birthday. Since *their* fifteenth birthday. Theo looked his brother in the eye.

'Torres. You're . . . here,' he said, and in spite of everything his voice shook.

'Apparently,' Torres said, closing the closet door behind him and coming further into the room.

Theo took three involuntary steps backwards. His eyes tracked the shape of his brother's left hand in his front trouser pocket. He would feel a lot better if he could see it out in the open. Torres could all too easily be holding a handful of Nightmare material in there, and then all he would have to do is get close enough and the Horn would do the rest.

Maybe that was the plan all along. Maybe the baby was only meant to lure Theo out into this trap, with no Magistrates between them and no one who knew where he was. Iara, and even Salvador, had warned him about the possibility of this a long time ago. The likelihood that the other two Majors—Nightmare and Dream—were as satisfied as Theo was with the peace that the Gates brought was very small. If one of them had killed the All-Mother, it made sense that they would come for him next. This was why they had to be kept apart, to stop one Major from getting rid of the other two. How ambitious were the Major gods? How much power did they crave?

Theo's eyes darted to the basement door. Should he make a run for it? He was further away from it, but was he still faster than Torres, as he had been when they were five?

Then as if he were reading his mind, Torres moved position so that he was standing between him and the exit.

Theo's heart sank. He was going to die. There was no doubt in his mind now.

Torres pulled his hand out from his pocket. Theo flinched.

Torres noticed but said nothing. His hand was empty and he lifted it up to scratch his cheek, looking at his brother curiously.

Pull yourself together. Theo told himself. *Don't let him catch you off guard. Don't let him see that he already has.*

Torres folded his arms. 'You know, my realm almost just got destroyed,' he said, speaking so casually that it took a moment for Theo to process what he said.

'The Mountains too?' Theo asked, steadying his voice despite his surprise.

'Too? The same thing in Zion? Interesting. So it probably wasn't you then.'

'No. I thought . . .' He trailed off, but he didn't have to complete what he was going to say for Torres to nod in understanding anyway. Suspicion was nothing new between them.

'There was a baby,' Theo said, watching his brother's face to see if he showed any surprise. 'I think he was the one who caused this. I woke him up, then the earthquakes stopped.'

'A mortal?' Torres asked.

'Yeah. That's why I came down early, to see if I could find him.'

'Hmm.'

Torres's eyes narrowed in thought and Theo held his breath as he watched him. Would his brother believe him? Theo wasn't a good enough liar to come up with a story like this, plus he had no reason to, but Torres might not necessarily see that. If he decided that Theo actually was the one who attacked his realm, then it would mean they'd finally reached the point they'd been circling for years. Because if one of them really did have a weapon that could get through the Gates, then they had moved past the point of accusations: it would be war.

If only Theo could know what Torres was thinking at that moment. His face used to be as familiar to Theo as his own, but now, apart from his perpetually laughing eyes, his expression was unreadable, and Theo knew no matter how much he tried, he'd never know again what was written there.

'Okay, so what are we waiting for? Let's go find this kid,' Torres said, turning towards the basement door.

Theo was left standing in place for a moment, shocked by how easily Torres had believed him. But before Torres could reach the door, he remembered why he had been waiting down there in the first place.

'Wait! The Magistrates!' he hissed, suddenly aware of how loudly they'd been speaking this whole time. 'We can't let them see us.'

Torres turned back to him and scanned the basement room. He went over to one of the many boxes and pulled out two frayed robes.

He wrinkled his nose in disgust. 'The Magistrates are still wearing brown? Isn't that so . . . five centuries ago?'

* * *

Lines of brown-robed Magistrates passed by the basement door like a brood of ducklings following their mother. Some had their hoods up, covering their faces; others walked in pairs or small groups, conversing in hushed tones.

Before they left the basement, it had taken some effort for Theo to convince Torres that they should begin by seeking out the First Magistrate instead of going to find the child straight away. On their own, they wouldn't have the first idea of where to start looking and the Magistrates would save them a lot of time. Torres led the way down the corridor as if he knew where he was going. He walked with his hands clasped in front of him and his hooded head bowed, and no one batted an eyelid at his presence. Even though he walked behind him, Theo could sense the laughter in his brother's eyes at how easily the Magistrates accepted this parody of themselves. The robe was surprisingly rough against Theo's skin. He thought the Majority primarily made things for rest and comfort, but the robe felt like dry soil.

The gods turned down the first left-hand corridor they came to, which was significantly less crowded. Torres stopped a Magistrate who tried to hurry past them and kept his head down as he spoke.

'Excuse us, Magistrate, we have a message to deliver to the First. Could you tell us where he is?'

The Magistrate rolled his eyes. 'You out-of-city Magistrates shouldn't even be in the temple until the ceremony starts. All you do is get in the way. Give me the message for the First, then be on your way,' he said, holding out his hand for an expected slip of paper.

Theo took a step forward, prepared for Torres to make an excuse so they could leave, but instead his brother reached into one of the overly large pockets of his robe.

'Oh, thank you very much. We've never been to the main temple, you see, it's so much bigger than the prayer rooms at the hospital. Anyway, if you could tell the First that the faecal matter sample he provided for us at his last check-up wasn't enough. If you could just have him fill this and then return it to us at the hospital—'

'Uh, no, no,' the Magistrate said quickly before Torres could remove his hand from his pocket. 'That sounds like hospital business, I probably shouldn't get involved. Go to the end of this corridor, past the courtyard, and then a little further down the right. The First should be in his office, third door down.'

He hurried away and, as soon as he had turned the corner, Torres burst into laughter. 'Did you see his face, *irmão*?'

Theo offered a hesitant smile. 'You don't really have . . . anything in your pocket, do you?'

Torres looked at him seriously. 'No more than the usual vial I carry around with me. But it's already a little too full of my own for the First to have added any more.'

Theo couldn't help but smile.

There were no windows down the rest of the corridor, and if Theo didn't know any better he would say they were still underground. Torches lined the walls, casting a bare minimum of what could just about be called light. The brick walls trapped the damp, cold air. Theo had never seen this part of the temple before. The way the Magistrates usually led them to the prayer hall was much nicer. Here, wooden frames hung from the low walls, with detailed carvings etched into their surface. It was only as Theo passed the third or fourth one that he realised they were telling a continuous story. Two large hands held the earth in its palms; by the glow of anti-light emitted from the delicate fingers, it was clear that they were supposed to belong to the All-Mother. In the next panel she tore a piece of the giant landmass away and sent it off across the sea to become an island of its own: Pangaea, with all the All-Mother's worshippers on her back. The next panel was the longest and showed the destruction, plague,

49

and fear that swept through the rest of the world at their renouncement of the true goddess.

Theo didn't know if the carvings were an accurate depiction of life outside the island. If any of this was history instead of myth, then it all happened long before he was born. The story came to a sudden end halfway down the wall.

They came to another corridor with windows looking out onto the courtyard. Here were benches but only a few Magistrates were using them; their heads were bowed, as if in prayer.

'*Mãe de todos*, do you see that?' Torres cursed, stopping suddenly at one of the windows.

Theo followed his gaze. 'Oh. Yeah. They presented them to us a couple of Majoracles ago.'

Three stone statues sat in the centre of the courtyard, the Major gods on their thrones, looking off into the distance. The sculptor who had created them had been both remarkably talented and terrifyingly inaccurate. The faces, although recognisable, were still somehow wrong. Theo's youth had been exaggerated, making him look even younger than he had at seventeen when it was created. His cheeks had been rounded out and his eyes made bright and large. He had an almost cherubic look to him, which verged on offensive. Yet it was definitely him. To his left, Fanta's statue showed her as beautiful, and that was accurate. But the sculptor had made her too fragile, like a Zionese flower, instead of her real desert cactus beauty. Torres, on the right, had received the opposite treatment from Theo: age had been aggressively carved into the edges of his face, making him look mean. The sculptor had forgotten his smile.

Theo had forgotten that Torres wouldn't have seen them before. A lot had changed in the four Majoracles since Torres had last stepped foot on the island.

'And you let them get away with that?'

Theo smiled. 'They were supposed to be complimentary.'

'If that's a compliment then I'd hate to see what they'd do to insult us,' Torres said, running a finger around his own chin as if comparing its shape to what he saw out the window.

'We can't blame them. The only way they really know what we look like is through bad art.'

'They can see us every Night in the realms.'

'But Zion water makes them forget.'

Torres's hand paused against his goatee. 'Hmm. How is Iara, by the way?'

Theo stiffened suddenly as he remembered who he was talking to and where they were. 'We should get going,' he said quietly.

Torres looked over at him, obviously noting the change in his voice. He smiled and shrugged it off but didn't speak again until they reached the third door of the right-hand corridor. He knocked.

'Come in,' a hoarse voice said from the other side.

Inside, a cluttered desk took up most of the space in the room. There were two comfortable-looking chairs facing the one behind the desk. Next to the door was a queen-sized prayer bed with thick sheets and plumped pillows. Leatherbound volumes filled the waist-high bookshelves that ran around three walls of the room. Many of them were just one repeating title: *The Holy Theologos*, with different numerals next to the name depending on the edition. The Majority's Holy Book had been through several revised editions since the original First Magistrate put it together. The most notable revision in recent years had followed the death of the All-Mother. Theo had never read that version but, if it was anything like its predecessors, he wasn't missing out on much. To say the *Theologos* tended towards exaggeration was an understatement. The Holy Book claimed events that had never happened, put words in the gods' mouths that they had never said. According to its narrative, Theo was already a fully grown man at times when in real life he was still a child. *The Theologos* could not be trusted. When they were young, and Rogan was their schoolteacher, he had made all three of the Majors read the Book. He said it was important to understand how the Majority saw them. The answer? The Majority saw their gods as poetry—and struggled just as much to understand them.

Above the bookcases there was a round window with spiderweb panes on the back wall, but it was already dark outside on the island so no light penetrated the glass. Trident candle-holders stood in all corners of the room and it was their light that fell on the old man who sat behind the desk. He glanced up as Theo and Torres entered and closed the door behind them.

'Yes? Can I help you?' he asked.

As if they had agreed on the moment beforehand, Theo and Torres both pulled back their hoods. The old Magistrate gasped and in a flash that belied his age, he was out from behind the desk and on his knees with his face pressed against the faded carpet.

'Milords. Forgive me, I had no idea you had arrived already.'

'It's okay. You're First Magistrate . . .?'

'First Magistrate Arthur, Milord.'

Theo came forward and helped the First to his feet. Everything about the man gave off the impression of great age, although his hair wasn't yet grey. He had slim rectangular glasses and hair stuck out like fireworks from his ears. Theo held up his hand, curling his fingers into the three-fingered sign of the Major, and blessed him. After a moment of apparent hesitation Torres did the same, then hopped into the closest armchair. Arthur pulled out the second armchair for Theo. Usually, Theo would have shrunk away from such treatment, but Arthur gave him such an easy smile that Theo decided right there that he liked him. The Magistrates he had met at other Majoracles had been so rigid with formality and tradition, Theo had always been tempted to grab a pair of scissors and cut the air over their heads to see if that would loosen their strings. Whereas, as Arthur sat down on the other side of the desk, Theo imagined this was what it would feel like to be visiting an old grandfather.

'We're sorry for being early, Arthur,' Theo said.

The First shook his head. 'I can only apologise for not having my Second stationed by the staircase or personally attending to it myself in case of this eventuality. Please forgive me, Milords. And to greet you amidst such mess! Inexcusable.'

The First shook his head in embarrassment as he looked over his desk. There was a pile of wooden sticks in front of him, some with sewing string wrapped around them. An open notebook lay facing him by his elbow, filled with symbols that Theo couldn't read upside down. There was also a wooden bowl with sanded-down sides and a pyramid of tiny coloured glass balls. Three small bottles were cushioned next to each other in an open case. The first was filled with a liquid the colour of stained teeth, the second held something thick and black, and the last appeared to be nothing but smoke.

'What is all this, anyway?' Torres asked.

'This, Milord? It's divination equipment.'

Torres laughed. 'Don't tell me you use that nonsense in the Majoracle ceremony now.'

'What's divination?' Theo asked.

Arthur picked out the first small bottle and handed it to him. 'We use it to read the meanings behind certain obscure Dreams and Nightmares.'

Meanings? From twigs and marbles and smoke? Theo thought, disbelievingly. It sounded like Obeah magic to him, the kind that mortals used when they were neither Magistrates nor Magi but still wanted a taste of divine power.

'Is this a new practice?' he asked, examining the bottle.

'Not at all. It must have been around for several Majoracles already. But no, it's not used in the ceremony. May I ask if this is the reason for your early arrival, Milords? Because I assure you the ceremony is in good hands.'

'No, it's not that. We actually need your help with something and it couldn't wait,' Theo said. 'We're looking for someone. A child.'

Arthur stayed silent, waiting for more. Theo shifted uncomfortably in his seat. He realised now that it wasn't much to go on.

'Perhaps we have a name for the child? A gender? Or a specific age?' Arthur said patiently.

'A boy,' said Theo.

'Less than a day old,' Torres said.

Theo looked at him, surprised, and he shrugged.

'We know he's only gone to Sleep once. He can't be older than that,' he said.

'I see,' Arthur said, pushing up his glasses. 'Well, we should have a copy of all the island's birth records here in the temple. They are updated every day, though there may have been some delay today, since it is the Majoracle.'

'He'll be in the city,' Theo said as the thought occurred to him.

Pangaea was geographically identical to the celestial realms, down to the shape and size. Where the mortal's body fell asleep on the island dictated the rough location their soul would appear above. The boy they were looking for had appeared in the centre of Zion, which would place him somewhere in the main city on the island. He couldn't be far.

'And when do you need this child located by?'

'A couple of hours ago would have been great,' Torres muttered.

'Before the Majoracle starts,' said Theo.

'Ah.' The First Magistrate pushed his glasses up the bridge of his nose. 'Then we haven't much time to lose, have we?'

CHAPTER SIX

Thirty-six cots lined the temple hall.

A sermon stage at the front of the hall held the First Magistrate's pulpit and the gods' three thrones. Theo's was the middle of the three gold-leafed, ornately carved seats. Around the high walls of the hall were galleys with enough room to hold all the city's Magistrates. Arched stained-glass windows lined the room.

As Theo, Torres, and Arthur entered the room, the cots were just starting to be filled with a selection of screaming babies. Second Magistrate Varseer had been tasked with rounding up all those who fitted the gods' criteria, and he had put himself to the task with surprising efficiency. Only two cots were still empty. As they approached the first line of babies, Theo was the first to see the slim back of a young woman standing over one of the newly occupied cots. He noticed the kinks of her short hair, like a black woollen halo. Her hands were out of sight under the fabric of her green- and yellow-patterned kanga. And then the Dream Goddess turned around.

Her dark skin was pearlescent, and her features were round and still as she locked eyes with Theo. It was only as her gaze found Torres that her expression contorted into a vicious snarl.

'You!' Fanta said.

Torres was completely unfazed. He grinned. 'You too, *irmã*. I'm assuming that the missing part of that sentence was "nice to see."'

Fanta reached under the front of her kanga and tugged at a piece of string that hung around her neck. As the end of the necklace came into sight, Theo stumbled backwards in pure panic. Torres did the same; he wasn't laughing now. There was nothing funny about the finger-sized carving of pure Ivory hanging around his sister's neck. Fanta let the necklace hang in front of her as she straightened her back and looked at Theo.

'At least you've already caught him. I thought I might have to do it myself,' she said, much more calmly than when she first spoke.

Theo couldn't take his eyes off the Ivory. 'C-caught him?'

'Surely you know what he did? He tried to kill us!'

Torres laughed but it sounded forced to Theo's ears. 'And which time are we talking about now?'

'Dream Country was almost destroyed a few hours ago. I spoke to Rogan before I came here, and I know the same thing happened in Zion. It's a little convenient that two of the three realms were attacked on the same day that you decide to show your face at a Majoracle again, isn't it?'

'It's a little *convenient* that the good Gatekeeper neglected to mention that the same thing happened to *Os Pesadelos.*'

Theo shivered at the name of his brother's realm. He had spoken it in the tongue that he sometimes interjected into his speech, and which always made Theo nervous, for no real reason. When Theo spoke of it at all, he only ever called Torres's realm 'The Mountains.'

Fanta, obviously not affected by the language in the same way, snorted in disbelief. 'You're a liar,' she said simply.

Torres smiled. 'And you, *irmã*, are a—'

'Why don't we just assume for now that we're all telling the truth?' Theo interjected hastily. He spoke in hushed tones so that the Magistrates wouldn't overhear more than they already had. After bowing to Fanta, Arthur had made a hasty retreat to the other side of the hall once it became obvious that this wasn't about to be a happy family reunion.

Four Majoracles was a long time for the three of them to have stayed apart, but it had passed in the blink of an eye compared to the old memories that were still fresh to them—memories from further back than four Majoracles, to when they were six, when the Gates first went up. That day when concepts like trust and family had become too heavy, too dangerous for them to believe in, because look, *look* what it had done to the All-Mother, their mother, the Night. Dead, with no body to bury or mourn; killed, with no love behind the hand of whichever of her children had done it. It was clearly matricide; who else but a Major would have the power to kill the Night? Not to mention the strange circumstances in which the children were found at the time, or the blood-soaked weapons that were later discovered . . .

But the culprit wouldn't confess. Suspicion in the celestial realms went three ways like the triangle of their gazes now, all these years later, in the island temple.

Fanta folded her arms. 'So all of us were victims and none of us did it? Why does that sound so familiar?'

As suspicion had grown, so did the death count. One by one, the Minors who showed too much allegiance to one Major over another began to fall, by sips of poisoned drinks and worse methods. No one thought the six-year-old triplets had killed *all* of them. But everyone was certain that one of them had committed the first murder, the most important one, and that was enough. Then, on the brink of civil war, when the gods were at a breaking point, came the Gates. Came safety.

In the end, Theo never had to admit he didn't remember that day, didn't remember where the weapons had come from—if he ever knew—and didn't remember why he had done what he'd done on that day. He had found ways to justify his own actions to himself. But even then, he never spoke it out loud. No one needed to know.

Now, he said, 'I know who did this to our realms. I'll tell you if you promise to calm down so we can work together. Don't you want to know why we have all these babies here?'

Fanta paused, staring at him as if she was trying to decide whether or not to believe him. Theo tried not to blink. Blinking felt like something a guilty person would do.

Eventually she nodded. Only slightly, and she didn't break eye contact as she did, but it was like she was giving Theo permission to do so. He was slightly ashamed that he did look away first.

After he explained who they were looking for, he thought that she might throw her necklace at him. She had a look on her face that said, *Do you really think I'm that stupid?* That, or, *Are you really that stupid?*

But, surprisingly, all she did was glare at Torres and stand quietly to one side as the rest of the cots were slowly filled. He was left standing between Fanta's and Torres's two turned backs. Just as Zion was closed in, between Dream Country and the Mountains. Somehow he always ended up being the one keeping his older siblings apart. And it always left him surrounded and vulnerable on both sides.

One by one, Theo checked the screaming, wrinkled faces of the mortal children. Their distress might have been due to the cold that permeated the cavernous hall, or it may have had something to do with being separated from their mothers who were being looked after by some lower Magistrates in another room.

He moved quickly, to end the traumatic experience for them and for himself.

'He's not here,' he announced, tugging anxiously at the ends of his dreads as he came to the last cot.

'You barely looked at them,' Fanta accused. 'They're babies, they all look alike.'

Theo shook his head. *Not this one. I would remember his face anywhere.*

'We don't have time for this!' Fanta said. 'Let's just deal with *him* now.' She stabbed her chin at Torres.

Theo tried to remain calm as he answered her, though he was sure his own nerves showed all too plainly in his voice.

'Since we're still assuming that we're all innocent,' he reminded her carefully, 'we need to find out who the boy is and how he did what he did. Rogan will probably know. We just have to get the boy up to him so he can tell us.'

'And how do we do that? Rogan won't leave the realms and if we let the boy fall asleep again all we get is a repeat display of what he can do,' said Torres.

Theo hesitated. It felt good to know that at least one of his siblings was taking his plan seriously—but Fanta was right: he hadn't had time to think it out very well.

'I was thinking, maybe, that what he did only happens when he enters the realms normally,' he said finally. 'If we take him up the staircase with us—'

'You intend to allow a *mortal* on the staircase?' Fanta interjected.

'He's a baby, he won't remember it,' Theo reasoned.

The Dream Goddess straightened her back. Self-righteousness had always been her great postural aid. 'That's not the point. There are some things that a god cannot show their followers. Divine mysteries.'

'The mystery is why you think that's important right now,' Torres said.

The hall doors swung in and Varseer entered. He awkwardly held what appeared to be a bundle of cloth in each arm. As he got closer Theo saw two tiny faces peek out from behind their wrapping. Pale faces, like calcified fingernails. Theo sighed.

'Here are the last two children, First,' Varseer said.

'It's not them,' Theo said before Arthur could present them. 'You're sure you got them all?'

'Our records show seventy-four children born in the city today. Thirty-six males,' Arthur said, double-checking the papers in his hand.

'Could he have been taken out of the city?' Torres suggested.

'I doubt he would have got far enough for us not to know about it, Milord. All island transport shut down last night for the Majoracle.'

Theo's shoulders sank. This had been their only plan. Theo knew that mortal time moved much faster than his own, but he'd never felt it pressing down on him so much on the island as today. There were only two more hours until midnight, the official start of the Majoracle. The Gates of Horn and Ivory would close to Sleepers as soon as the clock struck. What would they do with the boy then, even if they did find him? How would they get him back to Rogan?

A sudden commotion out in the corridor caused everyone's head to turn towards the closed doors. Something crashed and the sound of raised voices reached their ears. Varseer hurried over to find out what was going on, but before he got there the double doors crashed open and a robed figure practically fell into the room, scrambling away from three others who were trying to grab a hold of a flailing limb.

'What's going on here?' Arthur said, raising his voice more than Theo would have thought him capable of.

The three Magistrates who had been in chase flushed as they found themselves standing face to face with the two highest Magistrates and the three gods. It seemed as if they were about to bow down until the first figure, who had come in ahead of them, got up and tried to run again. Then they all started forward but Varseer got there first. His hand tightened around the fleeing Magistrate's forearm and—

No, not a Magistrate, Theo realised.

The woman wore similar robes to the religious leaders, similar to the ones Theo and Torres still wore, but lighter in colour, almost golden brown—and, without the high neckline and tight belt of a Magistrate's robes, they were hanging loosely open, revealing the shape of her naked body underneath.

'You?' Varseer growled in disbelief. He pulled back the woman's hood and grabbed a handful of the blonde ringlets of her hair so that her face was forced to look up at him. She cried out but Varseer ignored her and turned on the other three—the real Magistrates. 'How dare you bring her here?'

One of the Magistrates began to explain. 'Second, we—'

'Varseer! Not here!' Arthur said. He tried to place himself between the gods and the scene unfolding in front of them, but Fanta stepped around him.

'Why are you treating this woman so roughly? Explain yourself!' the Dream Goddess commanded.

'I work only in your service, Milady!' the woman cried. Her voice was strained as Varseer continued to pull on her hair. 'The Dream Goddess guides me in all that I do. I am her servant, I am her vessel.'

'Shut up!' Varseer said.

'Release her. And let her speak,' Fanta ordered.

She watched the woman as Varseer reluctantly let her go. She fell to her knees. Theo recognised the look on his sister's face. It was the one she put on at every Majoracle choosing ceremony as she let her Magus candidate grovel before her in gratitude for being chosen. Theo remembered one Magus who had delivered a forty-minute ode to the Goddess's benevolence and, while the rest of the congregation blinked in bemusement at his amateur poetry, Fanta drank it all in. Mortals never interested her more than when they were worshipping her.

'Oh, Milady,' the wrongly-robed woman said. 'My name is Belmira and I *am* your humble servant, unlike these vicious Magistrates who claim to be, though they raid my home with no warning and drag me through the streets before my neighbours. You've seen how they treat me, Milady, with no provocation. Please, I throw myself at your mercy.'

Fanta looked at Arthur. 'Is what she says true, First?'

'Does it matter?' Torres asked. 'You do remember why we're here, right? Let the mortals deal with their own affairs, we have something a little more important to do right now.'

'So go do it then,' Fanta snapped. 'Leave me to handle this.'

But even though Theo agreed with Torres, he knew they couldn't do anything until Fanta was with them. If they went off on their own to find the child now, Fanta would take it as 'evidence' that they were conspiring against her. All they could do was wait.

'It's not as she makes it sound, Milady,' Arthur explained. 'She is a criminal, that is why she was brought here.'

'Under what charges?'

Arthur shifted uncomfortably on his feet and the tips of his hairy ears turned pink. In the end it was Varseer who saved him.

'She will be tried under the laws of trafficking, unlawful body labour, and blasphemy, among other things. She's a Sister.'

Fanta frowned. 'What's a "Sister"?'

This time Varseer looked to Arthur for permission before he spoke. The old Magistrate nodded.

'The Sisters are a group within the Majority who dedicate themselves to pleasure. They claim that it is only through physical pleasure that we come close to spiritual connection with the gods. They place a particular significance on yourself, Milady, the link between Dreams and pleasure, as they sell their bodies to this end.'

'So?' Fanta said, completely unfazed. 'I don't hear that she's done anything wrong.'

Varseer cleared his throat. He looked deeply uncomfortable. 'While being a Sister is not illegal, there is a particular group of them who take it too far. They have begun to force, trick, and blackmail people into the profession, as a form of cheap labour. They are even suspected of kidnapping some of their workers. Poor people are particularly at risk of falling into their clutches. We have been trying to track them down for a while but the information we get on the location of their Houses is always one step behind them. This woman here is one of the known affiliates of this group.'

Fanta looked at the still-kneeling Sister without blinking. 'You do this in my name?'

'I do everything in your name, Milady.'

Amazingly, her eyes still shone with expectation, as if she thought Fanta would congratulate or even reward her for what she so brazenly confessed to doing.

Fanta approached her and lifted her chin with one hand, more gently than Theo would have expected. The woman's whole body shook at the goddess's touch but Fanta made sure to hold her head steady as she spoke.

'I've allowed poor men and princes to Dream of being kings. I've allowed broken hearts to Dream of love and empty stomachs to Dream of feasts. There is nothing that I cannot put in a mortal's mind if they so wish it and ask it of me.' Her voice was gentle, her face unreadable. 'I've allowed the beaten child to Dream of whittling his own knife, so that when he wakes the movements are familiar to his hands. I've allowed the hunting cat to Dream of where the mouse is hiding—and when she wakes she finds her prey right where I told her it would be.' With the slightest movement her hand went from the Sister's chin to wrap around her throat. 'I've allowed the skies of the celestial realms to Dream of Night. But I have never, *never*'—fingers tightening—'forced one person to fulfil the Dreams or pleasure of another, taken away their free will, or invaded their body or mind. *How dare you use my name?*'

The Sister's face was swelling up, colouring with stagnant blood. Her fingernails scratched against the temple floorboards as she stifled every instinct in her body that told her to fight. She wouldn't raise her hands to the goddess, even if it was to save her own life. That would be one blasphemy too many. No one else was willing to come to her aid either. The Magistrates looked awkwardly at their feet or straight ahead, unblinking. Torres was watching Fanta, his eyes narrowed, though not in concern, not in anger—in curiosity, maybe. Only Theo had his eyes on the Sister. Her lower body had gone limp and her fluttering eyelids were beginning to close as she descended into unconsciousness. He wondered if she could see the Gates of Zion opening for her already.

'Stop it, Fanta,' Theo said. 'Enough.'

She didn't listen. Her fingers tightened.

'Fanta!'

'She deserves to die,' Fanta snarled.

'No, she doesn't. Trust me, death is too good for her.' He was speaking quickly but calmly. He couldn't let Fanta hear the panic in his voice. She already had the scent of blood in her nose and, if she smelled his weakness too, there'd be no calling her back from that. 'Let the Magistrates deal with her as they must. We'll have her exiled, taken from the island, her and everyone like her. But please, Fanta, let her go. Let's leave this and go find this missing baby. He must still be in the city somewhere and we're running out of time. Please.'

Finally, Fanta raised her gaze and met his eyes. Theo couldn't tell what look was more venomous, the one she gave to him or to the woman at her feet. He could see the disgust plainly written on her face. *You would beg for a mortal's life?*

I would.

And then she let go. The Sister fell on her back gasping for air and the loitering Magistrates immediately rushed forward to pick her up by her elbows and drag her out of the gods' sight.

'Baby—' the Sister croaked when she was almost out the door. A fit of coughing silenced her but she grabbed onto the door frame so the Magistrates couldn't move her until it passed. 'Baby—'

'What is she saying?' Torres asked.

The Magistrates dropped the Sister to let her speak now that she had caught yet another god's attention.

'You're looking for a baby in the city,' she said, her voice a vacuum. 'I know where you can find one. I'll take you.'

'You think we'll let you escape that easily?' Fanta scoffed.

'I won't try to escape. I promise, Milady. Milords,' the Sister's eyes filled with tears as she turned to Theo and Torres, who had already shown mercy and patience with her once. 'There is an infant in one of the Sister's Houses. A boy, who was brought in with his mother last night. I've seen him with my own eyes.'

And what else have your eyes seen within those walls? Theo suppressed a shudder. *She just admitted they have children in those Houses.*

'I don't believe her,' Torres told him quietly.

'It's the truth! His mother was in the middle of birthing him when we found her so she's not yet . . . um, been put to work.' She glanced nervously at Fanta who glared. 'I'll give you directions. I don't even want to come with you, so you know I'm not trying to escape.'

'And your fellow Sisters don't have to know you betrayed them?' Varseer sneered.

'I have nothing to gain from doing this. Except . . . except, Milord, if you find that I am telling the truth, perhaps the sentence of exile can be reconsidered. Please,' she said desperately, 'Pangaea—the Majority is all I have.'

Theo considered her. *What if she's telling the truth?*

'Give the Magistrates directions. But, since we know you have experience lying to them, I want you to know that they won't be going alone. We'll be going with them to check out the House and see if this baby exists.'

'Outside the compound?' Arthur asked, eyes widening behind his glasses.

Theo looked at his siblings who both nodded in approval. Then he turned back to the Sister who had practically collapsed with relief.

'Yes. Outside the compound.'

CHAPTER SEVEN

When the All-Mother died she left her corpse on Pangaea. It had been so long Theo had almost forgotten what it looked like.

Night-time.

As they came out into the temple courtyard, the darkness dazzled him. After all the years of blue skies and constant sun, Theo found himself having to turn his head away from the moonlight and stars as his chest constricted with memories. He turned his attention instead to the view on the ground, where points of candlelight around the island marked the darkness like holes in a net. It may have been late, but the island was still very much awake.

None of the Major triplets had ever really seen how their worshippers lived before. Every other trip down the staircase had seen them confined within the four walls of the temple, where the Magistrates could control everything they saw and everyone they came into contact with. Arthur already saw the Sister's interruption of their meeting earlier as a lapse in his duties and he was reluctant to allow a second. The First Magistrate spent several agonising minutes trying to convince his gods to take a retinue of Magistrates as security. But Magistrates were rarely seen together in large groups and on the First Day of the Majoracle when they were expected to be walled up within the temple, they would attract more attention than ever. So it was that, as Theo, Torres, and Fanta stepped out of the temple compound for the first time, only Second Magistrate Varseer was with them.

Theo watched the Magistrate in secret fascination. Varseer held himself with an imposing confidence that most other mortals dropped in the presence of their gods. Theo was sure they would be safe under his protection.

They emerged amongst the crowds of the main street where people were waiting at the temple doors for a chance of securing a seat inside once the ceremony began. They rolled up the tents they'd slept in while staking their place in the queue over the last few days. Theo pulled the hood of his robe closer to hide his face. Fanta had been given a robe of her own to match the ones her brothers had stolen and, so far, their disguises seemed to be working well. Even those he came close to didn't meet his eyes but ducked their heads and addressed him in low voices.

'Bless me, Magistrate.'

He curled his fingers into the familiar three-fingered sign of the Major and then moved on, leaving his petitioners unaware that they had just received the most sacred blessing of their lives.

They soon turned off the temple street and there was a noticeable change around them as they went further into the city centre. The buildings here were tall and thin, though none reached so high as the temple spire behind them, and their roofs were flat instead of domed. Children ran across the roofs without fear, easily hurdling the gaps between each building.

There were women in thin, airy skirts and trousers and men in wide-brimmed hats with ribbons tied around them, like the Zion Minors would wear. Teenage girls seemed to prefer clothes like Fanta's kanga, while young boys wrapped themselves in the island's green flag as they danced the samba. Everyone had some area of skin bared, showing off their various complexions, as the press of bodies only increased the island heat even at Night. Tattoos were strewn across plump thighs and muscular forearms, self-decoration being common here. The crowds were the only constant in the ever-changing streets of celebration.

The effect was dizzying. One second a smell of spiced meat in the air made Theo gag and wish to close up his nostrils, but then a new smell of roasting fruit on the next street made him inhale greedily. Colourful ribbons were strung up overhead and banners hung out of open top-storey windows like drying laundry. Music played from somewhere—many different songs that joined together to create one that seemed to come from the moon.

Theo looked up at the sky again. Just looking made his heart ache but somehow he couldn't keep his eyes away from it. He felt as if he had stepped into the past with the Night sky above him once again, on an island which reminded him so much of what Zion once was. All around him, words from Torres's and Fanta's languages nestled together comfortably in the same sentence as words from their common language. The loose and open tones of one dialect met the guttural and nasal tones of another. It sounded like everyone he passed was in the middle of a song. Theo had almost forgotten that once it was all one language, that to the Majority it still was. It was even harder for Theo to remind himself that he had once spoken this all-encompassing language as fluently as anyone he heard around him.

The streets became more crowded as they walked. There were so many people! Theo had never before seen the full scope of the mortals' numbers; on a normal Night only a third of their population entered Zion, with the other two-thirds going to his siblings. Even though as he looked around he was aware that he wasn't seeing all of them, there was still an overwhelming number. And all of them out here—to celebrate him? Had everyone he had seen in passing so far at some point whispered his name in prayer?

They had. Theo only had to think about it and he could even know what they had prayed for.

That woman over there, a farmer from out of town, had prayed for a plentiful harvest after the torrential rains of last season.

That dancer over there had prayed that the man he was supposed to marry really was just busy with work lately and wasn't trying to avoid him.

That child over there had prayed that Nana wasn't lonely in Zion, now that she had gone to stay up there for good.

All these people had different prayers, different paths that they had chosen for their lives. None of them had their destiny chosen for them from birth. Even the idea of being able to think of a different life was a dizzying kind of freedom. Theo wouldn't give up the peace of his realm for all the riches in the Celesterra, but sometimes . . . sometimes he wondered what kind of life he would lead outside Zion. If he were not a god, what kind of man would he be?

As he craned his neck not to miss any of the faces of the people he passed, he almost walked right into the back of a child, skipping between two ropes with her friends.

Theo disentangled his feet from the ropes but when he looked around, Torres, Fanta, and Varseer were nowhere in sight. His heart pounded in his chest.

Don't panic, he told himself, *nothing will draw more attention than panicking.*

He forced himself to walk calmly to the end of the street where he hoped it would be easier to scan the crowd for three Magistrates. Pangaeans jostled him until his hood almost fell back from his face. He grabbed hold of it and took another look around. He knew that they'd been moving in this direction when he lost them. From what little Theo knew about the island's geography, he knew that if they kept walking in a straight line he would eventually reach the docks. He couldn't see the others anywhere on this avenue but there were two narrow streets branching off near him. A group of teenagers bumped against his shoulder, knocking him towards the left one. And there was Torres. Waiting for him.

Theo hurried towards him and mumbled a thanks. Torres only smiled, as if to say, *That's what big brothers are for. If I wasn't here to find you when you were lost, who would be?*

They walked on together. There was a different atmosphere to the new crowds than on the main streets. Festive excitement was still palpable but it felt muted and heavy like a long-held secret. People spoke in whispers.

'Bless me, Magistrate,' someone hissed in Theo's ear.

He held up his hand to them automatically, but a strange feeling of guilt overcame him as the person accepted it and moved on. For some reason on these narrow avenues, blessings felt like sin, immoral and unclean. Theo hurried along.

Outside a house that looked like any other, with the number nine painted on its door, a small group of two women and one man watched the crowds go by, wearing what he now recognised as Sisters' robes. As he watched, a lanky young woman approached one of the female robed figures. She handed her a handful of silver coins and the Sister smiled charmingly as she took first the money, then the woman's hand. The Sister held up her hand and blessed the woman, then kissed her on the mouth and led her back into the house.

Fanta and Varseer were waiting for them in the shadows of number eleven.

'It seems she wasn't lying. This is the group she belongs to, I recognise several of them,' Varseer mumbled as Theo and Torres joined them.

Theo snuck a glance at his sister, but her eyes were so fixated on number nine and her face was so rigid with anger, she appeared almost catatonic.

'Maybe we should have come with more people,' Varseer said, 'so we could have arrested everyone inside. Now they will all escape once they realise we know about this location.'

But as much as Theo wanted to see these people brought to justice, it wasn't what they were there for.

'We have a plan?' Torres whispered to Theo.

Before he could formulate an answer, Fanta stepped out of the shadows and towards the House. Her brothers hissed after her but the Second was the first to react, falling into step after her, his back already tensed in a protective stance.

'Oh. Happy Majoracle, Magistrates,' the remaining female Sister said with a forced smile as she noticed them approaching. She glanced over at her male companion who immediately slipped inside, presumably to warn the others. 'Can I help you with something?'

Theo expected Fanta to start making demands. Accusations. Threats.

Instead, the Dream Goddess said very simply, 'We're coming inside.'

'Ah. I'm afraid that won't be possible. You see, my friends inside are deep in . . . prayer. Meditation. It wouldn't be good to disturb them before the Majoracle. Perhaps, if you come back—'

Fanta dropped her hood. The woman gasped and fell to her knees, almost into the goddess's arms.

'Milady,' she wheezed. 'I, we . . .'

Without a word Fanta stepped past her to the doorway and rattled the handle.

'He locked it,' she said and Varseer went to aid her.

Theo, who was busy nervously scanning the street to see if anyone else had seen Fanta's dramatic revelation, didn't see what the Magistrate did next, but he heard the House door click open and turned just in time to watch them go inside. Torres waited for Theo to go in ahead of him, then he closed the door on the still kneeling figure of the Sister outside.

As soon as he took one step through the door Theo felt the atmosphere of the House press down on him. The walls were lined with candles which, through some art Theo knew nothing of, emitted a purple flame that made the shadows they cast seem deep enough to drown in. After the Sister's confession Theo had braced himself for what he might see coming into this place; he hadn't considered what he might hear. The reverberating echoes of grunts and cries painted a more vivid picture of the illicit acts on the other side of the walls than anything he could have been confronted with in that narrow hallway. Mercifully, the numerous doors of the lower level were closed and only Varseer took it upon himself to peek his head inside and check for the child.

'Upstairs,' he suggested, leading the gods.

Fanta's fingernails scraped the wood of the banister as she ascended, whether to mark her territory or physically scrape away any association to herself like a layer of dead skin, Theo didn't know. The noises of the House became clearer as they got to the second floor and heard, mingled with them, a rhythmic chanting, the unmistakable sound of prayer.

'Sound familiar, *irmã?*' Torres muttered from a few steps behind her.

She snapped around and threw him a vicious look. 'What's that supposed to mean?'

Torres shrugged. 'You make pretty speeches but you and I both know that you're not too upset about all this. Whether these mortals are forced to be here or not, they're here for you. You must really love it.'

Fanta spun around fully to face him and her left hand twitched up as if to reach for her Ivory necklace—but before she could do anything more Theo's voice halted her in her tracks.

'Stop!' he shouted.

The Dream Goddess turned her pre-loaded anger towards him. But Theo hadn't been talking to her. At the other end of the corridor, where the ceiling sloped down almost to crouching height, a cluster of five or six Sisters were in the middle of slipping quietly into a small attic door. Each one held a pale and disoriented-looking youth closely to their side, in various states of undress. One Sister had been holding her hand over her hostage's mouth, but let it fall when she saw the group on the stairs. With his hand still at the keyhole, the male Sister they had seen outside spun around at Theo's call and his eyes went wide.

'Ah! Magistrates . . . I didn't see you there,' he said, straightening up with an easy smile.

'Evidently,' Varseer said coldly. 'But spare us your excuses for now. Where is the child you have hidden here?'

'Child? I don't know what you mean. Of course, if your preferences lean towards one of our younger Sisters, I'm sure we could accommodate you,' he said as he pushed forward the boy at his side. He was maybe sixteen years old but with the wide-eyed look of terror he gave Varseer, as if the Magistrate might take the Sister up on his offer, he looked even younger.

Fanta growled. The Sister turned to look at her, but while some of his companions cowered away, no flash of recognition sparked in his eyes. Theo almost wanted to laugh. The Sisters pretended to have been instructed in what they did in their Dreams, and yet this one had been out of Dream Country for so long he couldn't even recognise the Goddess when she stood ready to pounce.

'We could accommodate all of you,' the man continued, oblivious. 'It wouldn't be the first time we catered to the Magistrates, after all. We know what you like, and we'd be happy to consider it a Majoracle gift from our House to yours. Pleasure before rest, isn't that what *The Holy Theologos* says?'

Theo had no idea, but the fact that this person was now quoting scripture at him made his heart pound in his chest. And what did he mean by, 'we know what you like'?

The Magistrates don't come here, do they? They wouldn't!

Theo glanced at Varseer but if the Second knew anything about what the Sister was referring to, he didn't show it.

'I have a better idea. How about you show us where the child is and when I have you and your friends arrested afterwards I won't add the charges of attempted bribery of a temple official? Who knows, if you take us to the boy before I really lose my temper, perhaps I will send a prayer to the gods so they might repeal your impending exile sentence.' He glanced at Fanta. 'Although somehow I doubt it.'

With all the arrogance wiped out of him like fog on a warm summer morning, the Sister visibly paled and gulped. Wordlessly, he pointed. Second door on the right.

Torres was the closest and within two strides he was there and pushing it open. Theo and Fanta followed while Varseer stayed behind to monitor the potential runaways.

'Oh, *Mãe de todos*,' Torres whispered as he looked into the room.

Theo had to look over his brother's shoulder before he saw.

A dark-skinned woman huddled in the corner of the room, her hair a matted shock around her bloodied face. One of her eyes was swollen shut and the cheek underneath was like a large apple fallen to the hard ground from a high branch. A gag pinched tightly around her face and over her ears, and her eyes, which had been tightly shut, snapped open to find the group of strangers staring at her. She began to mumble desperately into her gag, pushing herself further into the corner as she locked eyes with the gods. She was dressed in rags and the soles of her feet were crusted over with something brown and foul-smelling. No one turned their heads away or pinched their nose: they were all focused on the loosely wrapped bundle inside the woman's arms. And now, with the door open and the cooler air of the hallway blowing against his face, the baby began to cry.

The woman's ankles were bound with rope and probably her wrists too, though they were hidden under the wailing bundle in her arms. She cowered away from Theo as he came closer, her whimpers filling the room to match her child's.

'It's okay,' he said gently, holding out his hands. 'I'm not going to hurt you.'

She didn't seem to understand him. Her eyes were wide and shone with fear. Theo pulled down his hood and tried a smile but that only seemed to terrify her more.

Did these people smile before they did this to her?

He wondered if he should have let Fanta come in here first, instead of him. She wasn't gentler than Theo, but would this woman feel safer to see *her* smile? He should have thought of it before, but as soon as he had seen this woman's face and heard her baby cry . . .

I recognise that cry.

It seemed impossible, but he did. It might sound the same as any other child's cry, but he would bet Zion that *this* was the one he'd heard, followed, and brought an end to only a few hours before.

'It's okay,' he repeated, turning back to the boy's mother. 'I'm not going to let anyone hurt you. I'm not like those people, you're safe with me. I'm Majority.'

Why did he say that? As if that one word proved anything. The Sisters also claimed to be Majority—and look where that had got her. Theo immediately felt foolish for the words that he knew the woman didn't understand anyway. He sighed and straightened up, prepared to let Fanta take over.

The woman moaned under her gag. She must have been in pain. There were cuts on her body that looked fresh and Theo also caught sight of her inner thighs under her bunched-up dress, which were coated in blood and other signs of afterbirth. The woman moaned again. Theo wished he could help her. If the Majoracle was not so near, he wouldn't hesitate to put this woman to Sleep to help her heal. He briefly considered reaching for the minds of some of the nearby Sisters and taking the Sleep energy out of them to give to her. But even though they would deserve it, Theo couldn't bring himself to seriously consider doing what he had long ago promised himself he never would. His purpose was to give energy, not take it.

He looked into her eyes once more, hoping to convey at least his sympathy, and then he saw it. There was no fear in her eyes anymore. They were narrowed as if she was asking him a question. Only then did he realise that her noises were not the wordless moans of before. She was trying to say something.

Carefully, he crouched down again and reached forward to untie her gag.

The woman licked her cracked white lips before she spoke.

'Majority?' she croaked.

'Yes. Yes, I'm Majority.'

The woman's eyes filled with tears. She nodded down at herself with her chin. 'Majority.'

'You're Majority too?'

She nodded. Theo smiled and this time the woman returned the gesture. Her two front teeth were cracked and her gums were bloody, but she had a wide and beautiful smile. Theo untied her and this time she made no objection. She simply raised her baby closer to her chest, hiding the face.

'Please,' the woman said, removing one hand from under her baby's head so she could grab Theo's wrist. It was only as she spoke this second word that her accent became obvious. She lisped it, shortening the sound of the vowels: *pliss.*

Through the thin walls of the House a sudden volley of explosive noise made the woman jump and the baby's cries louder. There was a small window in the woman's prison, too high for a person to reach, but offering a clear view of the Pangaean sky as a flash of fireworks marked the clocks striking midnight on the First Day of the Majoracle.

Theo, Torres, and Fanta exchanged a glance that said all that needed to be said:

Too late.

But still they turned back to the beaten woman and her child.

She'd fallen silent and now just rested in exhaustion with her head against the back wall as if she knew the danger had passed.

Theo held up the three-fingered sign of the Major before her half-closed eyes.

'Majority,' he said.

She nodded and he blessed her. He then lowered his hand so it was hovering just above the bundle in her arms.

'Majority?'

She hesitated. Then unfolded her embrace, revealing the child who had found her breast and was suckling peacefully for its milk. Theo recognised his face. Tiny, ink-spilled, powerful.

Hello, little Realm-destroyer, he thought. He felt suddenly like a great weight had been lifted from his shoulders. He'd found him. *Now what are you?*

'This is him,' he confirmed in a voice that was barely a whisper.

Fanta and Torres stepped forward for a better look.

'He looks like any other mortal to me,' Fanta said.

'So we should take him, right?' Torres said. 'I know it's too late to get him back to Rogan but—'

'No. We're not going to part them like that.' Theo spoke firmly and both of his siblings seemed surprised by the sternness in his voice.

'Maybe this is a good thing, he won't be able to get into the realms for the Majoracle, so we can just come back in five days when we have a better plan in place and take him then,' Fanta said. 'Or better yet, since his mother's not a Pangaean, we just get them both taken off the island and not be allowed back. Then he won't ever be able to get into the realms again.'

Torres snorted. 'Is that what you do with all your problems, *irmã*? Send them far away so you don't have to think about them?'

Fanta scowled at him. 'It's what I would *like* to do for quite a few problems I can think of.'

Theo shook his head. He hadn't yet spoken to his siblings about everything he'd seen in Zion during the quake. He was hoping he wouldn't have to, at least not until he'd spoken to Rogan first. Now he had no choice.

'The Gates might not stop him,' Theo admitted. 'Either during the Majoracle or off-island. When I woke him up earlier, I saw something in my realm sight. He wasn't just causing an earthquake. He was shaking the Gates.'

Torres and Fanta fell silent. Theo found that he couldn't take his eyes off the baby's face to be able to see their expressions.

'Are you sure?' Fanta asked softly. She sounded younger and without turning around Theo could almost believe that it was his six-year-old sister standing behind him.

He nodded.

There was a heavy pause within the room and for a moment all that could be heard was the woman's shaky breaths and the male Sister's resumed pleading and bargaining as he stood outside with Varseer.

'We could ask Rogan to open up the Gates for a second so we can bring him in,' Fanta suggested finally.

'But if we break the Majoracle for even a second we sacrifice the whole thing for all of us,' Torres said.

They all remembered that lesson. Rogan had taught it to them early on, back when they still shared the same classroom.

'Maybe it's worth it,' Fanta said.

Theo thought about all the tired Minors he had left back in Zion. They'd been waiting for this Majoracle for a long time, for a chance to temporarily put aside their power and responsibility and just get some rest. They deserved it. Would they forgive him if he made this choice?

'Maybe,' Torres agreed. Then paused. 'But we're forgetting the obvious here. Not *all* mortals are forbidden in the realms during a Majoracle.'

Theo's first thought was of the Duppies. Was Torres suggesting they kill the boy? But then he realised what his brother really meant. Magi.

Magi were allowed through the Majoracle Gates.

Full of milk, the baby nudged away his mother's nipple and began to cry softly, as if from lack of anything else to do. His mother rocked him.

'We take him back to the temple and one of us chooses him as their Magus,' Torres said.

Fanta frowned. 'But Theo and I always choose our Magi in advance. We can't just change now.'

Torres opened his mouth to say something but just then Theo remembered something. 'I haven't chosen anyone yet.'

Torres's mouth snapped shut and Fanta looked shocked.

'You haven't?'

'I . . . left it too late.' He should have given Rogan his Magus's name before he left for the island, but what with the surprise party and the earthquake he had completely forgotten to even look for the girl's name in his mind. Which meant he hadn't yet chosen a Magus. If they had gone back to the temple without thinking of this, Theo would have had to forfeit Zion's Majoracle anyway. This was the perfect solution.

The baby's screams intensified and the mother began making gentle noises between her teeth like the sea lapping against the dockside.

'But—' Torres began.

'Why should you get to take him?' Fanta said.

Theo shrugged. 'What difference does it make?'

'He was in Zion when this whole thing started. And I'm still not convinced that you're not the one behind all this,' she said, folding her arms.

Theo stared at her in disbelief. He looked to Torres for support but his brother's eyes were downcast and he didn't seem to be listening.

'He should come with me,' Fanta said.

'But you already have a Magus.'

'So you take her. I'll take him.'

'Why would I agree to that?'

'You should be grateful I'm offering her to you in the first place. I could just let you forfeit.'

Theo spluttered and stood up from where he'd been crouching this whole time. 'Grateful? I—'

'Maybe I should decide.'

They both stopped and looked at Torres. Even the woman looked away from Theo with a wide-eyed expression as if she suddenly understood what everyone was saying.

'You must be joking,' said Fanta.

'Well, why not?' He shrugged.

'I don't trust you.'

Torres smiled slightly and, Theo thought, a little sadly. 'I know that, *irmã*. You've both made that very clear in the past.'

Theo couldn't help looking away. There were decisions he had made a long time ago about Torres, decisions he didn't regret but wasn't proud of either. But did that mean he didn't trust him?

Torres continued. 'If we want to keep things fair and speed this up a little, I should pick who gets to take him for a Magus. What do you think, *irmão*?'

Theo stayed silent as he considered what Torres was saying, but he was distracted as the baby started to cry once more. If he didn't let Torres decide, he would have to make the decision himself and risk stoking Fanta's anger or just making the wrong choice.

'Okay. You pick.'

Torres grinned and gave Fanta a better-luck-next-time kind of shrug. Theo could remember him taunting her the same way when they were kids and she frowned, probably remembering the same thing.

'Fine. But hurry up, this baby is getting on my nerves. I wish he would just shut up.' She folded her arms tighter across her chest in annoyance and glared down at the child.

'Okay, well, I'll try not to let your natural maternal instinct sway me too much in this decision,' Torres said and grinned when he caught Theo trying to cover his smile. 'But I think I'm going to have to give it to Theo. For the simple reason that Rogan was already in Zion when we left. It should save some time getting the kid to him and getting some answers.'

Fanta grumbled something under her breath. She couldn't argue with Torres's logic, but she still did not look happy about it.

It also helped Torres's decision that Theo seemed to be the only one that the woman trusted near her child. She flinched away from Fanta when she tried to help her to her feet, and she snatched the baby away from Torres after she saw he was struggling to hold him, but she leaned on Theo's arm as they left the room. She stayed close to him as they came back out to Varseer, smiling whenever he caught her eye.

Theo smiled back, shakily, trying not to let his concern show. No Magus had ever been taken under the age of sixteen before. The price was considered too high for someone that young. Because along with the prestige and the power, being chosen came with a death sentence. Something about spending five unfiltered, uninterrupted days in the celestial realms shortened a Magus's lifespan. In Pangaea, those who died young were said to have made their Magus's bed.

The longest-living Magus was one of Fanta's, who'd lived for fourteen years after being chosen.

Theo looked again at the boy and then at his mother. If trying to explain that he was taking her child away from her into the celestial realms would be hard, how would he explain that their actions would mean her son probably wouldn't live past the age of fourteen?

As Varseer led them back towards the entrance of the House, the woman stopped Theo by waving the baby in front of his face.

'Ereon,' she said.

'Ereon,' Theo repeated, relieved that he could finally give the strange boy a name.

'Majority,' his mother said, still displaying him proudly.

'Majority,' Theo agreed.

THE HOLY THEOLOGOS,
BOOK ONE, VERSE II.I

And because the weight of the world is heavy, and the length of eternity is long, our gods, holy-be-their-names, were not afraid to admit that they were tired.

The gods alighted upon the earth and said unto the masses: 'Who shall provide Sleep for the Sleepless? Who will heal the healers?'

And the Majority fell upon their knees and submitted themselves to the duty.

'For five days,' the gods announced, 'we shall take our rest. For five days the Gates of our realms shall be closed to you. You will be tired. You will be weak. Yet you will be proud, for you shall know that your deprivation serves us.'

Hence it was decided that on the anniversary of the Major triplets' birth, the gods would take their rest. This would take place once every several centuries, for mortal time and divine time do not coincide and the triplets are more ancient than their years.

These five days came to be known as the Oracle delivered by the Majors, and so it was the week of the Majoracle.

Then, because the gods are good, they said: 'Your sacrifice shall not go without reward. During the Majoracle each god shall choose one of your number to come with us into our realms. This person shall become our Magus and they shall be anointed with our divine attention and gifted various heavenly secrets. They shall return to you at the end of the Majoracle, holier and wiser than they left you. Yet since the divine may only ever be temporary amongst the mundane, the Magi's lifespans will be cut short. Step forward, those who wish to have honour conferred upon them, and we shall name you first of the Magi.'

Many stepped forward but only two were chosen. Before the God of Nightmares could make his choice for the third, the God of Sleep and the Goddess of Dreams stayed their brother's hand.

'Brother,' they said as one, 'to be a Magus is our followers' reward. To be your *Magus would be their undoing.'*

For the gods are not cruel and do not seek to torment us. Even Torres's Nightmares are not given to cause pain, but merely to act as a reflection to the innermost fears and hindrances of our soul. And it is for this reason that the Nightmare God alone of the Majors does not take a Magus at the Majoracle; for even our own reflections would harm us if we kept their company for too long a time. Yes, a week in the mirror of Os Pesadelos *would cause such abuse that even the goddess's country of* Dreams *could not amend it.*

CHAPTER EIGHT

Ereon's skin still smelled of the hibiscus oil in which the Magistrates had bathed him. It reminded Theo of the field in Zion where the flowers grew wild and tall. As he lay his hand over Ereon's anointed forehead, he wondered whether that field would survive the boy's re-entrance into the realm. Whether anything would survive.

The young god took a deep and ragged breath. This should be the easiest thing in the world for him. On Theo's first birthday, he had been held in a Magistrate's arms and taken through the temple halls. The first Pangaean he reached for was considered to be his choice for a Magus. The woman who'd been chosen had been smart; a young mother who knew how to get a baby's attention. She wore bells in her hair and had applied glitter along her cheekbones, and if Theo hadn't reached for her, Fanta would have. After that, it was never so easy for the mortals to sway his choice. With every other choice in his life Theo was always open to persuasion and other people's leadership, but not when it came to choosing his Magus. That was his sacred duty, and his alone.

The easiest thing in the world: all he had to do was put the boy to Sleep and keep hold of his soul on the other side.

Even so, Theo's fingertips were clammy as they hovered above Ereon's oily skin. He would not actually touch the boy. It wasn't necessary. But it didn't help his nerves that he had a room full of people watching him. That was enough to make him sweat on a good day. None of the packed Majoracle congregation knew just how important this Magus selection was, not even the Magistrates. Varseer stood with his head bowed, ready to take Ereon's unconscious body once the selection was complete. Arthur stood at the temple's pulpit, *The Holy Theologos* open in front of him, and every three seconds he smacked his palm against a bell he held in his right hand. The noise rang out surprisingly loud for such a small instrument, making the stained-glass windows and the hundreds of Majority in the congregation shake with the sound of it. Ereon's mother, in her place of honour in the front row, shook like she held an earthquake in her womb.

Ereon's eyelids drooped heavily and his breaths deepened into little repeating sighs of exhaustion as he listened to the resonance of the bell. As their souls reached out to each other, god and Magus, Theo was overcome with a wave of what the child was feeling. He gritted his teeth to suppress a yawn.

To the side of him where they sat occupying two of three gold-leafed thrones, Theo felt the eyes of his siblings watching him. Fanta's part in the Majoracle ceremony was already over. When her Magus's name had been called, Theo was surprised to see that he recognised her. Pale face, square jaw, tired eyes . . . it was the girl from the hibiscus fields, the one Theo had intended to take as his own Magus before Ereon.

Arielle, Theo repeated to himself when he heard her name. He was glad she was still being chosen. Dreams would still give her some of the rest she needed. After her Magus collapsed into Dream Country, Fanta had returned to her throne. Torres's hands were clenched around his own throne, jaw tense as his sister joined him, but Theo thought nothing of it. His siblings became just some more members of the congregation of bated breaths as Ereon was brought forward.

On their return journey to the temple with Ereon in tow, the siblings' temporary alliance had come to an end. The space between them grew; Torres started walking faster as if he couldn't wait to get away from them. Fanta slowed down, to ensure that neither of her brothers were at her back. Theo felt almost sad about the change. For a moment out there, it had been just like before.

But as they had walked away from that House of sin, Fanta had set that illusion of family, that nostalgia of innocence, aflame. Before the Second or either of her brothers could say a word—Theo wanted to believe that he would have said something, even if it was only, *let them all come out first*—she had removed a matchbox from one of her pockets, struck the match, and thrown it. The dry, cheap wood of the House's walls burned well. They lit up the island Night almost as well as the fireworks or the ever-watching moon. The siblings hadn't stayed to hear the first Sister find the flames, or to watch the smoke rise. They had walked away with enough distance between the three of them for a country's borders, none of them admitting that they were grateful for the reminder of what happened to those who played at being a sister, or even a brother, in their world.

But now at least Theo felt that their gazes were with him even if nothing else of theirs was. Fanta and Torres wanted him to succeed at this; it was just as important to them and their realms as it was to him and Zion.

He took a deep breath. Ereon was still only half-asleep. It didn't usually take this long but Theo wanted to be careful. He made sure to repeat the boy's name in his mind, hoping it would give Rogan enough time to catch it and make up for the fact he had not given him a name before he left. *Ereon, Ereon, Ereon.* Theo sent another wave of Sleep energy into the child—but this time something felt different. There was some kind of resistance in the boy that forced Theo to *push*. Ereon gave an unhappy gurgle of protest and almost woke himself up. Theo pushed again. This was strange. A bead of sweat rolled down the side of the Sleep God's face. He gasped.

This was more than strange, it was *painful*. Ereon's resistance to Sleep made Theo so dizzy he lost all sense of orientation. He could no longer find Zion. Where was it?

Theo fumbled with the boy's spirit and almost lost it forever. The child would have found Zion that way, but the wrong way.

No, he needed him alive.

Theo concentrated his energy into the small figure in front of him. And then he saw it. There were the Gates of Horn and Ivory. And suddenly, just as it should be, Ereon's spirit was being pulled into the realm that was behind them. At last. He went through the Gates easily, but Theo stopped just short of following him.

This wasn't his way back. The staircase was waiting for him.

CHAPTER NINE

A silence settled over Zion as Theo ascended the celestial staircase. It was a fragile silence like confectioner's sugar pulled gossamer-thin. Theo found himself holding his breath, afraid to break it. After the explosive hedonism of the island celebrations, returning felt like coming home to an empty house after a long day; welcome, yet lonely.

But Zion wasn't empty. Theo's first instinct was to track down Iara and Bede and see how they were getting on with repairs, but he knew that could wait. First, he had to get Ereon to Rogan.

It was impossible to guess what kind of knowledge Rogan might hold to help them make sense of this. Theo was certain nothing like Ereon had ever existed before or he would have heard of it, but there was a part of him that still believed there was nothing his old schoolteacher didn't know. As Theo made his way through the Garden, his body vibrated with anticipation. He felt as if he was on the verge of a great discovery, like a prospector who had found a new plot of land to explore. But what was underneath, gold or a landmine, was yet to be determined.

All Magi appeared in Zion in the same spot, at a particular bend in the River that corresponded to the location of the temple stage down on the island. Theo always found his Magi, wandering, disoriented, in this area. It wasn't far from the staircase.

When Theo was halfway there he heard someone calling his name and suddenly Iara was beside him, matching his long strides. She had always had a talent for finding him wherever he was, almost like she had realm sight of her own.

'When did you get back? Why didn't you come and find me?' the goddess asked.

'I just got here. How are the repairs going?'

'The Minors are still working on them, but the damage wasn't as bad as it looked. I sent Bede to the Duppy villages in case they needed more help there. So? What happened, did you find the boy?'

'Yeah, we found him. Just in time too, he—'

'Wait, what do you mean "we"? You mean the Magistrates?'

'Yes. Well, no . . . Fanta and Torres were there.'

Iara stopped in her tracks. She grabbed hold of Theo's arm, stopping him too. Her eyes scanned over him like she expected parts of him to start falling off as she watched. 'Torres too?' she asked quietly, even though he knew she'd heard what he said the first time.

Theo nodded. 'The boy didn't just affect Zion. It was their realms too,' he said, moving forward again. 'I wanted to take him up the staircase, but we got to him too late. I took him as my Magus instead.'

'You what?' Iara gasped. 'Why would you do that? We don't know anything about him, how do we know he's safe for us?'

Theo held out his arms, gesturing to the intact world around him. 'He seems to be, doesn't he?'

They arrived at the riverside just as the post-midnight sun was in perfect position to send rays of light glinting off its surface. It looked like the gentle waves were made of light instead of water; even at a distance, Theo felt Iara relax at the sight of it. She could never be too stressed as long as she was around her water, which was good for him because he needed her firmness right now when he had so little of his own.

His own shoulders tensed when he couldn't see Ereon at the River, but then he remembered his Magus's size. When the baby had been laid out in front of him on the temple stage, he'd seen that he could hold him with one hand. He was small, even for a typical newborn mortal.

Theo looked more carefully among the riverside reeds and Iara, following his lead, did the same on the other side. There were no cries to direct them this time.

Maybe he can only do what he did when he's crying. Was he hungry? Or scared? Is that why it happened?

If Bede had been there, then Theo would have had someone to bounce his theories off. Iara always preferred facts over speculation, whereas Theo's mind seemed always to be full of questions that even a god couldn't know the answers to. For instance—

'Where is he?' Theo asked, frowning and raising his head. There was no sign of Ereon anywhere. 'Have you found him?'

Iara straightened up. 'Maybe he came through somewhere else.'

'But they all come here. The River—' A new thought cut Theo off as he spoke. He looked down at the sunlit waves of the Zion. 'You don't think he could have fallen in, do you?'

Iara frowned and crouched by the water. She peered in and trailed the tips of her left hand over its surface. Theo could tell that they were conversing, though the meaning was lost on him. Iara stood up again. 'He didn't fall in,' she said certainly.

Theo felt his heart race. He'd lost a Magus. The most important Magus he'd ever had.

'Keep looking,' he told Iara.

They did. Half an hour later Ereon was still nowhere in sight.

'Why don't you look for him?' Iara asked.

'I *am* looking!'

'No, I mean—' she pointed two fingers at her own eyes then waved them vaguely in the air above her, '— *look*.'

Of course, stupid!

How could he not have thought of it earlier? Theo slipped into his realm sight and immediately began to search around. The realm was damaged, the people were confused, but there was one essential similarity between the realm and the riverside: not one mortal baby in sight.

'He's not here,' Theo said quietly. He was in such shock that he forgot to return to normal sight before he spoke. He didn't see Iara's reaction to his words, except from a very great distance. It looked like she frowned.

'How can that be?' she asked.

To Theo it seemed as though the clouds were talking to him in her voice. And they were a lot more judgemental in their interrogation than she was.

How can that be?

How could you let this be, Sleep God?

Theo's gaze shot out to the borders of Zion. He scanned the Gates, but Rogan was nowhere in sight.

Have I lost everyone today? Gatekeeper and Magus both at once?

But then he found him. Not the Magus, the Gatekeeper. Rogan had left the realm's borders and was moving inland, coming towards them. Now Theo's heart, which had been only a little agitated before, threatened to fly out of his chest. Rogan never left patrol of the Gates during a Majoracle. *Never.*

Theo snapped his sight back and without a word to Iara he began jogging off towards Rogan. The Gatekeeper and the Major god met each other halfway, one with his knees trembling from the walk, the other panting from his run.

They both began to speak at the same time.

'Rogan, have you seen—'

'Theo, did you—'

They both stopped. Theo waited for his old mentor to go on but for a second it didn't seem like he would. He had a look on his face, like disappointment, that Theo hadn't seen in a long time, not since classroom days when he'd answered a question wrong even when he knew the answer. He just wasn't paying enough attention.

Rogan sighed. 'Theo,' he began again. No *Milord*, not now. He was a child with the wrong answer, not a god to flatter with formality. 'Theo,' Rogan said, 'are you aware that there is a mortal in your brother's realm?'

CHAPTER TEN

The twelve mountains were shrouded in fog. The monsters liked it this way, when all their favourite activities could be performed under the cover of the thick white air. No one else dared be caught out in *Os Pesadelos* alone when the sky looked like this.

A solitary crow broke through the fog. It swept down to the base of the third mountain, then glided on the back of a gentle breeze to where Torres was standing by the Gates, bending to pick Ereon up from the hard ground.

Abilo landed on a rock by his master's head and dipped into a strange, hopping bow.

'*Senhor*. Was your trip fruitful? *CAAW!*'

Torres grinned. 'Here's the fruit,' he said, lifting Ereon slightly. He held the struggling boy awkwardly in his arms.

Abilo cocked his head to the side. 'I don't understand. I thought you were going to find out what caused that earthquake?'

'This *is* what caused it,' Torres explained. There was a hint of curiosity or amazement as he looked down at the mortal in his arms. 'He almost brought down three realms. *And* the Gates.'

'He did that?' Abilo asked, unconvinced. He hopped closer to Ereon to take a closer look. The child looked back into the face almost as dark as his own and began to cry.

Torres rocked him erratically. 'Theo saw.'

'And—forgive me for asking—you trust him, *Senhor*?'

'*Claro.* Theo wouldn't lie. I don't think he knows how.' Torres chuckled.

There had been something comforting about seeing how little his brother had changed over the years. When they were younger, Theo had always seemed to him like a shaking leaf faced by a strong wind. Fragile, apparently hopeless, but hanging on nonetheless. When he locked eyes with him in the temple basement he'd had to resist the urge to pull him into a hug and ask, 'Still hanging on, *irmão*?'

'Is there a reason why you have him, *Senhor*?' Abilo asked over Ereon's screams. 'Your brother gave him to you?'

Torres shrugged. 'Kind of. Not really. He didn't *give* him to me, but he didn't exactly stop me either.'

Torres had been surprised that Theo hadn't stopped as soon as he felt something wrong when he was choosing his Magus. Everyone in the temple had seen the moment when it happened, how the Sleep God had recoiled from the boy, but he had raised no alarm. He'd pushed on, even though, surely—Torres felt a little guilty—it must have hurt him. But he pushed past it and opened the Gates anyway. Torres had almost laughed out loud in relief.

'How did you do it?' Abilo asked.

Torres was glad he'd asked but he would have told him anyway; he'd been too clever not to tell someone.

He pushed back the sleeve of his left arm to just above the wrist. Lying flat against his skin was a thin Horn bracelet with a delicate clasp. One half of the *boitatá*'s goat-poaching fine. Torres then pushed back the cloth that was draped loosely over Ereon's kicking feet. A bracelet encircled his ankle, identical to Torres's. The other half of the fine.

'I got it on him after we found him, before Theo chose him in the temple. His mother almost stopped me, pushing me away when I tried to get near, but in the end I don't think even she noticed when I put it on him. The Magistrates will find it, of course, now that they have his Sleeping body, but by then it'll be too late for them to interfere.'

'So . . .' Abilo said, in that slow, avian way of his, 'when Theo was taking him as his Magus and the Gates were supposed to open into Zion, the Horn made the Gates to *Os Pesadelos* open instead?'

'Nightmare material to open the Nightmare realm.' Torres hoped that if Abilo had hands he would have clapped. It was brilliant.

'Did you know it would work?' Abilo asked.

'No. But it did.'

The half-formed plan, that had come to mind immediately after Theo explained who they were looking for, hadn't involved the bracelets at all. He had worked out long before standing in the Sister's House with his siblings that the only way to bring Ereon back to the celestial realms, if they couldn't take him up the staircase, was to make him a Magus. The first thing to do was to make *sure* they couldn't take him up the staircase. All he could do then was try to delay the search party until after midnight so that the staircase would be closed. His opportunity came as they walked through the Pangaean streets. He made sure Theo was behind the rest of them, and then all it took was some fast walking and some careful manoeuvring to make his little brother get lost in the crowd. By the time Theo found his way back to them, half an hour had passed and he knew it was unlikely they would find the boy before the ringing of the midnight bells.

The final stage of his plan, in which he grew more and more confident with every passing second, was to volunteer himself to take the boy as a Magus. He would have been the only available option, since Theo and Fanta would have pre-selected their Magi long ago. At least, that's what he'd thought.

When Theo claimed him, for a second as Torres stood there on the second floor of the House, he'd felt his whole plan crumbling before him, felt his Magus—*his* by right, by compensation, by a nineteen-year delay—being taken away from him. But by a last-minute stroke of pure genius, that Torres was almost tempted to call divine intervention, he had slipped one of the bracelets onto the boy. Torres had managed to convince his siblings to let him pick who should take the boy for his Magus and of course he had chosen Theo. There was no way the Horn would have slipped past his sister's watchful eye if the boy had been under her care. Luckily no skin-to-skin contact was required to formally take a Magus, or Theo also would have noticed the Horn right away.

Overall, stealing his brother's Magus had been easier than he thought.

'So what will you do with him, *Senhor*?' Abilo asked, bringing Torres's mind back to the present.

'I'm just going to let him do what he does. Theo said he shook the Gates. I'm just going to watch what happens if they keep shaking.'

He would have shaken them himself if he could. Grasped the Gates with both hands, his own Horn, and the Ivory his sister had only just threatened him with, and never stopped shaking, until the whole of the Celesterra shook with him and then, maybe then, his own mind could be still.

The mortal screamed louder. He hadn't stopped this whole time. A moment of anxiety gripped Torres's heart. Was it possible that was all he was—a screaming mortal? *Could* Theo have lied to him?

No, if Theo said it was this boy, then it was. Torres still remembered his brother's face down on the island when he told them about waking him up. He'd seemed . . . spooked.

Of course, it had never taken much to frighten Theo. When they were younger, Torres had taken Theo into the rock caves of what would eventually become *Os Pesadelos* and left him there. He hadn't blocked the exit, hadn't stopped Theo from leaving in any way, but for some reason his brother never managed to find his way out. He just stood there, paralysed with fear in the dark, until Torres came back for him. Once they had walked out together, Theo rushed off to tell someone. Torres couldn't remember who he told—Fanta? Rogan? Their mother? Theo ignored him for a few days after that but soon he forgave him. Forgiveness came easy back then.

Torres looked down at the unforgivable child in his arms.

Maybe a familiar face would make him feel less restless. He thought back over every detail he could remember about the boy's mother. Dark, scrawny, beaten—he would get rid of that last part. He imagined her face as it would look when not painted with blood.

The image inside his head slowly materialised in front of him, the boy's mother standing frozen like a golem waiting for the holy word to bring it to life. Torres could tell who she was supposed to be, but there was something not quite right about her features. Usually when creating illusions of real people he would tap straight into the mind of the person who knew them. But babies' minds were difficult. At Ereon's age, mortals usually only went to Zion rather than the other two realms. Their minds were not sophisticated enough for the illusions. Torres would just have to do the best he could.

He imagined the boy's mother smiling. She had smiled at Theo, probably Fanta too. Had it brightened her eyes? Lifted her cheeks? Torres thought he had it. He cast the image of these features onto the apparition in front of him.

She smiled. She held out her hands for her baby. A warmth filled the air, reminding Torres of the scent of the woman he had found in the Sister's house, only a little less bloody and a little sweeter. Ereon's cries died down as he recognised his mother.

Torres let out a breath. He'd done it. He'd made a *good* Nightmare. A Dream. Was this what the Majority revered Fanta for? But it was so easy—

Ereon's mother's smile grew wider. It did not stop. The smile spread like a disease across her face. Her eyes were bright with mania. Ereon screamed.

She began to laugh from in between closed teeth, drooling out a pink mixture of saliva and blood from the upturned corners of her mouth. Her claws reached for Ereon.

Torres sighed and snapped his fingers. The illusion disappeared with a pop of displaced air.

Just another Nightmare, Torres thought, but he couldn't even work up the will to be disappointed. He hadn't truly expected anything else.

The ground beneath him practically shook with the force of Ereon's terrified screams but this was not the kind of earthquake he was looking for. The Gates were completely unaffected.

'Maybe he needs to be close to the Gates,' Abilo suggested.

Torres replaced the child back on the ground, where he had found him. 'Take him, Abilo.'

Without need for further instruction, the bird obediently glided down and picked up the back of the boy's shirt in his beak. Abilo hopped backwards as he dragged the boy across the hard rock, careful not to knock his head. He was a much stronger creature than he appeared and soon he had the child within touching distance of the Gates. Torres frowned to see how close they were, but he knew the Ivory did not affect Abilo as it would him. Only the Majors were truly held back by the poisonous materials of the Gates.

If the boy did what he should, Torres would not be held back any more.

From where he stood, Torres could see into both Zion and Dream Country, but only one of the realms held his gaze. He didn't even dare to blink. It had always been close.

It had never *felt* closer.

Now that he actually held the power to break through and enter, he almost felt sick to think how near he was to his goal. All he had to do was to make his and his sister's realms one again, as they once were, then everything would be different and Dream Country would be his.

What was the difference between two illusions? What separated them besides a barrier so inconsequential that Torres could have snapped it in half with his bare hands if it were made from any other material? What, *really*, was the difference between a Dream and a Nightmare?

To the Majority, and to his sister, it was a world of difference. But Torres had thought his brother understood. He thought Theo saw him for who he was and not just the God of Nightmares. So, naively, stupidly, on their fifteenth birthday Torres had asked his little brother for a Magus.

And what had happened?

His brother had said no.

Or more accurately, the voice behind his brother, the wind blowing the leaf, said no.

Fanta! It would have meant nothing to her for Torres to have a Magus. Nothing would have changed, for better or worse, for *her*. Yet Torres had recognised that it was her voice using Theo's mouth like a ventriloquist's puppet that day. There was no one else it could have been. The Dream Goddess must have picked up a hint of what Torres wanted and decided to shut it down, because she knew that her having a Magus, and him not, was the only thing that really separated them. Not the Gates, a Magus. And if he was granted one, it would only be a matter of time before the Majority came to that conclusion themselves and finally remembered they had three gods, not just two.

Torres's thoughts went back to the island. He had forgotten how hard it was to sit idly by while Fanta and Theo took their Magi. He had had to hold himself back from jumping up from his conciliatory throne and shouting out, 'What about me!' After her Magus was chosen, Torres caught the triumphant look Fanta had given him out of the corner of her eye, as she felt the eyes of the congregation following her, like a moth to a flame, and Torres was left only with the ashes. Her pride was as potent and as repulsive as her Ivory.

A tense silence fell by the mountainside as Torres and Abilo watched the Gates now with bated breaths.

Torres looked just as closely at the mortal. He wasn't what he'd imagined for a first Magus, but he was an opportunity so obvious that he jumped up and down waving in Torres's face. An opportunity that asked aloud the same question that had been going around in his head for the last four years, since he had stopped attending the Majoracle ceremonies that had nothing to do with him: what would happen if there was one less barrier between you and her? How could they ignore you then?

He'd had to take that opportunity. He'd had to take *him*.

Theo would forgive him.

Like I learned to forgive you, irmão.

CHAPTER ELEVEN

How?

The question repeated itself like a stuttering breath.

How?

Ereon or Torres? Did Theo prefer to believe that the wrong Gates opening was some other symptom of the boy's dangerously strange abilities? That what he could do was so vast and unimaginable that what they'd seen the day before was barely even a fraction of it?

Or did he prefer to believe that this had nothing to do with Ereon, that his powers, although mysterious, were limited, and therefore that Torres had done this on purpose?

That's what you get, he thought bitterly.

He'd allowed himself to get comfortable around his brother, to trust him, throwing away the knowledge of thirteen years that *he couldn't be trusted.* In the space of just a few hours he'd allowed himself to forget that, just because Torres hadn't tried to kill him immediately when they were alone in the basement. In a way, a *painful* way, he was grateful for this reminder. Theo had needed his siblings in order to find the child who could shake the Gates. But he had to remember: the reason he had to find the child was so that he could protect the Gates that protected him from his siblings.

They were only temporary allies. They weren't family, not really. Family didn't hurt each other like they'd long ago learned to hurt him.

But how?

'Did they come into contact at any point on the island?' Rogan asked. They'd found a nearby uprooted tree for him to rest, though Rogan wasn't using it. He paced up and down beside it, his stick digging into the mud. Theo sat instead, his head bowed.

He shook his head. 'She wouldn't let him. Ereon's mother, I mean.'

Why didn't Theo know her name? He'd been so pleased just to learn the boy's that he'd forgotten to ask. But most of a child's mystery comes from their mother. Didn't he know that best of all?

He frowned. He was latching on to all the details he'd missed while on the island, except the most important one.

How?

He was sure that if he just kept thinking, he would find an answer.

There's no point overcompensating now, he told himself. *Thinking should have come first, not afterwards. Idiot.*

Rogan had already shown his disapproval of Theo's whole island endeavour when he recounted it to him. The Gatekeeper had stopped short of chastising him, but still made his thoughts clear with a lot of 'maybe you should have' and 'why didn't you just.' Theo had no answers for him or for himself.

After Iara caught up, she tried to provide the answers for him. She stood with her arms crossed, facing the Gatekeeper who was just as much her old schoolteacher as he was Theo's.

Rogan sighed. 'I really wish you hadn't rushed down there, Theo. If you'd come to me first—'

'It's not his fault. We encouraged him to go,' Iara said.

Theo winced. Somehow she made it sound worse. Like he'd needed help even to come to a terrible decision.

'Anyway, there's no point wishing now. It seems to me like we're being way too dramatic about this. Can't you just go into *Os Pesadelos* and get the boy, Rogan?'

Theo straightened up. Would he have ever come to that suggestion himself? It didn't matter though because, thank the realms for Iara, it was the perfect idea, it would solve everything, it—

'I can't do that,' said Rogan.

Theo slumped. 'You can't?'

Rogan shook his head. 'All we know for sure is that boy was taken as a Magus. He could be yours or he could be Torres's, either way I can't take a Magus between realms.'

Iara and Theo fell silent, eyes slightly wide as they looked first at each other and then at Rogan.

'What do you mean, he could be Torres's?' Iara asked.

'I mean just that. I heard you sending me the boy's name, Theo, and I sent the appropriate permission to the Gates, but it wasn't limited to Zion's Gates. As you both know, the only way for a living mortal to enter the realms during a Majoracle is to be a Magus. He's in Torres's realm. I don't think it's a wild assumption to make.'

'Oh,' Theo breathed.

A Nightmare Magus.

A mortal spending five days and Nights with continuous Nightmares. It was unheard of. It was unthinkable. It was unkind.

Theo had seen how relieved a Sleeper was to find themselves in Zion after *one* night of Nightmares. Even if River water made sure they didn't remember the substance of their fears, they remembered the feeling. And there was no Zion water for a Magus. It was considered a privilege for the Magus to remember. Five days and Nights of unrelenting peaceful Sleep or pleasurable Dreams. Not Nightmares. Never Nightmares. Theo had made sure of that himself a long time ago, when he'd had to learn how to say no.

But what could he say now? If Ereon really was a Nightmare Magus . . . it was worse than a death sentence. It was permission for torture.

But how could he be a Nightmare Magus when *Theo* had chosen him? Zion's Majoracle hadn't been forfeited, the Gates were closed and there were no Sleepers, meaning Theo must have met all the criteria of taking a Magus. Could he and his brother be *sharing* a Magus? It was an odd thought—they'd hardly shared anything since the womb. And what would that mean for Ereon?

As Rogan had said, it was impossible for a Magus to go between realms. Even after the Majoracle ended, the Magi's visits were confined to the one realm. Only when a Dream Magus died would they again re-enter a realm they'd not been chosen for, when they joined the Duppies of Zion.

If Ereon died he would come here.

Theo looked up and caught Iara's eye. It was almost like they were having the same thought, but where she seemed to be rolling it over her tongue, savouring it as a possibility, Theo wanted to spit it out like rancid meat.

Ereon's mother had trusted Theo with him. That meant he couldn't let him stay a Nightmare Magus—but he couldn't let him die either.

There had to be another way.

* * *

Theo Major approached the Gates of Horn and Ivory, Iara and Bede at his back. At first, Theo had wanted to leave the goddess and the Duppy behind, but Iara had insisted and Bede couldn't be kept away once he had found out what was happening. Theo halted ten paces from the radiant Horn and Ivory, and although his friends could have gone closer, they stayed by his side. The Mountains stood just before them, but if they walked for longer alongside the Gates they would reach the intersection of the three realms, where Salvador had gone through just the day before. Everything on Torres's side of the Gates seemed to be tall and made of rock. Even the few trees that clung on for dear life through the gaps of the mountainside looked grey and hard. Nothing like Zion, but so close.

Now, we wait.

'Do you really think he'll come?' Bede asked, shuffling on his feet. He had never met one of Theo's siblings before, only heard of them in name and deeds, and he didn't seem to be looking forward to the introduction.

Rogan had gone through the Gates to bring the message to Torres, telling him that Theo was there waiting for him. It was possible that Torres would come with Ereon in his arms, sheepish or confused, and then Theo would know this had all been some big mistake and they could work together to figure out how to get Ereon back in Zion.

'Of course he won't come,' Iara said. 'He took the boy on purpose. Bad things don't just happen around Torres. He makes them happen.'

She seemed to speak with the bitter voice of experience.

'Either way, we have to get Ereon back,' said Theo. 'If what Rogan said is true, Torres and I might be sharing him as a Magus somehow. But that means he has just as much right to be in Zion as he does in the Mountains. I'm going to try to put him to Sleep again. Maybe that will bring him to me.'

'Even though the Gates are closed for the Majoracle?' asked Iara.

'I don't know. I don't know how this will work because I don't understand how Torres did it,' Theo admitted.

'But even if the Gates do open, how will the boy get to you? He's a baby, right? It's not like he can just walk over here,' said Bede.

'That shouldn't matter. If he was a god or a Duppy he would need to be able to bring himself here physically, but he's only Sleeping. All Torres really has over there is his soul, not his body. As soon as I get hold of him and direct some more Sleep energy to him he should just appear in Zion. It's the same way a mortal can go between all three realms in one Night, from Sleeping to Dreaming to Nightmares.' Theo took a deep breath. 'Okay. It would help if I had a rough location for where Ereon might be, but I'm going to try this now.'

'Who's that?' Bede said suddenly before Theo could even begin to close his eyes.

Theo followed his gaze.

A small child, of no more than eight years old, was dancing on the other side of the Gates. The bronze puffs of her hair swirled around her face, obscuring it from view as she held her arms out to the side and laughed. After the sixth or seventh turn she came to a stumbling stop and turned her face in Theo's direction. She grinned toothily and waved as she caught his eye.

'Watch!' she called.

And then she began to spin again. Without a word between them, Theo, Bede, and Iara watched her as her dress flared into the shape of a temple tower bell around the clapper of her thin legs. When she had successfully completed ten turns she stopped again and laughed and applauded her own achievement. Without thinking, Theo and Bede joined in the applause. Only Iara frowned. The girl skipped closer to the Gates until her uncovered toes were brushing against the bottom bar.

'Who are you?' she asked, looking at Theo. Her voice was soft, almost musical.

'Wait, I know!' she said, before he could reply. Then she cocked her head to the side, narrowing her eyes appraisingly. 'But you don't look much like him.'

She meant Torres. Theo, assuming the girl was a Minor goddess, forced a smile.

'You're right. We're related but we're not the same. Sometimes even things that are the same can have different faces.'

The girl gasped and clapped again, almost as if Theo's words were a performance more impressive than her own dancing. Theo waited for her childish joy to taper off, smiling patiently through it, and then he asked her a question.

'Do you know where Torres is?'

'Yes.' She nodded her head confidently. 'He's in *Os Pesadelos.*'

'Where in the Mountains is he?'

'Somewhere that's not here.'

'Look, little girl, we don't have time for this,' Iara said, stepping forward. 'Just tell us what we want to know.'

The child's eyes widened as she looked at Iara for the first time. She seemed to shrink into herself with sudden shyness as she realised that she was talking to three adults, and strangers. Her eyes filled with tears.

Theo shot an accusing look over at Iara. He crouched down so he was at eye level with the girl even though ten paces and the Gates separated them.

'Please don't cry. We just need your help. We need to speak with my brother. Can you help us?'

'I'm not supposed to,' the girl snivelled. 'You're on that side of the Gates. I'm not supposed to talk to you. You'll hurt me.'

'No, we won't, no one here is going to hurt you.'

Suddenly the girl's head snapped up and she fixed Theo with a dry-eyed stare. He felt his heart ache as he looked at her, and in that moment he knew he would do anything to keep her from crying.

'Do you promise?' she asked flatly.

Theo nodded. 'I promise I won't hurt you.'

The girl's brilliant grin broke forth again. 'I know where Torres is. Don't worry, I'll tell him I've seen you.'

And then, in an instant, she had spun around and was dancing away over the rocks and into the shadows of one of Torres's Mountains.

Theo took a deep breath and raised himself up to full height once more.

'That was . . . strange. For a second there, did you feel like . . .' Bede trailed off.

'Like what?' asked Iara.

'Like someone had a hold of your mind . . . someone who wasn't you.'

Iara only frowned in confusion but Theo felt he knew exactly what Bede was talking about. It had been the oddest sensation of his life.

'Let's find this boy and get away from here, Theo,' Bede said.

Theo agreed. He closed his eyes and let his mind sharpen its focus to the point of a needle as he searched for a familiar soul. There were unbreakable ties between a god and their Magus, a bond formed in the temple and kept forever. Theo sifted through the familiar souls of his old Magi, all seventeen of them now safe in the Duppy villages of Zion, and Bede who stood beside him. And then, finally, he found what he was looking for.

It was a small soul that could only belong to a baby. Theo tugged at the thread that connected them and felt Ereon slide towards him, but the child moved barely a few inches before something stopped him: he slammed into an obstruction and screamed. Theo was sent flying out of his own mind.

Iara caught him under the arms and then immediately lost her grip on him again. The ground around them was shaking; behind them the River water was rising.

A tremendous rumbling noise filled the air.

'Are you doing that?' Iara asked.

Theo didn't get a chance to reply. In the distance he saw a horned figure silhouetted against the intersection of the Gates.

'Theo!' Rogan shouted. 'Run!'

* * *

'Oh, *Mãe de todos*,' Torres cursed, looking into Zion, 'wrong Gates.'

CHAPTER TWELVE

The Gates between Zion and the Nightmare realm were falling. Theo had to blink twice before he could believe his eyes. *The Gates were falling.*

One bar after another, collapsing like a row of felled trees, starting from just behind Rogan. The Horn and Ivory pieces, the material of his own body, lay there at the Gatekeeper's feet but he ignored them. He was looking only at Theo.

'Run!'

'Come on!' Iara said, dragging him by the arm.

Theo willed his feet into action as he followed Iara towards Rogan. Even as he moved he couldn't take his eyes off the Gates.

Falling.

There was no baby for him to wake up this time to stop it. Theo felt the taste of the air changing around him, as his brother's realm mingled with his own as significant gaps in the Gates appeared. The first of many.

Iara tugged at him more urgently. By now the River water was flooding around their ankles, watery fingers trying to get one last grasp on their mistress before the end of the world. Each step was harder to take than the last, as the force of the uncontained River kept knocking them backwards. As another shock hit the earth, a wall of Zion water rose up and came down over Iara and Theo, sweeping them into the River itself.

Just as he felt himself going under, a large hand grasped the front of Theo's shirt and pulled him back into the air. Then Bede was there, grim-faced, lifting him effortlessly back to the bank. His stomach collided with the side of the bank as Bede brought him over, knocking all of the air out of him. But Iara was still down there. Theo wasn't sure how much the River could really hurt its own goddess, but he was afraid to find out.

'Theo!' Rogan called.

Theo stared back in shock. The Gatekeeper hadn't moved from where he was standing before, but a great change had taken place: there were no Gates between him and the Mountains. The domino-like chain of destruction ran far into the distance, so that now Theo had to strain his eyes just to find the place where the Gates were still standing.

'Go to him!' Bede roared. 'I'll get Iara.' And with one final push to Theo's back, Bede dived under the frothing white surface of what used to be the Zion.

As Theo tried to keep his balance on the rocking earth, a loud whipping noise accompanied the appearance of a giant crack in the ground all the way from Theo to Rogan's feet. Theo couldn't hear what the Gatekeeper was saying anymore but he didn't need to. He ran.

When he reached Rogan, Theo had tears rolling down his cheeks.

'Rogan,' Theo breathed. 'Bede. And Iara—'

'I saw,' Rogan said. 'There's nothing we can do. We have to get you out of here.'

'Out?' Theo felt dazed and slow as he tried to get his thoughts into words. 'To where?'

Rogan half-turned and nodded behind him. 'These Gates are holding.'

The Gates around Dream Country. It was amazing how serene the other realm looked, not thirty paces away from all this destruction.

Theo shook his head. 'I can't go in there. Fanta—'

'Isn't tearing down your Gates right now. Which makes her a better option than Torres.'

A huge tree tipped over and fell into the increasingly widening chasm in the ground next to them.

'I'm sorry, Theo, we don't have time.'

With that, Rogan turned and hurried up to the Dream Country Gates. He held out his hands in front of the Horn and Ivory as if he were reaching for the handles of two large double doors, then pulled. The Gates opened smoothly for him.

'Quickly!' Rogan said, turning back to Theo.

The Sleep God's stomach lurched and he swallowed; the acidic taste of vomit slid down his throat. Less than a day ago he had been willing to risk assassination just to keep an old friend—and now new enemy—from walking through these very same Gates. Did Rogan really expect him, willingly, to follow that same path?

He couldn't do it. More importantly he didn't want to do it. He couldn't just run away and abandon Zion, the Duppies, the Minors. He should have been going back down to the River to find Bede and Iara. He couldn't just leave.

Theo looked down and found his feet moving. It seemed he'd already been taking steps towards the Gates this whole time.

Coward!

His own mind screamed at him but he ignored it, forcing himself closer to Rogan. The smell of Torres's realm was so strong now it made him dizzy. He almost didn't notice the gut-wrenching pain as he approached the Horn and Ivory. It was only once he was standing right next to the opening in the Gates, closer than he had ever been in his life, that his stomach gave another heave and this time the vomit splattered out the corners of his mouth. He wiped it away with a shaky hand.

'Be careful,' Rogan said. He was looking at him intently, and for a second he raised a hand as if to place it on Theo's shoulder but he only dropped it back to his side. 'Now go!'

On trembling legs, Theo stepped into Dream Country.

And with a resounding thud Rogan closed the Gates behind him.

THE HOLY THEOLOGOS, BOOK ONE, VERSE I.IV

Once, in time immemorial, there existed a world where gods and mortals walked the same earth. It is not known to us what took place thereafter; perhaps the gods were angered by the mortals; perhaps the mortals became erroneously disenchanted with the gods. Nonetheless, the earth split into a realm of mortals and a realm of gods and became the world as it is now, the Celesterra.

Some time after that, the All-Mother saw that the rest of the world had turned its back on her children, the Majority, and so the All-Mother wept and Her tears formed oceans. These oceans separated the land, forming an island that held the Majority, and carried them away from the rest. The island was named Pangaea, because as far as they were concerned, that was the world entire, and the All-Mother decreed that from that point forth, Her true essence, the true dark of midnight, may be experienced nowhere else but on Pangaea.

Many years later the All-Mother died. In response to the death, the realm of Zion was split into three. The land, the cultures, and the gods who were once one, were torn asunder—the smallest division thus far but certainly the most painful.

Once, in time immemorial, the Major triplets could walk across the sands of Zion, through the fields and woodlands, and arrive to play in the mountain caves, all without ever leaving the side of the sky-blue River.

These are those things that the gods remember when even time forgets.

CHAPTER THIRTEEN

As Theo took his first returning step into the realm that was once one-third of his home, one thought prevailed in his mind:

I shouldn't be here.

He turned back to the Gates, the ones that were still standing. The ones between Zion and the Mountains had not finished falling yet. Clouds of dirt rose up with each crash the Gates made as they hit the ground. The River was muddy and still unsettled, but Theo had to turn away from its frothy surface before he thought about what he left underneath.

Coward!

The only figure Theo could see was Rogan as he hobbled away, following the line of destruction. Perhaps he thought there was still some part of the Gates he could save. Or he just wanted to get started as soon as possible on rebuilding them. Theo couldn't remember how long it had taken the Gatekeeper to put them up the first time; in his memory, one Night they weren't there, then the next day they were. Would it be so quick again? He hoped so. Theo was only one minute and one step out of his realm, but he already missed it terribly. Its absence was like a chunk taken out of his heart, out of the very essence of himself, since as soon as he crossed the border between the two realms he felt his second sight and his power being left behind.

The next thing Theo knew he was bent over, the rest of the contents of his stomach spilling out of him, soaking into the thirsty ground. When he raised his head again there were new figures on the other side of the Gates. He couldn't see their faces from where he was, but the inhabitants of the Mountains hovered by the line that had once separated them from Zion, exchanging anxious glances. And then, some brave pioneer took the first step and they all went flooding in.

Theo screamed as the Mountain people invaded Zion. If they heard him they showed no sign of it. Most of them walked in on two legs, but some of the creatures scampered on six or slid on none. As they went in, the final bars of the Gates in the distance came crashing down. The two realms were connected once more.

In a cold stupor, Theo watched every creature that passed by, licking their grotesquely blood-gorged lips or chuckling maniacally. They went further and further inland until they disappeared from view. No more groups followed them over the once-border, but Theo was sure they would come later. The Zions wouldn't stand a chance. Their god had always been too reluctant to prepare for an eventuality like this.

Just as he thought this, Theo locked eyes with a group of Duppy children crouching over the remains of the Gates. The smallest among the children reached out a hand for a piece of Horn and Theo let out a cry.

'Don't touch that!'

The children's heads snapped up and their eyes went wide. They stood completely still. Theo's heart lurched in guilt as he realised how he must have appeared to them. Safe on the other side of the Gates. He hadn't even tried to help anyone but himself out, and shreds of Nightmare material was the last thing they had to worry about now.

Overwhelmed by his own selfishness in that moment, Theo wanted nothing more than to look away from those children's eyes, to look away from Zion. He turned and ran, not knowing where he was going.

Everything from the hot, unstable sand to the dry, heavy air was different in Dream Country. Even the sun seemed hotter, and when he risked a glance up at it, he saw that it was redder than it ever appeared in Zion. Although Theo knew it, had lived it, if anyone told him then that this strange, unwelcoming place had once been the same realm as Zion, he wouldn't have believed them. A desert couldn't be separated so completely from lush grasslands merely by a well-placed fence, no matter what the thing was made of. There was something else going on here and as Theo came to a panting stop after a few minutes, unused to moving through such thick air, the answer came to him. Zion was more than a part of him, it *was* him, an environmental representation of who he was.

Dream Country was the same for Fanta.

When the lands were all connected, the transitions between the landscapes would have been less harsh, because back then there wasn't much to separate *them*. People, followers, and gods spoke only of the Major triplets; they gained their separate identities only when they lost so much more.

Theo kept moving, even though the air made it difficult. His one thought was to get away from the Gates—there was no doubt that Fanta was aware by now that he was in her realm. She could be watching him at that very moment through her second sight. All Theo knew was that when his sister found him in person, he did not want to be standing conveniently next to a structure of Ivory for her to use against him.

'Milord Theo! Milord!'

Theo jumped at the sound of his name.

She's found me already, he thought—but immediately afterwards he realised that his sister wouldn't be calling him *Milord*.

When he looked around he was surprised to see how close he was to the Gates. He had been so distracted in his contemplation of the new realm that he had not noticed himself wandering back to the very thing he was trying to get away from.

The girl who had called his name was on the Zionese side of the Gates. She was only a child, about the same age as those in the group he had scared away from the Horn earlier. As he got closer, Theo tried to recall if she had been with them but he could not. He came to a stop in front of her.

The girl was not someone he could put a name to. He didn't know all the Duppies, it was true, but he was sure that if he had seen this girl before, even just once in passing, he would have recognised her. She was no more than eight years old. Her face was cratered like the surface of the moon with pockmarks, which was not an unusual sight in Zion considering that the Pangaean Plague had brought a lot of them there. When she opened her mouth to speak he saw that half her teeth were missing and the rest were stained and rotting in her gums. They would never fall out.

But the girl's unfortunate looks were not what would have made her memorable. On the side of her neck, reaching up over her chin, was the sign of the Major tattooed on her in blue ink, looking grotesquely like the veins of an old person showing through thin skin. The practice of getting this tattoo, to show that you had been dedicated to the gods from birth, had died out long ago.

'Wow,' the girl breathed, her eyes wide. 'How did you get over there?'

'I, um . . .' He wasn't ready to think about it yet, to consider how the Gates, that impassable and omnipresent circumference to his life, had opened up with such ease. The pain of crossing had been bad but not deadly. Here he was, still alive on the wrong side of the barrier he had trusted all his life. If it was that easy to get through all along, was it any wonder the Gates had fallen?

He decided to divert the Duppy girl's attention from her question. 'How is everyone doing over there? Were many people hurt?'

'Lots,' she said cheerfully.

Theo flinched but made no comment. It was not the girl's fault that she was too young to understand all that one word encompassed, or how it hurt Theo to hear it.

'Are you okay?' he asked. 'Are you hurt?'

'I'm okay.'

Theo gave a sigh of relief. This one girl's safety was inconsequential in the grand scheme of things, but it made him feel less of a failure to know she existed, and maybe many others like her around Zion: the unharmed. Of course, that didn't help Iara or Bede or the other 'lots' she had mentioned.

'What's your name?' he asked the girl.

'N—Godspawn, Milord.'

That was a naming tradition as old as her tattoo.

'Listen to me, Godspawn, I need you to go and find Rogan for me. Tell him: I need to come back. Can you do that?'

Rogan would object but Theo would just have to insist. He couldn't simply stand here, hiding from his sister while his realm became a mongrel breed of Sleep and Nightmares. Even so, Theo hesitated to cross back without the Gatekeeper. He knew he didn't need Rogan to be able to re-enter his own realm, as the Gates had only ever been there to stop him from *leaving*, but it made his heart race to just think about going back without Rogan there with him.

Godspawn began to nod, then stopped, and a smile spread across her face. She smiled with her lips closed, as if she knew that showing the inside of her broken mouth would ruin the sweetness of her expression.

'You want to come back?' she asked, watching him with unblinking eyes.

'Yes, I—' Theo said.

'Are you sure?' she blinked, once. Twice.

Theo hesitated. '. . . yes.'

She shook her head. 'But what can you do if you come back? You wouldn't be safe. You should stay over there, I think.' Theo began to speak but Godspawn cut him off with childish enthusiasm. 'Don't you think so too?'

Theo nodded, slowly. 'Yes.'

He was filled with complete certainty. There was no point going back into Zion just to suffer alongside his subjects. They wouldn't want him to. They'd want him to be safely out of the way in Dream Country.

Godspawn smiled again. This time she showed her teeth.

'Okay! I have to go now,' she said and spun around on her heels to leave.

Theo shook away the fog of his thoughts.

'Godspawn!' he called after her.

He had only noticed as he watched her leave what he was seeing behind her. He had assumed that he had walked back on himself and come to the Gates between Zion and Dream Country. But now he realised that Godspawn was standing in front of a mountain: she was in the Nightmare realm.

'Don't come back here, okay? Stay in Zion.' A lump formed in his throat. 'In where Zion was. The Mountains are a bad place, you don't belong there.'

The child smiled at him and dipped into a clumsy curtsey. But before she ran away she pointed over Theo's shoulder and said, 'You're in a bad place too.'

Theo turned around. In the distance a small cloud of sand was moving steadily towards him. It was the only movement besides his own that he had seen on Dream Country's plains since he had got there. Theo squinted closer to see what it was.

'Oh no,' Theo said, as his sister's face emerged from the dust.

CHAPTER FOURTEEN

'Let me explain!' Theo called, hands held out in front of him as if to ward her off.

Fanta held her hand up too, in a mirrored position of his own and for a second Theo thought she was reaching out for him. That is until he saw the loop of string that dangled from her thumb and the small piece of Ivory attached to the bottom of it.

He stumbled backwards as pure, natural panic rose inside him. 'No, Fanta, wait! Please, I'm not here to hurt you.' His words were coming out in a barely intelligible rush. 'Rogan let me through. Didn't you see what happened?'

She might not have. If she hadn't been facing either of her brothers' realms at the moment the Gates fell, then what she saw before her was not a refugee, but an intruder. But Theo couldn't tell if it was curiosity, or just a moment of reflection on how best to lead the attack, that made his sister slow down as she came near to him.

She's having second thoughts, he realised.

She must have rushed over as soon as she noticed his presence; she had come alone, with nothing more than a necklace to protect her if he had really come to do harm. Theo took a few deliberate, deep breaths and began to speak again, more slowly. He felt like he was trying to hypnotise a lion, whose claws were already out.

'Torres has Ereon. I don't know how but he has him, and now the Gates between Zion and the Mountains are gone. Rogan had to get me out and there was nowhere else to go. Please, Fanta—'

'Get down on the ground.'

'What?'

'Get. Down,' she snarled.

Arms still raised in front of him, Theo slowly lowered himself to the sand.

'Fanta—'

'Shut up. I'm thinking.'

Whatever she was thinking about, she didn't take her eyes off him for a second. Theo wondered if she could hear his heart pounding. It seemed loud enough to him that she must be able to.

Eventually, after what felt like an age, Fanta narrowed her eyes.

'If you're lying . . .' she threatened.

'I'm not. You can go and see for yourself. The Gates are gone.'

'I will go and see. And I will speak to Rogan.' And the way she said it made Theo glad that he wouldn't be a part of that conversation.

Although he wasn't currently much better off himself.

'Okay,' Fanta said, thrusting the Ivory necklace towards him again, as if he might have forgotten about it. 'Take your clothes off.'

'What?'

'Theo, I swear in my own name, if you keep making me repeat myself I will shove this Ivory down your throat right now. You are *not* taking *one more step* in my realm until I know what you're carrying with you. Now take your clothes off!'

Theo nodded so vigorously he felt like his neck had broken a hinge. Without another word, he began to lift up the corners of his shirt. It clung gently to his skin, still wet from the River Zion. When it was off, and in his hand, he shivered, although he was as hot as he'd ever been and sweating.

'I-I have to stand up,' he said, indicating the rest of his clothes.

Fanta nodded. Theo got back to his feet and removed his trousers, his shoes, and his underwear. When he was standing completely naked before her, Fanta had him spin around so she could look him over from all sides, like an ant under a magnifying glass. She then began rifling through his discarded clothes. It took a while for Theo to register what she was pulling from his trouser pocket.

'Rogan gave that to me,' he said quickly. 'It's just a birthday present.'

Fanta flipped the pocket knife open. Theo watched in mute shock as she ran the tip of the blade over the pad of her thumb, drawing a thin line of blood. She licked the trail clean.

'Hmm. Okay,' she said, pocketing the knife. 'Back on your knees.'

Theo reached for his shirt and Fanta growled.

'Did I say anything about the clothes? Leave them.'

So this is how I die, Theo thought as he knelt once more before her, *naked and far from home at the hands of my sister.* He was surprisingly calm at the prospect of imminent death. There was nothing more he could have done for himself. He only wished he could have done more for Zion.

Fanta came forward, retying the Ivory amulet around her neck as she moved. From somewhere within the depths of her kanga she produced a length of rope. Apparently she had come more prepared than Theo first thought. Unless she always carried binding rope in her pocket.

Obediently, Theo held his hands behind his back and kept very still while Fanta tied them. He knew that one wrong move just then and Fanta would kill him, whether intentionally or not; while she was wearing that necklace her skin itself was poisonous to him. After his arms were immobile, Fanta passed the rope around his chest so that they were pinned against his back. It was an awkward position that made his shoulders ache, but he didn't complain. With the trailing end of rope in her hand, Fanta inspected her work. Theo realised with a rush of humiliation that she intended to use it as a leash.

'Is this really necessary?' he muttered.

'I'm going to find somewhere to put you until I can verify your story. Come,' she said, turning away and, with a slight tug at the rope, compelling him to follow.

* * *

The Gates were falling.

Theo couldn't get that image out of his mind. He didn't want to. Forgetting would only bring insult to injury. As Fanta walked ahead of him, her sandalled feet left footprints in the sand, but all Theo thought about were the steps he'd taken as he was leaving Zion behind.

He couldn't even talk to her about what was happening, though she was one of the only people who would understand what it was like to have their realm be in danger. Fanta had made it abundantly clear that she didn't want to hear anything he had to say when, after his second question, she had stopped to shove a gag into his mouth. Even though the cloth quickly sucked the moisture from his tongue, Theo was just glad it wasn't the Ivory.

They were in a valley of sand dunes which gave them the first shade Theo had felt since entering the realm. Although they were much smaller and more numerous, to Theo the dunes looked exactly like Torres's mountains. He fixed his gaze on the third one that they passed: that would be where the castle was, where Ereon was.

As he turned the corner of the last dune in the valley, it was like stepping out of Torres's realm and back into Fanta's. He stood at the top of an incline, and from there he could see what seemed like the whole of Dream Country stretched out before him.

The seemingly never-ending flat brown plains turned out on closer inspection to be rolling hills stretching towards the horizon. A blur of blues and greens marked out Zion in the distance, made hazy and insubstantial through the veil of hot air. Theo narrowed his eyes as he peered into the distance, looking for any discernible figures moving around in Zion, but his vision was blocked by a reflection of sunlight as it glanced off the standing Gates of Dream Country. Further along the Gates, Theo could just vaguely make out a herd of some large creatures trudging slowly across the land.

Fanta tugged at his leash and he stumbled forwards. But she didn't seem angry, in fact there was a hint of pride in her eyes that she had caught him stopping to admire her realm. He wouldn't have told her, even if he could, that he did not think her realm was beautiful. Perhaps, after the beauty of Zion to which he had become so accustomed, he just couldn't see it, but he was pretty sure that, objectively, Dream Country was not beautiful at all.

It was a strange place to make Dreams, if he really thought about it.

Theo felt the ground begin to decline until he found himself in front of a sandstone cave, which, while not very deep, blocked out the sun entirely. A pillar of sandstone protruded at the back of it and Fanta tied his rope securely around it. She turned to leave. Theo's mumbled protests from behind his gag didn't stop her as she went.

Time passed. How long was even harder to tell now that the cave hid the sun from sight. Theo considered trying to escape, but decided against it. Fanta would only find him again and then things would be much worse for him. He slumped back against the cool rock and began to blink rapidly, trying to make the shady interior of the cave more visible. Eventually his eyes adapted and he began to make out the shapes of things around him—rock, sand, more rock, girl—

Theo's eyes snapped back to what they had just passed over. There was a mortal girl standing hesitantly at the front of the cave, chewing her bottom lip nervously as she watched him.

'Hmhm-mm. Hmhmm,' Theo mumbled.

The girl's pale skin paled even further as if his incoherent mumbles were threats on her life.

'*Hmmm.*'

Overcoming her fear, she stepped closer. Theo could see now who it was. Fanta's Magus. The same one he had wanted to be his, before Ereon came into the picture.

What was her name again?

In a quick, birdlike movement, the girl darted forward and removed the gag from Theo's mouth, before flinching back to where she had stood.

'Ah,' Theo groaned, wetting his lips, 'thank you! Do you think you could get the ropes too?'

'I'm sorry, Milord. Milady Fanta has forbidden it.' She hesitated. 'Though I don't understand why she would do this to you.'

'I'm not exactly in my sister's good graces right now.'

The girl frowned. 'The *Theologos* tells us that you and your siblings have the ideal relationship and we should all aim to emulate you in our daily lives.'

Theo shuddered to think of an island full of people treating each other the way Torres and Fanta had treated him in the past few hours.

'I think your *Theologos* needs an update,' he said.

Her frown deepened. 'It *has* been updated, many times. The *Theologos* is never wrong. I owe everything to what I have learnt from its pages. If I had never read the *Theologos* as closely as I had, I would never have been chosen as a Magus. It taught me how to respect the gods, to never harm them or keep secrets from them, and to never disobey their wishes . . . and Milady Fanta didn't say anything about not taking the gag out so I haven't disobeyed her,' she added hurriedly.

Theo didn't know which one of them she was trying to convince.

'Um . . .' The girl's cheeks flushed red and she wouldn't look Theo in the eyes. She threw the gag she had just recovered from his mouth with almost perfect aim so that it landed in his lap to cover his . . .

'Oh,' Theo said, feeling his own cheeks flaming.

After a while he had completely forgotten that he wasn't wearing any clothes. He cleared his throat, hoping to recover the situation. The Dream Magus seemed like she wanted to help him, and she could be useful before Fanta returned.

'I didn't catch your name,' he said.

The girl curtseyed. 'Arielle, Milord.'

'Arielle. Do you know where—'

A loud thud from outside the cave sent the walls shaking and Theo tried to jump to his feet.

The Gates! The Gates!

'It's only the sand, Milord,' Arielle said, seeing his wide eyes. 'The dunes collapse in on themselves sometimes. It scared me at first too.'

Theo's whole body sagged with relief. And then to his own surprise, his eyes filled with tears.

'What kind of a place is this?' he whispered to himself, as he slumped back against the rock.

'Oh, Milord, it's a wonderful place! If I told you some of the things I'd seen here—' Arielle cut herself off, presumably as she realised she was preaching to Sleep about Dreams.

But for a moment there, when she began to speak, her brown eyes had lit up like lanterns in the dark and her lips trembled into an unaccustomed smile. Theo found himself fascinated.

'Tell me about them,' he said.

Arielle blinked at him shyly but lowered herself to the ground so that they were facing each other when she began to speak again.

'There's nothing to fear here,' she whispered, 'sometimes you'll hear noises that seem to come from nowhere, and voices, although nobody will have spoken. When you're on the island and you hear the same sort of thing, they say you're mad. Here, you're blessed. I hear things that I recognise, voices from my childhood, my father's voice. Maybe you'll hear things from Zion?'

Theo flinched. It was the first time he'd heard someone else say the name of his home since he'd been forced to leave it. But Arielle misinterpreted the reaction.

'Whatever it is, it won't hurt you,' she assured, 'nothing here does. My mother—she's very sick, bedridden ever since I learnt to walk—she appears to me in Dreams sometimes. I always recognise her, but she never looks like she really does. Once, she appeared like one of those creatures the poets speak of. Her skin was like glass, so I could see her bones underneath and they were made of coral. Her eyes were pearls and her hair was seaweed. She was beautiful.'

Theo smiled. He imagined Arielle's mother looked like Iara, and Arielle was right: at the bottom of her watery grave she would be beautiful.

'There's music to wake you up in Dream Country. In your realm,' she looked away, embarrassed again, 'you sort of fade awake. And in your brother's realm it's kind of like being *pushed* out and back into the world. But here there are bells and other instruments, even singing; it's like a song only you can hear, a lullaby, as if Dream Country itself doesn't want you to go. Then you wake up and . . . you're back. And everything's still the same.'

She fell silent.

'I guess . . . a place that gives you music for nothing can't be all that bad,' Theo said softly.

Arielle smiled and after that Theo couldn't bear to tell her that it had never really been the *realm* that scared him.

The Magus jumped up as soon as she saw Fanta approaching and ran to stand behind her.

'I've spoken with Rogan,' Fanta announced. 'It seems you were telling the truth.'

Theo released the breath he seemed to have been holding for the past few hours. 'So you'll let me stay?'

'Don't be ridiculous,' Fanta snapped. 'This is between you and Torres. It's your Magus and your Gates—so you can go back to *your* realm to sort it out.'

'You do remember that it isn't just any Magus he has, right? That it's the same boy we risked our lives to find on the island because of what he can do? What's to stop Torres from using him against Dream Country next?' He struck a nerve with that one. Fanta's whole body tensed at the thought of her home in danger.

'*I'll* protect my realm.'

Theo shook his head. 'It took less than five minutes, you know. As soon as the first section of Gates began to fall, I *felt* Zion changing. When I left, I barely recognised it; it took only five minutes. Dream Country will change. Even you won't be able to protect it when you won't even be able to recognise its music.'

Fanta shot a sharp look at Arielle who bowed her head in embarrassment. Theo hoped he hadn't got her in too much trouble by revealing what she had told him, but for the moment all he could do was hold his breath and wait to hear what Fanta would say.

'Letting you stay here won't stop Torres.'

Theo relaxed a little—that was an argument but it wasn't a refusal; it was progress.

'So help me stop him. Have you ever looked across into Torres's realm?'

Fanta nodded, slowly, not yet sure what she was agreeing to.

'So you've seen that castle on the third mountain? Near the peak? I think that's where he lives. He probably has Ereon there. If we can get to him, I can take him back and we'll end all this. Everything will go back to normal. Without him Torres won't be able to cause any more damage, so Zion can be repaired, and Dream Country will be safe. Let me stay in your realm so I can get close to the castle from this side. At least, that way Torres won't be able to use his realm sight to see me coming. We're more likely to get Ereon back if we catch Torres off guard; then we can all go back to the way we were.'

Theo couldn't say where the sudden inspiration for this plan had come from but, now that he had said it, it sounded right—it sounded like something he could still do for Zion and his Minors, despite his betrayal and abandonment of them. It was at least an apology, if not a solution.

'And how do I know that you won't do exactly what you're accusing Torres of as soon as you have your hands on the boy?'

Theo began to shrug but the rope digging into his shoulders quickly reminded him he couldn't.

'You'll just have to trust me.'

Something surprising happened then. Fanta threw her head back, her mouth opened wide, and she began to laugh. Theo, who had not heard his sister laugh in over a divine decade, was amazed to find how familiar the sound was to his ears. But when she had finished, her face was suddenly very still again as she examined him; there wasn't the slightest trace of the merriment that she had the ability to sound inside of her. The music.

'If you stay in my realm,' she said, her voice cold, 'the only safety guarantees I make are my own. You will not be untied, you will never be left unguarded, and if you take so much as one step without my permission then it will be the last step you take. These are the conditions of my assistance. Accept them or go home and die. I have no preference either way.'

Theo met her gaze. He had no doubt she was serious. He sighed.

'Can I at least have my clothes back?'

CHAPTER FIFTEEN

Torres looked out at his realm. He looked for what had once been half of his realm's artificial horizon: the imposing Gates of Horn and Ivory.

There was nothing to see but sky.

He blinked. Slowly, forcefully, he removed his gaze from the scene in front of him and looked down at what he held in his arms. The baby was swaddled tightly in an envelope made of Torres's shirt, leaving only his face visible. He had one of Torres's little fingers in his mouth, sucking contentedly at it. He looked half-asleep.

Torres could only stare at him in shock. It seemed amazing to him that this boy could not be aware of what he had done.

'*Senhor* 'Mare?' Abilo coughed, recalling his attention. 'Might I suggest I take out some crows and scour Zion? It may be best that we find your brother sooner rather than later.'

Torres inhaled sharply. Theo. He hadn't even thought about Theo.

He looked out again at the rubble of what once had been the Sleep realm. It was hard to believe that *that* patch of grass and *that* fallen tree and *that* pile of rocks had once stood together as Zion. Torres felt as if he was looking at the pieces of his brother, laid out before him on the coroner's table.

Except Zion wasn't dead. Broken, yes, but alive. Just transformed. Already the denizens of *Os Pesadelos* were out en masse, like children discovering their new playground with uncontained excitement. They skipped over the chasms in the earth. They danced in the shadow of destruction. And Torres didn't know whether to feel proud that he had given them this, or ashamed that *he* had given them *this,* what was never his to give. And, since he didn't know how to feel, for now he felt nothing at all, as he followed the winding path of the River further than he had been able to in a long time.

'Yes,' he said, 'find Theo. Make sure he's okay and then bring him to me.'

Abilo squawked and flew off as if his instructions had been clear.

Make sure he's okay? Torres brooded. *Of course he isn't!*

There were people who had been physically hurt when the Gates fell and if the Zions would only stop hiding from his monsters long enough for Torres to tell them, then they would realise that he only wanted to help them too. He had no intention of hurting them—though he was certain there were at least some Zion Minors who wouldn't pay him the same courtesy. After all, that's what the Gates had been for: to stop the gods from hurting each other more than they had already.

'Torres.'

Ah. What took you so long?

Torres turned and found Rogan Minor staring him in the eye. Torres only met the right side of his gaze; the other side was blinding in its blindness, so white it made Torres dizzy to look into its depths.

'Rogan!' Torres said and smiled hugely. 'I thought you'd stopped coming to see me long ago. How long has it been since you entered my realm?'

Rogan looked pointedly at the soil he was standing on. *Zionese* soil. 'I still have not entered your realm, Milord.'

The Nightmare God's smile didn't falter. This is how it had always been between them, back in the classroom days when Rogan laid the words 'Milady' and 'Milord' like a carpet at Fanta and Theo's feet, and in the next breath threw it at Torres like a missile to the head. In return, Torres would call the Gatekeeper 'Goatcreeper'—to his face, too—as he imagined the illicit activities his mother had performed to earn him his horns. It was almost comforting to find how little a relationship such as theirs really *could* change.

'Have you met?' Torres asked, holding up Ereon's restless form next to his own relentless smile, for Rogan to see both at once.

Rogan didn't even blink. 'I won't get involved with matters between you and your siblings, Milord. All I ask is that you don't get involved in mine. I've begun the process of rebuilding the Gates. I expect them to stay up this time.'

Torres's smile widened. Before Rogan had a chance to walk away, he called out:

'Oh, Rogan? You haven't happened to see Theo around, have you?'

'I should be asking you, Milord. You see almost as much as I do now.'

Torres watched him stride away, back bent but gait long, until he disappeared behind a copse of evergreen trees.

Is it true? he wondered as he readjusted Ereon in his arms. He hadn't even thought of it but, if it was true, then by rejoining the realms he had also expanded his own realm sight—two-thirds of the Gatekeeper's vision was currently in his *own* eyes. He closed them and waited.

Zion was never expected, never *wanted*, the way Dream Country was. But now here it was, and it was his. What would he do with it? Only a moment later he returned his sight to himself. He was breathless with awe.

'What *are* you?' he mumbled to the bundle in his arms.

Of course, he didn't expect the baby to reply, so he almost dropped him when he heard the voice in the back of his head.

I am the Key to the final Gate. I am Destruction. I am Fear.

I am You.

His body stiffened. He felt it rising inside him, from the bottom of his stomach to the base of his chest. He began to stumble backwards—though, it had always been impossible for him to escape from himself.

No, no, no, no, no . . .

The heel of his foot hit something solid and he fell. Instinctively, his hand tightened on the back of the mortal's head to keep him steady and, either with the impact of the fall or the sound of Ereon's screams, the foetal Nightmare ceased to grow inside him. Lying there, Torres breathed out in relief. Not yet ready to rise, he rolled his head so that his cheek rested against the grass. And came face to face with a Dream.

'Iara,' he breathed in wonder.

She *wasn't* breathing. She lay half out of the River on the bank, as soaked and torn as a tissue in the rain, but still beautiful, as beautiful as he remembered. After so long in the water, her wild hair had shrunk to half its normal size and her lips were gently parted. A Duppy man's arm was around her waist and he was panting heavily as he tried to draw her out of the waters. By the time Torres had laid Ereon down and got to his feet, both the Duppy man and the Zionese goddess were collapsed safely on dry land. Without thinking, Torres rushed over to Iara and knelt by her, laying his hand over her heart. He could feel the flutter of it beating weakly under his palm and he began to press down to the same rhythm, over and over again, until she was coughing up water and gasping for air.

'Iara,' he repeated, because she hadn't heard him the first time, hadn't heard how her name in his mouth still sounded like river-water tears and regret and love.

Confusion flashed across her water-filmed eyes as she saw him.

'Torres?' Confusion and haunting and fear.

Oh, Mãe de todos, *don't let her be afraid of me too.*

'What happened? Where's Theo? Where's Bede?'

She was too weak to sit up, despite her struggles, and Torres had to hold her down.

'I'm here, Iara,' the Duppy man that Torres had forgotten about said between racking coughs.

'Theo?'

'I don't know. I just managed to keep our heads above the water. I didn't see what happened to him.'

This time when she looked at Torres she did it properly, angrily. 'What did you do?'

He was so ready to say the word that would take that look off her face, the one that she needed to hear, that the first syllable of 'nothing!' was already on his lips, when Ereon cried out again, interrupting their reunion and making a liar out of him before he even spoke.

He didn't stop her from sitting up this time, so she could get a good look at the child.

'That's Theo's Magus. He did this.'

Torres's eyes darted between the boy and Iara. 'Yes!' he said enthusiastically. 'He did! I tried to stop him, Iara, really, as soon as I realised what was happening. I don't even know what he's doing here in the first place, I just came back from the Majoracle and found him in my realm.'

'Sure. And you didn't think to return him to Theo?' asked the Duppy man, who Torres had once again forgotten about. With Iara sitting in front of him, it was hard to remember *anything* else existed, but already he could tell the Duppy man was going to be an inconvenience.

'I tried everything I could think of to get in contact with Theo,' Torres lied. 'I sent out crows, I patrolled the Gates—'

'You didn't come with Rogan when we sent him to you.'

Torres frowned. 'Rogan never came to get me. *Really,*' he said in answer to the doubt in their expressions, 'I only just saw Rogan a few minutes ago, but not before that.'

Iara must have been able to tell that he was being honest, with that part at least, because her expression softened and she let him help her to her feet.

'Well, then, we'll find Theo now and you two can talk. Maybe we can still fix this.'

'Of course. I have crows looking for him already.' *Honesty again. Wow.* 'While we wait, I'll get you indoors. You wouldn't be any use to the search in this condition,' he said, cutting off her protest. 'I have clothes and food at my house. We'll take a goat cart up. The crows will probably have already found Theo and he'll be waiting for us by the time we get there,' he smiled.

Iara's whole body shuddered with cold and, begrudgingly, she nodded, turning to her Duppy friend who had managed to haul himself to his feet. He was taller than Torres and sturdy as the mountainside.

'Come on, Bede.'

'Are you sure?' Bede asked with a suspicious glance at Torres.

Torres grinned. He almost liked the man—he had never known a Pangaean, Duppy or not, be brave enough to show what they really thought of one of their gods. Torres understood why he and Iara would be friends.

'You are, of course, invited too, Bede.' He bent down to the ground and picked up the still-screaming mortal child, with one arm holding him against his chest, while he wrapped the other around Iara's waist. 'Any friend of Theo's is a friend of mine.'

* * *

When the goat cart arrived to take them to the top of the mountain, Iara was still shivering with wet and cold. Even though he wanted to be the one to warm her up, from the inside out like the molten core of the world, Torres instead gave her a blanket—and some space. With his natural sure-footedness on the rocky terrain, he led the goats up the path while Iara and the Duppy squeezed into the cart together. The whole journey, he could hear the two of them whispering, although, whenever he turned to look, their conversation always came to a quick end. No doubt the Duppy was still trying to convince her that Torres couldn't be trusted. He didn't mind. He was so amazed to be hearing her voice again he didn't care what she was saying. The idea that he could just reach out and touch her was still so new to him that he hardly knew what to do with it. The idea of Iara in his mind was like Dream Country, something unreachable, unattainable.

The last time he saw her they had been fifteen, and even if there hadn't been a severed realm, an impassable Gate, and the suspicion of murder between them, adults would have said that their minds were too young and their bodies too small to hold a concept as ancient and massive as love. But they *had* loved each other. They had grown up together and, before the Gates, Iara had been close to both Theo and Torres. But she had chosen to stay with Theo when the Gates went up and Torres didn't see her again for nine years, until he caught sight of her through the Gates one day, when they were fifteen. He'd recognised her immediately and they had fallen immediately, once again, into the rhythm of their friendship, like picking up the tune of an old song. Later it became something else, something more. There were stolen meetings away from prying eyes, when Iara would get as close as possible to the Gates but he would have to keep his distance. He had spent whole afternoons by the River Zion, running his hands through the water just so he could feel close to her. It had been Iara he talked to when he first started thinking about a Nightmare Magus.

'Think about it, Iara,' he had said, pacing excitedly up and down in front of her. 'A Magus is supposed to be our gift to the Majority, our way of showing them that we appreciate what they go through during the Majoracle when they can't enter the realms. A Magus gets to spend a whole week with us and then go home with powers no other mortal can ever have. *Imagine* what I could do with a Nightmare Magus.'

'You mean besides talking them to death?' she'd teased as she combed out her wet hair.

But the more the idea of a Nightmare Magus took over Torres's mind, the more Iara saw how serious he was about it and the more uncertain she became.

'There's a reason you don't have a Magus, Torres. Nightmares hurt mortals, Dreams and Sleep don't.'

'Just ask Theo for me. Please, *amor.* If he decides I can have a Magus, no one will be able to stop me.'

It might have seemed strange that Torres had never been bothered by the amount of power his brother wielded, but he just knew that it wasn't in Theo's nature to use his advantage as the God of Sleep for his own purposes, even in a religion that worshipped him second only to the All-Mother.

Iara had eventually agreed to his request and one day she returned to him, as he paced impatiently by the *Os Pesadelos* Gates, with three words on her lips: '*He said no.*'

Torres had gone still. 'That's all? Just . . . no?' He had thought about it for a second. 'Theo wouldn't do that. He would think about it at least. It was someone else. Someone else told him to say that, didn't they? Who?'

Iara said nothing but she'd hung her head as if she knew and didn't want Torres to see the answer in her eyes. His first thought was that maybe she had told Theo herself to refuse his request. But, no, no matter what they might disagree on, Iara loved him. She wouldn't do that. Who else? Who had the influence over Theo to tell him what to say? Who was it that least wanted to see Torres with a Magus of his own?

'Fanta,' he'd whispered.

He was an idiot. Why did he think that just because he only had contact with his siblings at Majoracles that they weren't still regularly talking to each other? Of course they were! It *would* only be him that they cut out. He was the one they both suspected and he knew why. It was because he never wanted to talk about that day, because he refused to admit to his siblings that he didn't remember anything about it. The day the All-Mother died was a blank in Torres's memory—but no one could ever know that.

Torres never did hear what Iara said in response, if anything. The world seemed to have been silenced and even the voice of the goddess he loved couldn't reach his ears. Feeling as if he had cotton in his ears, Torres had stepped closer to the Gates, closer to *her,* than he had ever been or ever expected to be again.

And because he had closed his eyes, he felt, rather than saw, the Ivory between them. Between him and the rest of the world. In that moment he had finally come to the realisation that he was in a cage made of his sister's shadow and bone, and that everything outside that cage, Iara most of all, was out of reach until he learned to tear the cage down.

At that moment he let the Nightmare out. And what he saw when he opened his eyes again would be imprinted on his mind forever: Iara, wide-eyed and shaking, staring at him in horror. Until that moment, he realised, he had never seen the River Goddess cry.

'Oh, *Mãe de todos,*' he kept repeating afterwards, '*Mãe de todos, Mãe de todos, Eu sinto muito,* Iara, I'm so sorry, *amor.*'

But Iara had run away from him at the Gates that day and had never come back. Torres wasn't sure exactly what Nightmare he had shown her, but from that day on he started holding his Nightmares in.

Goat cart unhitched and back inside the castle, Torres called the house crows down to meet them.

'Please take my friend Bede into your care and see that he has everything he requires to feel comfortable.'

'Iara . . .' the Duppy said, refusing to move as the crows tried to lead him into the kitchen. There was a hint of warning in his voice.

'Go. I'll be fine.'

Torres gave the dead man a satisfied smirk as the crows gently caught his sleeves in their beaks and led him away, leaving Torres and Iara alone by the staircase.

'He's very friendly with you. Do you let all mortals call you by your name?'

Iara shrugged. 'That's how it is in Zion. We don't use formalities there, not even to Theo.'

'Just one big happy family, huh? And is that all you are, you and the Duppy?'

'His name is Bede.'

'Only, it's not like you to be cuddling up in a goat cart with just any mortal.'

'How would you know what's like me and what isn't?' Iara snapped, dropping her blanket at her feet.

Torres met her gaze steadily. 'Who is he really, Iara?'

'If you must know, he was a Magus of Theo. From three Majoracles ago, which is why you don't know him, since you've been hiding yourself away for four. At least now you can be really pleased with yourself; you've got two of your brother's Magi in your castle instead of just one,' she said, glaring at Ereon, still in his arms.

Torres knelt to pick up her blanket but before he handed it over he took one of her hands in his. She shivered.

'Have you missed me, Iara?'

She kissed her teeth and grabbed the blanket. 'You're unbelievable,' she said as she followed the crows who had taken Bede and left Torres standing there with a smile on his face.

She hadn't answered the question.

Just then, Abilo flew through the hallway and swooped down onto the staircase bannister. Torres could see the bad news on the crow's face as soon as he landed.

'You were gone for a long time,' Torres said. 'Let me guess—you couldn't find him?'

'I'm sorry, *Senhor* 'Mare, we looked everywhere. Your brother is nowhere in sight.'

Torres sighed and ran his fingers through his hair.

'It must be Rogan,' he said finally. 'He's helping him hide somehow. I saw him earlier, he seemed way too *calm*. The Gatekeeper knows something.'

Abilo straightened his back. 'Orders?'

'None. If Theo wants to play hide-and-seek, then we'll play too. I'll smooth things over with him later, it'll give me more time to figure out how to get into Dream Country.'

Perhaps, after he had taken Dream Country, he would return Zion to Theo. After all, he'd never wanted all three—he *barely* wanted two. He only had one realm in his sights and as long as Theo didn't stand in the way of that (he wouldn't; Torres knew his little brother wouldn't stand in the way of a butterfly), then he wouldn't be a problem.

'And what about the boy, *Senhor*?'

'What about him?'

'Aren't you curious to know what he is?'

Torres looked down at the boy who gurgled serenely back at him. 'You don't have to know what a hammer is made of before you start swinging. Besides, I already know what he is.' Torres looked over at the kitchen door into which Iara had disappeared. 'He's my good luck charm.'

CHAPTER SIXTEEN

Fanta's monsters had skin like dried leather, dusty grey and loose around the stomach. Their bodies were bulbous and awkward, and with every flat-footed shuffling step they took, their already tremendous size seemed to increase even more. Their ears hung like sails on either side of the mast of their long trunks. And there, at the bottom of their horrifically impassive faces, were two long tusks of pure Dream-blessed Ivory.

'For goodness sake, Theo, they're harmless! They're not going to attack you.'

'You mean unless you tell them to?'

Theo cowered at the mouth of the sandstone cave, fully clothed now, his hands more loosely bound, in front of him. The last thing he'd expected after he and his sister had just come to the semblance of an agreement was to be confronted by some of the deadliest creatures in the celestial realms, creatures that he and Torres had spent their childhood avoiding while Fanta treated them as pets. Yet there they were, two phantelles standing together, each with a flimsy throne-like chair strapped to its back, one of which was already part-occupied by a pipe-smoking Minor god with short hair dyed red with ochre.

'Actually, they won't attack even if she tells them to. These ones only listen to me,' the unknown Minor said.

Fanta frowned. 'Only because I allow it to be that way, in case you've forgotten, Onkwani. They would listen to me if I really wanted them to.'

Onkwani Minor inclined his head and smirked in a way that inexplicably reminded Theo of slugs coming out after the rain.

'I'm not getting on that thing,' Theo said.

'Yes, you are, because I'm going to get you to Torres as soon as possible and phantelles are faster than walking. We're just lucky Onkwani was around.'

'I've already been on one, Milord, they're not so bad. It's a smoother ride than the horses we have on the island,' said Arielle.

'You see, even the mortal isn't afraid of them. You're going to be sitting on *top* of them anyway; their tusks are all the way down here. They would have to literally break their own necks to get to you. There may be some things in Dream Country that would be willing to sacrifice their own lives just to kill you, but I assure you the phantelles are not among them. So get on.'

Onkwani jumped down from his own seat to help Arielle onto the second beast. He offered a hand to Fanta, but she was obviously practised enough at mounting that she could do it alone and she pulled herself up beside Arielle. They looked down at Theo from above, Fanta with a sneer, Arielle with some sympathy, and waited.

'May I offer you my assistance, *Bwana*?' Onkwani said, offering his hand with that same smirk.

Theo looked at him and wondered if he was being sarcastic. The top of his head reached Theo's shoulders and he was obviously a few years older than any of the Majors. Theo couldn't remember his face to decide whether he was one of those people Fanta mentioned might not be too glad to see him there. The fact that he was in Dream Country at all suggested he had taken her side after the Gates went up, and therefore wasn't exactly Theo's biggest fan. But that didn't mean he hated him either; some of the Minors were just as indifferent to, or as suspicious of, the Major of their own realm as of the other two. After a moment, Theo decided Onkwani probably wasn't his enemy, although he still wasn't exactly sure what to make of the Minor god.

Theo allowed him to help him onto the phantelle and, once he was safely seated on top, he realised he would be needing Onkwani's help to get down again, since he had been paying more attention to those sinister Ivory tusks than to the process of mounting. Resuming his own seat next to him, Onkwani made a clicking noise and the phantelles both began to walk forward at once. As Arielle had promised, the ride was smooth, although Theo couldn't help thinking that he was sitting on top of a landmine. The Dream Magus looked over at him encouragingly.

'Everyone is afraid of something. It's blood for me. And small spaces,' she admitted with a shudder. 'I hate the idea of being closed in.'

Theo frowned. 'But if you're closed in that means you're safe. It means you have something around you to keep the bad stuff out and the good stuff in.'

Arielle nodded, slowly. 'I guess what we're afraid of doesn't have to make sense.'

There was something about that sentence, or about the resigned way she said it, that made Theo feel for the first time in his life that he was speaking to someone who understood him. He smiled at the Magus that wasn't his. But when she spoke again she seemed just as concerned for the phantelles as she did for him.

'How do you get them to do what you say?' she asked Onkwani. 'You don't hurt them, do you? On the island the Magistrates outlawed whipping the horses.'

'Oh, there would be no need for something so brutally *mortal* here. My phantelles like to obey me; they're like puppies.'

Theo frowned at the comparison. 'You're God of Beasts?' he asked, seeming to remember that Minor to live in Dream Country.

But Onkwani shook his head. '*Mama wa wote*, that animal? *La hasha*, I am the God of Reason. Phantelles are highly intelligent creatures. I simply use logic to show them that working with me is a mutually beneficial arrangement. So you have nothing to worry about, *mpenzi*.' He winked at Arielle who blushed.

'How long will the journey take?' Theo asked.

'If we want to get close to Torres's castle we have to get to the opposite side of Dream Country from the place where you came in. So, I'd say no more than two days,' Fanta called back.

It was a long time. Maybe too long. What would Torres be able to do with Ereon in the two days it would take to get to him?

'Is there no faster way?'

Fanta shrugged. 'Can you fly?'

In the end, Theo wasn't sure that using the phantelles was the quickest way to travel. Sure, the beasts had longer strides, but they also moved in such lumbering gaits, like a spoon being pushed through honey, he thought he might have been able to overtake them on foot. It also didn't help that Onkwani refused to make them run. He said that all it would do is tire them out when they were a long way from the River Zion where they could stop to refresh themselves.

Theo found himself imagining how amazed Iara would be if she could see him now, on the back of this creature. She was always telling him he needed to face his fears. And then Bede was always telling her that the purpose of fear was to warn you *away*, not to stir your misguided sense of bravery. At which point she would tell him that, while that may be true for mortals, Theo was a god and there was nothing he needed to be warned away from. Causing Bede to then point out that gods could still die, so while we're on the subject, what *really* made them gods anyway . . .

Right now, Theo couldn't think of what Iara's reply to that would be, because, with such an argument, Bede would have made an unanswerable point. After all, the River goddess herself might now be dead. And Theo was pretty sure it wasn't possible to die twice, but whatever state Bede was in now, he probably wished he could. Theo missed them.

A real god would have been able to protect his friends, he thought.

Preoccupied with his grief, he was nevertheless vaguely aware of being watched: Arielle watched him out of the corner of her eye, and Fanta made no attempts to hide the fact that she had her eye on him, and Onkwani divided his gaze between him and—more leeringly—Arielle.

Theo hated being watched. He always had, whether at his own birthday party or on a stage in front of the Majority. When he was a child, he used to close his eyes and pretend that anything he couldn't see could not see him. So now he let his eyelids fall.

As long as he ignored that nagging feeling that told him his realm sight ought to be engaging, but it wasn't because he wasn't at home (*you're in a bad place, too*), then it was almost pleasant to ride through Dream Country with his eyes closed. They passed no one as they went, and the only sound was Onkwani's incessant speech. The air felt like he was constantly sitting too close to a warm fire but eventually even that ceased to bother him.

He heard distant instruments playing, their sounds floating on the air like birdsong and wind chimes. He heard a voice begin to sing in the language of Dream Country and though he couldn't understand it he felt like he could. Falling into a trance, he felt his body rise away from the phantelle's back, as now he realised he didn't need them after all.

He *could* fly.

He could *fly*.

* * *

Theo was flying and he was laughing, two things it felt like he hadn't done in a very long time. He had missed them.

The land was miniscule beneath him, and the places he saw as he flew and the things beneath him were not real places and they were not real things. The sandy path had heated under the red sun, until it became glass, and Theo could see his reflection in it. He looked like a creature of air and wings.

A dark shadow fell out of the sky and as it got closer Theo saw that it was a hand. It tried to swat him as he flew around, like a fly at the fingertips of a giant, and then, pinching its two fingers together it grabbed him by the back of the shirt and lifted him up into the clouds. He wasn't laughing anymore, but he wasn't scared either.

The hand deposited him on the back of a giant mango-coloured bird, with feathers fading from red to orange to yellow to green, and it flew with him ever higher.

'Kirrrrbeee,' the bird trilled.

At the top of the hill where the bird landed, there was a giant waiting for him. The bird grazed on purple grass as Theo approached. The giant's face was a blur, but Theo knew that it was Rogan. He held out his hand and there was a tree in his palm.

'Plant this, my boy, and see what grows.'

Obediently, Theo took the large tree, struggling with it yet somehow managing to keep it in his grip as he knelt on the soil. He began to dig out a hole with his hands and while he worked Rogan took out a giant version of the pocket knife he had given Theo. Casually, he began to cut the heads off flower stalks, all of which had the faces of gods.

'Didn't you ever know your father?' Rogan asked.

'I don't think I had one.'

'Of course you did! Everyone has a father. Yours just so happened to be your mother. She was beautiful once. Dark and wide as the sky,' Rogan sighed nostalgically. 'Look, there she goes!'

Theo turned just in time to see the mango-bird take flight. 'Kirrrrbeee,' came her voice. She spread her wings until her shadow darkened the sky and Rogan's plants and Theo's tree shrivelled up in their hands. Theo didn't notice. He was watching the bird, which wasn't flying anymore but falling, falling, falling . . .

* * *

Theo tipped off the phantelle and fell to the warm sand, screaming, every muscle in his body stiff and every bone shaking, as pain racked his mind.

CHAPTER SEVENTEEN

Torres couldn't remember the last time he had eaten a full meal at his dining room table. Over the years he had learnt to sustain himself on snacks, enough to stave off the hunger but never enough to make him feel full. If he was ever going to sit down and eat properly, he would want to find a bowl of *feijoada* or a nice cut of *picanha* meat, with a brown crust and rosy pink on the inside, that fell apart when he put it in his mouth, meltingly tender.

Torres looked down at the leafy pile on the plate in front of him and wrinkled his nose in disgust.

'It's Ital. Just try it, it's good for you,' Iara insisted as she crunched down on another forkful.

She was illuminated by candlelight that lengthened the shadow of her teeth as she ate, making her look like a rabbit pinned against the dining room's walls. The sun was shining as brightly as ever and the candles weren't really necessary, but Torres had instructed the crows to put them out anyway, thinking Iara would like them. So far she had made no comment.

He sighed in resignation and picked up his fork. It would be rude not to finish everything on his plate, especially after Iara had come to him and asked if they could have dinner together, without her Duppy pet joining them. Surprised, he couldn't help asking what had changed her mind after she had seemed so intent on avoiding him before.

She'd shrugged, embarrassed. 'Maybe I *have* missed you.'

Over a day had passed since Torres found them and she'd been practically bouncing off the walls with impatience to get back down the mountainside and join the search for Theo, which Torres had told her was still ongoing. He was torn between telling her that he couldn't find him, in the hope that she might offer a clue as to where he could be, or keeping her in the dark for as long as possible, since he knew that as soon as they found Theo, his lies about just finding Ereon in his realm would be revealed. Theo wasn't stupid. He must have figured out the truth about Torres taking his Magus by now, even if he didn't know how or why. Yes, it was best for the time being for Theo to remain unfound.

'How's the search going?' Iara asked, as if she could read his mind.

'The quake tore up a lot of the land. The new theory is that some earth or rocks got overturned and trapped Theo underneath. That would explain why I can't see him in my realm sight, since I can't see underground.' Torres doubted this had really happened. Rogan would have thought of something more clever than that.

Iara went still for a moment. 'Torres, if . . . if something had happened to Theo, would you know?'

He thought about it. 'If Theo died someone else *would* have to become the God of Sleep . . .' *Unless we're like the All-Mother and can't be replaced.* Torres didn't want to speak this thought out loud. 'But it would have to be another Major, so . . .'

'It would probably be Fanta.'

Torres dropped his fork. 'Why?' he snapped.

Iara shrugged. 'She's the oldest.'

Torres felt his jaws clench until his teeth were grinding together. 'You see these tapestries?' he gestured around them.

'Well, no, I can't see them. Why are they all turned around like that?'

Torres pushed his chair back and got to his feet. 'You remember Attai?'

'Minor of Time? First generation?'

The 'first generation' Minors were those who were around before the Major triplets were born. There were very few of them, but Rogan and Attai and one or two others were first generation. Third generation Minors were those who came around *after* the All-Mother's death and never knew her. Minors like Iara were second generation, the ones between birth and death.

'Every Majoracle, Attai used to make me one of these tapestries,' he said, walking over to the first one. 'I think he knew how much I hated Rogan's lessons and was trying to trick me into learning history. He showed me a time before we were born. He wanted me to see what things were like back then.' Torres flipped the heavy tapestry and looked at the image for the first time in years, as Iara looked at it for the first time ever.

At first glance, it seemed to be a depiction of an anthill under a burning sun and Iara frowned at such meaningless imagery until, getting up to stand beside Torres, she took a closer look. She gasped. They were not ants; they were mortals. And what she had mistaken for the sun was actually a fire of tremendous proportions, with cities and countries burning beneath it.

Torres moved on to the next tapestry and turned it around. This one showed, from a god's-eye view, two mortal women in close combat, each with hands soaked in the other's blood. Iara shuddered as she looked at the expressions that had been so expertly woven into their faces. Torres couldn't blame her, it was hard to say which was more terrifying. The woman on the right had the anger of destruction in her; her gaze was the eye of the tornado. But the woman on the left was laughing as she stabbed her opponent. Enjoying the pain. In the background a child looked between the two death-marked warriors and looked completely unaffected by what he saw.

Torres moved on to the third tapestry. He actually felt bad about the moment of false relief he offered Iara as he revealed to her an image of still and peaceful waters. But again, inevitably, looking closer, she saw this was no lake, no river, but a grave. Mortals floated dead in the flood, indistinguishable from the drowning rats around them, except it seemed that more rats had survived.

'These are horrible,' Iara whispered. 'Why would Attai show you this?'

'Because he wanted me to see what things were like before we were born.'

'You mean they're real? The All-Mother allowed this?'

'There was nothing she could do to stop it. It was a force that wasn't her—another god, but one that hadn't manifested yet, so she couldn't even fight it. She couldn't control it, so do you know what she did?' Iara shook her head. She had gone pale and Torres wrapped an arm around her waist. 'She gave birth to it instead.'

'What do you mean? How . . .' Iara stopped, her eyes widening as understanding dawned.

Torres nodded solemnly. 'It was me, Iara. Me before I was me. I was the force that even my own mother couldn't stop.' He kissed the goddess lightly on the top of her head. 'So don't tell me that Fanta deserves the most because she is the oldest. There's *nothing* older than a Nightmare. You understand, *amor*?'

Iara nodded. Torres led her back to the table and pulled out her chair for her to sit down. She was quiet until Torres resumed his own seat and then he found her watching him, her food untouched.

'I did try to convince him, you know. I was on your side, I know you think I could have done more but . . .'

He knew exactly what she was talking about, even though this was a conversation they had dropped years ago. And he found himself hesitant to pick it up again now.

Nevertheless, he said, 'but you never really believed I should have a Magus, did you? Even while you were trying to convince Theo.'

Iara hesitated. *Don't lie to me*, he begged silently. He didn't know if he should feel relieved or disappointed when she nodded.

'But not because of the reasons everyone else was saying,' Iara went on. 'I think that now a mortal *could* be your Magus without it being dangerous—but not back then. We were all still just kids and you didn't have enough control over your Nightmares yet. It was harder for you than . . . the other two,' she said, hesitating to bring Fanta's name up again.

Torres heard it implied anyway. 'Because I'm weaker?' he asked bitterly.

Iara shook her head. 'Because you're the only one who doesn't match the power you were given. Even in the short time I've been here with you now, I've seen how you've learnt to take control; there are fewer Nightmares running around than ever. Theo is perfect as the Sleep God, because what he loves more than anything is peace. I think you two are a lot more alike than most people realise.' She raised her chin, as if preparing herself for a physical blow. 'And if Theo really is gone, the Majority would be lucky if you were the one to take his place.'

Torres didn't know how to respond. He felt shaky as Iara's words echoed in his heart. She really meant it, he could tell. She had never lied to him. When she reached across the table and took his hand, he raised it to his lips. He pulled her up from the table and into an embrace, at the end of which he brushed his cheek against hers as he brought their lips together. She kissed him back. After they pulled apart, his voice sounded heavy with love when he spoke again.

'Enough talking. Enough eating. Come,' he said, pulling her towards the doorway.

She hesitated, then nodded. 'Okay. But Torres, you have to let me help you while I'm here. When this whole misunderstanding is cleared up, I want to be able to help you explain things to Theo. Let me take care of the Magus until you find him.'

'I'll think about it,' Torres said huskily.

After that there was no more room between them for words.

* * *

At the flattest part of the base of the eleventh mountain, the *Os Pesadelos* market stalls overflowed with customers. Ever since the collapse of the Zionese Gates, that unexpected event of two days before, the Nightmare business was booming. No matter how monotonous it could be playing with mortals, the monsters always dreaded the week of the Majoracle when they didn't even have that. And while they could always find some quick entertainment in torturing each other, there was a strict ban on attacking the *Os Pesadelos* Minors. No such ban existed for the Zion Minors, and certainly not for the Duppies.

Os Pesadelos was the only one of the three realms to have implemented a system of commerce, and the gold had never flown so rapidly between hands as it did now. As he approached the eleventh mountain, with Abilo gliding over his shoulder and Ereon dragged along in a rickety goat cart, Torres noted the grins on the faces of his people, even the haggling, spitting, fighting people, and he realised he had never seen them happy. He realised that, for them, the gold in their hands was as much a Dream as anything Fanta could produce. Just as much an illusion too, since the shiny material only had value in his realm as long as he said it did. He could change his mind tomorrow and leave his subjects as simple magpies in a worthless nest.

But, for now, he liked to see them happy. One stall was piled high with scrolls that claimed to know all Zions' worst fears. Another displayed little carved figures of Torres on a mountaintop, in flowing robes and both arms outstretched to either side, with little signs underneath, reading 'made from the seeds of the palm trees of Zion.' Another, crowded with vats of boiling potion, with nothing advertising what they were; the proprietor simply wrapped his tentacles around any interested customer and whispered into their ear. Every single one of them walked away with a potion.

'I've never seen them like this,' Torres said in awe.

'The Zions are interesting, *Senhor*. Even the Duppy ones are nothing like the mortals we know. I've seen some of the Nightmares their minds can produce and it's . . . not pretty.'

Torres smiled broadly. 'Don't tell me *you* were scared, Abilo. I've never been able to scare you before.'

'There's a first time for everything, *Senhor*. Don't let it be said of me that I count my chicks before they hatch.'

'Two for one! Two for one, over here! *Ei, vem ver!* Let me guess, you're still using the same old tricks—dismemberment, chasing 'em down never-ending, dark corridors. Why not try something new, *hein?* Your loss, buddy. *A maldição!* You, sir, you look like—oh, *me desculpe, Senhor* 'Mare, I didn't recognise you.' The merchant bowed so low he almost chewed off his own head with the teeth protruding from his belly. 'Why, that's a pretty little Nightmare, *Senhor*! Is he for sale?' the merchant said leaning over Ereon in his cart. The child screamed.

'Not a Nightmare. A mortal,' Torres corrected. 'What are you selling?'

There was nothing on the merchant's table apart from a large sign written in letters of green sludge proclaiming, 'Vitor's 2-4-1!'

'Ideas, *Senhor*! *Compreende?* Times are a-changin' and the Nightmares of the first generation just don't cut it anymore. It's a time for unattainable lusts and disappointed fathers. Subtlety is the new skill of the Nightmare! And I just want to take this opportunity to say, *Senhor* 'Mare . . .'—the merchant took off his hat and twisted it obsequiously between his stubby fingers—'I just wanted to say, in case no one else has, how much I appreciate everything you've done, *de verdade*. I mean, bringing down the Zionese Gates like that was a stroke of genius. And so subtly done too! No one even knew you were planning it. To be honest, *Senhor* 'Mare, all those years you shut yourself away in your castle, not seeing anyone, and decreasing the Nightmares, we all thought you was going soft. Well, everyone else thought that anyway,' he corrected himself quickly. 'Me, I always said, *não, não Senhor* 'Mare, *ele tem algo grande planejado, é só esperar pra ver,*'

'I appreciate your confidence in me,' Torres said smoothly. He reached into his pocket and tossed the merchant a coin. 'I'm looking for *Senhora* Barrera, have you seen her?'

The merchant caught it deftly and the glint of the gold reflected in his eager eyes. 'Where she always is, I'd say, *Senhor* 'Mare.'

Torres nodded and walked away just as the merchant's tongue flopped out to taste the gold coin he'd just received.

He'd known exactly where to find the Minor goddess, but it didn't hurt to have the rumour spreading around the market that he was going to see her. It would make the monsters happy. *Senhora* Barrera, a first-generation Minor, had been one of the monsters' best advocates against the Nightmare restrictions during Torres's self-imposed four years of reclusion. There had hardly been a week when the old goddess hadn't dragged herself out from her caves and made her way to the peak of the third mountain, only to be sent away by Abilo at the door, without having received an audience.

Torres had to admit to himself he regretted treating the old goddess so badly. Now she would have a list of her own demands ready when he asked for her help.

'They think that's what this is, you know, *Senhor*,' Abilo said suddenly, landing on Torres's shoulder. 'They think that now you've taken Zion, the Nightmares are going to go back to the way they were before. Maybe even more this time.'

Torres shrugged, feeling the bird's talons digging into his shoulder. 'I can't help what they choose to believe. I've told them many times that the old level of Nightmares isn't coming back. But they'll be grateful in the end, once they see what I really have in store for them.' Abilo cocked his head to one side and crowed disbelievingly. 'Well, okay,' Torres said, 'maybe not grateful. Compliant, at least.'

They made their way to the centre of the crowded market, where the rock face of the mountain suddenly rose in a sheer cliff on one side of them. The merchants here used the mountain itself as their selling platform, hanging tapestries on the cliff face, similar to the ones Torres had in his dining room. The sight reminded him of his dinner with Iara, and all that came after, and he let out an involuntary sigh. He hadn't wanted to leave her, but this trip was something he had to do, if he planned never to content himself with just Nightmares.

The row of tapestries ended where the rock suddenly dipped inwards, as if someone had taken a large scoop out of it with a giant spoon. The cave went deeper than the light of the sun could reach.

Torres hitched the goat cart to a nearby pillar of stone, picked Ereon up, and led the way inside. He had been tempted to leave the boy behind at the castle, especially considering how eager Iara was to help out and take care of him. Before he left, in fact, he had found her kneeling over Ereon's basket, about to lift him out.

'What are you doing?' he'd asked.

Quickly, she'd snapped upright and spun around. 'I . . . I was just going to hold him for a little while. He looked like he was about to start crying.'

Torres had smiled. She was just so considerate like that. Even so, he had decided to take Ereon with him. He couldn't trust everyone in his castle like he could Iara.

Torres's eyes adjusted quickly to the darkness of the cave as he used his realm sight to enhance his vision, and he knew Abilo would have no problem with it either, but, almost immediately, Ereon began to scream and writhe around in Torres's arms like he was possessed.

'*Mãe de todos*, what's wrong with him?' Torres said quietly.

'Perhaps he's scared of the dark.'

Torres shook his head in bewilderment. Sometimes the Pangaean poets referred to the Magi as 'the All-Mother's grandchildren': it seemed ridiculous that Night's grandson would be afraid of the dark.

No more ridiculous than her son being afraid of it, Torres thought. He hadn't failed to notice how Theo had shied away from the sky while they had been down on the island. But was that fear? Or was it grief? Or even guilt? After all, there was that inescapable fact about the circumstances of the All-Mother's death that pointed right at Theo. Maybe . . .

The ground gradually sloped downwards and he could feel the texture of the rock changing beneath his feet. Each step became a little smoother until it was almost slippery and he had to start placing his feet with great care. Some way in, he reached a silk curtain blocking off the rest of the path. He took a deep breath, knowing what the curtain was hiding. It had been a long time since he'd been down here, but it wasn't a place that allowed itself to be easily forgotten. Torres pulled the curtain aside.

Glowing white light shocked his eyes, like an ambush of fresh snow. Even Ereon was blinded into silence. They were no longer standing on simple mountain rock but at one end of a wide crystal bridge. Torres looked over the side. The bridge was wide enough for three more people on either side of him. Still, it was a long way down. And it was more than a little disconcerting to see that the only thing holding the massive slab of crystal above the gaping pit was more crystal: pillars of crystal as thick around as a Pangaean building sticking out of the walls, ceiling, and floor of the cave at odd angles. As Torres and Abilo made their way across the bridge, a particularly low-hanging crystal forced Abilo to the ground and Torres to get down on his hands and knees to pass under it. Although, when looked at from a distance, the crystals seemed to be the purest white, closer up it was possible to see the colours in them. Some were pinkish or tinged with blue; others sparkled more brightly than any trinket of gold. The only sound was the faint whisper of routine Majoracle prayers to Torres resonating up from Pangaea through the crystals. They were extremely faint, but so few that Torres could pick out every word. Somewhere in the distance a loud crack broke the rhythm of voices, and the echoes of the broken crystal were thrown around by the walls long after the fallen rock had splashed into the unseen waters of the Zion below. The source of the River was in these mountains and that made Torres smile, thinking about how even in nature, he and Iara were joined.

'It's beautiful,' Abilo said, even his whisper echoing around them.

'Yes,' Torres said, his mind still on Iara. He shook himself out of his reverie. It was about time for him to announce his presence. '*Senhora* Barrera!' he shouted.

The whole cave shook and a few more of the weaker crystals broke loose and fell around them. Ereon looked around with wide eyes and Torres wondered if he felt at home here, where his wasn't the only voice that could shake the world.

'*O que? Quem é esse?*' There was a whistle in the disembodied voice as it came to them, painting a perfect picture of the wide gap between *Senhora* Barrera's two front teeth.

'It's me, Torres Major. I heard you came up to see me at the castle. It's a shame, I must have just missed you, but I thought it was only polite for me to return the visit as soon as possible.'

'Ha!' the voice exclaimed. 'And it hasn't been possible for the last four years?'

'I'm a very busy man.'

'You're a fool surrounded by other fools who have crowned you and allowed you to believe you're not so foolish after all. I'm surprised you even left your so-called castle. You were always one to hide from trouble when it came.'

'Funny. Other people always told me that I *was* the trouble.'

'You are. And it's not just been four years that you've been hiding from yourself.'

The woman waiting for them, as they turned the corner of a crystal at the end of the bridge, was crouched in a rocking chair in the middle of an extremely incongruous-looking set of living room furniture. *Senhora* Barrera was shrouded in clothes that might have fitted Torres but were at least five sizes too big for her. Her bottom eyelids drooped over her cheeks, exposing red flesh underneath and giving her an air of permanent exhaustion, though Torres wasn't fooled by it. He could see the alertness in the old woman's gaze, despite her body's genuine frailty. It was something of a miracle that she had managed to make so many trips up Torres's mountain on her own. But then again, she hadn't been alone.

On a woollen rug on the other side of the living room three monsters were harnessed together, curled up into Sleep. He couldn't see their faces, but between the wings of the one nearest to him, he saw the red marks of torn skin. He frowned. He had seen how *Senhora* Barrera whipped her monsters as they carried her around *Os Pesadelos*. There wasn't much he could do to stop the beatings even if he tried; and, in fact, the monsters seemed to like it.

'*Senhor* 'Mare,' the old goddess greeted him coolly. 'I see you brought your pet.'

Abilo bobbed his head. 'It's a pleasure as always, *Senhora*.'

Barrera ignored him. She was looking intently at the bundle cradled in Torres's arms. 'What's that?'

'You haven't heard?' Torres asked, pulling up a chair. 'I took a Magus.'

'*Took* being the operative word. *Sim, eu ouvi.* News like that even gets to me way down here. Your brother can't be too happy,' she said and cackled wholeheartedly and unpleasantly.

Torres smiled but didn't join in the laughter. 'If I had left this boy with Theo the whole of the Celesterra would be up in smoke by now. He wouldn't have known how to control him.'

'And you do?'

'No,' he smiled sweetly. 'But I think you might. Have the crystals shown you anything?'

'These aren't your mountain-corner, market-stall scrying crystals, *garoto*!' the Goddess of Fortunes said, insulted. 'They won't divulge the secrets of the future at your whim. You and your sister play too much with the elements of my domain. They're to be taken seriously!'

'I do take them seriously, *Senhora*,' Torres said gently, his smile still in place, 'which is another reason why I came to talk. The crystals are why you've been wanting to see me, aren't they? You saw something, something to do with monsters and Nightmares.'

The old goddess hesitated. Torres could practically see the cogs whirring in her brain as she weighed up the pleasure of telling him to 'Get lost' against the benefit of finally being able to speak to him about what she'd seen. Torres didn't need a cave of crystals to know what the result would be.

Senhora Barrera sighed and rocked forward in her chair. 'You'll push them too far one day, *Senhor* 'Mare. These monsters like to be pushed, but only in the way *they like to be pushed*, if you know what I mean.' She gestured to the three monsters tied up behind her and Torres nodded as she went on. 'I really hate the disgusting creatures. And I hate even more how they've made me out to be some kind of folk hero to them, thanks to you. They don't realise that I was trying to get the Nightmares back for *your* sake, not theirs. Because of what I've seen. And even I wouldn't dare push them as far as I think you're planning to. I've seen the monsters lay siege on your castle. Nightmare-deprived. Angry. Your little birdy doormen won't keep them out . . . I haven't seen what they'll do to you once they get inside. But, when you've seen as many futures as I have, you develop a pretty good imagination.'

Torres nodded. He rocked Ereon absent-mindedly in his arms, trying to seem unfazed and project calmness to the old goddess who was watching him carefully.

'And do you know when this is going to happen?' he asked casually. He feigned indifference but in truth he really was interested to know. Torres didn't like not knowing things. There were already too many things in his life that he didn't know or had forgotten, including the mystery of his mother's death. Every time he encountered something he didn't understand, it took him back to that day when he was six years old, Rogan's hot tea in his hands and his mother's face already fading from his memory.

Barrera thought for a moment. 'No. But I'm thinking that boy you're holding can't be a good sign.'

'Speaking of the boy—no, I've heard what you had to say now,' Torres said, raising a hand to cut Barrera off. 'And I appreciate the warning. I really do. But I still need your help with the Magus.'

Barrera sighed again, more deeply. The whistle at the end of it sounded almost like birdsong. Torres could see her relief at finally having told him about her vision. Anything that happened from here on wasn't her fault. She was divulged of all responsibility.

Must be nice.

'I meant it when I said I hadn't seen anything. But the answers you're looking for might have been a lot closer to you than I was all along. Pigeon Eyes!'

One of the monsters sat up from the rug at the sound of its name. It looked around and Theo saw that it really was cross-eyed like a pigeon.

'Bring me the *Theologos*,' Senhora Barrera said.

Torres scoffed. 'The *Theologos*? Look, I'm looking for serious answers, *Senhora* Barrera, and if you're not going to help—'

'Sit down, *garoto*!' the old goddess snapped. 'I've been telling you for a long time that you underestimate the mortals. You want proof? Look at what you're holding in your arms. He's the reason you're here, isn't he? You have a mortal question, you look for mortal answers. That's just common sense, fool.'

Pigeon Eyes crawled as far as his chains would let him up to *Senhora* Barrera's chair and handed her the book and, seemingly just for fun, she smacked him over the head with it before sending him scampering back to his rug. She attempted to throw over the Holy Book, and though her arms were too weak to cope with its great weight, Abilo caught it in mid-air and took it to Torres.

The Holy Theologos was a dense tome with thick pages that almost made his knees numb under its weight. The pages of this particular copy were brown and dry and the ink of its verses and chapters was faded around the edges.

You'd think something this hefty would contain something more useful than toilet paper.

'Okay. Well, I guess it's never too late to find religion,' he joked.

Senhora Barrera didn't answer. She had fallen asleep in her rocking chair. That was another change brought on by the collapse of Theo's Gates. It wasn't just that the Zions were having Nightmares, but the people of *Os Pesadelos* were also Sleeping again. Most of them liked it but it didn't affect Torres, probably because he was a Major. It had always been harder for the triplets to work their abilities on each other than anyone else. He just had to put up with *Senhora* Barrera's snores while he read.

Hours later, Torres had only just reached the birth of the siblings in the long-winded narrative. Nothing else of interest had happened.

He sighed. 'Did you know that I weigh the souls of each of the Majority to decide the extent of the Nightmare I give them?'

Abilo did his best to look impressed. 'Well done, *Senhor*.'

Torres snorted. 'Honestly, these mortals would believe anything. I don't know why we let the old Magistrates write this stuff. I don't even know what half of it means.' He slammed the book shut. 'Let's get out of here, Abilo. This was a waste of time.'

Just as he got up from his seat a loud crack sounded in the air above him. Over the hours, Torres had become used to the sounds of the cave and he didn't even flinch until Abilo slammed into the back of him.

'*CAAW!*'

Torres stumbled forwards and the crow rolled past him in a heap as a large crystal dropped down from the ceiling and landed where he had just been sitting. In shock, Torres looked at the thing that had almost killed him and saw its surface starting to turn a milky white. A sudden wind whipped through the cave, and he bent over to shield Ereon as he heard the heavy pages of the dropped *Theologos* rattling wildly under the force of the gale. The monsters by the fireplace howled. When the wind passed a moment later, he looked up to find the *Theologos* open at its middle page and *Senhora* Barerra crouching on the floor with her eyes and mouth wide open and her arms spread around the foggy image of the crystal. When she spoke, her voice was not her own.

'*Ivory one and Horn the other,*

The child was born, and then the mother,
For the cycle to make, the Gates must fall;
Send a thief beyond the wall.'

She collapsed.

Abilo and Torres stayed frozen for another few seconds, staring at each other. Torres cleared his throat. 'Well, that was . . . terrifying.'

After he had helped *Senhora* Barrera's prone figure back into her chair, he picked up the *Theologos* once more and read the open passage out loud.

'"*When a Sleep Magus or a Dream Magus is chosen, an eternal connection is formed with their god's realm. It is for this reason that a Magus will be able to enter no other realm after the Majoracle is ended (unless they are a Dream Magus, who will still be permitted entrance into Zion when they die.) It is as though the Magus permanently carries a Holy material in their hands and the Gates will not open for them unless they recognise the correct one.*"'

'What does it mean, *Senhor*?'

'I think . . . I think it means that Ereon is still technically Theo's Magus. And that when I tried to bring down Dream Country's Gates before, he automatically brought down Zion's instead, because that's the realm he's connected to. When he was just born he wasn't connected to anything and he could affect all three realms. Since the Majoracle ceremony he can't do anything to Dream Country because he has no connection to it. But,' he said, excitedly stabbing a finger down at the page, 'it says here that the connection is the same thing as holding a Holy material. That's probably why I was able to override Theo and Ereon's connection when I put the Horn on him. So if I want him to connect with Dream Country . . .'

'Ivory,' Abilo completed. 'He needs to be holding Ivory.'

'Exactly!' Torres grinned. '*Senhora* Barrera said it herself. *Ivory one, and Horn the other.* I'm not sure what the rest of it meant and I probably can't ask her anytime soon,'—he nodded down at her—'but this has to be what she was talking about!'

Abilo cleared his throat. 'Might I ask why you're so happy about this, *Senhor* 'Mare? It means your plan is ruined.'

There was no Ivory in *Os Pesadelos*; usually, just the thought of having it in his realm made Torres's skin crawl. And the Gates were hopeless, even the broken one: the Ivory in them was too melded with the Horn to be of any use. But Torres's smile didn't falter.

'Not ruined,' he said, 'just delayed. *Senhora* Barrera helped us there too. *Send a thief beyond the wall.* Abilo, gather some crows and tell them they might want to pack for a long trip. You're going into Dream Country and you're going to get me some Ivory.'

CHAPTER EIGHTEEN

Feeling crept back into Theo's limbs like a shadow across a wall. The tips of his fingers began to tingle, then he found himself very aware of his own heartbeat in his stomach, his throat, his temple, his chest. He wanted to scream but all that came out was a wet groan.

'He's awake!' someone said, then Theo felt movement nearby.

He opened his eyes. Onkwani and Arielle were kneeling on either side of him with intense expressions on their faces.

'Yep, he's definitely alive,' Onkwani said.

'What happened?' Theo croaked, trying to sit up.

Arielle's hands fluttered nervously around him, but she didn't touch him. 'I don't know, you just collapsed. Are you okay, Milord?'

'I-I don't know. I feel weird. And I saw things, but—what was that? With that tree and that bird . . .'

Arielle frowned, her eyes blank.

'You didn't see that?' Theo asked, his voice wavering. The last thing he needed on top of everything was to be going crazy.

A voice said, 'You can't see other people's Dreams. Only the Dreamer and I see it.'

Theo looked over and saw Fanta standing a short distance away from the three of them, next to the two phantelles. Her arms were folded in front of her and she had a bored expression on her face.

'So you saw the tree then?' he asked her. 'What—wait. What do you mean *Dreamer*? Did I just have a Dream?'

The Dream Goddess rolled her eyes. 'Obviously. Not the most exciting one I've ever seen, but you're still an amateur, they'll get better.'

'No. No, no, no,' Theo said, laughing in disbelief. He pulled himself up to his feet and stumbled a little before he could look Fanta in the eye again. 'I can't Dream. That's impossible, we can't do that to each other anymore. It doesn't make any sense!'

Once it had made sense, when they were closer, but that was a long time ago. They were their own people now and their very definitions excluded the other two. After all, what would you call a Sleeping Dream? Or a Dreaming Nightmare?

Impossible.

'It obviously is possible, but it doesn't seem to be advised. That's why you reacted like that. Dreams are like Ivory for you. Which is interesting,' Fanta said flatly.

'Interesting? You mean, I could have *died* from having that Dream?'

'Probably.'

Theo ran a hand through his dreads, tugging at the ends. 'Okay. So, I guess this is a good thing, now we know what it can do. You can make sure it doesn't happen again, right?'

'I can't do that.'

Theo stared at her. 'Why not?'

She shrugged. 'I tried when your Dream first started. I tried to stop it, tried to change it. Nothing worked. It must have something to do with you being a Major, I have less control.'

That was the only thing Fanta said that seemed to bother her. She frowned at the thought of her powerlessness.

'So you're telling me it's going to happen again and there's nothing you can do about it? You're the Dream Goddess!'

'Hey, I'm not the one who told you to come walking into my realm.'

'But if he had stayed in Zion, wouldn't he have had Nightmares?' Arielle asked quietly.

'Good point,' Onkwani said, a slight smile playing across his lips. 'You think Torres is struggling to stay awake over there?'

'I doubt it, since Theo's not there. We probably need the god *and* the realm for it to work on each other. Since you have such a problem with my hospitality, Theo, would you have rather had Torres's Nightmares?'

'What difference does it make, if they're both going to kill me?'

Fanta smiled. 'Some ways to die are more pleasant than others.' She turned and patted the side of her phantelle. 'Shall we keep going? Your Dream has already delayed us and I assume you'll want to make even quicker time now, since the longer you're here, the more Dreams you'll have.'

Theo didn't like the sound of that at all. Without so much as a flinch away from its Ivory tusks, he let Onkwani help him onto the back of his phantelle and he remained silent and stony-faced as the Minor coaxed the beast back into motion. He could hear the voices of his travelling companions, but he wasn't paying enough attention to know whether they were talking to him, or about him, or if they were ignoring him as much as he was ignoring them. He kept his eyes firmly on the knuckles of his right hand, tensed around the edge of the phantelle's harness. Someone had untied his bonds while he had been unconscious and no one had suggested retying them afterwards. Apparently, Fanta was satisfied that the threat of imminent death by Dreaming was enough to keep him in line.

Theo shuddered at the memory of the Dream. It hadn't felt real—it had felt *more than* real, as if everything in his life until the Dream had been a shadow and only now, for the first time, was he discovering what it truly was to *see* and to *feel* the world around him. True, it was a world of imaginary creatures and meaningless conversation and Theo told himself that he never wanted to go back. But he also couldn't help looking at the real world a little differently, now that his sister had given him new eyes. Theo sneaked a surreptitious glance in Fanta's direction. She and Arielle were speaking in hushed tones and Fanta was frowning slightly as their phantelle lagged behind the one led by Onkwani.

'She is lovely,' Onkwani said, making Theo jump.

The Minor god's head was so close to his own that when he spoke, Theo could feel his hot breath on the back of his neck. It smelled like dead wood and burning pages.

'What?'

'I caught you staring. Don't worry, I won't tell.' Onkwani grinned. He pulled out his pipe and lit it with a well-practised hand.

Theo frowned. Why should Fanta care if he had been staring at her? He couldn't kill her with sight alone.

'I've snuck a couple of glances myself. *Ndivyo*, she is lovely,' he sighed. 'Alas, it can never be. It's forbidden, at least here in *Taifa la Ndoto*. *Bibi* Fanta doesn't like anyone to touch her Magi.'

Understanding dawned and Theo looked back at Fanta's phantelle. This time, his gaze settled not on his sister, but on her Magus. They were still in deep conversation, but as Arielle listened to something Fanta was telling her, her gaze drifted over to Theo. There was a moment of surprise to catch him staring, then a blush, a smile.

'Such a shame,' Onkwani continued.

'Hmm,' Theo hummed non-committally. He was trying to think of the politest way to tell the Minor god to shut up.

'Although if anyone has a chance with her it's you. *Bibi* Fanta wouldn't like it, but what could she do? Mortals have a right to, ahem, *worship* the Majors in any way they wish.' He cackled unpleasantly. 'I'll help you out if you like. At our next stop I'll convince *Bibi* Fanta to let me and the Magus swap places so you can travel together. Admittedly, there's not much you could do on the back of a moving phantelle, but I'm sure you'd think of something.'

'I don't want—'

'Oh, you really are a lucky one. I'm getting all excited myself just thinking about it. Her body. Mortal. Hot. Young. Naked and ready to—'

'S-stop! Stop!' Theo cut in. He was getting light-headed and Onkwani looked at him, eyes wide in exaggerated concern.

'What's the matter, *Bwana*? Not another Dream already? All-Mother, I hope it wasn't anything I said . . .'

Before he could respond, he heard the Minor god's voice fading to a whisper and the edges of his vision began to blur. He needed water.

And suddenly there it was: a glimmer of blue amongst the never-ending beige, an oasis in the shape of a question mark, surrounded by stumpy trees and tall grass. The very air around the place seemed cooler, settling against Theo's lips like a kiss. Three figures, whom at first he'd mistaken for more trees, detached themselves from the copse and stepped into the light. Goddesses. Three of them, as naked as the sun and all the other stars. As Theo watched, one of them rolled up her dreads into a bundle on top of her head, so that the other two could bend to the oasis and bring cupped hands of water to wash her exposed back. The closer he got, the easier it was to see their faces. It was a beauty for the poets, a beauty only a child could see. It was a heart-stopping beauty . . .

Theo's heart stopped—

'Ah!' Theo's hands flew to his chest as if to keep his hammering heart from escaping. It felt like a million hot pins were mapping out the layer beneath his skin; he suppressed another pained cry. He didn't feel in danger of fainting again, but he had to take several deep breaths before his vision cleared and the pain began to subside.

Fanta was watching him and when he had calmed himself enough to meet her gaze he saw amusement there. Theo felt his face heat up like a bonfire. She'd seen everything, his whole Dream. He snapped his head away from her and stared fixedly straight ahead. He was going to have to start ignoring Onkwani and everything else around him, now that he knew how easy it was to be dragged into a Dream.

After several hours of Onkwani's constant one-sided conversation and several more torturous Dreams, Theo was exhausted. What he wouldn't give now to be in Zion, to pull Sleep energy out of the air into himself as easily as his lungs pulled in breath. Every movement of the phantelle's powerful muscles under him made him feel like he was running a marathon. He just needed to be still for a moment.

'Can we stop?' he said, to no one in particular. His words ran together as he struggled to find the energy to form them.

'You'll regret it in the long run. More time for Dreams,' Fanta said.

'I need to stop.'

Onkwani clicked his tongue against his teeth and the phantelles began to head in a new direction. Theo couldn't raise his head to see where they were going, nor did he feel capable of repeating his request. If Fanta decided not to let them stop, there was nothing he could do about it.

But after a few more lumbering steps, the phantelles slowed to a halt. Theo managed to raise his head—and for a chilling moment he thought another Dream had claimed him. They were stopped in front of a gently running stream and a strange-looking tree, and, although he struggled to recognise any other Dream signs, by now Theo knew that water and trees were recurring components of his Dreams, perhaps because they reminded him so much of Zion. But Onkwani, Fanta, and Arielle hadn't disappeared as they would have done if this was another Dream. He was so exhausted that Onkwani practically had to drag him off the phantelle, leading him over to the strange tree. It was a weird, bulbous thing with branches like roots and a towering trunk. It looked as though someone had turned the whole thing upside down. Once Onkwani had deposited him on the shaded sand, Theo was able to discern the shapes of some hard-shelled fruit in the tree's branches, and suddenly he remembered the name of the baobab, as well as its taste.

Fanta removed Theo's pocket knife from her belt and stabbed it into the trunk of the tree. She had to dig a little into the thick bark before the knife would hold and then she used it as the first step of her climb. Through an ingenious mixture of knife work and using all the small natural knots that the baobab offered to her as footholds, Fanta scaled the tree like ivy up an old brick wall. She arrived quickly at the low-hanging fruit and used Theo's knife to cut a few free. Onkwani caught each of them as they dropped and placed them in a pile on the ground.

'Milord?'

Arielle was standing before Theo, holding a plump flask made of some kind of dried animal skin. Droplets of Zion water shone on its cap as she offered it to him.

'You looked thirsty,' she said.

Theo took the flask gratefully and didn't hesitate to take a deep drink. He felt like a phantelle, sucking water up its trunk, as he practically inhaled the familiar liquid. By the time Fanta got back down from the tree, the flask was drained and Arielle went to refill it without Theo asking. He leaned back against the trunk of the baobab, although he finally felt capable of sitting up straight without any support.

That water really does make you forget, he thought, but unlike a mortal forgetting their time in the realms, Theo felt the aches and pains of all his Dreams draining from his body as if they never were. He was finally able to take a good look at his surroundings without feeling too much blood rushing to his head.

Other baobab trees besides theirs grew along the Zion stream. For the first time since entering Dream Country, Theo felt as if there was something to see that wasn't an invention of his own mind. There was life in this place, running under the surface of things like veins under skin. Fanta and Onkwani were knocking at the hard shell of the fruit, trying to get to the flesh and juice underneath. Theo noticed that Fanta had placed herself at a careful distance from him while she worked, but she had also positioned herself so that she could see his every move, even if it meant sitting out of the shade of the tree's branches. He didn't mind; as much as he wanted his sister to believe that he wasn't trying to kill her, he still wasn't completely convinced that *she* wasn't trying to kill *him*, and so it was probably for the best that she kept her distance. On the bank of the stream, Arielle had just finished refilling the flask but instead of returning to the tree she was staring off, dull-eyed and motionless, into the distance. A moment of concern for the young Magus passed quickly as Theo realised what was happening—she was Dreaming. He had almost forgotten that he wasn't the only one going through the experience, that Arielle the Dreamer, not Fanta the Dream Goddess, was the one who would understand best what he was going through. Even though, of course, for her Dreaming was a pleasurable experience. It was the reason why she was here, after all. Theo looked away from the Magus's statuesque form. He felt like watching her was invading something private; he also didn't like to think that he looked like that whenever he Dreamed, so helpless, so exposed. She didn't even notice when the two phantelles, who were spraying each other playfully, soaked her with the water from their trunks. Theo smiled slightly.

Sighing, he rested his head against the trunk, exposing his face to the blue gaze of the sky. This was the most peaceful moment he had experienced since Ereon showed up in his realm. He could almost pretend that he wasn't a refugee with dead friends, running to confront his brother before the Dreams of his sister struck him dead. Almost.

A flurry of activity along the horizon caught his attention—a splattering of black dots moving across the clouds so that Theo could see their wings flapping in unison. Birds.

Crows?

Theo jerked upright and hissed at his sister. 'Fanta! Crows!'

Fanta looked up from her fruit and squinted impassively at the sky. 'Hmm. I see them.'

Theo waited for her to do something, to suggest that they leave immediately or hide. His sister knew as well as he did that the crows were Torres's servants and his spies. They were the only beings besides Rogan who could see into all three realms, since there was nothing to stop them flying over the Gates. When the Gatekeeper had tried to raise the Gates taller, the crows had simply flown higher until it was the god who had been forced to give up. In Zion, Theo had learnt to ignore them when they came to rest on top of a fence to watch him with their beady eyes. Back then, there was nothing he needed to hide from his brother and he'd never worried about the crows reporting back to Torres. He'd been sure that Torres wasn't really expecting to find him making plans to go to war with the Mountains or anything. He was just checking up on him, every now and then. Theo had even come to look forward to the crows' visits, even though he never worked up the nerve to say anything to them.

But now he definitely didn't want to see his brother's spies; more importantly, he didn't want them to see him, not here.

'Torres can't know I'm here. If he knows I'm travelling this way he'll figure out that I'm heading for the castle and he'll leave. I won't be able to find out where he is again without spending time in Zion.'

With the monsters and the Nightmares is what he didn't say, but he saw that Fanta understood.

'Don't worry, Torres's little blackbirds won't be telling him anything. They can't see us.'

Theo looked around in confusion. The sparse foliage of the baobabs wasn't enough to hide them from sight, especially not from anything that was really looking.

'It's called a masking Dream,' Fanta said. She handed Onkwani the baobab fruit and he bent over it for a second before passing it over to Theo. He didn't even look at it. He had no appetite right now. 'I've made it to automatically engage on the crows whenever they pass above Dream Country. They're basically constantly Dreaming that whatever space I'm occupying is empty. The Dream's big enough to cover all of you too. To them this just looks like a stream and some trees with no one around.'

'That's . . . amazing,' Theo said. He didn't want to be impressed by what his sister could do, not after everything she was putting him through, but he couldn't help himself. A masking Dream—he couldn't do anything like that with Sleep. Fanta, however, wasn't so impressed with herself. She shrugged.

'Torres can do pretty much the same thing with Nightmares. When we were young we both used it to hide from Rogan's eye.'

'Wait,' Theo frowned. 'Why would you want to hide from Rogan?'

Fanta rolled her eyes and laughed bitterly. 'Yes, I forgot. Still the Gatekeeper's little golden boy, right?'

'I was never closer to Rogan than you or Torres were,' he said defensively.

'Maybe not, but *he* was a lot closer to you. He's the only Minor who didn't officially choose a realm to stay in, or a Major to support, but he's spent more time in Zion since the Gates went up than he has in Dream Country or *Os Pesadelos* combined. You think that's just a coincidence?'

Theo frowned as he watched Fanta crack open another baobab, using the knife that Rogan had given him for his birthday. He wondered what, if anything, the Gatekeeper had given her that same day.

'Personally, I wouldn't like knowing that the old stick was watching everything I did,' Onkwani said, lounging back on his forearms. 'Watching you bathe, go to the bathroom. When you have, ahem, *company.*' He winked at Theo, who looked away in disgust.

Released from her Dream, Arielle returned to the group and sat next to Theo. Theo caught what looked like a warning glance from Fanta, which made her Magus promptly shuffle away, putting more distance between herself and him. Theo frowned. Was Fanta really that protective of her Magi, as Onkwani said?

Onkwani quickly took advantage of Arielle's closer position, by throwing a not-so-casual arm around her shoulders. He raised his baobab in a toast.

'*Taifa la Ndoto!*'

Theo remembered the words from before. 'What does that mean?'

Onkwani laughed. 'It's the name of the land, *Bwana.* It's Dream Country.'

'Dream Country has another name?' Theo asked with surprise.

'Not one we share with outsiders,' said Fanta, glaring at Onkwani. 'Names have power when you know how to speak them properly.'

It occurred to Theo only then that, unlike Torres, Fanta never spoke her own language around him. She made sure to speak to him like an outsider.

'On the island it's said that's how the All-Mother was killed. Someone spoke her true name,' Arielle said softly.

Onkwani laughed. 'That would be an interesting theory—if the All-Mother were really dead.'

Theo frowned.

'What do you mean?' asked Arielle.

'You've never heard the story of the lizard and the chameleon?' Onkwani sat up straighter when Arielle shook her head. 'I'm surprised, I thought all mortals knew it. Perhaps it's a scholar's story, which is why I've heard it as the God of Logic. It goes like this:

'After the All-Mother created the world, she held a chameleon in her left hand and told him the secret of the shape of the circle and told him to go and put it in the world. In her right hand she held a lizard and told him the secret of the shape of a single line and told him to go and put that in the world. The lizard got to mortals before the chameleon, so their lives became a line, with death at the end of it. But the chameleon continued around the world, leaving circles everywhere he went and thus creating cycles: Night and day, Sleeping and waking. The lizard and the chameleon arrived at the gods at the same time and gave them both the line *and* the circle; from then on, the gods could die, like mortals, but return in the cycle of life and death.

'This is why a dead god will always manifest again in a new body. Some of the youngest Minors we have are really the oldest entities, on their third or fourth manifestations. I remember the old God of Chaos used to say he would be the first one not to re-manifest, just to shake things up a bit. But really the only god who has ever not re-manifested is—'

'The All-Mother,' Theo found himself saying.

Onkwani tapped his own nose and pointed at him. 'Exactly. And I hear you saying, *but Onkwani, oh wise and handsome one, that doesn't make any sense! Why would the All-Mother break her own cycle?* Well, I'm glad you asked! Why would the All-Mother leave this world without anyone to take her place? How could the oldest Major, the embodiment of femininity, leave no one to take up her titles, no one for the Majority to love and worship?'

Theo frowned as he began to see where this was going. Right on cue, a wicked grin broke out across Onkwani's features.

'But ask yourself—*did* the All-Mother leave us without an oldest Major? Without the embodiment of femininity? Without a goddess whom any mortal'— he nodded towards Arielle—'would be willing to shave off decades of their life just for a week in her presence?'

Theo had to take a second to compose himself before he replied. The God of Sleep could never be accused of being quick to anger but what Onkwani was insinuating, which was unmistakably clear at this point, was worse than insulting. It was blasphemy. And that was not something Theo took lightly, not when it came to his own mother.

'Fanta is the All-Mother's daughter,' he said at last. 'She is *not* the All-Mother.'

'What makes you sure?' Onkwani asked.

Theo looked at his sister, wondering why she was taking so long to dismiss Onkwani's nonsense and force him into silence once and for all. But Fanta's face was impassive and her mouth was firmly shut. She was watching Theo as if she also wanted to know his response to Onkwani's question. That only made things worse and Theo felt the back of his neck grow warm with rage.

'I'm sure because we were born before the All-Mother died, and any re-manifestation would have had to come *after*. Besides a god cannot re-manifest under a new domain. Fanta is the Goddess of Dreams, not of Night.'

He turned to Fanta again but she still showed no reaction. Confusion overwhelmed Theo's mind. Onkwani couldn't really believe all this. Fanta must have made him say it—but why? Wasn't it enough that their mother was gone? Did she have to try to replace her too?

'You look a little upset, *Bwana*. I hope it wasn't anything *I* said. Perhaps you should take a drink,' Onkwani said, reaching for Theo's baobab.

Theo opened his mouth to reply and jumped at the ear-splitting roar that came out. It took him a moment to realise it wasn't him that had made the noise.

'Theo Major, your time of reckoning has come!'

Theo's head whipped around, and he went cold at what he saw behind him. Salvador Minor was running straight for him.

CHAPTER NINETEEN

He stood by the Gates of Dream Country. He heard the call of Dream Country. On the wrong side of the Gates. Too far away for him to answer the call.

Torres got down on his hands and knees and began to dig, scraping his fingers against the rock until they bled. He tore up the land beneath his feet, lowering himself into the hole, refusing to stop until he reached the bottom of the Gates. He dug and he bled, and he bled and he dug, but the Gates just kept going down with him. Every time he looked up he still stood by the Gates of Dream Country. He heard the call of Dream Country.

He got back on his knees to dig.

* * *

Torres crouched on the library floor with Ereon in a blanketed fruit basket beside him. Impatient for Abilo's return with the Ivory, and tormented by more Nightmares of Dream Country than ever before, he had returned to the pages of *The Holy Theologos*. After the book had given him the idea to collect the Ivory, he had decided to read the whole text again, more closely this time, in case it held any further information. In the middle of a passage that he had previously skimmed because of its apparent irrelevance, he had found the words 'Vegetable Ivory.' Intrigued, he had read the sentence again.

'*Vegetable Ivory, found in palm trees* . . .'

The phrase reminded him of something. What? Finally he remembered his walk through the marketplace. One of the sellers there had been displaying little figurines of Torres, claiming them to be made from the seeds of Zion's palm trees. Torres immediately sent a crow to bring him one of the figures.

And now he held it in his hands, this tiny, statuesque version of himself, looking holier than he had ever felt in his whole life. He felt nothing as he held the material, none of the pain that would have come with authentic Ivory, but he had to admit that in appearance alone, the vegetable Ivory was indistinguishable from the true stuff. Ereon was just a baby, anyway; how would he know the difference?

Torres released a shaky breath and placed the statue on top of Ereon in his basket.

The boy went cross-eyed as he tried to look at it, then with a whine of apparent disgust kicked the statue back out of his basket.

Torres sighed and sat back on his haunches. He hadn't really expected it to work, but he'd had to try.

'I don't like your girlfriend.'

Torres looked up from the blurred words of the page and found himself face to face with an eight-year-old boy. He raised an eyebrow.

'How did you get in here?'

'The crows let me in.'

'No, they didn't.'

The boy grinned, shameless despite being caught in a lie. There was a gap between the two front teeth, stuck in a mouth framed by plump cheeks that looked like a squirrel hoarding acorns. Straight black hair came to the bottom of pointed ears. The boy stood on one of the library's only other chairs, looking around at all the books with an air of mild confusion, as if they had no discernible purpose. A short pink dress exposed grubby knees.

'Go away,' Torres said.

'No.'

He sighed. 'What do you want, Anansewa?' Torres asked. He used the Minor's full name in order to sound annoyed but they both knew he wasn't really. Nanse was one of the few Minors he could tolerate being around. But only in small doses, of course.

'I wanted to tell you something,' the young Minor said.

'Go on then.'

'I already *did.*'

Torres thought back to how their conversation had started. 'You don't like my girlfriend? You mean Iara?'

'She's mean. She told me to go away.'

'*I* just told you to go away. You don't seem so upset about it.'

Anansewa frowned. 'Yeah, but she told me to go away even *after* I told her to let me stay.'

Torres's eyebrow went up again. Iara had refused a direct order from Anansewa? Torres had known fully grown monsters who had been reduced to sobbing wrecks by trying to do the same. Even *he* couldn't ignore Anansewa when the Minor really wanted something from him.

'If she doesn't want to listen to you, you'll just have to find someone else to play with,' Torres said, but the suggestion did nothing to pacify his unexpected guest.

Anansewa had found Ereon's basket and the gurgling mortal quickly caught the child's attention. Torres darted a hand across to reach the basket first and pull Ereon out of reach.

'Not him,' Torres said firmly.

Anansewa stuck out a defiant tongue and jumped down from the chair.

'The other Zions have been a lot more fun than your girlfriend. I don't know why you don't bring some of them up here instead. She doesn't like you anyway.'

'I'm pretty sure she likes me well enough.' Torres smiled.

'Nope,' Anansewa said, arms folded. 'She likes that Duppy man better. That's why she told me to go away—so she could talk to him alone.'

Torres frowned. He had told the crows to keep Iara and Bede away from each other. Torres had known from the moment he met him that the Duppy would be trouble. What could he and Iara be talking about on their own?

'Show me where they are,' Torres said, picking Ereon's basket up with one hand and pushing back his chair.

With a flounce of the dress, Anansewa ran towards the library doors. Just before the Minor disappeared around the corner, Torres caught sight of the rodent-like features of the boy morphing and shifting, as if a sudden wind had blown across it. The boy's hair grew twice as long, lightening to a shade of honey brown. The nose widened and the ears became pointed and elfin, as the skin darkened. The Anansewa that left the library was a few centimetres taller than the one that had entered—and she was also a girl again. Torres followed her with interest; that was a face he hadn't seen her use in a while.

Anansewa led him through his castle and Torres was surprised when, instead of going to one of the other rooms on the same level as the library, she led him downstairs past the dining room and into the kitchen, which he had not entered in years. When he was younger he would come here to raid the cupboards for something sweet between meals, but ever since he started to lose his appetite four years ago the kitchen had become an unnecessary space. As they stood outside its closed door, Torres could already hear hushed voices coming from the other side. He made a sign for Anansewa to stay where she was and left her with Ereon in his basket to occupy her as he swiftly slipped into the room. On one side of the door a ceiling-high rack of pots and pans partially blocked the stovetops and cooking surfaces from sight, though holes in the wire meshing along its top formed useful peepholes. There was no sound of rustling feathers or scraping talons, so he knew that Iara must have cleared out the birds, as well as Anansewa. Crouching down behind the more covered part of the rack, he strained his ears to pick up the hushed tones of conversation.

'. . . more that we can do.' It was Bede speaking.

'What do you think I'm trying to do?' said Iara.

'Right now, I'm really not sure. You're having dinner with him. You're letting him lock us away from each other so we can't even *talk* about Theo.'

'I've been trying to get my hands on the boy ever since we got here. He doesn't let him out of his sight. Anyway, I don't think he wants to see Theo hurt any more than we do.' Bede must have made a face, because Iara spoke more insistently. 'I'm serious, Bede. You should have heard the way he was talking in the dining room earlier. This isn't about Theo. It's something else, some obsession he has about Fanta and Dream Country. He hasn't even noticed whenever we've left the castle to go searching for Theo, he's too busy up there with the boy and that book. As long as he doesn't think we're standing in the way of that, he won't stand in our way at all.'

'And are you? When it comes down to it, Iara, are you planning on standing in *his* way?'

There was a pause before Iara answered, in which Torres found himself holding his breath, as if exhaling would be the final push Iara needed for him to lose her again.

You're all I have, he thought desperately as he realised he had no idea how she would answer the Duppy's question.

'Getting Theo back safely is my priority. Anything else is irrelevant,' Iara said.

'Irrelevant? Iara, Torres is a maniac! He tore down Zion's Gates and kidnapped Theo's Magus. Can't you see that you have to put aside whatever childhood romance you had together if we're to stand any chance of stopping him? You can't just sit back and watch this happen while Theo's out there, possibly dead—'

'Don't you *dare* accuse me of not doing anything to help him. I've been helping the Majors, *all three of them*, since before you were even born, Bede. I've done things you couldn't possibly imagine to keep them safe. You have no idea what the realms would look like if it wasn't for me. After the All-Mother died—'

Iara stopped speaking so suddenly that her silence made Torres jump. He almost made the mistake of raising his head to look through the mesh and see what had happened but luckily the Duppy man spoke up before he could reveal himself.

'What? What happened after the All-Mother died?'

Iara sighed. There was a creaking sound, as if someone had just sat down on old wood. 'Haven't you ever asked Theo about that Night?'

'Yes, of course. But he doesn't like talking about it. He says he can't remember.'

'He's not lying. He *can't* remember, none of them can, although I've never heard Fanta or Torres admit it. But gods don't just forget things, especially not something that important. Someone . . . has to *make* them forget.'

'You? Iara, what are you saying? You gave the Majors Zion water after the All-Mother died? Why would you do that?'

Torres remembered . . . the blank fog of forgetfulness descending like a veil. The immediate comfort, then later, the fear and the guilt about what that gap in his memory could mean. He had never dared to examine his amnesia too closely, even now he had to suppress the urge to duck out of the room and forget everything Iara had said. But he was frozen in place. He had to know.

'I had to! Remember I was only six at the time too. And I was convinced—I thought it would be best for them. They were so obviously guilty: one of them did it and the other two *knew* who it was. If I hadn't made them forget, the truth would have come out eventually—and do you have any idea what would have happened next? I do. I've imagined it enough times.' She sounded broken. 'So I put Zion water in their tea. I had to.'

'And they really have no idea what you did? Not Theo, not even Torres?'

'No. And they can't ever find out. Promise me, Bede.'

Torres didn't stay to find out if the Duppy made the promise. As quietly as possible he slipped out into the hallway, where he was surprised to find

Anansewa still waiting, now in a different body. He would have thought her patience would have run out long before.

'Well? Told you, didn't I? She's planning to kill you or something.'

Torres shook his head. After everything he had heard he wasn't sure what to believe, but he was sure of one thing.

'Iara would never hurt me.'

Although he would have to be more careful to keep Ereon away from her, now that he knew Iara had been trying to get her hands on him, he still couldn't bring himself to be angry at her. She had made him forget, taken away his last memory of his mother, that of her death, but he could tell by the tone of her voice as she confessed it that she had genuinely believed it was for his own good. And for the good of his siblings. That was the craziest part of it all—Fanta and Theo didn't remember either. He had always assumed that they knew exactly what happened that day, that they had perfect alibis, which is why he'd never offered up his own. If he'd admitted he didn't remember, it would have been easy for those who didn't believe him to pin the murder on him. But what would the Minor gods say if they knew none of the Majors were sure who had killed their mother? Wouldn't they just assume they were all guilty? The realms would descend into chaos.

Torres had to agree with Iara. No one could ever find out. He had no intention of telling anyone himself and she had already proved herself capable of keeping the secret for the past thirteen years. That only left one person to consider.

'Nanse, I need you to do something for me. Go and gather the crows, tell them I have a special meal waiting for them in the aviary. Make sure they know that any dead meat they find up there when they arrive is theirs to have. I expect to see clean plates. Then I need you to go and find our Zionese guest . . . Bede, I believe his name is. I'd hate for him to say I've been a neglectful host. Give him a tour of the castle. Starting in the aviary.'

Anansewa was a smart young goddess. She caught on quickly. 'What if he doesn't want to come with me?'

Torres regarded the child seriously. 'Convince him.'

A wicked grin broke out on her cherub-like face. Then before Torres could change his mind she ran off to carry out her orders.

CHAPTER TWENTY

When Theo had seen his sister storming towards him a few hours after he first trespassed in her realm, he had thought there could be no more terrifying sight in Dream Country. Not even a herd of rampaging phantelles could have made his heart pound like it did when he saw Fanta coming with her necklace raised.

But then he heard the voice of one of his oldest friends:

'Theo Major, your time of reckoning has come!'

And he realised that until that moment he had not truly experienced fear in Dream Country.

He dropped his baobab at the sound of Salvador's voice and to his astonishment the fruit's liquid, flowing onto the sand, immediately began to hiss and spit as it burned a hole right next to his feet. As if she was standing next to him, he heard Iara's voice:

From now on, if anyone hands you a drink, you spill it.

The baobab had been poisoned.

Theo looked at Fanta. Fanta looked at Onkwani. Onkwani lunged.

His outstretched hands were aimed for Theo's throat but before he could get close, Arielle picked up a large baobab and swung it against the side of the Minor god's head. Onkwani gave a high-pitched scream of pain and fell to the side, rolling down the slight incline of the hill where the tree stood.

'Theo! Come on!' Fanta said, jumping to her feet as lithely as she had climbed the baobab tree earlier.

Theo didn't move. A shirtless Salvador Minor cut through the Zionese stream, screaming words of vengeance terrible enough to frighten even the phantelles from their play. The Sleep God could see the spittle flying from his mouth with each prolonged howl of rage.

Fanta grabbed Theo by the arm, pulling him up and dragging him along behind her as she and Arielle began to run. It didn't take long for the cold stupor of shock to pass and for Theo to engage his legs as he ran alongside his sister.

The three of them ran around the baobab stream and when Theo dared to look back he saw that Salvador was only a few paces behind and getting closer, Onkwani stumbling lamely behind him.

'Quickly!' Fanta shouted as they reached their two saddled phantelles standing by the stream and casting disparaging glances at the commotion going on around them.

Theo skidded to a halt next to his phantelle. Without Onkwani to help him, all he could do was take a bended-knee jump and grab onto the edge of the harness to pull himself up. The phantelle started moving before he was safely on top and he screamed in fear.

'Stop playing around! Get on!' Fanta's voice came from somewhere on the other side of the phantelle's bulk.

At last Theo pulled himself into position on the seat, sweating heavily, and saw Fanta and Arielle bumping up and down in their own seats, as both phantelles broke into a gallop. They moved faster than Theo thought they were capable of, and when he turned to look back, Salvador had come to a stop, watching them go. Theo and the ex-Zion locked eyes and his echoing roar followed the Sleep God until Salvador was nothing more than a blond blur in the distance.

Fanta eventually slowed their mounts to a trot but wouldn't meet Theo's eye, even when he cleared his throat to get her attention.

'Thank you,' he said. Though his voice was still shaky from all the excitement, he knew it was loud enough for her to hear. The way he'd frozen, there was no way he would have got away from Salvador if he'd been on his own. But Fanta had chosen to help him.

For a while it seemed she would leave him unacknowledged; then she gave a curt nod.

'Why did you decide to help me escape? When I first got here you said you wouldn't stand in the way of anything in your realm that came for me,' Theo reminded her.

'It was a spur-of-the-moment decision. Don't make me regret it.' She spoke sternly, but with a click of her tongue slowed her mount even more so that it was walking next to Theo's.

He smiled. That was the closest Fanta would ever get to saying, 'You're welcome.'

'And you, Arielle,' Theo added. 'Thank you for what you did back there. It was very brave of you.'

Arielle bit her lip and cast her eyes down. 'You shouldn't thank me, you should punish me. I attacked a god.'

'I'm surprised you care about that. The way Onkwani has been all over you this whole time, I thought you'd be glad to see the back of him,' said Fanta.

'But what if I hurt him?'

'I hope you did. Only a little,' Theo added quickly in response to Arielle's shocked expression—and Fanta's slightly impressed one. 'I can't believe he tried to poison me. *And* he was going to strangle me. It was like Salvador all over again.'

'Is he the other god who chased us?' Arielle asked, looking between the two gods.

'Yes. Theo's birthday present to me,' Fanta said drily.

'I didn't *send* him here. He wanted to come. I tried to stop him.'

Fanta raised an eyebrow. 'You mean you wanted him in Zion?'

'No, I just . . .' Theo hesitated, feeling silly. 'I didn't think it would be safe for him in your realm.'

'Well, now because of him it's not safe for *us* in my realm. Hopefully he will have lost our trail by the time we get to the caravan.'

'Caravan?'

'A group of Minors. They're nomadic but if I haven't lost track of time they should be settled at a nearby stop on their circuit right about now. We'll have to swap the phantelles for some camels there.'

They rode on in silence for a while. Fanta looked steadily ahead at the path in front of her as if she could see their destination. Arielle kept looking behind them as if she expected Salvador and Onkwani to appear at any second. Another Dream took Theo away. In it he was a child again and Fanta was there, but they were not the same age and Theo's Dream-self held closed the door to a cage of silent crows, while Fanta dipped her finger in ash and kept drawing circles on his forehead, over and over and over . . .

Now that Onkwani was no longer riding beside him, Theo could collapse along the full length of the seat once the Dream was over. His body spasmed convulsively and his tongue felt thick in his mouth. For a terrifying second he felt his heart seize up and his bladder release a small stream of hot urine down his leg. The seizure stopped right after and he was able to recover his breath and sit up straight again. Fanta looked at him out of the corner of her eye as if to make sure he was alright, but Theo was grateful she didn't say anything. Arielle was once again wrapped up in a Dream of her own. This time the Magus's jaw was clenched and her left hand gripped the side of her seat so hard that the skin over her knuckles appeared thin, almost translucent. She looked like she was in as much pain as Theo had been, which made him frown. There was no reason for Dreams to be unpleasant for her. Theo sneaked a glance at Fanta. Was she doing that to Arielle on purpose?

Can she make an unpleasant Dream? Wouldn't that be a Nightmare?

Theo realised for the first time how little he knew about the difference between his siblings' domains.

As they rounded the corner of an unsteady-looking sand dune, a herd of about twelve phantelles suddenly came into view. Theo tensed and sat up straighter. Just because he had spent so much time on the back of a phantelle, it didn't mean he was ready to get into a herd of them. His eyes were drawn to their Ivory tusks. As they got closer Theo noticed three calves hiding behind their mothers' legs. They weren't old enough to have developed tusks yet and he found himself thinking that they were actually rather cute.

Their own phantelles greeted the herd with trumpeting blows from their trunks that sent vibrations running up Theo's legs. But their calls were not returned. Huddled together, the other phantelles seemed preoccupied with some solemn task and with curiosity Fanta directed their phantelles into the crowd until they finally got a clear view of what was at the centre of it.

A dead phantelle lay on its side. Even Theo could see that this phantelle had not died of natural causes. One of its tusks had clearly been clawed or gouged out of its head. It lay discarded next to the body, the tip of it missing.

'Something hunts phantelles?' he asked in disbelief. He didn't want to imagine something in Dream Country that was bigger or more dangerous than what he was already sitting on.

Fanta was frowning. 'No.'

The lower half of the dead animal was covered in sand and, as they watched, the herd continued to flick piles of it over the body with their trunks. Fanta and Theo's phantelles let out a funereal blare of distress, then silently added their trunks to the burial effort. Dismounting, Fanta went over to the body and, though the mourners batted her away protectively, she swept past them to pick up the broken tusk. Theo tugged nervously at his dreads: what she held in her hands now was ten times bigger than anything she had threatened him with before. She wasn't pointing it at him, though. She was examining it curiously, running her fingers along its jagged edge.

'I don't understand this,' she said.

'Maybe one of the other phantelles did it?' Arielle suggested.

Theo's mount snorted indignantly at the idea.

'Or Salvador,' Theo said. 'He seemed angry enough to do this to anything that got in his way.'

'Maybe,' Fanta said.

She replaced the tusk respectfully next to the body. Theo only caught half of what she muttered over the dead phantelle but it sounded like a prayer.

He intended to wait for her in silence but, with a gesture, Arielle caught his attention. She shuffled over to Fanta's side of the saddle so that she could be closer to him.

'Milord,' she said so softly that Theo really only deciphered the words by the movement of her lips. 'Have you ever heard of "Lucid Dreaming"?'

Theo silently shook his head.

'It's a Dream Magus ability,' she whispered. 'I have already started to be able to do it, though it will be easier by the end of the Majoracle. It's a way of taking control of your Dreams. It means that you get to decide what you see and what happens next.'

Theo nodded slowly, not understanding. Lucid Dreaming sounded fascinating, but not so much so that it required all this secrecy. Arielle leaned even closer.

'I think you could learn to do it too. It's not that hard. All you have to do is, whenever a Dream starts, notice three things around you and ask yourself if they're normal or not. Like, if you should be able to see your reflection, but can't. Or if you can walk through objects that are supposed to be solid. Once you notice three things that aren't normal, your brain realises it's a Dream—and then you can start to control it.'

'But why would I want to do that?' Theo whispered back. 'Do you think it will make the Dreams less painful?'

'I don't know. But maybe there are things you don't want to see in your Dreams. Or that you don't want other people to see.'

Theo frowned. She wasn't making any sense. She was looking at him intensely as if there was more she was trying to tell him through her eyes alone. Close up, he noticed how clammy her skin was; she was a few shades paler now than she had been a couple of days ago. She was shivering and sweating at the same time. Her brown eyes had split into rainbows of different colours circled around her pupils. And, although she was looking at him, her eyes seemed unfocused as if she was staring through him, off into the distance somewhere.

'Arielle, are you feeling okay?'

Before she could respond, the background murmur of Fanta's prayer came to a stop and Arielle slid quickly back to the other side of the saddle.

'We'll have to walk from here,' Fanta said, offering Arielle her hand to get down. 'The phantelles don't leave their dead behind. They'll keep watch over it for a few days after they bury it. Come on, Arielle.'

The Magus stroked her phantelle's large ears in affectionate farewell before following Fanta away from the herd. Theo jumped down and tentatively patted his phantelle on the rump. After it had carried him in his escape from Onkwani and Salvador, and after he had seen how lovingly phantelles treated their dead, the beasts didn't seem so deadly or so dreadful to him anymore—though he still avoided their Ivory tusks as he ran to catch up with the others.

'How could that have happened?' Fanta was murmuring to herself when he reached her. She sighed. 'I would have seen it if only I'd been checking my realm sight like I usually do. But I've been distracted.' She shot a sidelong glance at Theo.

'You can't blame me for this,' he protested but she didn't bother to grace him with a response.

Theo noticed how close Fanta kept Arielle to her as they went on. Now that they weren't riding on separate phantelles, she seemed hyper vigilant of every move her Magus made towards Theo. At one point Arielle lost her footing and almost fell into a small ditch but, as soon as Theo reached out to steady her, Fanta made sure to get in his way and grab her first. Theo decided it was best if he kept his distance.

* * *

About an hour after they had left the phantelles, Theo heard the faint hum of music in the distance. They were walking in the direction of the dazzling setting sun, which prevented him from seeing where the music was coming from.

But the closer he got to the sound, the more Dream Country seemed different from the one he thought he knew. This new place still had the sand and the air of Dream Country but it was vastly overcrowded. There were people everywhere he looked. No wave of euphoria or pain hit him so he could tell that these were real people, not Dreams. They hung around outside tents, or roasted food over open fires whose smoke only added to the claustrophobic atmosphere, or sat grinding cornmeal to a heavy and grainy paste, or used a pestle and mortar to mash up peas and potatoes. Child gods and goddesses running up to the fires with their hands out for food were shooed away by the adults. At the edges of everything, small-humped camels stood with clueless expressions on their faces.

People turned to see Theo, Fanta, and Arielle walk by. They began whispering to each other or breaking off their conversations. The sight of Theo especially seemed to disturb them, and he avoided their gazes, not wanting to recognise any familiar faces of Minors who had denounced him years ago. So intently was he watching his feet that he didn't even realise there was someone standing in his path until he bumped into them.

'Sorry,' he said, jerking his head up.

The Minor was a girl of about sixteen god years. She had a shaved head and plump cheeks. Theo moved away but the Minor's friends giggled and pushed her after him.

'Go on! That's him!'

Theo hurried past her, following Fanta and Arielle. Although Fanta had told him that the purpose of them coming here was to get camels, she wasn't going towards any of them. The camp had obviously been set up to circle the place where the music was coming from, and Fanta was heading straight for it. There were two or three drums playing and a horn and some bells. The women playing the instruments shook their bodies as if they couldn't decide whether to keep playing or to stop and dance. Five other women were dancing in front of them, all with shaved or closely cut hair, the longest being about the same length as Fanta's. They wore brightly coloured robes and were heavily decked out in beaded jewellery—around their necks, across their foreheads, or through their ears. They had intricate patterns of dots and stripes drawn in some kind of white paint on their faces, though it was hard for Theo to get a closer look because of the way they were all moving around, shaking, hopping, and running around each other. Somehow their movements were never messy or anything less than graceful and spontaneous. As he watched, one of the dancers with bells strapped around her ankles crouched down, lifted her leg up and shook her foot violently, adding her cacophony to the music. They sang as they danced, chanting in a call-and-response pattern, taking it in turns to raise their voices to the sky and shriek in joy. But this kind of party was for participants, not audiences, and soon they beckoned Theo's group over to join them. One of the dancers left the circle and shimmied her way over to them. She was the heaviest of the dancers, her belly sagging through the bottom of her clothing, and whenever she moved she sent sand clouds up around her. Without warning she pulled Fanta into what looked like a bone-crushing hug.

Theo raised both eyebrows in surprise. There were very few people he knew Fanta would let touch her like that. But one of them was—

'Auntie?'

It had been hard at first for Theo to recognise her under all the layers of face paint and age. But then the older woman released Fanta and turned to him.

'Who else, child?'

And she pulled him into an embrace too. Theo smiled, his eyes filling with tears. He hadn't realised how much something as simple as a hug would affect him, but it was the first physical contact he'd had since watching the Gates fall and entering Dream Country. Auntie held him at arm's length so she could get a good look at him.

'But haven't you grown tall?'

Theo grinned. He hadn't seen the Minor goddess in so long he'd forgotten her strange habit of speech that turned everything she said into a question. There was no real relation between Auntie and the Majors but she was family in the same way Rogan was and she'd been very close to their mother. She grinned back at him. She had even applied paint to the underside of her lips.

'Auntie, we're going to need to borrow a couple of camels,' Fanta said, cutting short the reunion.

'Right now?' Auntie asked. 'You think you can just come and leave, just like that?'

'We're not leaving yet, we'll stay for a while.'

'Wait, we're staying? Aren't we . . . in a bit of a hurry?' Theo said, making faces at Fanta and hoping she would understand the message. Although he was sure all of Dream Country knew by now that his Gates had fallen, he didn't want Auntie knowing that Fanta was taking him to the Mountains.

'I have things I need to do. If that doesn't fit in with your schedule, that's too bad for you. Auntie, this is my Magus, Arielle. Can we use your tent for a while?'

'Do you have to ask?'

Fanta nodded her thanks and grabbed Arielle by the hand, but when Theo took a step to follow them she barred his path.

'You stay.'

He was mildly ashamed that he obeyed better than any puppy as he watched his sister and her Magus disappear into the crowds.

'You going to dance with me, *mpenzi*?' Auntie said, regaining his attention.

If anyone could have got him to join the dance it would have been her. But when Theo looked over her shoulder he saw that the other dancers, who were all much younger than Auntie, had changed the rhythm of their movements into something much more sensual and slow. They swayed their hips in a grinding motion obviously directed at him. He felt his cheeks go hot. But when Auntie turned around to see what had caught his attention they ended their seduction before she could catch them at it. Auntie tutted and turned back to him.

'Eh-eh, but wasn't there a time when you would have done the whole dance and not cared what anybody thought of you for it?' she said, mistaking his embarrassment for shyness.

'I was a child, I didn't have to care what people thought.'

She made a dismissive noise in the back of her throat. 'And what are you now if not a child? Aren't you and your brother both still acting like children?'

Theo avoided her gaze, tugging at his dreads. 'So you *do* know why I'm here.'

'You didn't know Fanta sent a Dream message telling me when you first came?'

He shook his head. 'But then you must know that Torres—'

'Started it? Isn't that what you used to say? And what do I say next?'

'"I don't care who started it, I'm going to finish it,"' Theo said, paraphrasing to leave out the question marks in case she thought she was being mocked. She would knock him around the head for less. 'But it's different this time.'

'How different?'

'He's gone too far.'

Auntie laughed. 'So what are you going to do about it?'

'I . . .' Theo hesitated. All of a sudden an image from his last Dream came to him: holding the door shut on a cageful of crows while all they could do was wait, docile and patient, for him to set them free.

He had never been really sure what he would do once he got into the Mountains. Take Ereon back, yes. But what about Torres? A part of him still wanted all this to be one of his brother's bad jokes; he still half-believed that Torres would simply give Ereon back, rebuild the Gates, and expect Theo to laugh. But he knew that wasn't enough.

He did this to me.

Magus gone, exiled from his own realm, battered by Dreams—and where was Torres while all this was happening? Theo could no longer think of an excuse for his brother not showing up to apologise or help to set things right. He must have done this on purpose. How much further would he be willing to go in the future if he got away with this now?

No. Something had to be done about Torres.

'I'm going to close his realm. After the Majoracle, I'll get Rogan to keep Torres's Gates locked so the Majority can't get through.'

Auntie stared at him. 'For how long? Forever?'

Theo thought again of the crows in his Dream. 'For as long as it takes.'

Auntie shook her head to herself. 'But didn't you just tell me you weren't a child anymore?'

She didn't understand. This was not a child's petty revenge, this was an adult's move, possibly the most grown-up decision he had ever made in his life, especially since he had come to it by himself. He wished he could articulate that to her but all he could do was repeat himself.

'Things are different now.'

'Is anything ever different? Isn't it always the same? Or I don't know what I'm talking about anymore?'

Auntie looked over her shoulder and this time she caught the girls swaying their hips at Theo. She shouted at them and they dispersed, taking the band with them.

'Didn't anybody ever tell these young goddesses you can't be so obvious if you're trying to get a man?'

'Um.' Theo wanted to ask why all of the Minors were throwing themselves at him, but Auntie seemed to read his mind and just smiled.

'But doesn't it come with the name of Major to make you so attractive? And now that Fanta's engaged, isn't everyone looking to snatch up you and Torres next?'

'Fanta's getting married?!'

'You haven't heard?'

Theo didn't know what to say. He wasn't surprised that Fanta hadn't brought it up herself, but if there was one thing the Gates couldn't stop spreading between the three realms it was rumours. Yet he hadn't even known that she was seeing anyone, let alone engaged.

'Who is she marrying?'

'Why don't you go find her and ask for yourself?'

She spun Theo around by the shoulder, directing him towards the edge of the camp. Tents of various sizes fanned out from the camp's centre like petals on a flower. Theo began walking in the direction he thought Fanta and Arielle had gone but the thought of what Auntie had said slowed him down. Was there a difference between doing the hard thing and doing the fair thing? Growing up and watching all the adults around him, they had always made it seem like the same thing. He didn't *want* to close the Mountains—and that's why he felt sure it was what he *should* do. But what if what he was doing was hard *and* unfair? Then what was the easy, fair thing that he was missing? He sighed. He wished Rogan was there to tell him the answer. He just wanted things to go back to normal.

He had wandered to a quieter spot, where everyone was inside the tents instead of hanging around in the open air. They must have been Minors who still remembered and followed the old day and Night cycle. The midday sun made everyone younger forget that it was just past midnight.

One of the coal pits hadn't been doused properly and a spark on the edge threatened to reach the timber pile. Theo went over to kick sand over it before there could be any accidents. As he got closer he heard voices coming from a tent behind the timber. Two voices speaking in hushed tones. He was almost too far away to hear them when, amongst all the indistinct murmurings, he heard his own name spoken. Careful to avoid making any noise, he approached the tent and leaned in to hear better.

'. . . nothing suspicious,' said the first voice. It was Arielle.

Breathing out in relief at having found her, Theo was about to pop his head in when he stopped himself. What was it she was saying about him?

'I still have to check.' That was Fanta.

'I don't feel comfortable with this, Milady.'

'With what? All you're doing is sitting there. I'm doing all the hard work.'

Something rattled and neither spoke for a while. Theo decided to risk crouching by the mouth of the tent and peeking inside; if Arielle or Fanta saw any movement hopefully they would think it was the breeze.

Arielle's back was to him, but Fanta was sitting directly opposite the mouth of the tent and, as he peeked inside, she inhaled sharply. He almost stood up to apologise, thinking he'd been caught, but immediately realised that his sister was looking not at him but at a bowl in her lap, and whatever had made her gasp was in there. He knew he should leave now before he was caught for real but a glance at what was around Fanta on the floor kept him in place. There was a glass container filled with what looked like blood and another of a different liquid, clear, but too thick for water. At her feet was a scroll of parchment covered with symbols which Theo couldn't read from this distance. She was tilting the bowl in her lap from side to side and Theo saw that she had placed her Ivory necklace in it; it rattled against the side of the bowl as it slid about. The edges of the necklace were stained with the liquids from both vials, dark stains crusted over with time—and now Theo recognised it all as divination equipment, similar to what Arthur had shown him in the temple.

'The Ivory is struggling to remember this bit,' Fanta muttered. 'The symbolism of the ash circles he Dreamed I was drawing on his forehead could be a sign of guilt. But . . . it's hard to tell.'

Theo glanced over at Arielle to see if she would reply but she was not even watching what was happening. She had her eyes turned to the ground, chewing nervously at her bottom lip.

Fanta also looked at her and noticed her distraction. She raised her voice slightly. 'What did you feel when it happened?'

'I don't know,' Arielle said.

'I'm not going through all of this just for you to lie to me, Arielle,' Fanta said firmly. 'Remember whose Magus you are.' And then, more softly, 'It's right for you to be careful of your actions when it comes to your gods. But I promise you what you are doing is *helping* Theo. It can't hurt him.'

Arielle glanced upwards, then back down again. 'We're spying on his Dreams looking for a murder confession. He'd be hurt if he found out.'

Fanta went stiff. She looked intently at Arielle's bowed head. If Theo had burst inside the tent then she wouldn't even have noticed, she was so focused on her Magus.

'And is he going to find out, Arielle?'

There was no response. And then, finally, slowly, as if she had the weight of the realms on her shoulders, Arielle shook her head. 'No, Milady.'

Fanta sighed. She put the bowl down. 'We're done for now. Go, I have someone else I need to meet with. I'll come to find you afterwards.'

Theo scrambled to get up and away before Arielle had finished bowing and left the tent. He slipped back into the shadows and held his breath until she was gone.

Somehow Fanta was tapping into the Ivory's memory of the Dreams it had been near recently. Fanta was trying to recreate his Dreams and keep a record of them. But what did Arielle have to do with it?

He remembered all the hushed conversations between the Dream Goddess and her Magus, how Fanta had seemed to want to keep Arielle away from him.

She was afraid Arielle would let slip about what they were up to. Every time I had a Dream and whenever I passed out, they must have been taking out that same equipment and been analysing what they saw.

He wondered if he should try to steal the glass vials, since she probably couldn't proceed without them. He didn't know where Fanta kept them, but Arielle would, and if she was as uncomfortable with violating his privacy as she seemed, she might be willing to help him stop Fanta. But why did he want to stop her? What did he think she might find behind the haze of his memory loss? Theo had always told himself that he hadn't killed his mother—could he really be so sure? It's not as if he had any memory of that day to go on. His Dreams had already revealed parts of himself he never knew existed.

What else could they be hiding? If Fanta really is looking for a clue, will she find it?

He was about to leave but before he could move from his hiding place the tent flap moved aside again and Fanta stepped out into the sunlight. She looked up at the sun, then gave an impatient sigh. Whoever she was meeting was obviously late. Theo wondered if it was her fiancé. Fanta walked right past his hiding place and went in the same direction as Arielle. Theo couldn't help but notice that she carried nothing with her, no bowl, not even her necklace. Which meant that she'd left everything inside the tent. Before he could have second thoughts, Theo went forward out of the shadows.

Inside Auntie's tent all the divination equipment had been left scattered across the floor. Theo crouched for a closer look at the notebook but still couldn't decipher what was written there, or even guess whether it was code or language. One line of writing was fiercely underlined, and Theo did recognise the string of question marks at the end of it. He thought back over all the Dreams he'd had so far. Was there anything in them that could be mistaken for incriminating evidence? He hadn't Dreamed of the All-Mother directly, but he didn't know enough about divination to know if that meant he was safe or not. He was about to reach for one of the glass vials when something else caught his eye: the pocket knife Fanta had confiscated when she first found him. He picked it up and absent-mindedly flipped it open. The blade shone even in the dimness of the tent. He turned it around to catch a sliver of light—and as he looked into its surface he saw in the reflection a pair of hands reaching out for him.

He was too slow in turning around; suddenly there were hands gripping him by the neck, pulling him down. He tried to call out but another hand clamped down on his mouth. He was thrown to the floor and in the next moment his hands were behind his back and tied together. He looked up. Onkwani was standing on Theo's feet so he couldn't struggle while Salvador was securing his hands. The pocket knife had gone flying into a corner, unnoticed by his captors. Onkwani grinned but there was nothing playful about him now.

'Hello again, *Bwana*,' he said cheerfully. 'Don't worry, I've got him perfectly under control.' He patted Salvador on top of his blond curls as if he were an impressive and obedient pet.

Onkwani held Theo by the neck while Salvador tied his feet and, when he was done, he straightened up, and kicked Theo ferociously in the stomach. When Theo tried to scream, Onkwani shoved a piece of cloth into his mouth to gag him.

'Much better,' he said over the sound of Theo's frenzied mumbling. 'Now— we have some questions for you, *Bwana*.'

CHAPTER TWENTY-ONE

Theo nodded. There was nothing else he could do. Salvador removed his gag.

'I would love it if you screamed,' he whispered.

Theo gulped. 'What do you want to know?'

'You *know* what we want to know. The All-Mother—her death. Everyone else might be willing to forget but we're not. You had something to do with it and we want to know what,' Onkwani said.

'I didn't kill my mother.'

'So who did?'

'I don't know.'

'So you don't know if you didn't kill her.'

'I do!'

'You did?'

'Wait, wha—ah!' Theo screamed as Salvador pulled his thumb backwards at the knuckle. He heard it pop.

'Get to the point, Onkwani!' Salvador growled. 'Or are you going to make me do everything myself?'

'For your information, I had everything under control before you came charging in. He was about to drink from that baobab.'

'You had a hundred opportunities to kill him before that, yet you did nothing.'

'Well, excuse me for not being a barbarian. I was waiting for the right moment.'

Salvador grabbed Onkwani by the front of his shirt. '*This* is the right moment. And if you don't hurry up, I'll—'

Onkwani sighed dramatically. '*Sawa, sawa*, fine, *amani*, my friend.' He cleared his throat and straightened his shirt as Salvador let him go. 'The point is, Theo, we don't care why you killed the All-Mother, we just want to know *how* you did it so that we can do the same thing to you, very, very slowly.'

'I don't know anything about how she died. I-I don't remember.'

'Ha! How convenient. But it's not just that you don't remember is it, *Bwana*? What were you and your siblings doing when Rogan found you to tell you about your mother's death?'

Theo bit his lip and looked down at the tent floor. He whispered his response downwards as if he were confessing a secret only to himself.

'What was that, *Bwana*? Speak up, we can't hear you!'

Salvador smacked him across the jaw and the words came tumbling out between waves of pain.

'We were asleep!'

And there was the truth. The reason why none of the triplets could bear witness to their mother's death, the reason why so many Minors had pointed their fingers at Theo in the days after the death. Wouldn't only a guilty person put their siblings to Sleep so that he could murder their mother and then claim to have been asleep too? But there was never anything Theo could say to defend himself, because although he remembered being woken up from the Sleep, and Rogan handing him and his siblings some tea as he told them that they were orphaned, he remembered nothing from the day before. Nothing.

Onkwani widened his eyes, even lowering his pipe for dramatic effect. 'Asleep? What, even Fanta and Torres? How did that happen?'

'I-I must have put us all to Sleep. But that was normal! We all used our abilities on each other back then. That's just how it was.' Theo said, in just the way he had said it to himself for years.

It wasn't you, it wasn't you, it wasn't you . . .

'So, then, you and your two siblings wake up from a state you admit only you can impose to find your mother missing, and therefore obviously dead, and you, her uncontested heir, claiming not to remember anything. Hmm. Yes, sounds like a likely story. Okay Salvador, let him go.'

Salvador walked behind him and for an insane moment Theo thought he really was going to untie him—but then the Minor god stomped down on his hands with the full weight of his large feet, crushing his fingers. Theo screamed.

He glanced in desperation at the tent flap. They were on the outskirts of Auntie's camp but not so far away that no one could hear him scream. Why wasn't anyone coming to help?

'Okay, *Bwana*, let's try this one last time, shall we—'

'The weapons!' Theo cried, before Onkwani could say anymore. 'What about the murder weapons?'

'What about them?' Onkwani asked stiffly.

'You're only focusing on the fact that we were asleep because it distracts attention from Fanta and you want to protect her. But you know that when Rogan and the others went searching for my mother they found two blood-stained weapons.' He remembered that part, remembered Rogan showing them where the weapons had been found and the pool of blood in which they had lain.

'That has nothing to do with—'

'A dagger of Horn and a dagger of Ivory! I wouldn't have been able to even touch either of them—'

'Enough! Tell us what you did! Tell us how you killed her.'

'I was only six! I've never killed anybody!' Theo cried. 'Why do you even care?'

'She was our goddess,' Onkwani said with exaggerated affront. 'And Fanta is our goddess now and we don't like how you've tricked her into letting you into her realm.'

'I didn—oof!'

Salvador punched him in the stomach. He raised his arm again to land another blow but Onkwani caught it mid-swing and, with difficulty, held the bigger god back.

For a second it looked as if Salvador would turn his free fist on Onkwani, but he paused when Onkwani shushed him.

'Wait. Listen.'

Both Salvador and Theo stopped breathing so they could hear what had caught Onkwani's attention.

Footsteps. Eventually they came up to the front of the tent. A long shadow was cast across the space inside and over Theo's helpless frame. A hand came up to the entrance flap but then pulled away at the last second, leaving the flap closed.

'I see you in there,' Fanta said. 'I see your shadows. Onkwani, is that you?'

Onkwani and Salvador nodded to each other. Without warning Salvador punched Theo across the back of the head. He must have intended to knock him out completely as he didn't bother to replace the gag before he left, but in fact the blow only dazed him. Onkwani and Salvador left the tent to meet his sister.

For a while, Theo couldn't tell if their voices were quiet or his hearing was fuzzy, but eventually he could make out their words. Theo wasn't gagged. He could cry out and let Fanta know he was inside, what her Minors were doing to him. But he didn't make a sound. For the second time that Night he found himself eavesdropping on his sister's conversation.

'. . . told us to do.'

'That was before. If I had still wanted you to do it, I wouldn't have run away from you with him, would I?'

'But you didn't send us another Dream message to tell us to stop. What were we supposed to think?'

'I wanted to be sure,' Fanta said.

'And are you?'

'I need more time. His Dreams are complicated, I can't read them easily.'

'Are you willing to let him go while you figure them out?'

'I'm not letting him go, I'm just delaying until I can be certain.'

'What if you never are? What if you get to the Gates of *Os Pesadelos* before his Dreams tell you anything? Then it'll be too late. Just let us take care of him now while we've got him where we want him. If certainty is what you want, we'll make sure to get a confession out of him before we're finished. Right, Salvador?'

A grunt, probably of approval.

Some feeling was starting to come back into Theo's body, radiating from the painful spot at the back of his head where he had been hit. He twitched his fingers and found that the Minors were not as good at tying knots as Fanta was. The rope was slightly loose around his wrists. He could see the pocket knife, still open, not far away in the corner of the tent. Making as little noise as possible, he began to slide his body over to it.

'I shouldn't have to repeat myself.' Fanta's voice sounded stern now. 'Untie him and then get out of here. You can keep following us. When he tells me about this little stunt of yours later, I'll pretend not to know anything about it. You'll have him back before we get to the Gates. I'm close, I can feel it.'

Her footsteps retreated from the tent.

Theo waited for the Minors to re-enter, his body tense. He closed his eyes and tried to steady his breathing in order to appear unconscious. Soon he heard the two pairs of footsteps enter the tent, one heavy, one light, and he felt their presence as they stood over him.

'What are you doing?' Onkwani's voice hissed quietly.

'I'm going to kill him anyway,' Salvador said in reply. Theo felt him move closer.

'You can't! Fanta will—'

In one swift motion Theo revealed his unbound hands and the pocket knife in his grip as he sprang to his feet. Onkwani let out a cry of surprise but Salvador's reflexes were quick and he lunged forward. Theo only narrowly evaded him, ducking under his outstretched arms. Staggering backwards, he brandished the weapon out in front of him, but Salvador was not put off. He charged at him with a feral roar, hurling himself onto Theo—and onto the blade of the knife. They crashed together onto the ground, Theo tangled up in the tent's fabric with Salvador on top of him. The deranged Minor tore the tent out of his way as blood gushed from his wounded side. Desperately, Theo managed to get a grip on the protruding handle of the knife. He slid it out, then plunged it back in through layers of bone and muscle, twisting as he pushed.

Salvador fell off him, screaming in agony or rage, Theo didn't care which. He was all too aware that Onkwani was still close by, and, before he could find out just how close, he got to his feet and ran.

He tore through the campsite, not caring who or what was in his way. All he knew was that he had to escape.

He came quickly to the edge of the campsite where he had to stop for breath. A quick glance over his shoulder told him that he was not being pursued. Deep breaths shook his entire body as he crouched with his hands on his knees.

He gave himself exactly ten seconds before forcing himself to straighten up and take stock. His thumb hung ineffectually at the side of his hand, still throbbing from Salvador's stomping. He prodded it and winced. Not broken, just dislocated. Biting down on his bottom lip to stop himself from crying out, he popped the bone back into place.

He looked around to see where he was. Fanta had said it was maybe a day's journey to the Gates on camel but taking one would draw too much attention to himself. Battered and bruised, he began to walk, leaving the camp behind.

'You're going?'

Theo whipped around so fast the air crackled around him. Arielle flinched, then went very still, not meeting his eyes.

'I suppose now you're going to run and tell my sister,' Theo said, surprised at the bitterness in his own voice.

'No. I'm not going to do that.'

'No? Why not? I thought you two liked telling each other secrets.'

A part of him recognised the irrationality behind his anger. What occurred between his sister and her Magus was none of his business. Even so, his blood boiled just to have Arielle standing before him. He had thought, stupidly, that they were friends, that she was his only ally in a realm full of strangers and enemies.

Obviously, he'd been wrong.

'I won't tell her you're leaving because if I did she would never let me come with you,' she said.

Theo stared at her for a moment in shock. 'What are you talking about?'

'I can't let you go out there alone, Milord. What if you have another Dream and there's no one to help you? You could die.'

'So that's what this is about. Dreams. What happened? Was my confession not clear enough in the ones Fanta already took from me? She had to send you after me to collect some more?'

'I never wanted to be involved but I had no choice. She would have done it anyway, even without my help, and I thought . . . I thought maybe I could help you both,' Arielle finished simply.

'Really? Name one thing you've done to help me, Arielle.'

'I tried to warn you.'

Theo scoffed. 'You mean all that stuff about Lucid Dreaming? Yeah, thanks, you really kept that information until the last minute. All you've done is tell me a beautiful fairy tale about Dreams the first day I got here and ever since then you've just been coming along for the ride to watch me suffer.'

The Magus's eyes filled with tears. 'That's not true.'

'Well, I say it is!'

It was all too much. Theo felt like he was about to explode. The agony of the Dreams, the desperate fight with Onkwani and Salvador, and now this. Mentally, physically, and emotionally, he was exhausted; he felt that the walls of his last defences were tumbling down as easily as the Gates around his realm had done.

That explains why it was so easy for Torres to take Zion then. Theo thought to himself. *A realm is only as strong as the god who controls it. You're weak. Weak!*

He clenched his fists, even welcoming the pain of his recent injuries in order to drown out his own thoughts.

'I'm tired of people calling me a liar, Arielle. I'm tired of being made out to be the bad guy when all I've ever wanted was peace. I'm tired . . .'

All-Mother, I'm just plain tired.

He needed to go home. He needed to let himself Sleep.

Raised voices reached him from Auntie's camp: the alarm had finally been raised. They were coming for him. Theo sniffed back his tears and straightened up to his full height. 'Well, I've had enough. I'm your god, Arielle, and you won't doubt me anymore. You'll do as I tell you and I'm telling you to stay here.'

He spun on his heels and ran out into the desert. He knew he wouldn't get very far. They had camels while he was on foot, and there was nowhere to hide in the open sands surrounding them. But though he knew he wouldn't escape, he would never forgive himself if he didn't try. No matter what Fanta or Onkwani or Salvador did to him after that, it wouldn't be as bad as knowing that he had been too much of a coward, too weak, to try to prevent it.

As he ran in long-legged strides, he heard a familiar voice behind him:

'He went that way, Milady!' Arielle shouted.

Theo's heart sank. He slowed to a halt and turned around, prepared to face his captors with a straight back.

A herd of camels, all with riders spurring them, were galloping at full speed— in the opposite direction. As he watched, only one camel split away from the rest, heading to where Arielle was standing. Even at this distance he recognised his sister's figure sitting astride the beast's hump. Slowing in front of Arielle, the camel's feet kicking up sand as it was spun around, she wasted no time in pulling

Arielle up behind her. Then, with a shout, they were gone, galloping off after the other. The last thing Theo saw was the pale moon of Arielle's face glancing back at him and her hand raised in a hesitant farewell. He didn't wave back. Theo turned and continued running.

THE HOLY THEOLOGOS, BOOK I, VERSE III.VII

Shall you fear mortality any more than you fear going to bed at Night? Death is the cessation of mortality, not of life. It is a transcendence from what we are into beings worthy of keeping the gods' constant company. Death makes equals of us all, in Theo's Arms.

Yet one cannot make a Duppy out of a god. Where goes the soul of a god when their time has passed? In what third tier of realms, past the understanding of the Celesterra, does the All-Mother lie now?

The All-Mother was the first to be born and She was the first to show us that it is possible for a god to die. Perhaps the faith of mortals is the life-blood of a god, and so the world's disbelief was the killing blow to our goddess. Perhaps a god's sole function is creation and once the All-Mother had completed that mightiest work of all creation, the birth of Her three children, Her function was complete. Perhaps She was simply, irredeemably tired and has gone elsewhere to rest.

'Tis a mystery that the gods do not wish us to comprehend. Wherever the soul of the All-Mother may be, undoubtedly Her children know of it and are at peace.

CHAPTER TWENTY-TWO

He stood by the Gates of Dream Country. He heard the call of Dream Country.

On the wrong side of the Gates. Too far to answer the call.

Torres held out his arms and stood still while his crows landed, shrouding him in their feathers. They made a living scarecrow out of him. He clenched his teeth as their talons hooked into every part of his skin. They began to flap their wings. He felt his feet being lifted away from the rock beneath him as the crows took him up to meet the sky. They would go as high as the Gates and then over the top. The higher he went, the thinner the air became, and Torres began to feel light-headed as he gasped for breath. Higher and higher and higher, and they were almost there, there it was, the top of the Gates, black dots crowded in his vision, his lungs burned, but still, higher and higher and higher, and they were almost there . . .

* * *

When the crows began to sing the next day, Torres knew that Abilo had returned to the castle. Their birdsong was like a death march coming from their macabre croaking voices, as the crows who had stayed behind greeted the ones who had gone.

Torres met Abilo in the castle's entryway with Ereon in his arms. The boy had been a lot more docile lately as he had become used to *Os Pesadelos* and to Torres.

He burbled in his arms as they stood at the bottom of the winding double staircase and to Torres's ears it sounded like mocking laughter. He looked down at him with a bitter glance.

The Dream Country Gates are still standing. What do you have to be so happy about?

Torres sighed in frustration. The mortal had one job and he couldn't even do that right. He still needed a way for Ereon to be connected to his sister's realm. Abilo was returning just in time to stop his patience running out.

'Do you have it?' he asked eagerly as the crow landed.

Abilo ducked his head and what he had been carrying in his beak fell out, rattling on the floor, sending up bright sparks from the stone. Torres approached cautiously. The Ivory was small but he didn't dare go too close. It had a pointy tip like the end of some kind of tusk, but it was jagged at the other end where it had been broken away. Torres couldn't take his eyes off it. When he spoke again, his tone was reverent and distracted.

'It looks so harmless,' he whispered. This was the moment he had been waiting for. 'Okay. Give it to him, Abilo.'

He bent and placed Ereon on the ground. The baby screamed at the sudden chill but Torres ignored him. He took several steps back and watched.

Abilo hopped over to the Ivory and snatched it up in his beak. The other crows lined the hallway, watching just as intently, though Torres barely noticed them as Abilo approached Ereon with the Ivory. Torres shifted restlessly. He would have liked to have been outside by the Gates so that he could watch them start to fall, but he was too impatient to take Ereon and the Ivory back down the mountain. He told himself that he would still be able to see it all with his second sight. But what Ereon was about to do deserved his full attention.

Abilo bent over the mortal's small chest. But just as he was about to drop the Ivory on it, a foot struck him solidly across the beak. The Ivory flew away, wide of Ereon, followed by Abilo's body, made limp by the force of Iara's blow.

The water goddess stood on the last step of the staircase, her foot still coming down from the kick as the other crows fell on her with collective ferocity to stop her reaching out for the baby.

'Don't hurt her!' Torres shouted.

He wasn't sure if they heard him over the sounds of their own cries and flapping, so he had no choice but to run into the mêlée and begin batting crows away with his own hands. By the time he had fought his way to Iara her face was slashed with claw marks, which made it look like she was crying tears of blood. But she didn't even tremble, just as she hadn't screamed or made any sound at all when the crows were on her. Her face was set hard as stone.

'It's okay,' he said, reaching down to help her up. 'I forgive you, *amor.* I know what this looks like but we're just fixing the Gates, that's all—'

'You killed Bede!'

A high-pitched screech of rage escaped her lips as she sprang up at him, knocking him to the ground. He would have smashed his head on the solid base of the stair banister had some crows not been behind him to break his fall. They squawked in alarm as Torres crashed onto them, crushing their small bones. As he lay there, blood pooled around his ears and filled his nose with a metallic stench, but he didn't have time to raise his head before Iara's hands were at his throat. They were soft, and he could still remember what they felt like when his lips were pressed against them, but now they gripped him fiercely.

The crows came down onto Iara's back with renewed fervour. She ignored them. Her river-bed mud-brown eyes were locked firmly on Torres as he tried to prise her hands off his throat. With her on top of him, he struggled to get any leverage; he could see the muscles in her shoulders popping with murderous intent. Finally, one of the crows managed to get a clear hit, smacking his wing into the side of Iara's head and dazing her long enough for Torres to get her fingers loose. Before she could readjust her grip, he swung his fist into her throat and she fell, gasping, off his chest. Now he was on top. He pinned her arms to the ground above her head, gripping her knees with his thighs so she couldn't slip away. She wriggled under him, growling like an uncaged animal.

He didn't want to hurt her. Not even after her betrayal. He still wanted everything to go on as before. There were ingredients in the kitchen that the crows could mix together to soothe those cuts on her face; it would be like none of this had ever happened. He would forgive her and then explain everything, and they would bring down the Gates to Dream Country together. He would make her his Dream Goddess once this was all over. She was breathing heavily but she had stopped struggling. Slowly, he began to release his hold on her wrists.

'Iara—'

She brought her knee sharply up and into his groin. Groaning in agony, Torres went down like a felled tree. Through watery eyes, he saw her fight off the crows and dive across the room. He suddenly realised she was going for the Ivory. With rising panic he twisted himself up into a kneeling position, still feeling like he was trying to hold everything in place.

'Abilo,' he groaned through gritted teeth. 'Abil—' But then he remembered that he had never seen him get up from Iara's first attack.

Not bothering to go after Iara, he crawled forward to the last place he remembered seeing Ereon. The child was still there, screaming and blood-soaked at the foot of the staircase. It could have been crow blood, or Iara's or Torres's own for that matter, but it didn't look like Ereon had been hurt himself.

Torres picked him up. He didn't know what the crows were doing to Iara behind him but she was screaming now too, a sound more of rage than pain. Torres just wanted to get away from it. He reached the castle's front door and fumbled to get it open. Outside, the cooling wind whipped against his face. Licking away the saltiness of his sweat, he looked down the mountain path. He turned away from it; he wasn't going to run screaming out of his own home.

It wasn't long before Iara made it out of the castle as well. She looked weak and dazed but had enough presence of mind to pull the door shut behind her, trapping the birds inside. Torres felt sick when he saw her. Her cuts had widened into gashes, her shredded skin hanging loosely around them; large bruises coloured her brown skin with reds, yellows, and purples, like the reflection of sunlight on water. Several of her fingers were broken, but with the ones that weren't she held the Ivory. Her bloodshot eyes fell away from Torres's face to Ereon's.

'You can't kill me,' he stammered. 'He's my Magus, I'm the only thing keeping him under control. If you kill me, all three realms will be destroyed.' He hoped he sounded more certain than he really was.

'Then I'll kill him too.'

'You'd kill a baby?'

She stepped forward. 'Yes.'

Torres didn't know what to say. This was not the same Iara he once knew. His gaze drifted back to the Ivory she held so tightly in her hand. It was doing something to her. That poisonous material, Dream material, was corrupting the only person Torres had left on his side, turning her against him. The memory of Iara standing in Zion while he stood in *Os Pesadelos*, the Gates between them, the Ivory between them, filled Torres's mind. Fanta was doing it again. She was ruining everything for him once again. A growl rose up from the pit of his stomach and suddenly he lunged at her. Instinctively, she brought up the hand that was holding the Ivory, though she couldn't have known that was what he was going for.

Torres didn't even think about what would happen when he touched it, his only thought had consumed him and that was to get the Ivory away from Iara.

Now she understood what he was trying to do and in her surprise she dropped the Ivory. They both tried to grab it at the same time, but Ereon's tiny thrashing arms were in Torres's way and Iara's injuries slowed her down. Torres tried to kick the Ivory away to where he could grab it more easily but at the same moment Iara lunged and his foot ended up hitting her ribcage, sending her sprawling. He looked around desperately, trying to find the Ivory but it was nowhere to be seen—Iara was laying on top of it. Torres put Ereon down by the castle doorway and tried to roll her over but she wouldn't move and her punches were becoming more and more painful. He pushed her harder and harder and . . .

He hadn't realised how close they were to the edge of the cliff until she screamed. She tried to pull herself back to safety, arms flailing wildly for something to grip onto, but the rock was smooth here and she slipped further until she was lying half over the precipice. She looked up at Torres and he looked down at her. Under the part of her back that was not hanging in mid-air he caught a glimpse of Ivory.

'Do it then,' Iara spat. 'Kill me, just like you killed Bede and your mother.'

'You think I killed her?' he asked. That actually made him pause and take a half-step back, though not enough to give Iara room to get away from the edge. 'Not Theo?'

'I know Theo,' she said, shaking her head, as if that was all the explanation required.

Torres's mouth felt dry. 'And not Fanta?'

Iara met his gaze. 'She's better than that.'

Torres didn't say anything. He only looked into Iara's face one last time—and then kicked her over the edge.

He shot a foot out just in time to step on the Ivory before it followed her over.

He turned away so that he didn't have to see her fall, but he didn't have to be watching to know that when her screams stopped a moment later it was not because she had reached the bottom but because the wind had drowned out the rest of the screams. The mountain was high—she still had a long way to fall.

Torres was already calm enough to know that it was not a good idea to try to touch the Ivory again without protection. Wrapping his hand in the cloth of his shirt, he gingerly picked it up. Without waiting a moment longer, he walked over to Ereon, got down on his knees and, with shaking hands, lifted the child's shirt to place the Ivory on his chest, right above his heart.

He waited.

And waited . . .

When, a few moments later, he re-entered the castle with Ereon in his arms, he found the crows still excitedly flapping around. A small group were huddled together on the floor and as Torres got closer he saw Abilo in the middle of them, being pecked at affectionately and having his crooked feathers readjusted by the other crows.

'*Senhor* 'Mare!'

'Are you okay, Abilo?'

'I'll be fine, *Senhor*. Is the Ivory—'

'Safe,' Torres said wearily.

'And Iara?'

Torres hesitated, then simply shook his head. He was exhausted. Although he had a lot to think about, he found himself unable to process even one coherent thought, even about Iara. He managed to get up to the second floor and put Ereon into his basket, before collapsing beside him. The boy was still screaming and seemed to have been doing so non-stop, for longer than was healthy. Torres could see the bulge of the Ivory against the boy's chest, kept in place by his shirt. The scene downstairs had obviously shaken him badly and for the first time Torres found himself having some sympathy towards him. It couldn't be a good experience to find yourself in the middle of a battle—which at the scale of a baby was a war—when you couldn't understand that it was being fought over you, couldn't walk away from it, and couldn't talk to ask everyone to stop. This midnight-skinned boy had the power of a god but was still just a helpless little baby. Torres knew what it was like to live at the whim of people more powerful than you, who claimed the right to think for you but never thought *of* you. He was struggling to change things for himself, but he didn't want to become that same powerful, inconsiderate force to somebody else, even if it was just a mortal child. Ereon began to quieten down as, without thinking, Torres reached down and took his hand.

'You and me, *maninho*. We're the same. But don't worry,' Torres said, engulfing the baby's chubby little fist in his own large palm, 'I won't let them hurt you.'

He couldn't have said how long he stayed like that, hardly moving at all, hardly blinking. At some point he began to cry. A Nightmare began to rise inside him but he was too tired to stop it. It spread throughout his body, making his fingertips tingle where they came into contact with Ereon's skin. He closed his eyes tightly as if by doing so he could also close off his ears and not have to hear the screams of the boy he had just sworn to protect.

When the Nightmare came, *Senhor* 'Mare was sobbing so loudly that he didn't hear that the mortal wasn't screaming at all. When the Nightmare came, *Senhor* 'Mare was sobbing so blindly that he didn't see the premature smile that lifted his Magus's cheeks.

When the Nightmare came, *Senhor* 'Mare didn't notice that it was the sweetest Nightmare he had ever made.

* * *

Some distance away, unnoticed by anyone, the Gates around Dream Country shook.

CHAPTER TWENTY-THREE

Theo was surprised that the search party didn't see through Arielle's ruse, turn around, and bring him back to camp like a child who tries to run away from home but only gets as far as the street corner. But it had been at least three hours since he'd left and there was still no sign of any of the camels or their riders. He would have liked to say goodbye to Auntie, but she would never have believed him if he'd tried to explain that Fanta had hired assassins to kill him. Auntie hadn't believed that any of the three of them were murderers and even Theo had shared her doubt sometimes. But, if he needed a wake-up call, Fanta had given it to him. It shouldn't have surprised him that she had taken her suspicions so far, but he'd be lying if he said it didn't hurt.

Soon enough he had reached the border of Dream Country and he was walking alongside the monumental Gates.

I could go through right now, he thought repeatedly, but every time the idea tempted him he had to remind himself why he couldn't do it. If he went through to the realm that was half-Zion and half-Mountains now, he would be giving up the advantage he had suffered to gain over the last five days—the element of surprise. If he crossed now he would still be too far away from the castle and Torres would see that he had returned and have time to plan against him.

Trying to keep this in mind, Theo kept going on the Dream Country side of the Gates.

'Hey, you!'

He looked up. There was a child on the other side of the Gates. Theo was too far away to see whether it was a boy or a girl and he couldn't find out by going any closer to the Gates, without risking the temptation to cross immediately. The child's voice didn't give much away; it was soft, even when raised to a shout it gave the impression that the wind could carry it away like a feather. Theo squinted, trying to make out the child's features more clearly, but after a while gave up, realising he should probably answer them. After all, there was no one else around to whom they could be calling.

'Yes?'

To his own ears his voice sounded weak and dry, but it must have carried well enough because the child waved.

'You're going the wrong way!'

Theo frowned. 'What?'

'You're going the wrong way!'

'I don't understand,' Theo said quietly, half to himself. He was sure, that time, that there was no way the child could have heard him.

'You *do* understand,' came the reply nonetheless, with all the exasperation of a child trying to explain something to an adult. 'Aren't you trying to get home?'

Theo nodded. Home. That's all he wanted.

'You have to go that way.' The child pointed over Theo's shoulder—away from the Gates. 'Do you hear me? Keep walking that way and don't stop.'

'Home?' Theo asked. He suddenly felt that this strange child was the only one who could help him. His mind was blank; all he knew was that he was lost.

You're going the wrong way . . . Aren't you trying to get home?

'Home?' he asked again.

'Yeah, that way will take you home. You just can't stop walking. Remember, okay?' Theo nodded. 'Go on then.' The child waved him cheerfully on his way and Theo felt a certain comfort knowing that they would stand there to watch him until he was out of sight.

He walked in a straight line, as if the direction of the child's pointing finger had left arrows for him to follow that he didn't dare to stray from. His heart felt light for the first time in ages.

He was going home.

* * *

Hours passed and Theo was no longer able to keep up the same pace. The further he went, the more the details of his conversation with the child faded. He wondered if it had just been a Dream but, even so, he couldn't stop his legs from moving forward. He was going home. He clung to that thought.

He didn't think it could have got any hotter than it had been over the past few days, but it had. It was incredible, considering that the sun was no longer even bearing down on him as storm clouds rolled in to cover it. He considered stopping for a rest. He felt unnaturally exhausted. It was as if his sister's realm had penetrated every one of his senses so that just when he was sick of seeing it on the outside he realised it was inside him too. The realm's aridity choked off his every thought, until all he felt was the desire for a cold glass of water.

His lips felt chapped and sticky as his mouth tried its hardest to produce whatever moisture it could. On top of everything, his stomach was starting to complain. He couldn't remember the last time he ate something.

The lizard was already dead when he found it. It was about the length of his hand, green with bulging eyes that looked up at Theo as he looked down at it. He couldn't remember the last time he had eaten an animal or even an animal product. It helped that he hadn't had to kill it, but it didn't help that it was going to be too big to fit into his mouth all at once. He could imagine the crunch of the bones in his mouth, the ooze of cold blood, and sliminess of the flesh clogging his throat. His stomach gurgled in protest but, holding the lizard's tail between thumb and forefinger, nevertheless he began to lift it to his mouth.

At that moment a grey mass moved across the sky, blocking out the final rays of the sun. More clouds were rising up along the horizon; at this rate there would be no blue sky visible above him within a few minutes. The clouds looked heavy and swollen with rain and Theo had never been so glad at the prospect of bad weather. He dropped the lizard, his hunger forgotten. A little rain would cool him off and give him something to drink. But he should have known better than to expect only a *little* rain. The desert didn't do little things, it did everything to extremes, storms as well as heat.

In the distance a dark wall was rolling towards him over the sand. It got bigger and darker as it went, picking up more and more sand. It wouldn't take long to reach him. The only extra protection he had with him were the rags Onkwani and Salvador had used to tie him up, still dangling from his wrist. He quickly untied them and folded them together, forming a strip of cloth that would wrap around his head. The rest of his body was covered well enough, all he had to worry about was his eyes.

Now he realised with rising panic that once he wrapped the cloth around his eyes he would have no way of seeing where he was going. If this were Zion, he could use his realm sight to guide him. But this wasn't Zion. Zion had never done this to him.

The wind had been picking up quickly and was already starting to swirl the sand up around his feet. He hesitated. Probably it wasn't a good idea to try to move in a storm anyway. Maybe he should just sit down and wait it out. But he had no idea how long sandstorms usually lasted and he couldn't afford to waste time, either to get to Torres or to get away from Fanta. Plus, if this initial wind was any indication, the storm would bury him if he sat down in it. No, it was best to keep moving, even blindly. He tied the blindfold. The cloth went around his ears as well as his eyes, though the wind was so fierce he could still hear it, a wild sound, like rushing torrents of water.

When the first grains of sand hit his cheeks and arms they felt no worse than tiny hailstones. They stung a little but they were tolerable. Then the rain came.

Immediately it drenched Theo to the bone, but that too was not unpleasant. It occurred to him then that since he really didn't have any idea how long the storm would last, he should try to drink as much as he could now. So he opened his mouth.

At that moment, the wall hit. Theo choked on a mouthful of sand. He couldn't spit it out without opening his mouth and letting more sand in. The grit clung to his teeth, drying out his mouth. Bringing up some saliva from the back of his throat, he swallowed, and it went down as a hard, congealed lump. He shuddered but already he had much bigger things to worry about. He could no longer feel individual grains hitting him, only one relentless onslaught. The storm battered the exposed flesh of his neck, face, and hands, leaving them raw and burning. Now the cloth around his eyes felt far too thin. Theo squeezed his eyes shut tighter to protect them. He took his first shaky step forward and was almost thrown off his feet as he tried to walk against the wind.

He struggled on like that for what felt like forever. He wondered how much progress he could actually be making when, with every hard-won step forward, it seemed like the storm pushed him back five.

His body was soon completely numb. Even his sense of taste was gone. He was disoriented and alone but he tried not to think about how much safer he had felt wandering this strange land when his sister had been with him.

He pushed on against the storm.

* * *

There was a whistle in the dying wind. It sang a lullaby without words and gradually Theo fell under its spell. The wind had switched direction so now he was no longer struggling against it but being pushed forward by it. The air was still electric with the memory of the storm, but he was sure now that this wind would not hurt him. He removed his blindfold and was amazed to see how much the landscape had been changed by the storm. There were more sand dunes than ever now, piled up to over three times Theo's height. Some of them were so monumental and sturdy looking that they almost looked man-made. Some distant memory told him he should be looking around himself for three things, trying to notice if they were real and that it was *very important* that he did this *right now.* But just then the tune of the breeze picked up, wiping all other thoughts from his mind as he stepped into a valley of dunes, accompanied by his windy lullaby. Without even noticing himself doing it, Theo began to hum along. Then another voice joined the melody. Theo wasn't afraid. It felt right that someone should be singing to him.

It only took a moment for him to realise that it was not singing, but someone, a woman, simply saying his name, making it sound like a song just for him. Her voice was husky and familiar somehow and she called to him as if she knew him too. Theo wanted to call back but he didn't know her name.

'*Theodore,*' she sang. '*Theodore, sweetness. I have to leave you now.*'

That seemed a strange part to the song, but her windy fingers were still brushing through his dreads and against his face so he knew she wasn't going anywhere. He could ignore her words as long as she was still there.

'*Theodore, amor, I have to say goodbye. You've killed me. They killed me. Who killed me?*'

Her hands continued to brush his cheeks and Theo sighed contentedly at her touch. He felt safe here with her.

'*Theodore, mpenzi, I'll see you again soon.*'

Her hand brushed his eyelids again but when it moved away, Theo noticed for the first time that it was Night. His heart leapt at the sight of the blue-black sky, speckled with stars and maternal instinct, and that felt familiar too. He'd seen this colour recently, in Ereon's skin, but it was different seeing it up there, where it was supposed to be. It was no longer strange that there had been no Night in the celestial realms for most of his lifetime, all that mattered was that it was here now. Brushing his face. The woman's singing voice was getting more insistent now, her hands began to brush his face almost fiercely. He cried out in pain. He tried to reach up to the sky but his hand struck something. He looked about him and realised he was in a glass coffin.

'Mama?'

'Theodore, don't you remember? The Night always comes back.'

Then Theo looked east and saw something which made him feel sick. His heart stopped and he went cold as he looked at the sunrise. Yellow rays of the sun were bleeding into the sky, lightening the Night to a cerulean blue, brushing away the stars. Someone was lowering his coffin into the ground.

'Mama!' he called, his voice rising in panic.

He couldn't understand why she wasn't helping him. Someone was trying to bury him alive! Where was she?

'Theodore, I said goodbye.'

Suddenly the full meaning behind her song hit him. She was not coming to save him. She was leaving.

More of the new sky chased away the old as it retreated under the horizon. Theo cried out again.

'Don't go! Please! I'm sorry! I'm sorry I don't remember!'

He pounded in desperation at the glass walls that surrounded him but they did not break. His eyes were fixed on the dawn sky.

Tears filled his vision as he screamed at the sky, screamed at the disappearing Night, begging it to stay. He wanted to run after it, to keep running even if he knew he would never reach it, because he knew, *he knew*, that the moment he stopped running to catch it was the moment when it would be gone forever. Dirt piled up on his tomb. He heard himself crying out, echoes of himself parodying his pleas, until he wasn't sure which voice was really his.

'Mama!'

'Mama!'

'Mama!'

'Don't go!'

'Don't go!'

'Don't go!'

'Please!'

'Please!'

'Please!'

'Mama!'

'Mama!'

'Mama!'

'No!' A new voice shrieked, breaking the cycle.

It was a female voice, higher pitched and younger than the one which had gone, and Theo thought he recognised it. The graveyard dirt disappeared and the glass coffin smashed. He blinked in shock.

Fanta was cowering away from him as if he was made of poisonous Horn. She clawed at her own tear-streaked face, screaming at him, 'I don't do Nightmares! I don't do Nightmares!'

CHAPTER TWENTY-FOUR

Theo had felt loneliness like this only once before, when the Night died. The pain inside his chest was telling him that *just* happened, just now, but his head was saying, no, that was years ago, and they couldn't agree.

He couldn't remember how old he was. His fresh pain was confusing him, it insisted that he was no more than six years old, an age before he had learnt to numb himself to feelings like this. But he felt older. He felt tired. He was the God of Sleep, was it right or wrong that he felt so tired?

And then he remembered. He was nineteen, and it was wrong, so wrong. He shouldn't be tired. Theo wished he didn't remember. Forgetting had felt good for a while.

He forced his eyes open. The last remnants of the storm had completely passed. There were only clear blue skies above.

He turned his head. Fanta was there. She was on her knees, her head on her chest. Her fingers were dug deep into the sand as if she were trying to hold on to a wild animal. She was like a statue of grief, so still that Theo could not even tell if she was breathing.

'Fanta,' he called softly.

She didn't look up. He tried again.

'Fanta. Please . . .'

But he didn't even know what he was asking for. Comfort? Did he want his sister to tell him that everything would be okay? Or did he want her to heal him? To lay her hands against his aching body, his tired mind, and take the pain away. She couldn't. Theo knew that, even if he found the words to ask her, she wouldn't be able to help him.

Maybe he just wanted her to look up. To look him in the eye and show that she was hurting too. Maybe he just wanted to know that he wasn't alone.

Theo let his head fall back to the ground. He was glad to let his tears go. The words of the Nightmare still spun circles in his mind.

I have to leave you now, I have to say goodbye.

Theo sniffed and wiped the tears from his eyes. Almost without noticing, he began to hum the song from his Nightmare. He recognised it now. It was the song the All-Mother used to sing to them at Night, when it had always been as though it was her voice alone, and not Theo's power, that was putting them to Sleep. Theo couldn't remember the real words anymore. Something about three little birds. Something about happiness. He turned again to face Fanta who had not moved.

'Has Mama ever spoken to you since she died?' he asked.

Fanta looked up. Her eyes were red and swollen with tears. She did not have the black pooling irises of their mother's eyes—of the triplets only Theo did—but something about her expression in that moment reminded him so much of her that he had to choke back another sob.

'What?' Fanta croaked.

He swallowed. 'Have you ever . . . felt like she was trying to tell you something?'

Fanta looked at him curiously, as if she was trying to figure something out. After a while she pushed herself up to her feet.

'I have something to show you,' she said. She held her hand out to help him up.

Theo considered it for a moment, his own hand tingling a little in anticipation of the Ivory shock he would feel if he took her hand.

But when he met his sister's gaze he saw that there was no violence there. She did not want to hurt him. He took her hand.

Theo let Fanta lift him to his feet and throw his arm over her shoulder to guide him to wherever they were going. As they walked he saw a figure standing between two camels in the distance. Arielle. They passed close enough for Theo to see the expression of relief that passed across her face when she saw him alive, but to his surprise Fanta led him further on. He stumbled to avoid a rock and would have fallen if she had not been there to support him. The further they went away, the more rocks there were, and he soon realised that they were not lying at random but had been arranged to form the borders of a path along which Fanta was leading him.

'You came so close to it on your own, it's as if something wanted me to show you,' Fanta said as she came to a stop.

Theo looked down. At his feet was another rock, a grey one, larger than those leading up to it though not so beautiful or noteworthy as many of them had been. Nonetheless he felt something inside pulling him towards it.

'What is it?' he whispered.

There was an atmosphere around the rock similar to that in the temple on Pangaea that made the Majority fall silent, but stronger. In the temple he knew that the silence was only for him. This felt as if it was for something greater.

Fanta replied in the same hushed, reverent tones. 'It's moon rock.'

Theo's head jerked up. He searched his sister's face, trying to tell if she was joking or lying. She looked perfectly sincere.

'I only found it here,' she added hurriedly. She must have realised at the same moment as he did how bad this made her look. The rock was the closest thing they had to their mother's corpse.

'When?' Theo asked.

'The day after,' she said, and nothing further was needed to explain what she meant by 'after.' 'Some of the Minors said they saw it fall.'

She fell silent. Theo looked at the rock again and felt his throat tighten with emotion.

'I could never bring myself to move it.'

If it had fallen in Zion, Theo wasn't sure if he could have just left it exposed, as Fanta had, but he understood not wanting to touch it.

'I don't remember,' Fanta whispered.

'What?'

'The day she died. It's just like . . . a space in my mind. I want to remember. I want to remember the last time that I saw her, but I don't. And for a while I was just so . . . angry with her.'

'With Mama?'

'Yes. She left us. I know it's stupid, I know it's not her fault, and not something she would have ever chosen to do. But she should have prepared us better. We didn't even know there was a possibility of a world without her and then all of a sudden we were living in it. I felt so much responsibility put on me as soon as she was gone.'

'Why?'

Fanta shrugged. 'I'm the oldest. Not by much, I know, but I still felt I had to take care of you and Torres. And . . . I failed.'

'You were a child. We all were.'

Fanta said nothing for a moment. 'She used to take me to sit by the top of the Staircase. We would look down and she would tell me about the mortals. She told me how most of the people of Celesterra had forgotten her but that one day she would reclaim them and they would be Majority. She said she would do that—for us. She told me that the world was mine for the taking and all I had to do . . . was take it. And then she was gone.'

They looked back down at the moon rock in front of them. The image of the phantelles throwing sand over their dead flashed across his mind. Shakily, he left his sister's side and knelt down to pick up a handful of sand. He dropped it on top of the moon rock and watched it fall into the small crater around it. Before he had time to pick up another handful, Fanta scattered her own in the same spot. They didn't say anything to each other as they buried the rock; working together, it didn't take too long.

When they were done there was just the suggestion of a rising mound on the flat earth to show where it had been. Nowadays in Zion there was a tradition, after a death, of 'nine nights' staying up at the house of the deceased. Nine nights was how long it was thought to take for a god's soul to move on to its next stage, wherever that may be. Although Theo didn't have time to do that for his mother now, the moment still felt as if it required some words, a formal goodbye which they had never had a chance to make before. He found, however, that he couldn't think of a single thing to say. All those times when he had wished that Mama was there—to witness some important occasion in his life or to offer him some advice, or the hours he had spent musing on what he would say if they could just have one more minute together, all of this fell upon the spear of the moment and died.

'I don't remember either,' he admitted. 'How is that possible?'

'A lot of impossible things have happened recently,' Fanta said.

She turned away from the grave, forgetting to help him along with her.

He struggled after her. 'Fanta,' he called. 'Whatever that was, back there, it wasn't you. It was Torres. He's doing something with Ereon that made that happen.'

'I know,' she said, stopping in her tracks, 'and that's why when you get to *Os Pesadelos* I don't want you to just take that baby from him or close his realm, as you told Auntie. I want you to kill him.'

Theo felt his heart thump, but he didn't even attempt to speak. She wasn't done yet.

'You don't owe me anything, Theo. I know you already know most of this, but I want to give you an explanation. When I left you tied up in that cave the first day you got here, I sent a message to Onkwani and Salvador. I only wanted them around as security, in case I needed them if you tried something. But I thought I could find out for sure, through your Dreams, whether or not you had killed Mama. I gave the Dreams to you on purpose, but I discovered it wasn't as easy as making a mortal Dream. I had to use a lot more Dream energy to get it to work, but it was also enough to kill you, which I didn't want. So I gave Arielle my Ivory necklace. Because she was Dreaming at the same time, the Ivory was already attracted to the Dream energy around her, so I could just direct it to take the excess that came off you and give it to her, so that I could make sure you stayed alive. The necklace created a connection between you and her and gave her insight into your Dreams that even I didn't have, which was also helpful when I started the divinations. But it meant that I had to keep you away from each other, so you wouldn't touch her and discover that she was the one who was wearing the Ivory, not me.' She tugged at the front of her kanga to show him. Her neck was bare.

Theo thought back to the expression of pain he had seen on Arielle's face the last time he saw her Dreaming. Could a mortal be hurt from having double the amount of normal Dreams?

A million conflicting emotions rose up inside him. The knowledge that Fanta had stopped her Dreams from killing him fought with the idea that she could have stopped them altogether. The way she had used Arielle as some kind of Dream-recycling bin also felt wrong, especially since she had only been doing it to get to him. But, when it came down to it, with Onkwani and Salvador she had helped him escape and made them let him go. Should he feel angry? Grateful? He didn't know.

Fanta frowned. 'If I hadn't been doing all that, I could have got us to the Mountains in two days. But it's taken all this—giving you a Nightmare—for me to realise the truth. It doesn't matter who killed Mama because Torres is killing us *right now.*'

'So you think that means I should kill him?'

'I would kill him myself if I could come into *Os Pesadelos* with you, but I can't get through the Gates, so I'm asking you to do it. To keep my realm safe. Just say yes or no.'

He couldn't give her the answer she wanted. 'I already told you, Fanta, I'm not a killer. Don't try to make me into one now. But . . . I'll do whatever I can to make sure Torres doesn't get into Dream Country the way he got into Zion. I'll keep the Nightmares over there. I promise.'

Fanta examined him for a moment and then nodded, reluctantly, before turning away.

'We're about two hours' ride away from the castle Gates,' she said and took his arm again. 'You were going completely the wrong way.'

The Sleep God leant on the Dream Goddess as they followed the rock-strewn path away from their mother's graveside.

Theo only stopped himself from looking back because Fanta didn't either.

* * *

The bells that marked the end of the Holy Majoracle always rang out at midnight on the Fifth Day on the island. In the celestial realms it was at the sun's second peak that the festival officially ended.

As Fanta, Arielle, and Theo came to the borders of Dream Country not one of them was looking up at the sky. Reunited with her Ivory necklace, Fanta rode alone on the back of the larger camel. She kept the beast hurrying along at a steady pace, as she rode with murder in her eyes.

Theo and Arielle could only try to keep up. The Magus sat at the front of the camel while Theo leaned wearily against her with his arms wrapped around her waist. At first Arielle was hesitant when Fanta took her necklace back, understanding that she had revealed everything to Theo.

'I'm sorry. For everything,' he told her with a shaky smile. None of this had been her fault, after all, and he and Fanta had both treated her terribly.

Now they rode in silence, unaware of the passage of time, until they were not far from the Gates and a man appeared in front of them, bringing them to an abrupt halt.

The man stared dazedly around himself for a second before he noticed the three of them watching him.

'How pretty,' he mumbled and wandered away.

Fanta watched him go. 'A Dreamer. They're coming back.' She looked at Arielle. 'Majoracle's over.'

Theo could feel Arielle deflate in front of him.

'Oh . . . really?'

Fanta was already dismounting from her phantelle. 'Let's get you back to the island.'

Arielle and Theo joined her on the ground. It was hard to say which of them moved most reluctantly. Theo had said goodbye to eighteen Magi in his life, but he couldn't remember ever feeling the way he did with *this* Magus, who wasn't even his.

'I'm sorry if I ruined your Majoracle, Arielle,' Theo said when she turned to him.

'You didn't. I had fun. I mean, apart from all those times when you nearly died, of course. Maybe fun isn't the right word. It was interesting, I mean.' She blushed. 'Do you think . . . I know that I'm only meant to come back here from now on, but do you think I could come and see you in Zion sometimes?'

Theo considered it. He knew that what she was asking for was impossible but he still smiled.

'One day we'll meet in Zion,' he said truthfully.

Arielle smiled back and then she lowered her head in preparation to be sent back to her body. 'Okay, I'm ready.'

She bit her bottom lip. The life she was going back to on Pangaea would not be the same as the one she left behind to come here. She would be a holy figure, a celebrity, holding a position in society higher than that of the Magistrates themselves. But she also had a death mark looming over her; her life would last no more than fourteen more years. Then, as promised, she and Theo would meet again.

Fanta touched Arielle between her closed eyes. The Magus sighed happily at the touch from her Goddess; the edges of her began to blur as her Dream-self was given directions back into her body. But before she could disappear like she was supposed to Fanta drew her hand back and exhaled sharply as if she had just been punched in the stomach.

'What's wrong?' Theo asked.

'I—I can't get her through. The Gates won't open.' She shook her head. 'I'll try again.'

And she did, but the same thing happened and Arielle almost had to catch her this time when she was knocked away. A desperate look passed across Fanta's face. Theo couldn't understand it either. The Magi Gates were not like the ones between the realms, they didn't require Rogan to work. They opened and closed at the will of the Major god of that realm. There was no reason that Theo could think of, nothing Torres could be doing, that would stop Fanta from letting Arielle through.

'What do you think it means?'

She wouldn't answer him but when she glanced over at the Gates she had a horrified expression on her face. Suddenly she was running at full speed for the border with the Mountains. Arielle helped Theo to follow and by the time they caught her up Fanta had already pushed herself past the pain of the Horn to get as close as she could to the Gates. She was staring at it, with an intensity that demanded silence. Theo didn't know what she was doing but he watched closely, holding his breath. The latticed bars in front of Fanta's face began to move, reforming themselves in the same way they did whenever Rogan walked through the Gates. The Horn and Ivory peeled back from each other like a wound opening and the gap kept growing until it was as tall and as wide as Fanta herself. Her hand was shaking when she stuck it through. Into the Mountains.

Theo gasped. 'How did you do that? You just left Dream Country!'

Fanta shook her head. The tears now ran freely down her cheeks.

'I wasn't leaving Dream Country. I was entering *Os Pesadelos*.'

Theo went pale.

'What's the difference?' Arielle asked looking apprehensively back and forth between the two gods.

In a cracking voice Fanta managed to reply, 'You can't enter a realm that isn't your own.'

She looked at Theo with a look of such total despair and helplessness that his heart winced to see it.

'Theo,' she said, 'what do I do?'

But he didn't have an answer for her. He didn't know what Nightmare Goddesses were supposed to do.

THE HOLY THEOLOGOS, BOOK I, VERSE IV.IV

In times unholy,
In times untrue
I Dreamed a Dream,
I Dreamed of you.
You All-Mother's daughters
You All-Mother's sons,
I Dreamed a Dream
Of everyone.

And in my Dream
What happened then?
I Dreamed of times
Of 'Once' and 'When.'
The Dream, it knew me,
The Dream outgrew me
And then the Dream,
It passed right through me.

When I awoke
The Dream, it ended,
The Dream, it broke
And never mended.
When I once Dreamed
I never thanked her,
The Dreams were hers,
Milady Fanta's.

CHAPTER TWENTY-FIVE

Dream God.

He liked the sound of that.

The day after Iara's betrayal, Torres slunk around his castle as if all the colour had been sucked from the world. Abilo and the crows tried to cheer him up by reminding him that he had everything in place for his plan at last; now that Ereon had the Ivory, the Dream Country Gates would fall and Torres would finally have the realm he'd always wanted. But all Torres wanted to do now was keep his Magus close by, cradling the child tightly to him as if he were as precious as the last rainbow in a grey sky. He didn't want to think about Dream Country just then. For now, all his thoughts were on the boy, and it seemed that Ereon's thoughts were likewise only on Torres. The boy wouldn't tolerate anyone else's touch and when he was in Torres's arms he had an almost constant smile on his face.

By midday, the newborn had learnt how to laugh.

* * *

At midday, the Gates around Dream Country shook again. At the one-time border between Zion and *Os Pesadelos*, the Gatekeeper looked up from his work and took notice.

* * *

Very, very slowly, the castle was changing. The shadows became a little less deep and the haunting moans of the walls were slowly coming to a rest. The crows flew like they were dancing and, without knowing why, the monsters of *Os Pesadelos* moved further and further away from the third mountain and that new atmosphere shrouding it.

Still Torres noticed nothing beyond the silence of his own mind.

Well into the afternoon of the Fifth Day of the Majoracle, Abilo found the Nightmare God in the dining room, staring absently at his realm through the floor-length windows.

The crow cleared his throat loudly. '*Senhor?*'

'Hmm?'

'I thought perhaps I should remind you that the Majoracle is over in a few hours.'

'Hmm. Yes, it is.'

'*Senhor?* The boy will have to be returned.'

'Returned? Returned where?'

'To his home, *Senhor* 'Mare.'

Torres winced. 'Don't call me that anymore, Abilo.'

A pause. And then Abilo said smoothly, bowing, 'As you wish, *Senhor.*'

Torres turned away from the view. 'Ereon is already home.'

'I meant to the island, *Senhor*. To his mother.'

'He *is* home, Abilo,' Torres repeated, more sternly.

The crow gulped. 'You—don't intend to let him leave, *Senhor?*'

'Why would he want to leave? Haven't you noticed how happy he's been lately?'

'No, *Senhor*, I can't say that I have . . . perhaps you've been imagining it.'

You too, Abilo?

Torres let out a sigh. He didn't have many people he would call a friend. Someone he trusted. But it seemed that this week every last one of that small number was doubting him. Mocking him, then torturing him with their disbelief.

You're the last one now, maninho, he thought, looking down at Ereon. *Just you and me.*

'You think I can't tell the difference between illusion and reality, Abilo?'

'That's not what I meant, *Senhor,* I—'

'You think I'm losing my mind?' Torres turned to look at the crow, who was perched on the back of one of the dining chairs, the one where Iara had sat just two days earlier. Torres readjusted his grip so that he held Ereon in one arm as he raised the other one in front of him, palm down. 'Let me reassure you, old friend. Come here.'

Abilo hopped around on the spot, squawking so convulsively they sounded like hiccups. But, as Torres knew he would, he obeyed the order, swooping over and landing gently on the back of Torres's hands.

'*CAAW! CAAW!*'

Torres ignored the bird's panic. If Abilo wanted to suggest that Ereon's happiness was only a product of Torres's imagination, the Nightmare God would have to remind his servant that joy was not the type of thing that got imagined in his realm. He closed his eyes and let his guard down.

Nothing happened. For the longest time nothing happened.

Torres peeked out from beneath his half-closed eyelids. Abilo's squawks had calmed down and the crow was watching him expectantly.

'*Senhor?* Should something be happen—oh! Oh.'

The white crow approached the flock with uncertainty. But Abilo raised his wing and took the newcomer under it and the walls of their cage had fallen around them by morning. The early birds sang for freedom and as their beaks drank in the sun's rays, the white crow turned to Abilo and said, 'You've done well and the journey's almost over and your destination's in sight. You'll get there by the morning of tomorrow's tomorrow if you go well and as the crow flies.' Abilo's eyes filled with tears as the white crow pecked his feathers affectionately, grooming them in preparation for the journey ahead . . .

'Oh,' Torres said too.

He and Abilo looked at each other, their eyes wide and tearful for different reasons. Torres was stunned. He knew Nightmares; that was no Nightmare.

'A Dream,' he whispered, afraid that if he spoke the name any louder he would catch himself in a lie.

Luckily, Abilo was there to confirm it, nodding his head in shocked silence and allowing Torres to speak the words once more, this time with more conviction.

'I just made a Dream.'

* * *

The first piece of Horn fell from the Gates that separated Dream Country from *Os Pesadelos*.

* * *

Once he had regained his composure a little, Abilo informed Torres that the white crow was a symbol among his species for the figure of Death. When he heard this, Torres's heart sank a little; in his experience if an illusion involved death, it was definitely a Nightmare. But Abilo reassured him: the white crow was a symbol of comfort for birds, and of destiny. It was not something to fear.

Torres had to take a seat and even laid Ereon to the side, to give himself time to process it all.

Dream God.

Had he done it? He didn't understand how he could have. He wasn't even in Dream Country yet—in fact, the Gates were still standing. He looked at Ereon and saw the slight lump above his chest. Torres pulled the top of the child's shirt down until the Ivory was revealed, sitting so innocently on his chest.

And then Torres remembered.

He pulled up the blanket around Ereon's ankle. The Horn bracelet, the one he had used to take him from Theo and bring him here, was still there.

Torres had never heard of anyone, besides the Gatekeeper, who could wear Horn and Ivory at the same time without the two materials reacting against each other in a fatal way. But here was this child, with a Dream on his heart and a Nightmare like a shackle around his ankle.

And now, not only was Torres making Dreams but he suddenly realised he had been holding Ereon, skin-to-skin, for the whole day without the Ivory affecting him.

In order to test his theory he had other crows summoned to him and laid hands on them all, one by one. He tried making them Dream on his own, with Ereon laid to the side: nothing happened. Not even a Nightmare. And then he picked Ereon up . . .

Every single crow walked away with the experience of a Dream. As Torres stared down at him in bewilderment, Ereon laughed.

I've been giving you Dreams, haven't I? That's why you've been so happy.

Torres didn't know how he hadn't noticed, how he hadn't *seen* any of Ereon's Dreams, but he didn't care. He told Abilo to gather all of the crows he could find and bring them to the dining room.

Where *Senhor* 'Mare had been hesitant to give Nightmares, he was generous with Dreams.

Something awoke in Torres which he suspected had always been there. He was not starting from scratch in understanding the Dreams. The process was pretty much the same as for Nightmares, only the outcome was different. But that knowledge only made the memories of how differently he and Fanta had always been treated burn more. If Theo or the Majority saw him as he was now, he bet they wouldn't deny him a Magus then.

The crows were the only ones he felt comfortable practising on for now. If he revealed to the Minors or the monsters that he could make Dreams, he would have to lock himself inside the castle to avoid what they would do to him.

A mutiny would not look good, especially since the Majoracle bells had rung and the Pangaeans were returning to the realm.

His only other option was Anansewa, and she was an unwilling participant.

She sat on the edge of the windowsill, kicking her legs and tugging at her earlobe, a habit Torres noticed she only adopted with this particular body, a sullen-looking white girl, tall for her age.

Torres was disappointed with how unimpressed Anansewa seemed. In fact, her lack of interest was starting to annoy him. After all, here he was, a Nightmare God, making Dreams! The paradox alone should have fascinated her.

'Are you sure you don't want a Dream, Nanse? I can make you something to play with or . . .' He paused as he thought of other good things that might interest her. He was back in the dining room with a warm bottle of goat's milk, holding it at a careful angle as Ereon guzzled hungrily.

Anansewa kicked her legs. 'No, I don't want one. Dreams are dirty.'

Torres frowned. 'Dirty?'

'Yes. Nightmares are clean, Dreams are dirty,' she stated matter-of-factly. 'I don't know why you wanted to swap anyway.'

'People like Dreams.'

'I don't. You should have chosen your brother. Sleep would've been cooler. And I like your brother.'

Torres snorted. 'You've never met him.'

'I might have done!' Anansewa protested and then a grin spread across her young face. 'In a Dream.'

'Well, you'll have to get used to them. I have Abilo preparing the goats right now to take me and Ereon down the mountain to the Gates. It's time for Dream Country to open up.'

A taste for Dreams had only whet his appetite and reminded him of his hunger. Now he was ready to feast.

CHAPTER TWENTY-SIX

Theo shivered.

Logically, he knew it was no colder in the Mountains than it had been in Dream Country; it was the same sun above him, the same air around him. Yet he felt like a man returning home to find he had left all the windows and doors wide open, and with the eerie suspicion that the cold wind had not been the only uninvited guest while he'd been gone. The cold shade of the rocky outcrops almost made him miss the relentless sun. Something about being in the Mountains made his skin crawl, even with the knowledge that the air he breathed was half-Zionese.

He had been surprised at how hesitant he'd been to come through, especially after all those hours of homesickness. But the problem was that this was not home. It had the air of home, the people, and even the land, but from the moment Theo set foot inside he could feel that this was just another thing that Torres had corrupted. Even if he could still get Zion back, there was no way it would ever be the same.

And if he felt that way, knowing that this realm was half his, he couldn't imagine how Fanta felt. She had only needed the briefest of mourning periods to recover from her shock before she let the anger replace it. It had been her, not Theo, who took the first step through the Gates, and once she was through she didn't stop once to look back at her realm, her brother, or the Magus she had left behind.

'She'll come back for you,' Theo told Arielle, who smiled weakly, unconvinced.

Unlike the other Dreamers who were appearing more regularly around her, Arielle couldn't wake herself out of Dream Country. All she could do was wait.

'Be careful, Milord,' she'd said.

And before he could change his mind, he'd stepped past the Gates and followed his sister. His own power hit him like an avalanche as it returned. He felt his ability to access his realm sight tingling behind his eyes. And the power of Sleep! He was used to taking breaks during Majoracles, and usually he even looked forward to the rest, but the last five days had been the first time without *being able* to put anyone to Sleep. Until the power was returned to him, he hadn't realised how stripped back, how exposed he'd felt without it. How much easier would his journey have been if he'd had his Sleep? He could have disposed of Onkwani and Salvador with a touch. Or, he could have put *himself* to Sleep and avoided all of those painful Dreams.

Tentatively, Theo drew some Sleep energy to himself. His head cleared and the throbbing in his bones from Onkwani and Salvador's attentions began to fade. He no longer felt hungry. He didn't dare to give himself any more than this though, afraid that it would make him slow and tired. He had a feeling he would need to be as alert as possible when he got to the castle.

Fanta was already out of sight by the time Theo got through the Gates but the way the rocks crowded around him, he could tell there was just one path she could have taken. It felt so different to be among the Mountains that he had been seeing from a distance for so long. Up close, they were daunting, imposing. He felt like a child among giants, half-expecting one of them to turn its rocky face to him and pick him up by the neck. He forced himself to get a hold of his thoughts. After a week in Dream Country he knew what kind of illusions an apparently innocuous thought could lead to. He did not want to see what they led to here.

From behind a rock, a line of five little old women came out and blocked Theo's path. Their skirts went down to their feet and two of them carried large handbags on their wrists. They wore head-scarves wrapped under their chin and their heads were bowed.

'Um, excuse me . . .' Theo sucked in a breath.

The little old women had all raised their heads at once to show their faces. If you could call them faces. They were just skulls, flayed of skin and flesh with bared teeth and gaping eye sockets. All at once, they were hissing at him with a thousand different voices out of each one of their mouths and a cackle behind each word.

'Well, if it isn't the little godling—'

'Come to play—'

'Your brother won't be happy, no, no, not at all—'

'I can't wait to watch you burn—'

'*Senhor* 'Mare will give you to us tonight!'

Theo started to push past them but, before he could take a step, the backs of their skirts lifted up and long, green, crocodile tails whipped out and wrapped around his ankles and wrists.

'Hey!'

The monsters laughed and began to sing.

'*Nana, neném,*

Que a cuca vem pegar,

Papai foi na roça,

Mamãe foi trabalhar.'

They got closer and closer as they sang until Theo could smell their rancid, hot breath.

'Let me go!' he shouted—and to his surprise they did.

Their tails recoiled and they stopped singing as they stood to one side to let him pass. Uncertainly, he stepped forward, thinking they would make a grab for him again any second. But they let him walk away and as he did he heard one of them say, sulkily, 'Only because you belong to *Senhor* 'Mare.'

Theo breathed out in relief. For a second he had thought they might be his first Nightmare, but they had let him go, meaning that they must be some of the monsters he had heard occupied Torres's realm. Theo looked nervously at the hard boulders around him. If those creatures were the normal inhabitants of the Mountains, how much worse would the Nightmares be when they came?

I won't be here to find out. Get the boy, get out. And with that thought, Theo hurried forward to catch up with Fanta at last.

He only managed this because she had slowed down. In fact, she had practically come to a halt ahead of him, looking around in disgust at all that lay ahead of her.

The Pangaeans were returning here too. As Theo and Fanta watched them, they saw that it never took longer than five seconds from a mortal setting foot in the Mountains and their Nightmare beginning. Unlike in Dream Country, the illusions here weren't private affairs between the mortal and the god. Every Nightmare was visible.

A child screamed as a hairy, hunchbacked creature devoured his legs and made him watch.

A pregnant woman choked on a torrential rainfall of blood.

An old man clawed the skin from his own back as a thousand invisible furies scampered beneath his skin.

And while all this was happening, an audience of monsters watched and laughed. Black-robed *capelobos* threw rotten fruit at each new mortal as they appeared. Shaggy *lobisomens* wagged their tails and howled in amusement and approval.

'This is sick,' Fanta said. She looked around at everything that was happening, unblinking, as if she wanted to take in every detail.

Theo had to take a moment before he replied to make sure that he wouldn't vomit instead. He gulped. 'Yeah. But he can't help it.'

Shaking her head, Fanta turned her slow gaze to him in bemusement. 'You're still defending him. Even seeing all this.'

'You did some pretty messed up stuff to me too, Fanta.'

'But not to *mortals*. Never to mortals.'

'It's who he is,' Theo said. He honestly couldn't say why he was still defending Torres; all he knew was that Fanta's judgement of their brother's power, her *disgust*, felt wrong. Too personal.

Fanta shook her head again. 'It's who he's chosen to be. A single spider would count as a Nightmare for some people. Standing naked in a crowd. Do you really think he *has* to take it this far?' She gestured around. 'He likes it. He likes to watch people suffer. If we'd ever taken the time to see what he did to the mortals, we would have been more prepared for what he intended to do to us. We were always next on his list.'

She began walking again, dodging the screaming, writhing bodies of the Pangaeans, but walking right through the incorporeal illusions with barely a shiver. Theo hurried behind her.

'You're acting like I'm not planning to do anything about it,' he called.

She snorted. 'What, close his realm? That won't do anything, Theo. He needs to die. But I'm not asking you to do anything for me anymore, alright?'

He watched her with suspicion. 'You don't want me to kill Torres?'

'No. Because I'm going to do it.'

Theo opened his mouth to reply but at the same moment the ground lurched under their feet as the Gates groaned under their own weight. For the first time in a week he closed his eyes and slipped into his realm sight. His double sense of self returned to him, his *I and I*, and he greeted it like an old friend. It took a moment to adjust to his expanded vision; at first his eyes couldn't navigate the Mountains the way they could trace the familiar lines of Zion, but he soon narrowed in on what he wanted to see. The doorway he and Fanta had created to get through the Gates was struggling to close itself. Though the Horn and Ivory reached for each other like separated lovers, they couldn't quite make it. Theo returned his sight. The Majority were too deep into their Nightmares to have even noticed the earthquake but the monsters were sitting up and paying attention. Every last eye in the horde of their brother's creatures turned to look at Theo and Fanta.

'I think we should get away from here. Quickly,' Fanta suggested.

But before he could take a step, a large hand grabbed hold of Theo's sleeve. It was covered in grime and gore and he instinctively moved to shake it off until he looked up into the person's face.

'Theo, thank the All-Mother you're all right.'

Bede pulled him into a full embrace.

'Bede? I-I thought . . .' Theo's eyes filled with tears as he remembered the overflowing River and Bede diving under. 'I'm so sorry I left you, Bede. Please forgive me, I'm so sorry—'

Bede only laughed, in that deep throaty way of his that told Theo that everything was going to be alright.

When Theo pulled back he looked at his friend with wide eyes. Half of Bede's left foot was missing and he had only one arm. But most disturbing of all was his stomach: there was a hole in it about the size of a fist that went through from the front to the back. Fanta took a step away from him in disgust.

'What happened to you?' asked Theo.

Bede shook his head. 'Torres tried to have me killed. He sent me as a snack for his crows.'

Theo couldn't take his eyes off the blood-ringed hole in his friend's stomach. It was incredible. He didn't even feel sick looking at it because he couldn't actually believe it was really there. Tentatively, he reached out a finger and put it through the hole. He drew his hand back quickly before it went all the way through. *Now* he felt sick.

'Does it hurt?'

'Everything hurts here,' Bede said vaguely. 'I don't know how you got out but I'm glad you did. I thought you were dead.'

Theo clenched his fists and his jaw tightened. The more he looked at what his brother had done to his friend, the more he wanted to race up to the castle and find him. Instead he forced himself to relax. It was harder to use his Sleep energy when he wasn't at peace. He breathed out then placed the palms of his hands on Bede's stomach and concentrated. It was difficult, but the hole slowly began to stitch itself together.

'How did you get away from the crows?' Theo asked as he worked.

'They all left to go watch something Torres was doing, I don't know what. They must have thought they'd already finished me off. But you know what I always say: you can't keep a dead man down! While they were gone I managed to slip out. But it's taken me a long time to get down the mountain.' He hesitated. 'He brought both me and Iara to the castle after the Gates fell. You can see what he did to me but . . . I haven't seen Iara in a while.'

Theo frowned. 'Torres wouldn't have done anything to her.'

Theo hadn't known what to think about his friend's relationship with his brother when it started. He'd made sure to warn her to be careful and he knew she wouldn't have forgotten what he'd said, even after it was all over. She'd refused to tell him what had happened or even to mention Torres's name again. But now Theo almost felt glad to know that she was with Torres. No matter what else he did, Torres wouldn't hurt Iara, which made being with him the safest place to be in the Mountains.

Sweat was beading on his forehead now, from the amount of Sleep energy he was giving Bede, but the dead man's stomach was once again closed.

'I'm on my way to the castle now. I'll make sure to find her while I'm up there,' Theo added when Bede still looked unconvinced.

The big man perked up. 'I'll come with you.'

'No, Bede. I can't ask you to go back up there after what you've been through.'

'Lucky you didn't ask me then.'

Fanta sniffed. 'Don't tell me you let all your subjects speak to you this way, Theo,' she said. She cast a disdainful look at Bede, then walked away without saying anything else.

'I see she has your brother's charm. Are you sure you're related to those two?

How did she even get into this realm?' Bede asked, then without waiting for an answer, or even for his foot and arm to grow back, set off after her.

Theo caught his friend by his whole arm. He knew there would be no stopping the Duppy man if all he did was ask him to stay away, but Fanta mentioning his subjects had reminded him of a way that he could keep Bede safe while still having him be useful.

'Listen, Bede, have you seen many other Zions around?'

Bede's face twisted into an unreadable expression. 'I've seen them since I got away from the castle. They . . . it's bad, Theo. The way they're having Nightmares, you wouldn't be able to tell the difference between a Zion and one of these mortals,' he said, gesturing around.

'But you haven't had any Nightmares?'

Bede didn't even need to answer that. He just looked pointedly at his missing arm and Theo's cheeks flamed for having forgotten so easily.

'Yeah, right, that was probably enough.'

Bede nodded. 'Although I did notice something strange while Iara and I were in the castle. No Nightmares there either.'

'Really?' Theo thought for a moment. 'You think it's the boy? Ereon? Maybe he can do more than bring down the Gates, maybe he can dampen our abilities somehow.'

'Maybe. But Torres never let him out of his sight so he must have noticed. He wouldn't even give him to Iara.'

'Are you coming or not?' Fanta called from a distance ahead. She must have finally realised that Theo wasn't following her. He was surprised she even bothered to check back for him.

'We really should get going, Theo,' said Bede.

'Wait,' Theo said. 'I need you to do something for me. The Gates where me and Fanta came through are open but they're unstable. They could close at any moment. I need you to find as many Zions as you can and go with them into Dream Country.'

'What? Why?'

'Because I'm not sure what's going to happen when I get to Torres. I may be able to keep the Dream Country Gates up, but if for some reason I can't get our Gates up again, at least the Zions will be stuck with Dreams instead of Nightmares.'

Bede frowned. 'Is this a good idea, Theo? Are you sure that we can trust Fanta any more than Torres?'

'I've spent the whole week with her. I haven't seen her do anything bad,' Theo lied.

'That doesn't mean that she *didn't* do anything bad, just because you didn't see it.'

Theo smiled slightly. 'If a tree falls in a forest and no one is around to hear it, does it make a sound?'

Bede smiled too, more enthusiastically than seemed possible for someone who had half his limbs missing. The two friends embraced and then Theo watched him limp off, the stump of his left arm swinging to keep him balanced, carrying the escape message for all the Zionese Minors and the Duppies.

'What took you so long?' Fanta said irritably when he finally caught her up.

Luckily, she didn't seem to notice that he said nothing in reply. For now, it seemed best not to tell her that he had sent hundreds of refugees over to her realm, uninvited.

Hopefully, he thought, *she'll never have to find out.*

They would find Torres and Ereon, send the boy back to the island, close the Mountains to mortals for a while, let Rogan rebuild the Gates—and then everything would go back to normal. Theo wrapped his arms around himself as he passed through another of the many dark shadows cast by the Mountains. He shivered.

Optimism felt wrong in a place like this.

CHAPTER TWENTY-SEVEN

'*Senhor!*' Abilo burst out into the dining room in a flurry of feathers, almost crashing into Torres as he tried to stop himself at the last second. '*CAAW!*'

'*Mãe de todos*, Abilo, where's the fire!'

'I'm sorry, *Senhor*. But you asked me to inform you immediately if there was any activity at the Gates,' the bird reminded him as he righted himself onto his talons. 'You said that only my life was more important and maybe not even that.'

'So? What's happening at the Gates then?'

'Your sister, *Senhor*. She's in the Mountains. And Theo is with her. They came together from Dream Country.'

'What!' Torres jumped to his feet. 'How did this happen, why wasn't I told earlier!'

'I'm sorry, *Senhor*, the crows on duty were distracted, too relaxed. They aren't used to all the Dreaming you kn—*CAAW!*'

This last squawk came in response to the bottle that Torres hurled at him.

'Meaning of course, *Senhor*, that their distraction was entirely their own fault, a result of their innate laziness. They will be punished.'

But even as Abilo spoke, his master was letting his mind go out of the castle to survey his realm. He directed his attention to the borders where the post-Majoracle crowds of the Majority were entering the realm. There were more of them than Torres had ever had to deal with before, since those who should have gone into Zion found themselves here instead. It made it harder to sort through their faces to find who he wanted.

Torres brought his attention back to the castle and growled. Abilo watched him nervously.

'Well, don't just flap there, you fool! Send out some crows and don't let them get to the castle before I come back. *Vai!*'

Torres took Ereon to the back of the castle where he left him in the care of the kitchen crows.

'I'll be back,' he whispered to the boy in his basket. But he found himself still hesitating to move away. If he could have been sure that he could have kept the child safe, he would have taken him with him. But he couldn't. And it broke his heart to hear his Magus's tears as he left him behind. Nevertheless, he hardened himself against it. There was only one way Theo could get into Dream Country and Fanta into *Os Pesadelos*. He let the anger inside him grow until it was so hot it almost physically hurt, but all feeling fled from his mind before he made it to the front door.

One day you'll push them too far.

Senhora Barrera's warning rang suddenly in his mind as he froze at the sight of what was waiting for him.

The monsters had seized the castle.

Besta-fera, cuca, jurupari and *mapinguari* blocked his path. Some of them had crows pinned to the ground beneath them. They were all growling and hissing and spitting at him though not one of them dared to get too close. A pack of reeking *boitatás* were obviously the ringleaders of the rebellion.

It was hard for Torres to distinguish between the twenty or so *boitatás* that faced him. But one smelled distinctly more terrible than the rest and he could only assume stench was a sign of rank. It was to this one he addressed himself.

'Can I help you?' he asked calmly. He had to be careful. In her visions *Senhora* Barrera had not seen any further than this.

'We want our Nightmares back. It was bad enough when you started making fewer of them,' said the leader.

'Now you're making Dreams as well,' another monster interjected.

The others in the group began to howl and urinate down their own legs.

Torres raised his voice to be heard above the noise. 'If you're unhappy, why don't you find the Dream Goddess and complain to her? She's the one who gave me the Dreams.'

One of the monsters gave a high-pitched yelp of anger. 'You mock us!'

'I assure you I do not. In fact,' Torres almost ruined it all, by laughing, imagining his sister actually *handing over* her Dreams to him, 'you should have got here a little sooner, I've already sent my crows after her. But if you lot can get there first and bring her to me,'—he hesitated—'*and* my brother, I will guarantee that my previous plans for the state of Nightmares in my realm will not change.'

The leader hissed at the rest of the group before they could get too excited. He turned to Torres, his eyes twitching in excitement. 'Do you promise?'

'On my honour,' Torres said, holding up his left hand and creating the sign of the Major, as if he were swearing on a *Theologos*. 'I promise you the Dream Goddess will not stand in our way any longer.'

The monsters bounced into the air, scrambling over each other in their rush to the door. Torres called to them before they reached it.

'Alive! I want my siblings alive.'

He watched them go.

* * *

Torres sent the crows ahead of him when he found Rogan. He saw everything through his realm sight.

The old god was walking with his head down so he couldn't have seen the sky darken with crow wings. He was taken by surprise by the murder of crows as they came beating down on him with a ferocity that could only have come from a direct order. He made an effort to defend himself, shaking his horns from side to side to hit the birds, but the crows were not as unprepared as they had been during Iara's attack in the castle. They attacked in alternating groups, diving in to claw at his face and quickly retreating before he had time to toss his horns at them. By the time Torres arrived, Rogan was on his hands and knees, mouth foaming through gritted teeth, blood dripping from cuts on his face and hands.

'Aren't you going to bow, Gatekeeper?' Torres asked and kicked his arms out from under him, forcing him lower.

Rogan groaned with his face against the rocks.

'Correct me if I'm wrong, Gatekeeper—get up, you idiot! Look at me when I'm talking to you!—correct me if I'm wrong but is it not your *job* to keep people *out* of my realm? Actually, no, excuse me, I *am* wrong, I'll correct myself. *People* are allowed in my realm, it's *gods* that you're supposed to keep out. More specifically, two gods in particular. Do you know who I'm talking about?'

'Yes . . . Milord.'

'Who?'

'. . . Milady Fanta and Milord Theo.'

'And where exactly are *your lady Fanta* and *your lord Theo* at this moment in time, Gatekeeper?'

Rogan looked down at the ground he had just raised himself from. His blood had stained the rock there in a pattern like raindrops and he stared at it for a while. Torres waited for him to answer. He was waiting patiently, as if he really didn't know the answer to his question and Rogan was the only one who could give it to him. They had been in this position many times before, in fact, Torres and Rogan in a classroom years ago, when the same face which cowered from him now, only younger, had looked down at him, even then unable to answer all his questions. Torres had waited then too.

'Your siblings are in *Os Pesadelos*, Milord.'

Torres sighed, as if he were disappointed that there wasn't a more exciting reason why the sky was blue.

'You let them in.'

'No, Milord, they let themselves in.'

He laughed. 'At least have the decency to value my intelligence a little, Rogan. We can't get into each other's realms.'

'But as I understand it, Milord, your actions have made some changes as to whose realm is whose. This is half-Zion now.'

Torres clenched his jaw. 'So what's your explanation for how he got into Dream Country in the first place?'

Rogan hesitated. 'I let him in.'

'Ah! Finally, a confession!'

'But that's all I did,' Rogan added.

'And the Gates just opened up to Fanta because she made them feel comfortable?'

For the first time since the crows got to him, Rogan met Torres's eye with a kind of steadiness that made the younger god almost take a step back. A cut on his forehead bled into Rogan's eye.

'You've been making Dreams.'

Torres stood up straighter. 'So?'

'So, every time you make a Dream instead of a Nightmare, the Nightmare still has to go somewhere—and it goes to the person whom you took the Dream from.'

'You mean . . . Fanta's been making Nightmares?'

Torres knew that he shouldn't find it funny but he laughed anyway.

Rogan remained serious. 'It's more than that. The realms recognise the ability, not the person. She's been making Nightmares, so the Gates let her into *Os Pesadelos*.'

Torres considered this. 'And I could go into Dream Country?'

'I wouldn't advise it.'

'It's a good thing I wasn't asking for your advice then.'

'That boy, Torres. He can't stay here. The Majoracle is over, he shouldn't still be in *Os Pesadelos*.'

'So now you concern yourself with who should or shouldn't be in my realm? I suppose my siblings told you to say all this to me.'

Before Rogan could reply, Torres stepped past him to face the Gates. He felt that Horn and Ivory feeling, as always, pushing and pulling him in different directions. Could he really just walk through? It seemed too easy.

Torres imagined Dream Country's Gates opening up for him. It was not a new image to his mind—it was something he'd been Dreaming about for years.

He reached out a hand and the Gates began to pull apart.

His breath caught in his throat. It was right there. He could smell the clean air of the realm crossing into *Os Pesadelos* like it had been waiting to find a way in all along. Finally, there was nothing to stop him walking right in.

'Torres,' Rogan coughed, 'I meant what I said. Though you and Fanta are changing, there's still time to make things right again. But not if you go over there. Think about it; if this becomes her realm and that becomes yours, you won't be able to come back.'

Torres hesitated. If he went over there now he would have everything he had ever wanted, he would have Dream Country—and without the complications of the other two realms that bringing down the Gates would have brought. One step. That's all it would take. Then he could be the God of Dreams and leave everything else behind, the past, the Nightmares, his very name. But . . . it would also mean leaving Ereon behind and, with Fanta on her way to the castle, he couldn't risk that. What would happen if she got her hands on the boy while he was still wearing both the Horn and Ivory? Would she be immune, like he was? Would their abilities begin to swap back again? Torres shuddered at the thought of being made a Nightmare God again, after everything.

No, Rogan was right. He had to go back for Ereon.

But the air in Dream Country was so tempting, it was as if it was taking him by the hand and pulling him through.

'You let Theo into Dream Country, right?' he asked. 'So you can let me out after I've gone through. I just want to look around.'

He began to take a step forward.

'No, Torres,' Rogan said gently. 'You just want to be her. But you can't be. You never will.'

'Shut up.'

'You're different, Torres. You can't change what you are.'

'I'm only what I am because people made me that way!'

Rogan shook his head. 'You were born this way. That's why I told Theo not to let you take a Magus all those years ago.'

Torres spun around. He stared uncomprehendingly at his old mentor for a few moments. 'That wasn't you. It was Fanta. Fanta did that to me.'

'You wanted to believe she did,' Rogan said. 'You wanted an excuse to justify your jealousy. You've always been jealous of her, Torres. Ever since you were young, dropping your own toys so you could snatch up hers. I saw the evil in you then, even before all this. I saw it then and I see it now. I'm just telling you what I see.'

All of a sudden something inside Torres snapped. 'Well then, if only I was as wise as you, Rogan! If only I could *see* what you *see.*'

He lunged forward and grabbed Rogan by the back of his hair, pulling him forward with one hand. The old god cried out but couldn't escape Torres's vicious grip. With his other hand, Torres reached out in one swift motion and dug his fingers into his old mentor's eye socket. Rogan screamed in horror as his left eye watched his right eye come away in Torres's fingers.

He would have preferred to have taken Rogan's all-seeing left eye but in the heat of the moment he had ended up with the normal right one. He held it gently for a second, holding it up to his own eye to examine it with mild interest. It felt gelatinous between his fingers. Then, disgusted, he tossed it onto the ground, where the crows began fighting to pick it up.

Rogan dropped to his knees, screaming, his hands clutching his empty, raw eye socket.

With a last, lingering look at the opening between *Os Pesadelos* and Dream Country, Torres turned and walked away, not waiting to see how the crows eventually managed to divide the Gatekeeper's eyeball up into equal shares.

CHAPTER TWENTY-EIGHT

If Torres had chosen the location of his castle for its inaccessibility, Theo had to grudgingly admit that he had done a fantastic job. He and Fanta spent so much time wandering around the base of the third mountain looking for a path that wasn't too steep to climb, that Theo was sure his brother must already be aware of their presence. He doubted that any advantage of surprise gained by going through Dream Country remained; he still had a whole mountain to scale across unfamiliar terrain with just the vague hope that Torres had decided to sit and wait for him. Perhaps his brother was even watching him and Fanta now through his realm sight.

The idea of his brother's eyes on his back made Theo so uncomfortable that he began flinching at the sound of every rolling pebble.

Fanta turned to him in exasperation. 'Would you stop that? You're making *me* nervous.' She pushed aside a small boulder that blocked their path, her neck muscles straining as she worked, but when Theo made to help she shooed him away, like an annoying insect.

'You're already exhausted. Your dead friend looked better than you do. It seems like we can go up this way—but if there's anything else in our path let me deal with it, okay?'

Theo didn't protest. He could imagine how terrible he looked, even if he hadn't noticed it when he used his realm sight earlier. His days in Dream

Country hadn't done him any kindnesses; his normally slim frame was now positively bony, his cheeks hollow, his dreads crusted with sand and unravelling at the ends. Until this week, he'd always walked at the pace of a casual stroll; now he hurried along in clumsy strides like he had demons at his back.

Fanta climbed over another obstruction in their path that she couldn't move this time. Theo struggled to follow her but his arms wouldn't allow him to pull himself over.

'I could use a hand,' he said between heavy breaths.

'Sorry, I can't touch you right now. I've got Ivory on.'

It was another five minutes before he got over and they could continue on.

'What's the Ivory for?' Theo asked. 'A weapon?'

'Defence, actually. I don't want to risk having any Nightmares while I'm here . . . or giving any.'

Theo went silent for a moment. 'Everything will go back to normal soon.'

'Or a better version of normal,' Fanta said.

Their path snaked up the mountain at a gradual incline but, even so, after a few more minutes of climbing, the backs of Theo's legs began to burn; at some corners he almost had to go on his hands and knees just to keep himself from falling backwards.

A sudden cacophony of hisses tore through the still mountain air. At first he didn't even look up to see what it was—they had already passed worse-sounding Nightmares—but Fanta came to a sudden halt, forcing him to stop behind her on the narrow path.

'What—what is that thing?' she stammered.

Theo looked over her shoulder and froze. A creature that looked like a snake with stumpy legs and fiery eyes stood upright on the path in front of them. As they watched, it licked the flaps of its lips and blinked slowly with see-through, veiny eyelids.

'Is it real?' Theo asked. They couldn't afford to be delayed by a Nightmare, no matter how hideous it was.

At that moment more of the creatures came crawling down the mountainside. One slid ahead of the rest and joined the first.

'You take sister, I'll take brother,' the new creature croaked.

'I think they're real,' said Fanta.

Theo was already taking a step backwards towards escape, when a taunting voice echoed in his ear.

Coward! Coward!

Theo looked around. Fanta clearly hadn't spoken.

'What was that?' Theo asked.

'What?' Fanta hissed. She hadn't moved and the creatures hadn't attacked yet. More than likely, so long as they didn't try to run or make any sudden moves, they would be okay.

But Theo couldn't stay still. 'I heard something. It sounded like—'

'*CAAW, CAAW!*'

Theo's head jerked up towards the sky. And at that moment, the monsters lunged.

'Run!' Fanta shouted.

They stumbled backwards, the way that they had come. But half the slinky creatures slid past the fleeing gods, blocking their escape route. Theo spun around, but no matter where he looked he saw death closing in on him.

'What do we do?' he cried, his voice high with panic.

Coward! Coward!

'Shut up!'

'What?' Fanta asked in confusion. 'I—'

But before she could say any more the crows were on them, beaks and wings and claws battering every inch of Theo's body. He screamed. Someone else screamed too.

Fanta, his mind vaguely recognised.

He was drowning in pain; he couldn't breathe. He felt his mind separating itself from his body, abandoning ship like a rat. His second sight took over. From the height of the sky, he felt like one of his attackers, looking down on his own struggling body underneath an agitated heap of crows. He saw Fanta, struggling just as hard as he was against the crows and, as he watched, her skin turned grey, her cheeks collapsed in on themselves, her lips crusted over, and her hair matted together. Flies appeared, swarming around her, attracted by the stench of rot.

Theo forced himself to think. *One—Fanta's corpse; Two—that voice in my head; Three—I'm not breathing. That's three things that aren't real—it's just a Nightmare.*

With that thought, Theo took control of the Nightmare, just as the last of Fanta's body disappeared beneath the bodies of the scavengers.

He called his mind back, like a stray dog. It came shyly and his body shuddered to receive it back. He tried to calm down enough to remember himself. He needed to do more than the healing he had performed on himself and Bede. The last time he had done something like this had been with Ereon. He reached out and found the crows' minds. There were so many of them and he wasn't as strong now as he once was, but he could still do something to give himself a fighting chance; it made it easier that he was in physical contact with all of them as they piled on top of him. So he clutched at the crows' active minds and with all his strength tugged them down, dragging them from wakefulness into Sleep.

Their bodies fell limp against him, almost crushing him with their weight, suffocating him under feathers. Then he felt something grab hold of his ankles. Crow's talons? Monster's claws? He thrashed against his new captor with the last of his energy—Fanta pulled him out into the open air.

'Are you okay?' she asked, clearing away the rest of the Sleeping birds.

Theo could only nod as he gasped for breath.

Coward, the Nightmare voice said, fainter now.

'Why aren't you asleep too?' Theo asked as she helped him up.

'I was still wearing my Ivory when you did that.'

'But you're not now,' he pointed out obviously, as her hand lay bare against his arm.

Something dark flashed in Fanta's eyes. 'I took it off.'

'You took our Nightmares,' a spitting voice said from behind Fanta.

Theo sagged. He'd thought it was over.

In the confusion of battle, the crows must have inflicted damage on their own comrades as the Nightmare creatures limped towards them, whining in pain.

'Get behind me, Theo,' Fanta said calmly.

'What? No, we—'

'Behind me!'

He barely had time to step out of the way before she was flying past him, clashing in mid-air with one of Torres's monsters. He watched in amazement and then, suddenly, blind panic. Did she intend to fight these creatures on her own? He rushed forward to help but, before he could get too close, a wall of hissing, chittering creatures blocked his path. He backed up to the rock face. Now they were toying with him, snickering with laughter as they stalked closer. Behind them, he could see their leader's sharp teeth were already bared as he pinned Fanta to the ground.

'No!' he cried out.

But at that moment Fanta twisted her arm free and held her hand against the creature's head and everything went still. The creature couldn't seem to understand what was happening, why its prey was suddenly petting it like a lapdog. Sensing their leader's stillness, all the monsters surrounding Theo turned their heads to see what was happening. A moment later a thunderclap boomed in the air and Fanta's foe fell onto his back, howling as a Nightmare erupted out of his chest like a spring flower.

Theo recognised it as a Nightmare immediately, as the air around him suddenly went cold and his stomach lurched. The Nightmare swirled above them as red fog before its shape fully formed, rolling into a giant ball, a miniature sun with lightning and fire crackling around it, pulsing around the edges. Theo ducked as a stream of flame shot over his head. The monsters went crazy, running about with their eyes closed, screaming for mercy. As Theo dropped to the ground, narrowly avoiding the line of fire, one of the creatures jumped over the side of the mountain as the Nightmare turned in their direction.

'The *morte-de-ouro* has returned! The *morte-de-ouro* has returned!'

'Run away!'

Theo was amazed to see that the creatures couldn't tell the difference between their leader's Nightmare and a real *morte-de-ouro*. They scattered in such a rush that they trampled obliviously over Theo where he lay, pounding him with their many feet.

He only felt it safe to lift his head again when he felt the residual heat of the *morte-de-ouro*'s last eruption cooling on his back. He got to his knees and warily looked around then gave a sigh of relief. They had gone. He was alone.

He went tense. He looked around again.

He was *alone*.

'Fanta?' Theo called. 'Fanta!'

He didn't care if the creatures heard him and came back. He ran in panic to the place where he had last seen his sister, but all he found there was her discarded Ivory necklace. Heart pounding in his ears, he opened his realm sight and scoured the Mountains.

There was no sign of Fanta anywhere.

I have to find her, he thought. *No*, another part of his mind replied almost immediately. *Get to Torres. Find her later.*

He picked the necklace up by its string, holding it carefully between two fingers. He couldn't leave it here. Who knew what the monsters would find to do with it? Swallowing his revulsion, he dropped the necklace into his back pocket. It wasn't touching him, but he could feel its proximity, sucking his energy from him like a leech.

He had to get going. The crows that carpeted the mountain behind him were beginning to rouse. At his feet were some spots of blood—Fanta's or the monster's, he didn't know. He stepped over them and continued up the mountainside.

He was halfway there.

CHAPTER TWENTY-NINE

The journey was slow but, to his surprise, nothing else came to meet him.

Crows and monsters. Is that the best you have, Torres?

As Theo's feet dragged him higher and higher, he forced himself not to think of his sister. He had to think about what was waiting ahead of him, not what he had left behind.

He found himself grateful for the Ivory that he carried; even though he felt its power radiating through the fabric of his pocket, making his legs numb, he knew it kept the Nightmares away. But his progress was slow. He stumbled even more than he had when he first entered the Mountains. Back then he'd only been tired and Dream-weary—now he was bruised, cut, and half-baked by a Nightmare.

As he neared the peak of the mountain and Torres's castle came into sight, he felt no relief, or anything else, at having finally arrived. If, at that moment, his heavy eyelids hadn't slipped shut for a moment, engaging his realm sight, he would have forgotten completely why he was even there, why he had put himself through this last week of hell. But his eyelids did close and he found himself looking down, not on himself and the Mountains, but on Zion.

His home, his sanctuary, his place of rest. His heart ached for it.

By the time he opened his eyes again, the God of Sleep knew exactly why he was there.

He found a stick on the ground and cleared a patch of earth with his foot.

ROGAN, he scrawled in large letters. He hadn't seen the Gatekeeper when he looked through his realm sight, he had been too tired to really look for him, but he knew the Gatekeeper's eye would eventually be drawn to his own name written on the ground. As long as he didn't find it too late. Theo had a message for him.

When he got to the mountain's peak, he found a little girl there waiting for him.

'Hello,' she said, moving so that he couldn't get past her.

Theo paused. The little girl spoke with a sweet smile on her face and she didn't seem dangerous. Her face was hidden under layers of dirt and Theo couldn't tell if her ruddy colour was more filth or her natural complexion. There was something familiar about her.

She cocked her head to one side, her eyes filling with laughter. 'Don't you talk?'

'Yes. Hello. Who are you?'

'I'm Nanse Minor. I'm a goddess.' Her eyes sparkled again. 'You're supposed to bow to me.'

Theo was too weary to argue. He bowed.

She laughed and began dancing around him in dizzying circles.

'Come on, I'll take you to Torres, he's been waiting. I have too, for ages and ages. What took you so long anyway?'

'I was delayed.'

'Well, yeah, obviously, or you wouldn't be late. But why were you *de-layed*?' she pronounced the word carefully, as if she had struggled with it before. 'And where's your sister? Is she dead?'

Theo's head whirled from all the questions that he didn't have the answers to.

'I don't know,' he said as a general response to them all.

'I thought you would have killed her. Or she would have killed you. That would have been fun.' Nanse sighed with all the cares of someone twice her age. 'But you're here now. What are you going to do when you get to the castle?'

Theo shook his head. His mind felt foggy. 'Torres . . .' he began uncertainly. 'I'm here for Torres. He . . . did something.'

Why was it so hard to think?

'Are you really sure you want to go in?' Nanse asked.

Am I really sure?

'Maybe you should just go home.'

It was as if someone set a live electric wire against his skull. *Home.* Who had been the last person to send him home? Wasn't there another little girl once, that he saw through some gates, pockmarked with Pangaean Plague—no, that was wrong. That was *another* little girl. How many had there been?

Why do I always do what they say?

'You,' Theo breathed out, as realisation dawned, bringing him back to himself, 'what are you doing to me?'

Nanse's eyes widened in obvious surprise. 'You remember?' she couldn't stop herself from asking, then her hands flew to her mouth as if she could take the words back in.

'I-I didn't. I kept forgetting, but . . . I was going to come back to Zion, before Fanta found me in Dream Country. Then something happened and I changed my mind. And I was by the Gates, I was close, before I had that Nightmare, but then I felt like I was going in the wrong direction, like home was the other way. Something happened . . . I spoke to someone. Was that you?'

'No,' Nanse said quickly.

Theo's eyes narrowed. 'It was. What did you do to me!'

He lunged forward. He only intended to grab her by the shoulders, to stop her from escaping, but before he could touch her he suddenly found himself on the ground.

I promise I won't hurt you.

It was his own voice, echoing in his ears; the promise he had made the very first time he saw Nanse, when he had just wanted to stop her from crying. Now, Nanse's face loomed over his prone body.

'You can't break your promises. Not with me. And it's not very nice of you to try to hurt me. I'm only a child. I think you should apologise.'

'N—' Something clicked in Theo's brain. His first instinct was to struggle against it but soon all he could do was relax. It felt right. Like coming home. 'I'm sorry.'

'I forgive you.' Nanse beamed prettily. 'Now, tell me what you're going to do once you get inside the castle. Are you going to fight your brother? Kill him?'

'No. Fanta wanted to, but I won't.'

'Well, you should at least try!' the goddess said, stamping her foot. 'You can't come all this way and not at least *try*.'

Theo was shaking his head, but it felt like a movement disconnected from himself, like watching a stranger dance. 'No.'

'Stop saying no to me!' Suddenly five or six faces flashed across the features of the little girl, boys and girls flickering past in the blink of an eye. Nanse's former face reappeared and she took a deep breath. 'You don't mean it do you? You're just not thinking straight? Right?'

'I-I don't . . . I can't think . . .'

'Do you want me to think for you?'

He had no willpower. He nodded vacantly and Nanse grinned, pleased.

'Look over there,' she instructed.

His body reacted to her words as to an irresistible urge. He followed the line of her finger and found himself looking over the sheer edge of the cliff. The castle door was right behind him now, but Theo no longer thought of it.

He looked out over Torres's realm. The mountains in the distance seemed to have been painted in greyscale, the closer ones only slightly less monochromatic. There was no movement anywhere; the whole realm seemed rigid with cadaverous beauty.

'It's pretty,' Nanse said. 'Listen to that.'

Theo strained his ears and heard what she wanted him to. It sounded like a waterfall. He looked down expecting to see water coming out of the cliff face but there was nothing.

'You're sad,' Nanse told him and he nodded.

'You don't want to live anymore,' his mind told him and he agreed.

'You should jump,' he thought to himself and one foot was already over the edge.

No, no, no. Theo thought desperately. He reached out for the part of himself that Nanse was holding down. His other foot was inching forward. Part of him recognised that what she was doing was not so different from what he did—it was just that instead of putting the body to Sleep, she suppressed the sense of self and free will and replaced it with something that was all her. A gust of wind almost blew him back to safety, but his foot persisted in going forwards. He just had to wake himself up. But trying to wake yourself up once you've realised you're Sleeping is like trying to stop a sneeze once you've noticed it coming. If anything, it only makes it more inevitable. His body moved slowly as it tried to fight against what it was being told that it wanted to do, but Nanse was not impatient. Out of the corner of his eye he caught her mimicking his movements in slow motion, making faces, and dancing around. She had changed bodies again.

Theo poked his unconscious mind, trying to stir it into life. For a moment there was a sluggish sense of self-awareness, then it disappeared and Nanse was there again. Theo's second foot was half over the edge now but before he could move forward anymore, Nanse stopped him. She was playing with him, just waiting now for him to tip over. He made one last desperate attempt to wake himself up but he already knew it was too late. The ridiculousness of it, of all he had been through, getting across Dream Country, fighting the crows and the monsters and the Nightmare, losing Fanta—only to be stopped at the very door of the castle, by a child! It was almost funny. He would have laughed if Nanse had let him.

The wind reversed itself and nudged him, almost encouragingly, at his back. He tipped forward. Before he fell his head went light with vertigo and his mind was shocked awake by the sudden sensation of falling. His arms shot out, too late, trying to save himself. He clutched at the air as he fell, but he fell all the same. A familiar feeling swept through him, a loud feeling which muted the sound of Nanse's laughter. He was going to have one last Nightmare before he died.

As the Sleep God plummeted off the highest peak of *Os Pesadelos*, he felt the half-Zionese wind trying to hold him up, forming a bed of air under him, but the wind native to this realm resisted the attempt and he continued to fall between its chill insistent fingers. The familiar sensation pulsed in Theo's heart, stopping his scream there. He felt his tears spread across his face, stinging his cuts, whipping off his cheeks as he fell. He decided to close his eyes. He would rather die in darkness than in terror.

And then he landed on feathers. He felt the simultaneous beat of a giant heart and two wings drumming through his body. He opened his eyes and another scream, this time of joy, escaped his lips. He was flying! On the back of the mango-bird that had appeared in his first Dream.

Nightmares in Dream Country and Dreams in the Mountains. Theo couldn't help but laugh out loud and the bird trilled in response. '*Kirrrrbeee!*'

'Thank you, Kirby!' Theo yelled.

But she was taking him the wrong way, away from the mountain and the castle. Theo tried to pull on her feathers to direct her but it was like trying to harness the wind. Desperately, he tried to think of a way to turn the bird around or just get her to set him down before the illusion ended and he fell out of the sky. And then he remembered the Ivory in his pocket. This was the first Dream he'd had that wasn't painful—the Ivory was close enough to him to suck up the excess Dream energy, even more than when Arielle had been wearing it. Fanta had told him that Dream energy was attracted to Ivory and here he was riding on the back of a Dream. He pulled the necklace out and waved it in front of the rainbow bird's beak.

'This way! This way, Kirby!' he called, leading her with the Ivory as he might lead a donkey with an apple.

Kirby turned around, flying a full circle and setting him down on the edge of the mountain. This time he was in no danger of falling as he looked down on the little goddess.

'No fair!' Nanse said, pouting, as she watched him land.

But now when she looked at him she didn't see anything to amuse her. In her fright she flickered between four faces in rapid succession, one of them pockmarked with Pangaean Plague, then spun around and fled to the castle. As Theo jumped off Kirby's back the bird snapped up the Ivory in her beak and before he could snatch it back, both bird and necklace disappeared with a pop.

He ran after Nanse. She tried to close the door on him but he got there just in time, lodging himself in the doorframe and stumbling inside as the resistance behind the door suddenly disappeared.

He looked around the empty entryway: there was no sign of Nanse Minor. But from behind a double-arched doorway of solid metal, next to a winding staircase, there came the sound of a baby crying.

CHAPTER THIRTY

Torres didn't bow when he saw him, but he did tilt his head slightly in deference to his younger brother, as Nightmare must defer to Sleep.

Ereon was lying on the long dining table behind Torres. Theo closed the door behind him, his hands shaking as he pushed his hair off his face and locked eyes with his brother across a distance that seemed a lot further than twenty or so paces.

'You going to sit down or just stand there?' Torres said finally as he resumed his own seat.

Theo sat. He was too tired to remain standing. He chose the seat at the furthest end of the table from Torres and for a moment just allowed himself the pleasure of being still. Graciously, Torres allowed him his time. When he was ready, Theo raised his head to hear Torres speak.

'You don't look too good, *irmão.*'

'Well. There was a little girl outside who tried to kill me.'

Torres smiled. 'Yeah. I saw.'

'She wanted me to try to kill you too.'

Torres nodded but showed no other reaction. 'Sounds like her. She is the Goddess of Chaos, after all. She has fun with it, messing with people, getting inside their heads just because she can. But you look terrible anyway.'

Theo shrugged. 'I've come a long way.'

'Yeah. Through Dream Country, I hear.' Torres hesitated and then in a voice that was barely a whisper he asked, 'What was it like?'

Theo shook his head, sitting up straight in his chair. This wasn't what he was here for. 'I came for the boy.'

'You can't have him,' Torres said simply.

'Torres, he's destroying the realms.'

'He's not destroying the realms, he's destroying the Gates.'

'And what makes you think he'll just stop there?' Theo asked with exasperation. Was it possible that Torres really didn't see it? Didn't see the harm he had caused?

Torres shook his head. 'You should be thanking me. We were never supposed to be separated. I'm putting things back to how they were. We'll be one realm again, *Os Pesadelos*, Zion . . . and Dream Country. Tell me what it was like. Please.'

Theo sighed. His body still felt heavy with the memory of the journey and it sagged at the question. What was Dream Country like? He thought back. When he had first entered the realm, he had wondered at its plain appearance. Now, Theo thought he finally understood it.

'Dream Country was beautiful, but . . . difficult.'

Torres laughed. 'Like its goddess,' he said, and Theo laughed without thinking, then frowned as he reminded himself what he was there for.

Torres laughed again. 'You've changed, *irmão*. It's happened quickly, but you're definitely different. I like it.'

'And you haven't changed?'

He shrugged. 'You know me. I'm like the sunrise. Predictable.'

Unnatural, Theo thought instead. *Broken*. Enough was enough. Theo got up from his seat and walked around the table.

'Give him to me, Torres,' he said, holding out his hands.

Torres stared back at him, unblinking. 'You never told me Rogan was the one who said I couldn't have a Magus.'

Theo stopped in his tracks as he tried to keep up with his brother's train of thought.

'It never seemed worth telling you,' he said eventually. 'I knew it would only make you angrier if you knew it didn't come from me. And I was right. If *this* was how you were going to react, I was right. Give him to me.'

'Take him,' Torres said. He pushed his chair back so that he was no longer between Theo and the baby.

Theo looked at the boy. He seemed happy enough, unharmed by his week in the Mountains, but there was no way for Theo to be sure. There was no way that he would be able to see the mental damage that had been inflicted on his Magus.

A week of Nightmares.

Theo shuddered. But he didn't take him.

'He's wearing Horn, isn't he?'

Torres merely smiled. 'Only one way to find out. Take him.'

'Take the Horn off.'

'Take him!'

'Enough, Torres!' Theo snapped. 'Give me my Magus, now!'

Torres only looked at him for a second and then his whole face contorted with anger and disgust.

'*Your* Magus? You would actually try to give me an order, while you're standing here dying in my realm? You've only been here for a day and look at you,' he spat.

'You didn't do this to me,' Theo pointed out and that made him angrier.

'No, I didn't,' he agreed. '*Fanta* did it, so I didn't have to. *Dreams* did this to you. She's not special, you know. I can do the same things she does. I can do Dreams and desire just as well as she can.' He laughed.

Someone tapped Theo on the shoulder and he turned around. Fanta was standing behind him.

'Fanta!' he said. He felt the air rush out of him in relief as he looked his sister in the eye. She was here, she wasn't dead, she was safe . . .

But then Theo looked down and saw that she was naked. It took him a while to understand what he was seeing; for a wild second he wondered if the *morte-de-ouro* had burnt off her clothes. Then a beam of light came out from behind a cloud and swept in through the high windows behind them, and when it touched Fanta he could see that her flesh was transparent and misty around the edges. This was not his sister. This was a half-formed Dream made by someone who had only ever dealt in Nightmares.

'Oh no,' Theo whispered.

'Oh, yes,' The Nightmare replied.

The illusory Dream Goddess swayed her hips as she began to circle Theo like a predator. She smiled, showing a hint of fangs at the corners of her mouth, licking her lips in a way the real Fanta never would. When the thing got too close Theo felt his senses fill with her phantom scent and he became dizzy. This wasn't desire, this was fear. He was revolted by this anti-Fanta, stripped by Torres of her personality, her family relation, and her clothes. He had nowhere to go; the wall and the windows were behind him, she was in front and Torres stood with his arms folded on his left, looking so confident that Theo felt there was nothing he could do. But by backing him into a corner the anti-Fanta had also pushed him into the shadows, away from the sunlight that always drained his power. He felt his power surge inside him, still weaker than before, but hopefully enough.

Despite the overwhelming fear still coursing through his body, he forced himself to relax. His eyelids fluttered and his breathing slowed as he sought out the nearest mind. Torres's mind.

He hadn't used his power on his siblings in over thirteen years, but as soon as he touched Torres's mind it felt familiar, how he imagined his own mind would look in the reflection of a warped mirror. Before Theo could do anything, Torres noticed his brother's presence inside him—and panicked. With as much force as possible he threw his own power outwards, not towards Theo but towards his illusion.

Roses and vines sprouted suddenly at the anti-Fanta's feet, climbing up her legs. One plant shot out and wrapped around Theo's waist, pulling him away from the wall. The room was filled with the nauseating smell of perfume but Theo didn't let go of his brother's mind, he kept hold of it until the Sleep paralysis took over Torres's body and he froze. Even then, though Torres's body was still, his mind was still pushing his illusion towards Theo. And Theo could feel his brother's frustration building at having allowed himself to be trapped.

Anger was rising inside Torres, bringing with it something dark and long suppressed. A shadow. Theo held it back as long as he could but most of his defences were already gone. It was something inside Torres that had been waiting for release for a long time, like a long-held breath and now, finally, finally, he released that breath—and the Nightmare came out from behind it.

A horde of bloodthirsty mortals burst through the dining room doors, their faces pale and starved, and when they caught the scent of Theo they ran towards him, arms outstretched like he was the last morsel of food on a dead planet.

A booming voice, coming from nowhere, shook the glass out of the windows. LET ME SHOW YOU HOW YOU DIE, it said, and then, inside Theo's mind, it did show him.

Theo's muscles roared in pain as the mortals finally reached him, grabbing his limbs, pulling him in every direction, ripping his flesh with blunt teeth, sucking his blood . . . The horror, more than the pain, tore him apart.

But he still remembered what he had come here for. He could still feel a corner of his brother's mind in his grasp and, before his senses fell to the Nightmare again, he did the one thing he said he would never do. He took the Sleep *out* of someone's mind.

Waves of energy flowed out of Torres, making him cry out and leaving him slumped on the floor as it found its way into Theo. The room was suddenly brighter, his blood hotter. The Nightmare continued, but the voice and some of the mortals had disappeared when Torres had collapsed, and now Theo knew what to do with the rest of them. He thought of Bede, escaping from the crows by letting them think they had already finished him off. If you wanted to beat a Nightmare, you had to make it think it had already beaten you.

'No!' he screamed. He didn't have to exaggerate the pain in his voice. 'Don't carry me away! Please!'

Thinking that carrying him away would be the scariest thing they could to him, the mortals immediately lifted him up and hauled him across the room—back over to the dining table, where Ereon still lay.

Theo wasted no time. Throwing himself out of the Nightmare's hands, he lunged for the boy, taking care to touch him only where his skin was covered. He had him! Theo could hardly believe it. It had only been five days since he last held this child in his arms, taking him from his mother and choosing him as his Magus in front of the Majority congregation, but it felt like they had been separated for a lifetime.

He gently pushed back the folds of the baby's wrapping, looking for the Horn he knew Torres had hidden on him. And then the whole world went white. He screamed and almost dropped Ereon as he was flooded with the most excruciating pain he had ever felt. As he sank to his knees, he saw what his hand had just brushed against: a piece of Ivory the size and shape of the end of a phantelle's tusk, falling from Ereon's stomach and a Horn bracelet falling off his ankle.

The pain felt like some animal burrowing beneath his skin from his heart to his pelvis, trying to gnaw its way out, a terrible biting pain that Theo thought would drive him mad before it killed him.

His eyelids drooped and the sound of everything around him became dull as he instinctively put himself to Sleep to try and repair the poison of the Dream and Nightmare material.

Theo could hear a voice speaking to him again but couldn't understand what it was saying. Maybe it was 'You'll be okay,' maybe 'You should pray'—though it probably wasn't the second one; after all, who could a dying god pray to?

He wanted to call for help but his tongue felt loose and watery; it fell against the back of his throat whenever he opened his mouth, almost choking him. He tried to roll over onto his side but he was so dizzy he couldn't tell if he was moving or not. He didn't want to die here, where the ground was hard and wouldn't recognise his bones. Especially when, back home, there were cool riverbanks where he could rest his head on grass instead of rock as he died. But he would never lie by the riverbank again. This had all been too much. The whole week had been slowly chipping away at his energy and now he knew that he had reached his limit of Dreams and Nightmares; this last one would kill him, he had no doubt. The Sleep God was going to finally get the rest he needed.

He closed his eyes and sent his mind out into the realm. The Mountains were entirely emptied of Zions and Dream Country's Gate was closed. Rogan must have got the message he left for him in the mud:

GET THEM ALL OUT. CLOSE DC.

Close Dream Country. It might not be enough. But Theo knew he had to try, had to make sure there was something he could save, no matter what happened when he came to the top of the mountain.

With Theo down, Torres had managed to get back up on his own feet. He crawled over to Theo and took Ereon away from him, cradling him in his lap. The next moment he cried out as Ereon began to shake violently in his arms.

'Help!' he shouted, 'What have you done? You've hurt him! Theo!'

It was too late. For the first time in a week, the Sleep Magus was not in contact with either Horn or Ivory. And the Majoracle was over. He was freed of his connection to the realms and now he was ready to go home to his mother. He cried for Theo and Theo heard him. He found his Magus's mind and just like the first time he found him, he gave him a simple command.

Wake up.

The ground shook. It began to turn black, to crumble in on itself, but Theo kept control of the boy, trying to hold back the child's destruction before it reached Dream Country's Gates, and when he tried to go too far Theo made him *stop!*

Stop!

The Gates would hold, he had to believe it, he had to believe that the last remaining Gates in the celestial realms would hold, that everyone behind them would be okay. The conjoined realms of Zion and the Mountains rumbled hungrily. Cracks appeared in the very fabric of the air; it became thin and hard to breathe. Torres gasped and dropped to his knees. Equally breathless, Theo lost control of Ereon. The Dream Country Gates shook harder.

He made one final effort and in doing so he used the last of himself. He fell asleep.

And his and his brother's realm fell with him.

* * *

Torres fell too.

It was a long way down to Pangaea from the celestial realms and as they fell the Major brothers reached for each other, whether to bring each other down or hold each other up, it was hard to tell. The shock of the fall had temporarily re-awoken Theo from his self-inflicted slumber. He felt Zion pulling at him, even as it collapsed. Ereon was still, looking so peaceful in Torres's arms. Bodies fell around them: the Minors of *Os Pesadelos* and the crows who couldn't keep themselves airborne at this strange lower altitude. Only the Pangaeans who had been having Nightmares were not there. They would have woken up sweating and safe in their beds on the island, and in the morning they would tell each other they had all Dreamt of falling.

Fanta might be somewhere among the rain of bodies. Theo wished he could see her. He looked over at Torres and saw the panic in his face and heard it in his screams. Meanwhile, Theo leant back against the air current and laughed.

Torres heard him over the sound of the wind.

'Are you crazy?' he screamed. 'We're going to die!'

'The Majority will catch us,' Theo said and laughed again.

Torres could hardly believe what he was hearing. This was a situation they had been in a million times before, one of them joyful, the other serious, but now their roles were reversed. As they tumbled in the air, up was down, right was wrong, brother was brother.

'Oh, Torres, I'm so tired, *irmão*.'

Suddenly Torres began to lose his grip on Ereon's tiny body. His fingers scrabbled to keep a hold of him, but it was as if there was some invisible rope pulling the boy towards the sky—because as he fell out of Torres's arms, he fell *up*. Torres watched in such complete shock that he forgot to keep screaming. Ereon floated like a bubble, up and up and up, until finally, he burst.

Darkness spread across the sky like paint spraying across a canvas that had been empty for far too long. As Torres watched, Ereon's body darkened the sky and, for the first time in a long, long age, Night descended in the celestial realms.

'Theo?' Torres whispered, not wanting to take his gaze away from what he was seeing, but *needing* to see if his brother was seeing it too.

The ground below was fast approaching and Torres had to accept the fact that there was nothing more he could do. He looked over at Theo. His brother was pale, bloodied, and bruised but he looked almost peaceful, with his eyes closed, as he fell. They looked like they would never open again.

For a second as he looked at his brother Torres forgot that he was falling too.

'Theo?'

THE HOLY THEOLOGOS, BOOK I, VERSE I.I

This is how the All-Mother created life:

She lay down on Her back and Her breasts heaved with the exertion of Her own creation, which She could not remember, although She knew that She had done it herself. Her darkness was still spreading to fill the light that was Nothing before. She felt a phantom babe suckling for her milk and so She fed it, and the earth was made.

Afterwards, the All-Mother lay down again. As She carries all elements of creation in Her, She also carries the man as much as the woman. It is by this that She impregnated herself when the time was right. The All-Mother's belly swelled with the life of Her children and it was the moon. But the Children of Night were premature and when they came they tore their Mother's body, stretching her skin and ripping it, and Her stretch marks were the constellations and Her wounds were the stars. The All-Mother would do nothing but birth a girl first; and so she came and she was named Fanta of the Major. She was Dream. Next She brought forth her daughter's counterpart and he was named Torres of the Major. He was Nightmare. Finally She created balance for Her two firstborns and he was named Theodore of the Major. He was Sleep.

The triplets were dissimilar in appearance, even to their Mother. She was the blue-black of Night, and She gave them each a shade of Her.

It is said that when the time comes the All-Mother will un-birth Her children in reverse order. And those will be the end days.

ACKNOWLEDGEMENTS

First, I would like to thank the wonderful team at Onwe Press, especially Reni and Alice, whose dedication, patience and belief in this story were critical to making it what it is.

Thanks to my editors, Amanda and Simon, and to all the talented artists that made my imagination visible, Andrea Mendez, Shady Curi and Viktoria Vinichenko. Thank you to Edwin Otwori and Fabio Lindner who helped to translate the Swahili and Portuguese words.

To Colin, for his advice and support.

To the online communities of writers and beta readers who encouraged me on my journey and allowed me to follow them in theirs.

To the University of Birmingham Library whose resources I relied on throughout.

To every English teacher I have ever had, who saw that I would not speak and allowed me to write instead.

And, of course, I must thank my family:

Mum, who read to me every night and never stopped asking me "when's your book coming?" until I had no choice but to start writing it.

Dad, who always believed in me.

My brothers, Loran, Rhys and Adley, who made me want to make this story about siblings, about growing up, growing apart and growing back together again.

And finally, Nana and Grandad, who were taken from us only a few months before they could see this story brought to life. This story is their story – no matter how much one country might sell you a dream, you never stop thinking about going "back home".

DICTIONARY AND PHRASEBOOK

Word/Phrase
Language
Meaning

Amani
Swahili
Peace

Amor
Brazilian Portuguese
My love

Besta-fera
Brazilian Portuguese
A beast that has the body of a horse and a human torso. The sound of its hooves is enough to terrorise people. A pack of dogs follow it; the Beast whips these, and any other animals it comes across

Bibi
Swahili
Lady

Boitatá
Brazilian Portuguese
Boitatá is a mythological serpent from Brazilian mythology. Boitatá appears to be a green, orange, flame or black huge serpent with flames around his body, it's sometimes described by having two horns.

Bwana
Swahili
Sir

Capelobo
Brazilian Portuguese
A vampiric creature from Brazilian myth, particularly in the states of Pará and Maranhão. These creatures have two forms, animal and humanoid. In animal form they have a shaggy coat of black fur and a snout that appears similar to an anteater's or a pig's

Claro
Brazilian Portuguese
Sure

Compreende?
Brazilian Portuguese
Do you understand?

Cuca
Brazilian Portuguese
A witch who kidnaps and eats naughty children

De verdade
Brazilian Portuguese
Really

Ei, vem ver
Brazilian Portuguese
Hey, come see

Ele tem algo grande planejado, é só esperar pra ver
Brazilian Portuguese
He has something big planned, just wait and see

Estou com fome
Brazilian Portuguese
I'm hungry

Eu sinto muito
Brazilian Portuguese
I'm so sorry

Fulano
Brazilian Portuguese
So-and-so

Garoto
Brazilian Portuguese
Boy

Hein
Brazilian Portuguese
huh

Irmã
Brazilian Portuguese
Sister

Irmão
Brazilian Portuguese
Brother

Jurupari
Brazilian Portuguese
Crooked-mouth beast

La hasha
Swahili
Not at all

Lobisomem
Brazilian Portuguese
A human with the ability to shapeshift into a wolf

Mãe de Todos
Brazilian Portuguese
All-Mother

Maldição
Brazilian Portuguese
Curse

Mama wa wote
Swahili
Mother to All

Maninho
Brazilian Portuguese
Little brother

Mapinguar
Brazilian Portuguese
A Brazillian beast sometimes described as a hairy humanoid cyclops, other times a giant ground sloth. The creature is often said to have a gaping mouth on its abdomen

Me desculpe
Brazilian Portuguese
I'm sorry

Me perdoe
Brazilian Portuguese
Forgive me

Morte-de-ouro
Brazilian Portuguese
Golden-death

Nana, neném, que a cuca vem pegar, papai foi na roça, mamãe foi trabalhar
Brazilian Portuguese
Sleep baby, that the witch comes to get you, daddy went to the farm, mommy went to work

Não
Brazilian Portuguese
No

Ndivyo
Swahili
Yes

'O que?
Brazilian Portuguese
What?

Os Pesadelos
Brazilian Portuguese
The Nightmares

Por favor, tenha piedade
Brazilian Portuguese
Please have mercy

Quem é esse?
Brazilian Portuguese
Who is this?

Sawa
Swahili
Ok

Senhor
Brazilian Portuguese
Mister

Senhora
Brazilian Portuguese
Lady

Sim, eu ouvi
Brazilian Portuguese
Yes, I heard

Taifa la Ndoto
Swahili
Dream Country

Vai
Brazilian Portuguese
Go